THE PRECURSORS

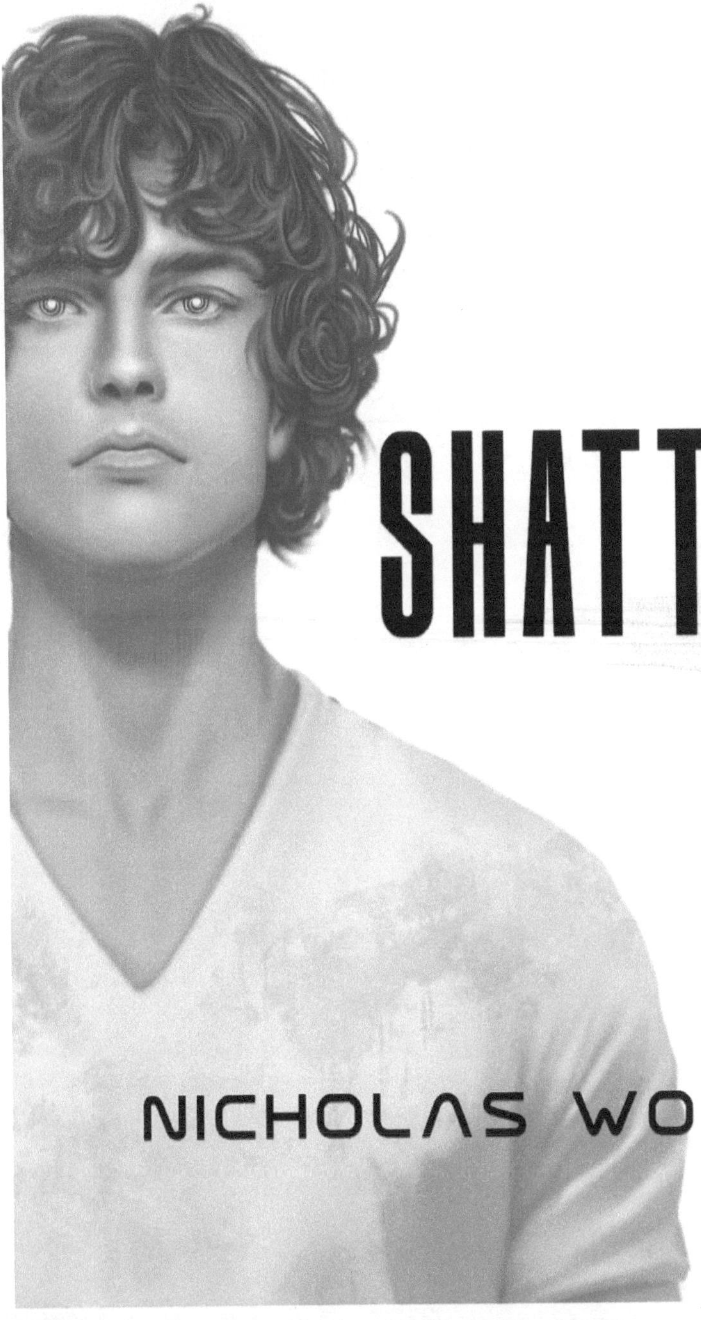

SHATTER

NICHOLAS WOLFE

Hardback ISBN **979-8-9992339-2-9**
Paperback ISBN **979-8-9992339-1-2**
Digital Online ISBN **979-8-9992339-0-5**

DEDICATION

Dedicated to my mom, who taught me one of the most valuable skills one can possess: how to learn. Before I knew what I was missing, as a child, she forced me to read, giving birth to the creative imagination that gave you this book.

CONTENTS

SHATTER

SHATTER

ACKNOWLEDGMENTS

First, I would like to thank God, for without him none of this would be possible, and I would not have written this book.

Next, in no particular order, I would like to thank my mom for typing the book, Blake for listening to me for six hours nonstop as I talked to him about the book, Amilee for believing in me to get the book out of my head and into the world, Stacey for editing the book and treating it like it was her very own work, Olivia for designing the book cover and putting together images straight out of my mind, Win Wilkins for putting an author's eye on it and giving me last minute help when I didn't even know I needed it out of the kindness of his heart, Georgiana and Alisha my first two ARC readers for seeing the book how it was meant to be seen, and Justin for more reasons than I can name, but chiefly marketing. Lastly, I would like to acknowledge myself for putting in the hard work that comes with writing a book.

STRATEGY

PROUD PARTNER AND SUPPORTER OF NICHOLAS WOLFE'S JOURNEY.

_____

"SOME PEOPLE WANT IT TO HAPPEN, SOME WISH IT WOULD HAPPEN, OTHERS MAKE IT HAPPEN."
- MICHAEL JORDAN

SHATTER

Visualeyez

Do what you love !

Love what you do !

Visualeyez.org

PROLOGUE

"Are you ready, young master?"

I turn to see Walcott standing in my doorway, looking impatient, if a stone can be said to look impatient.

"Walcott, you may be my mother's favorite servant, but that does not mean you can rush me."

He's been with my family since before I was born. I'm not sure if that's why he's my mother's favorite, but it would be reasonable.

"Rush you? I would never. However, your mother is, so . . . hurry up."

His bushy beard, which is peppered gray and black just like his hair, hides his face well enough that I can't tell if he's amused, but his tone suggests it. I smile, not being able to be as mean as my father to the servants, especially Walcott. He's something like a grandfather to me. I wonder what my mom would think if she knew that.

"Fine, then, if you don't have to be proper, then neither do I.

How do I look, you old fart?" I asked excitedly.

Today I'm going to go train with my mother, so I want to make sure I look good.

"You look like you need more dirt behind your ears. Now let's go," he replies indifferently.

"But what about my outfit?" I contest.

"You're wearing all black, who cares?" he says, disappearing out of the doorway into the castle hall.

I must run after him because his legs are longer than mine.

"But what about the white dragon on the back?" I ask when I catch up.

"You expected me to see the back of your shirt when you didn't turn around? I have no idea why your mother thinks you're smart," he says, continuing to lead me through the castle.

"You know I could punish you, right?" I say, not really meaning it.

"Yes, but you won't," he replies smoothly.

"And how do you know that?" I ask, eyeing him curiously even though he's walking ahead of me.

"Because you are not your father," he says, turning a corner and leading us down a hall that ends in an open doorway that goes outside.

Am I really that easy to read? Maybe I need to be more like my father.

Sunlight blinds me for a moment as I step outside, causing me to raise my hands to block out the sun. When my eyes adjust, I see my mother standing in the middle of a dirt field in an all-white dress, gold hair blowing in the wind behind her. Despite the wind kicking up dirt all around her, not a speck of dirt is on her dress.

"Mother!" I yell, and run toward her. My little legs carry me past Walcott and into my mother's open arms.

"Luca, my baby!" she yells back just as excitedly, picking me up and spinning me around once in the air, causing me to giggle. When she sets me down, her gold eyes settle on me.

"I trust you were polite to Walcott," she says to me questioningly.

"He was a gentleman as always, Lady Yuna," Walcott says from behind me. When I turn around, he winks at me, then bows to my mother.

"Oh, come now, Walcott, there's no need to be so formal. Stop that," she says, moving closer to him and raising him from his bow.

"Do all the other servants have to bow?" Walcott asks my mother, knowing the answer.

"You know they do, but you also know that is not my doing," she says apologetically.

"Nevertheless, they do, and so do I. Don't be sad. If I must bow to anybody, I'm glad it's you," he says, smiling.

This seems to lift my mother's spirits. I don't think my father would like them to be so familiar, but it doesn't bother me at all.

"So . . ." my mother begins, turning her attention to me ". . . are you ready to show me what you can do today?" Her smile makes me want to do my best.

I nod eagerly.

"Okay, we'll start small," she says to me while motioning Walcott backward, lest he get hurt. I doubt she'd let that happen though.

Once he's about fifteen yards away, my mother pulls out a knife from a secret fold in her dress and slits her wrist.

"Oh my, I seem to have cut myself. Whatever will I do?" she asks, playing the perfect damsel in distress. Her eyes lock on mine as blood leaks down her hand and drips into the dirt. "Young prince, will you save me?" she pleads.

The first time she did this, I passed out. I don't like it anymore now than I did then, but now I know what to do. I walk up to my mom quickly, take her hand into my own, and place my other hand over the wound. Closing my eyes, I begin to concentrate. Certain. Sure. Definite. Decided. Specific. Precise. I feel the power begin to flow from me into her wound, healing the cut.

"It appears your wound has closed, my good lady," I say, opening my eyes and looking up to her.

"My hero," she replies kindly, bending down to kiss me. "But . . ." she says, raising back up to her full height. She makes a gesture with her hand in the air, as if pulling a string between her thumb and all her fingers, and pulls water out of seemingly nothing, allowing it to fall on her bloody arm, rinsing it off. ". . . this water . . . seems to have spilled on my dress," she says purposefully, getting only water on her dress but no blood. "This is my favorite white dress, and the water will stain it. Do you think you could do something about this?" she finishes, holding out the stain on her dress to me.

"It would be my pleasure," I reply with a low bow. I have no idea how she pulled the water out of thin air like that, but now that it's in the dress, getting it out will be simple. Closing my eyes and concentrating, I reach toward the dress. I feel the water with my mind before I touch the dress, and I smile. Without touching the dress, I make a pulling motion with my hand and then feel the water come out of the dress. Then I feel it splash against my face.

"Well done, young master," Walcott yells from his vantage point, humor clear in his voice.

I open my eyes, embarrassed.

"Be quiet, Walcott, he did well," my mother yells back, coming to my rescue. Her approval means the world to me.

"If you would open your eyes while using the power, that wouldn't happen, you know," she says to me lightly.

"Yes, but it's easier to concentrate when I don't have so many things to look at," I complain.

"It's okay. We'll work on it, little one," she says reassuringly. "The next will be a little more complicated. Are you up for it?"

I nod eagerly. My mother smiles at me before taking a step back and raising her hand, palm up, shoulder height. In the spot where she just stepped back from, a small patch of daisies grows up from the dry dirt as if they were just hiding there the whole time. I stand and stare in awe, and my mother does not miss the look of loss on my face.

"Try feeling the dirt in your mind. It's alive and wants to become more. It's almost like healing, except instead of righting what is wrong, you must feel the desire for growth coming from the dirt and feed it."

I nod, even though it sounds impossible. Again, I close my eyes. I feel for the dirt with my mind, and surprisingly, I find it. But I don't feel the desire to grow. I feel its anger at being nothing more than dirt, and it spreads through me like a fire. I ball my fist up by my side, fighting against the anger trying to overtake me. I hear crackling under my feet and all around me. Somehow, I know the ground is splitting under my feet.

"Luca, you must calm yourself," my mother's voice calls worriedly. "The dirt can't control you. It doesn't have a mind." She places her hands on my cheeks. "Let go of the power, now!" Something about the way she says "now" causes me to let go and open my eyes. My mother is kneeling in the dirt with her hands still holding my face. She looks sad.

"You did well, but promise me you will never try that again," she says desperately,

"I promise," I say, confused.

"That's not something a six-year-old should be able to do," Walcott's voice calls.

I turn to find him approaching us. I am about to ask him what he is talking about when my eyes see the ground beneath him, beneath all of us. The ground is cracked in a spider-webbed pattern thirty feet in every direction centered on me. Did I do that?

"Walcott, I must protect my son," my mother says from behind me. I feel her stand.

I turn to look at my mother and find tears in her eyes. What does she mean by "protect me"?

"I understand. It's been an honor, Lady Yuna. I trust you'll send my regards?" he replies.

I turn and see my mother nod. Just as I'm about to ask what is going on, my mother holds out her hand, palm up, and a circle no bigger than she can make using her hand appears. I can almost see something in it. It looks like—. The circle shoots out of her hand toward Walcott, and my eyes follow. Walcott gasps, falling to his knees. I don't understand what happened until blood begins to leak from his chest. Where his heart should be, there is nothing but a hole the same size as the circle that was in my mother's palm. Oddly, Walcott dies with a smile on his face.

"I felt the power. Was that my son?" my father's voice yells excitedly from behind us.

My mother turns to face him, placing me behind her. "No, that was an assassin who came to kill your son," she says, pointing to Walcott's body. "It seems you are not doing your job," she spits venomously.

That is the first time I've ever heard my mother lie to my father. My father is not powerfully built, but the presence he gives off is overwhelming. Maybe I just think that because he's my father. His black eyes search my mother's. He closes his eyes and takes a deep breath. When he exhales, the world begins to quake. Is he doing that? Suddenly he opens his eyes, and it stops.

"That is unfortunate. Had I even suspected, he would have been dead like this." My father snaps his fingers, and I feel flames spring into existence behind me and mother. I turn to look and notice Walcott's body is gone. Not even ashes remain. Had I not felt the heat, I wouldn't have known there was a fire.

"I will tighten security around the castle, but should I find out that you are lying to—" my father begins, only to be cut off by my mother.

"I know very well what will happen if I am caught lying to you. There is no need to keep throwing it in my face. Besides, do you think I would kill a man for no reason? I am not you, X'avion."

My father's face is thoughtful for a moment. A lock from his curly black hair falls in his face. "You are right, of course; you are not me. See to it you keep me informed on the boy's progress." With that, he turns around and begins to walk off. "Keep up the good work, Luca," he yells back, glancing at me briefly and gracing me with a smile.

I don't respond because too much has just happened for me to keep up with. What I don't understand is why my mother killed Walcott and then lied to my father about it. Little did I know Walcott's death prevented me from becoming a monster.

1 PERFECTION

It is a week before my eighteenth birthday, and I couldn't be more excited. Well, maybe if I could learn how to wield Potentia, like my father, instead of Certus, like my mother, but that's still a maybe. I'm about to be of the age at which my mother and father agreed I would be allowed to leave the castle and travel the kingdom.

I've read books that my mother forced upon me about what lies beyond the stone walls of my home, but that is different from experiencing the world beyond. People are said to only be able to touch one form of the power anyway, Potentia or Certus. We've already determined that I've inherited my gift from my mother, so I don't understand why he goes on about it. In fact, he should be happy, considering most people can't touch either form of the power. I know I feel blessed.

Blessed, we live in a world where just about every deity that has ever been known is worshipped by someone, or so I'm told. That being said, the origins of what we call "the power" remain a mystery. I like to think of it as a force, like nature. My mother preaches to me about the one true God who is supposed to be a combination of every good quality you can think of and then some because he is infinity, and therefore infinitely good. I don't know what to believe. My mother's never lied to me before, but can something or someone truly so good exist, even if it is a deity? My father thinks it's all non-sense, but my father has steadily grown apart from me after we discovered which of the powers I can touch.

"Luca, you're doing it again," comes a soft but familiar voice from behind, startling me. I do my best not to jump. Picking my head up from where I was staring, lost in thought, at the family emblem, which is a black dragon head, on my blanket, I turn to see Shari.

Shari is a few inches over five feet tall and has long, curly red hair. Her skin is the color of caramel, and her eyes are a penetrating green. Sometimes when we talk, I feel as if her eyes see straight through me into my soul, if there is a such thing. If that wasn't enough, her body, suffice it to say that if she got her body from her mother, her father never stood a chance. All in all, Shari is a very distracting individual. Physically, she's stunning, but her personality is so straightforward and aggressive that it makes it really hard to deal with her. However, I've known her since I was a kid, so I can justly say I know how to deal with her—at least as much as a man can deal with the confounding species we call women.

My mother brought her home one day when I was eight. I don't know her back story, but I do know she was a lot quieter and less annoying then.

"The last time I checked, this is my room, so I can do what I want," I say flippantly. "How did you get in here, anyway?"

Something silver flashes in her hand and then disappears up her sleeve. "A real lady never reveals her secrets," she says, sounding much too gratified, gifting me with a distracting smile. "I know you see what I'm wearing," she adds.

"You aren't a real lady, because if you were, you wouldn't be sneaking into my room or wearing competition robes; you'd be courting someone by now. And to your second statement, I did not comment because I didn't believe you wanted a reminder that you are about to lose."

Normally we wear gray robes when we train. Today ours are both black because we will face each other in combat and, my favorite, archery.

I rise from my bed and walk over to the case on my dresser behind which sits a personal body mirror.

"Do you actually believe the things you say, or do you just like to hear yourself talk?" she asks in mock disgust.

I unclamp the two holders on the case. "Both," I say, smiling at myself for knowing I can get on her nerves, too, and at what's inside the case.

Inside the gold gilded oak case rests the most beautiful bow this world has ever seen. Made of a white wood I've never seen anywhere—and by that, I mean in books—it is hard enough that a sword could not slice through it. The bow is spiraled with gold lines that start at the top and bottom then travel the length of the wood toward the center, forming two distinct three-ring concentric circles just above and below the grip, which was custom made to fit my hand. There is no string because I can create one using Certus in the process of nocking an arrow and firing. Useful, to say the least.

"If you weren't so full of yourself and rich, you'd be really attractive," Shari whispers in my ear playfully as I stare down at the bow.

Surprised by her sudden presence behind me and what was whispered in my ear, I jump, then stumble, knocking over the oak case, nearly dropping my bow. Innocent yet melodious laughter fills the room from behind me.

"How and why can you do that? And why do you say things like that? And you live here too, so you're just as rich!" I exclaim, startled, but soon regain my composure.

"Yeah, but I don't wear it like you, Princeling, and to your first statement," she mocks, "we all can't touch the power like you and your precious parents, so we adapt by becoming relevant."

"Sneaking up on people isn't relevant. And to the second?" I ask.

"Is this my mouth?" Shari asks.

"What?" I say, not understanding the question.

"Is. This. My. Mouth?" she repeats, slowly tracing a finger on her lips while coming uncomfortably close.

I go with the obvious answer, trying to sound more confident than I feel, "Yes."

"So I can say what I want," she says, then simply moves away from me over to where the glass door to the balcony sits closed. She opens the door and then moves on to the stone balustrade to overlook the three-story view from my room to the castle yard.

"Hurry up, archer boy, or you're going to be late. I've already got a head start on you."

I turn to face her. "No you don—" She's gone.

"Her and her games. Two can play games, Shari," I say to no one in particular due to Shari's dramatic exit.

I grab the oak case off the floor and set it back on the dresser. Taking my bow back in hand, I pause before the mirror. My reflection staring back at me, I admire what I see. Standing six and a half feet tall, a little darker than Shari, the man in the mirror is as skinny as a reed. Short, brown, unruly curly hair rests atop my head. I do need to pick up some muscle; a hard wind could probably blow me over. No matter. Although my body is defined, it is not my main attraction. My eyes are.

Circling two white pupils is a vortex of black and gold, as if when I was in my mother's womb, my eyes could not decide on a color, and both colors wanted to be dominant, so they went to war. My father has black eyes, my mother gold. The white pupils seem to be an anomaly no one can explain. Black eyes are fairly common. I know this because a lot of the servants around the castle have black eyes. Gold eyes, however—there are a little over one hundred servants in the castle, and none of them have gold eyes. If Shari's eyes penetrate my soul, my mother's eyes discern the fabric of reality itself. Needless to say, my eyes make me very confident. So much so, in fact, that the servants whisper that I am conceited when they believe I can't hear, and I let them because . . . well, it's true. I mean, look at those eyes. I can't wait to leave this castle.

I exit my room to find the comings and goings of the servants, no doubt on random errands for my mother, father, or simple castle maintenance in general, through the vast hallways of the third floor. The entirety of the floor belongs to me as much as any child owns their own room in their parents' home. The first floor is really for show. Its main feature is one massive chamber big enough to host a thousand guests comfortably. Of course, that alone doesn't make it special. Inside the chamber everything is made of gold . . . chairs, tables, walls, floor, plates, cups, goldware, chandelier . . . you name it.

If I am conceited, my father is vain, showing riches and power openly as if in challenge for those who dare. The second floor is divided between servants' quarters, my father's war room, my mother's state affairs room, and a family room. The family room is entirely too big for three people, four if you count Shari, and unused. For some reason you will not catch Shari in the same room as my father. If you do, it won't be for long. I think he frightens her, which is understandable. Not many people can look at the strongest person ever to wield Potentia and not be scared. What I don't understand is why my mother seems to avoid my father. It's been that way for as long as I can remember too. She doesn't call him endearing names, only Your Highness or Your Majesty, and she doesn't show him any type of affection at all. I don't think I've ever seen them hug, let alone kiss. I try not to let it bother me, and for the most part, I've gotten good at it over the years, but from time to time it still gets to me. Surely, my father is strict, but he's not a monster. Just the leader he needs to be to run a kingdom unchallenged.

The third floor belongs to me, and it consists of my room, an indoor pool, the garden, a sweat room, and Shari's room. The last is the only place I've never been on my own floor. I wonder what her room looks like, but aggravating creature that she is, I deem it best to steer clear of it. The fourth floor and final place belongs to my mother and father. Except when they are sleep, which they almost never are and never do together, it remains empty.

Winding my way through the castle, heading to the training yards, I stop a few servants on the way and ask them about my upcoming birthday arrangements. They all shoot me down as if I were not the prince, murmuring apologies and something about not ruining the surprise. Although, the last man I asked told me to be patient and the festivities would be to die for. Remembering his smile and ominous tone of voice, I shall be sure to mention him to my mother. Strolling out of the back of the castle and approaching dirt grounds that mark the beginning of the training yards, I see Shari and Alrick. Shari is Shari, but Alrick is a brute of a man with no hair and a thick, bushy, but well-trimmed beard. Secondly, he is my father's strongest martial general. He cannot touch the power, but he can fight. He is said to have commanded the armies my father used to take control of the kingdom. Although, I'm not sure how much that means because through servants' gossip, I've heard my father was such a monster with his power that they didn't have too much resistance. Regardless, Alrick has never been bested, and whenever my father marches to war, Alrick follows. Lastly, Alrick is my personal trainer. Well, mine and Shari's now. Truth be told, I'm not one for violence; I get bad anxiety, and I have anger issues. Well, I did before my mother taught me to control my anger. For all the legend surrounding Alrick, he is a good man.

"Luca," Alrick's deep voice calls out to me in greeting.

"Alrick," I say back evenly in greeting as well.

"You're late," he says, tone demanding me to explain myself.

"Fashionably, but I am the prince, and I had a point I wished to illustrate to someone about relevance." My eyes flicker to Shari as I speak. Shari crosses her arms and no doubt swallows a fiery retort. She doesn't speak as fiercely to me when we are in public. Usually it is the only time I can get under her skin.

"Be that as it may, you are still late, and because you are late, and not Shari, we will start the competition with the sword. A duel. Between you and Shari," Alrick says. He then approaches and drops his voice to a whisper. "I hope you still feel relevant, Luca, because as good as you are with that bow, Shari is your equivalent with a blade, long, short, curved, or dagger. She trains every morning before you wake and every night while you sleep. She has devoted her life to this, and the result is beautiful swordsmanship. In fact, she is my star pupil, and I believe one day she will become a blade master better than even me."

I swallow the lump in my throat and look up at him. "Any advice?" I ask desperately.

"Yes, as a matter of fact," he says, picking his voice back up to its deepness. I listen eagerly for any help, tip, or advantage I can get. "That bow will not help you here. Set it down outside of this white circle," he says, amused, then walks to the other side of the circle, chuckling all the while.

2 SKILLS

The wind from a hot summer day kicks up dust as I stand in the middle of the dirt training circle, two sword lengths from Shari. A devilish smile plastered on her face is the only thing about her that looks intimidating. We have been given the choice of two wooden blades, one short and one long, or a long sword and a shield. Shari chooses the former. I choose the latter, thinking about the need to defend myself from Alrick's "star pupil." Whatever that means.

As far as I know, he only teaches Shari and me. Shari can't be that good. I've seen her train before, and it's nothing special. As I look at her now, she looks so soft and pleasant.

"You know the rules," Alrick says loudly from a seemingly random spot outside the ring. "No using the power. No dirty fighting, the duel is to yielding, and if you step outside the ring, you lose. Understand?"

Shari and I both nod our consent.

"Begin!" Alrick shouts.

Shari holds both her weapons down at her sides as she begins walking toward me, longsword scrapping across the dirt with every step. Somehow, I know this gesture for what it is: not a threat, but a promise.

I raise my shield because . . . well, put simply, I'm scared. I'm not even sure why. Maybe it is because Alrick said she was his star pupil, or maybe it's the confidence in her eyes coupled with the grace with which she steps. I reach for the only confident thought I can muster—*Alrick is my teacher too*—and then she attacks.

She swings her longsword in an overhead strike, and I raise my shield to meet it. My vision blurs, and my eyes tear up. What happened? I quickly blink the tears away and reposition myself. From what I can tell, she feinted with the long sword and hit me with the pommel of the short sword.

"Princeling," Shari whispers, "surely you can do better than that."

"I just let you get the first strike, you know. Ladies first and all," I say, trying to save face. She cocks her head to the side like she doesn't understand. No, she understands, and she's insulted. I know this because she rushes me. I try to sideswipe at her, but she ducks under the blade, sliding as if part of a dance, and drives both of her wooden blades into the shield to keep me from raising it again. Okay, well now she can't hit me again. Again, my vision blurs as she headbutts me in the nose. However, this time it begins to bleed. I fall on my butt close to the edge of the circle.

"Hey, the rules clearly state no dirty fighting!" I shout, furiously wiping my nose. Shari just smiles, and Alrick chuckles.

"Luca, despite what you believe, the world is far from fair, and that was not dirty. Uncouth, maybe, but not dirty. Kicking you in your manhood would be considered dirty, and she didn't do that. So stand up and fight or be bested by a girl," Alrick says with humor touching his voice.

I grab a wooden sword and shield and stand. "Some advice, Your Relevance, let go of your fear," Shari mocks.

"I am not scared of you," comes my heated reply.

"Luca, I see it in the way you stand, the way you grip your weapon and shield. This is just training. Relax, breathe." I don't know why, but anger surges through me at Shari's surprisingly modest-sounding lecture. I charge her and then swing three times. She blocks all three just like I expected, but there's a reason I chose a shield. As I retract the third swing, I use my momentum to push the shield forward as hard as I can and hit, nothing. I lose my balance and start falling face forward toward the ground.

Shari catches me by the collar of my training robes and whispers in my ear, "Calm your anger; it'll get you nowhere fast, and those are your mother's words."

She's right. However, I'm enraged. Why am I losing? Why is she mocking me? I grab her hand holding my collar, tuck, and roll hard, throwing her to the ground. Satisfaction. I swing my weapon at her from my knees, hoping to land a blow while she is lying back down in the dirt, but she rolls to the right and recovers fast. I try to stand, but I am halted halfway through the motion. Looking at the cause of my problem, I notice my shield pinned to the ground by a wooden short sword going through it, stuck in the dirt. Shit. I instinctively drop my weapon and cover my nose, just to feel Shari's foot hit my chin so hard the straps on my shield arm break, and then the force of the blow carries me onto my back. I'm dazed. There's pressure on top of me.

"Yield, Princeling," Shari whispers.

As I regain my senses, Shari is mounting me with a wooden sword at my throat. Damn, I lost to a girl. The second thing I notice is how soft she feels on top of me. The black competition robes aren't exactly thick, and Shari is a very . . . voluptuous female. The third thing I notice, she notices as well. Her face reddens furiously, and she jumps off me, but not before she stomps on my chest hard enough to make me wheeze.

"What happened?" Alrick calls to ask from across the circle.

I lean up hurriedly and yell back, "I yielded," looking at Shari, desperately hoping she would not give me up.

Our eyes lock for a split second while she gathers her short sword out of the dirt, and I'm not sure how to feel. Alrick looks to Shari and questions.

"You heard him, he yielded," she says in a tone I can't quite figure out. Thank you, Shari.

"Well, stand up, then. Target practice next. Your time to shine, archer boy."

"Just gathering my wits. That kick to the chin knocked something loose."

It definitely knocked something loose, but that's not the reason I still sit on the ground. I'm just biding my time so the blood in my manhood moves elsewhere.

"Yeah, your turn, archer *boy*," Shari says smugly before turning to walk in the direction of the archery course.

I could be mistaken, but I think she overemphasized the word boy. I blush, feeling severely embarrassed about what happened. She turned red too. "Just relax, breathe," I tell myself, choosing to take Shari's advice. Well, it's really my mother's advice. I had an incident I can't clearly remember when I was six involving my anger, and she's been quite adamant about me controlling my anger ever since.

Finally, I stand up and follow their tracks to my domain. I've always been gifted with the bow even before I could work with Certus. My concentration and attention to detail are alarmingly good, and that is being humble, which is why it frustrates me so much that Shari is always sneaking up on me. At eight years old I could see a man once and remember everything about him for weeks. At thirteen I could hit any target within range of my short bow without looking. That's the rumor, anyway. Honestly, I would steal a glance in the general direction of the target first, then look away, wait a moment, and then fire. I wasn't strong enough for a long bow back then. I also was nowhere near as good as I am with Certus now. Now, I can pin a fly to a tree by its wing from a thousand yards away. I'm certain my abnormal eyes help with that; most people can't see something so small from so far away. Whatever the reason, whether deities exist or not, I am a God with the bow.

The day is hot, but the sky is beautiful. Spectacles like this are why I dislike violence. As I walk up to the archery course enjoying the moment, I also spot all the targets that have been placed for us to shoot and the one hidden from everyone except me.

"Forget something?" Alrick asks knowingly as he tosses me my bow and quiver of arrows. I didn't forget it. He just took it as he left before I decided it was alright to stand up.

"Thank you," I choose to say instead.

"Save your thanks and hit the targets," he says sternly.

"Yeah, hit the targets," Shari adds playfully to let me know the awkwardness has passed.

Shari is distracting, straightforward, and aggressive, but she is also kind and sweet. At least when she wants to be. Right now, I am beyond grateful for the latter.

I go to turn my head but am stopped short by Alrick's hand grabbing my chin. "No, I saw you spot the targets on your leisurely walk here. Look at me and shoot."

Shari looks at me curiously, and then, as if to boast, she says, "I hit the first five 300 yards away dead center and . . ."

She is stopped short by a wave of Alrick's hand, followed by his deep voice. "Quiet, Shari, he needs no help." Shari is doubly confused now.

I'm not sure if she's ever watched me shoot a bow before, consumed with her own training as she is. I can imagine she's heard, with all the gossip from the servants around the castle, but hearing about something never gives you proper respect for it. Especially this. She also doesn't understand why Alrick thought she was trying to help me. He thinks her saying the number of targets and their distances will help me, but he should know better.

I raise my bow and nock an arrow on a string made of Certus. I think someone needs to learn the lesson about relevance. I take my eyes off Alrick and lock them on Shari's green soul piercers. He may be my father's general, but I am the prince. Without taking my eyes off Shari, I hit the five targets she mentioned in quick succession. Then I proceed to hit the six she didn't, three of which are 600 yards off deep in the trees. Two of them are 750 yards off in the open but are angled to the left and right, respectively, by forty-five degrees. The last one is 1,000 yards away, dirty, rusted, and filled with arrows that split each other sticking out of the bull's-eye because I'm the only one who shoots at it. All dead center. I blow a kiss to Shari and give a dramatic bow. The speed and accuracy with which I shoot is unprecedented.

I know Alrick is amazed, but he simply walks off, back in the direction we came from.

"How—" Shari begins, but it's cut off by Alrick's backward yell.

"Further training is postponed till after your birthday. Enjoy the rest while you can, Prince. Shari, in lieu of you kicking the prince's ass, or his chin, rather, you are off too. Both of you enjoy." With the last, he is gone.

I exhale a deep breath I didn't realize I was holding. It's still early in the day, and it is still heating up. I think I fancy a swim.

"You hit all ten targets dead center," Shari says, amazed, looking through a pair of binoculars she grabbed from a barrel full of arrows.

"Eleven," I say, positioning her binoculars so she can see the farthest target. Her breath catches. She looks at me in wonder, then back in the binoculars, and back to me again. Is she excited or angry?

"How did you do that?" she asks, stepping toward me.

Reflexively, I take a step back with thoughts of our mock fight still on my mind. She stops.

"Don't do that," she says, her voice slightly quavering.

"What?" I ask as she takes another step forward and I take another step back.

"That. You're keeping your distance from me like you're scared of me or something."

"I'm not scared of you, Shari," I say, clearly frightened.

Another step forward, followed by another step backward.

"So what, you think I'm some kind of monster now because I know how to use wooden weapons?" She sounds hurt. "I've never hurt you in twelve years. Why would I start now?"

I respond automatically without thinking. "I beg to differ." Cross doesn't even justify how I came off.

She stops, and the look on her face has transformed into betrayal. "That was only training. I would never—" whatever she was about to say, I'll never know.

Instead of explaining herself, she just loses a breath of frustration and storms right past me. As the moment fades, I stand there feeling a tad bit guilty because of the hurt in her voice. She just beat me as if I were nothing more than a practice dummy. How can she expect me not to be afraid?

"Your Highness," Shari's distressed voice echoes a few feet behind me.

I turn to see a teary-eyed Shari talking to my mother in hushed tones. Is she crying because of me? All the years I've known Shari, I've never seen her cry. My mother wipes her tears away and hugs her. They share a private joke, and Shari smiles and then lets loose a cute little laugh before she disappears toward the castle.

My mother turns to me to afford me her full majesty. Taller than Shari by a couple of inches, my mother is a golden-haired, golden-eyed beauty. She is a little lighter than Shari but nowhere near as curvy. She stands awaiting me to come to her, letting her straight hair blow in the wind. I say *letting* because sometimes she does not allow the wind to touch her. I've seen it; it is somewhat unsettling. She is wearing a sky-blue shirt and pants that look to be for riding. Where is she going?

"Luca," my mother calls in a demanding tone, but then extends her arms to me, waiting for a hug.

"Mom," I say evenly before a smile breaks my face and I rush toward her.

She stops me short by grabbing my nose and twisting until I hear a loud pop. Pain lances across my whole face, but it is quickly subdued by the healing my mother channels into me. When it comes to using Certus, there is no one better than my mother.

"That was broken, darling. Looked awful too," she says matter-of-factly before embracing me.

I return her hug by picking her up and spinning her in a circle. She and my father are both so busy I don't get to see much of either of them anymore. But up until a couple of years ago, she has been with me every step of my sheltered life. I cherish those times. I set her down.

"To what do I owe the pleasure?" I ask playfully, earning a swat to my recently healed nose.

"Forgetful child," she says just as playfully. "I told you I would be gone for a couple of days, so before I leave, I want to see how your power is developing. Come, accompany me to the gardens," she says. Then, with grace like you cannot begin to imagine, she begins to move toward the castle.

It's almost like she's not even moving and the world around her moves for her. "Hurry," she calls back, somehow knowing I have not moved. I move to catch up. I would be more excited about this if my mother would teach me, but she says if she does that, then it'll stifle my imagination.

"Certus is all about subtly bending reality to your will," I quote my mother aloud mockingly.

"I'm sorry, did you say something?" comes my mother's knowing voice.

"No, ma'am," I sigh.

"I didn't think so, just checking," she says cheerfully.

The only thing she has taught me how to do is shield myself and heal myself. The bowstring of power, I came up with on my own. I haven't worked on any new uses of Certus in quite some time. The walk to the gardens isn't far, and I use the rest of it to enjoy the scenery.

3 POWER

As I explained before, the power is broken down into two types: Potentia and Certus. Potentia is the type of power my father can touch. Potentia is a word in a language called Latin. I know this because I actually read the books my mother sends me, well, sometimes. Potentia means "strength, might, power, and force." And that is exactly what this form of the power is—the raw power to burn cities to the ground, draw lightning pillars from the sky, summon tidal waves out of thin air, and cause the ground to quake until nothing is left standing. As devastating as this sounds, these are only a few uses of Potentia. Through my studies, I've learned Potentia users draw upon a source of energy within themselves and use it to command fire, water, earth, air, shadow, and light—or anything that is a derivative of any or all of those sources, separate or combined. The more powerful the source of energy and the connection with Potentia, the more destructive one becomes. Some writing suggests that, based on personality, certain types of people are better at commanding different elements with Potentia. For instance, someone who is extremely stubborn might find it easier to command rock using Potentia instead of water. Someone who is full of rage might find it easier to command fire instead of wind. These are just theories, though, and until a week from now, I won't be able to find out myself.

My father has been unofficially crowned the strongest Potentia user since before I was born. Some people whisper he is Aries, the god of war, incarnate. I wouldn't know because I've never seen him in action. He must be quite a force to reckon with considering my whole life all I've known is peace. For all his power, though, the man cannot make a simple

24

shielding to protect himself. He must overpower his opponent or die trying. And he's not dead yet. Scary to think about. However, shielding is not Potentia. It is a product of Certus, my mother's domain.

It was no jest when I said my mother is the best when it comes to wielding Certus. What's scary about her is, I don't even know half the things she can do. Certus is a Latin word that means certain, sure, definite, decided, specific, and precise. Where my father is power, my mother is finesse. Certus cannot be properly explained due to the extensive realm in which the power touches. I like to think of Certus as the stitching that holds reality together, and though I don't fully understand it, I know that stitching is in everything material. My mother says it exists outside the material reality around us as well, but conversations like that always leave me with headaches. Basically, if you can think of it, my mother can do it, as long as it doesn't require too much power—shielding, healing, growing crops, and random lights, just to name a few. With Certus, the possibilities are endless. I saw my mother stop the rain around herself once when she thought no one was watching. Now, I only know she still does it because when it rains, her hair doesn't get wet, nor do her clothes.

Another bit of speculation from one of my mother's various books is that there is a spectrum of power on which Potentia and Certus sit at opposite ends of each other. Supposedly, the stronger you are, the less control you have. The more control you have, the less power you can summon. People normally fall on one end of the spectrum or the other, like my parents—except nowhere near as powerful or precise. Rumors have it in-betweeners exist. I wonder what they can do.

"So, what have you worked on besides the strings of force you use to nock your arrows on?" my mother asks me when the door to the gardens closes behind us.

I watch her move to the pathway that marks the entrance into the massive garden and am pleased by what I see. The beauty of the castle gardens never ceases to amaze me. The way . . .

"Stop gawking and focus," my mother calls to me without looking.

How well she knows me. Right. She asked me a question. "Shielding and healing as you have instructed, Mother," I answer.

"That's all?" My mother asks, sounding disappointed.

"Well, if you would teach me something new, I would work on that as well," I say somewhat rebelliously.

My mother turns to me and gifts me with a soft smile. "I told you I do not want to . . ."

I cut her off, "Yes, I know you do not want to stifle my imagination."

She nods, then turns from me so we can resume our walk. "You have been working on your healing, yet your nose was broken when I found you. Why?" she asks sternly.

"Because that heathen of a woman you adopted broke it," I complain.

"That is not what I asked you," my mother says impatiently.

"Yes it is, you just . . . Oh, you're asking me why I didn't heal it myself."

She twirls her finger for me to continue.

"Well, at the time I was distracted by other things," I say honestly, recalling the awkward experience between Shari and me. I feel my cheeks color.

"I thought you said she was a heathen," my mother states without missing a beat.

"She is . . . Wait, she is not the reason. I just forgot in the middle of training, that's all," I lie through my teeth, trying to avoid embarrassment.

"Shari is not a heathen," my mother says rigidly. "She's a beautiful young woman who's had the misfortune of a hard and unfair childhood. Secondly, I am your mother, I birthed you. The only thing that could make my self-centered son forget anything, especially the fact that his nose is broken, is a woman," she says knowingly.

I blush again.

"See," she says playfully. I can see the smile on her face as she walks toward a small fountain to inspect it, no doubt giving me a moment to myself. Soon, I join her.

"How was your shielding?" she asks as soon as I step next to her.

"Actually, I'm really good at that. Try—"

I'm cut off by my mother conjuring a water whip out of the fountain quicker than a wind breeze and splashing me with it. Well, she tried to, anyway. I smile and don't even look down, knowing how good I've become.

"Ha," my mother laughs. "Looks like you peed yourself."

"Where?" I ask, disbelieving.

"There," she says playfully, splashing me again, but this time I really do look like I peed myself.

"You tricked me," I complain, recalling Shari's first strike in our training session.

"You fell for it," my mother retorts nonchalantly. "You're getting better, but you need to make shielding a part of you just like breathing."

"Why?" I ask, bemoaning all the effort that comes with that.

"Because I'm your mom and I said so. Also because it might save your life one day. And before you go telling me it's too much, know I've watched you shoot a bow since you first began to shoot. So . . . Get. It. Done. Understood?"

"Yes, ma'am," I say, hating the next few days of my life already.

"There's a good lad," she says while extracting the water from my pants.

"Ow!" I yelp.

"What?" my mother exclaims in concern, searching my body, dropping her stream of water from my pants into the garden. I look up and smile.

"That is not funny," she says, sounding relieved.

"You fell for it. Apparently, you should also work on your—hmmph." My mouth feels like it's been stitched together by invisible strings. Rather than hurt, though, they tickle.

My mother walks to a bench and sits, motioning me to follow.

Grudgingly, I do.

"You need to be nicer to Shari. Despite your training session, she is not a monster." There's a pause, and then she looks up at me. "Nothing to say?" she asks smugly. I just point to my mouth. "Oh, well . . ." she starts playfully. "Until you can figure out how to undo what I did, you don't need to talk. So just listen."

I stare, wide-eyed, not believing she would do such a thing. Talk about—or don't talk about it, I suppose—motivation for learning. "This is not my story to tell, but since you lack the decency to converse with Shari about her past, I will enlighten you. Shari had a hard life before I brought her in. Her parents, who were close friends of mine, were chopped to pieces right in front of her face. She hid under the bed, not saying anything, barely breathing for fear of being discovered, but watching every single moment of her parents' massacre because she was powerless to stop it. I stopped by her house, her parents being friends of mine and all, and smelled death from outside the house. I walked into the door and saw blood trailing from the room at once. I rushed to the room and couldn't believe what I saw: Shari, just sitting next to the pile of bloody pieces that used to be her parents."

I was originally only concentrating on figuring out how to remove the stitches made of power from my mouth. By the time I figured out how to, I no longer knew what to say. Shari had to endure that at ten years old? I couldn't imagine losing my parents and the only life I've ever known. Albeit she did get adopted by the queen, but still. No wonder she was so quiet when she first came to live with us. I'm having trouble trying to empathize with something so . . . shattering.

"I know you've undone my power. Speak," my mother demands.

"What am I supposed to say?"

"Nothing, you learn."

"What am I supposed to learn from that?" I ask, horrified.

"Humility, courage, perseverance—you choose. But while doing that, be nice to Shari for me, please," my mother says softly.

"But she's dangerous and annoying," I complain.

"She is your best friend," my mother says, vexed.

"My only friend," I say, choosing not to back down.

"Please?" my mother asks longingly as she places me under the scrutiny of her reality-discerning eyes. I know when I'm beat.

"Yes, ma'am," I mumble.

"Thank you," she says, leaning forward to kiss my forehead and standing to leave.

"Where are you going?" I ask somewhat protectively.

"Are you my father, or am I your mother?" she asks evenly.

"You are my mother," I answer reluctantly.

"That's what I thought too." She smiles at me, then leaves.

I linger a while longer after my mother leaves, watching the sun move on its course through the sky. All the servants say you're not supposed to look directly at the sun, but it's never bothered me. I've been sitting, absent-mindedly playing with Certus, trying to replicate my mother's silencing trick while I think about what to say to Shari. It felt like small phantom strings were woven throughout my lips, keeping them shut. The string would be just like my bow string, made of power, but finer. But how do I weave it through someone's lips? I'm going to practice on myself.

I don't truly dislike Shari. She's beautiful and kind—who could honestly dislike her? She isn't annoying either. Our eccentric relationship is more like a game we've always played at since she opened up after coming to live with us. Just today, when she said I was scared of her in the training arena, is the only time I've ever been angry with her. Recalling the memory causes my fist to clinch, tightening the fine threads of power I've laced through my lips. I wonder if I can talk. "HMPF." Nope, I smile to myself. With a little more practice, I will have the silencing trick mastered in no time.

My mind wanders back to Shari. Until today, I never knew how good she is with blades, even if they are wooden. I've seen her practice before, but the firsthand demonstration was much more enlightening, and painful. She is dangerous, but even while she destroyed me during our fight, I felt no malice. If anything, it was the opposite. Her blushing face flashes in my mind again. Shit. I feel my face heat and heartbeat pick up at the memory. I must talk to Shari, and not just because my mother told me to. I rise from the bench and start heading to the pool. It's hot enough that the pool is going to feel really nice. It will also help me sort my thoughts a little more. The real question of importance is, what does one say to a girl who's been through what Shari has?

I stop by my room to drop off my bow and change into some shorts for swimming. Not really expecting different results, I continue questioning servants at random about my birthday, but still no luck. The random glimpses I keep catching of the sun through different windows let me know it's been steadily slipping toward the horizon and will set in an hour or two. The heat has gone nowhere. I approach the metal double doors, which have a dragon head emblazoned on them, that lead to the pool area. The dragon head is currently split in half because one of the doors is already open. That could only mean one thing: Shari is here. I gulp, not yet ready for this conversation. Going against my better judgment, I slip in and close the door behind me so no one can hear this sure-to-be-awkward conversation.

I turn from closing the door and find Shari exiting the pool. Eyeing me, she stands and is about to grab her towel but makes a split-second decision. Forgoing the towel, she walks over toward me . . . I'm stunned—no, more like scared. But not of Alrick's star pupil; I'm scared of the way her hips sway when she walks. I'm intimidated by the light bounce of her curves with every step. I'm scared of this woman right now because that's exactly what she is in every sense of the word. A beautiful woman. I don't think I've ever seen her in anything so . . . revealing. She is wearing a red two-piece swimsuit that compliments her hair but contrasts her beautiful green eyes. Water drips off her lovely frame, and she is approaching.

"You're blushing, Luca," she says playfully.

"No I'm not," I reply desperately, feeling my face reddening in the process.

"No, you weren't, but now you are," she says delightedly. I'm about to reply with some smart comment about women when I noticed the puffiness and redness around her eyes. She's been crying.

"Are you okay?" I ask, genuinely concerned.

"What do you want, Princeling? You're a lot of things, but sympathetic isn't one of them. At least not toward me," she says venomously. "Wait, I thought you were supposed to be scared of me now." She steps forward.

It takes all that I am not to take a step back, my nervousness having nothing to do with fear of our fight. Shari comes uncomfortably close and smiles when I do not run from her, then pats my chest for good measure. She then moves to a patch of grass in the pool area on which the last rays of sunlight still shine down on. As she walks past me, I can't help but admire the view. What real man could?

"If you're done staring, you could tell me what you want," Shari says, sounding pleased.

"If you didn't want me to stare, you would've grabbed your towel,"

I try to say confidently.

"Be that as it may, you still have not told me why you are here."

Well, this is my pool, but that is not what I want to say. "To talk."

"There's nothing to talk about. You are a boy or a man, I have yet to figure out which, and I am a woman. What happened on the training ground was just your body's natural response to that kind of contact," she says indifferently.

For some reason, my feelings are hurt. I speak without thinking. "Then why did you blush?" I mumble, hurt.

"Say it with your chest if you desire to be heard, Luca."

I will not play her game. "That is not what I wanted to talk about, but thank you for the clarification."

Curiously, Shari sits up. "Then what is it?"

"I wanted to talk about your past," I say softly.

She explodes. "Not you too!" She stands and gets in my face. Despite my earlier courage, I take a step back. "I'm so sick of everyone looking down on me, showing pity instead of general kindness. Oh, look, there's the girl the queen took in. Didn't she lose her parents, poor girl? They say these things right in front of me like I'm not there or like I don't exist as a person. They all just see me as some poor girl the queen took pity on. And you were HMPF—"

I silence her with the power just like my mother did me. She stares at me wide-eyed and shocked, but I will not be talked down to like a dog.

"All I wanted to do was talk to you and see if you were alright. The last time we spoke, you left crying, and when I came in here, your eyes were still red and puffy. Despite what you think about me I consider you my only friend. I know we play a lot and have our differences, but I enjoy your company. You are my only connection to the outside world. Eighteen years old and I haven't left the castle once. My mother said it would be good for me to listen to your story so I can understand more about you. You should know I would never treat you as the servants do. My one friend. I thought I really could learn something listening to your story, but all that got me was yelled at. Now . . . now, I don't know."

I release the power that stitches her mouth together. "You used the power on me!" she says, almost sounding scared.

"So," I reply, not understanding.

She ignores me and rushes past me through the double doors, not bothering to grab her towel. What did I do that was so wrong? My mom just did that to me just a few hours ago. Why is Shari so complicated? Why can't things ever just go the way I see them in my head? Frustrated, I jump in the pool and get out, dry off, and go to my room.

Over the next few days, I just stay in my room and practice my shielding as my mother asked. A couple of times I've woken up early and gone out on the balcony to see if Shari was out training. I know Alrick gave us the rest of the week off, but that's what she does when she's stressed. However, I haven't seen her, nor has she come to talk to me.

The servants are still as tightlipped as ever about my birthday. I only talk to them when I'm hungry or pass them on the way to search the gardens or the pool for Shari. My mother is still mysteriously absent, and my birthday is tomorrow. Is my mom even going to show up? Will Shari still be mad at me? My father is doing whatever it is he does, and I am not comfortable enough around him to willingly seek his counsel.

I can't wait until tomorrow. The first thing I'm going to do is go to a . . . what are they called? Tavern. Yes, a tavern, and I'm going to talk to all manner of people. I'll make more than just one friend, and I'll never be alone again. I wonder what ale and wine taste like. I always hear the servants talk about different kinds of drinks, debating which are the strongest or which taste the best. The wine the female servants seem to be so fond of smells deliciously sweet. My mother denies me the privilege of drinking.

"Wait till you're older."

Well, guess what? I'll be eighteen tomorrow, Mom. The servants say sometimes at taverns when folks have had too much to drink, they begin to fight for the stupidest reasons. Very few times, someone has died. I wonder if that's part of the reason my mom is so adamant that I control my anger. The thought of killing someone is staggering though. I have not, nor do I believe I ever could. It just doesn't sit right with me. I would never be in one of those fights anyway, as I really detest violence. I only train with Alrick because my father makes me. Although, I do love using my bow, I would never kill anyone with it. Excited as I am about my birthday tomorrow, I somehow manage to find sleep and dream of my first travels outside the castle.

I awake from the pressure of what feels like a blow from my hammer to my sternum. I wheeze as air forcibly escapes my lungs. What is going on? I struggle for air as I open my eyes, but it is pitch black. There's a bag over my head tied around my neck. Whatever is happening, somebody doesn't want me to know anything. I reach for Certus but cannot concentrate enough to touch it. Shit. While I lie trying to catch my breath, I'm powerless to stop myself from being hogtied and gagged. Another blow to the sternum almost makes me throw up. Already in need of oxygen, I dry heave and get lightheaded. I've never felt pain like this in my life. It hurts so bad, I can't even get mad. I think my sternum is broken as well as a couple of my ribs. One of my lungs might have collapsed. Soon, I am being carried over my captor's shoulder. Where, I do not know, courtesy of the bag tied over my head. Despite the pain, I feel confident because whoever is trying to kidnap me, the night before my birthday, just broke into the castle of the two most powerful users of the power and is trying to steal their son. They will never make it out alive. I may not like violence, but my father harbors no such sentiments. Very briefly, I wonder if I should fear someone who is crazy enough to try this. My thoughts are interrupted by shouting.

"Where is the boy?" It sounds like my father's voice, and it is borderline belligerent.

I knew it. This bastard is—. My thoughts are cut off by my mother's voice. "Far away from you by now," she says smugly.

What? What does that even mean?

"I'll kill you," my father roars.

Whatever else is said is lost to me when whoever is carrying me bends a corner, and my head smashes into something, and I lose consciousness.

4 SHATTER

I awaken to the smell of sage, rainforest, and some type of meat cooking over the fire. I open my eyes and find myself in what appears to be a hut. There are strange symbols all over the walls of this hut, and none of them are the slightest bit familiar to me. Besides the symbols, there is a very ancient-looking bookcase, a wooden table for two, and a couch, if the scraggly-looking thing can be called so justly.

I stand, expecting to feel pain in the entirety of my upper body, only to realize I feel better than I have in a long time. The next thing I notice is my clothes—or lack of, better put. Gone are my training robes, replaced by trousers made of animal hide. That's it. Who's cruel idea of a joke is this? I go from castle livery to this! I move to the only opening I see in the hut.

"Ouch."

I look down at whatever I stepped on and find the floor of the hut littered with all types of wooden weapons. I find a pair of boots on the floor by the exit that look to be about my size. I put them on— a little tight, but they'll do. Definitely better than nothing if I must run far.

I exit the hut slowly, looking around until I spot a man cooking meat by a fire to my right. He is clothed in similar garb, but unlike me, he has a wolf cloak around his shoulders and a quarterstaff lying on his right side. With his attention on cooking the meat, if I could just get that quarter—"

"Good morning, sleeping beauty," comes the man's voice, sounding older and more mysterious than time itself.

He didn't even look up from cooking the meat.

"This deer is about to be done cooking, and I imagine you have quite the appetite."

As soon as he mentions my appetite, my stomach looses a fierce growl. Well, he already knows I'm up, and I have no idea about my current situation, so I walk around to the other side of the fire and sit.

"What's the matter? Don't trust me?" he asks, chuckling.

"No, I don't know you, and you kidnapped me," I say flippantly.

"Good, trust will get you killed. However, I'm not the one who kidnapped you. I'm too old for adventures like that." He turns the meat in the fire.

"You were dropped off here. I was asked to look after you and teach you the basics."

What he says is true, at least in part; I noticed the grays in his hair before I sat down. Now that I look over his face, I can see creasing lines that mark age and crow's feet by his eyes. He has not looked at me yet, keeping his eyes downcast on the meat. Maybe he fears me. No, this man does not fear me. Old he may be, but his body looks as if it was forged between a hammer and an anvil. His hands are calloused; he is no stranger to the sword. Upon his body and forearms are scars older than me. Most people who play with blades don't live to see his age. That is a testament to his skill. He's at least twice Alrick's age.

"Do you always lose yourself to your thoughts?" he asks curiously when I take too long to speak.

"Who are you? What do you know about my situation? Where are my mother and father? And if you didn't kidnap me, then who did?" I ignore his questions and ask my own.

"So many questions, yet none of them the right one," he replies mystically.

"What should I be asking, then, old man?" He doesn't even have to think about it.

"Why? Why is always the right question because it leads to understanding. Why did you get kidnapped is the real question. By whom is irrelevant right now because they're gone and will not be returning."

I wait for him to continue. He doesn't.

"Well, are you going to answer the question?" I ask frustratedly.

"Which one?" He smiles.

I do not like this man.

"All of them!" I yell.

"That is no way for a grown man to act. Do not yell like a child because you find yourself frustrated. Anger will not solve your problems. And, no."

"No, what?" I ask, confused.

He sighs in annoyance. "No, I will not answer all of your questions."

This man, whoever he is, is worse than Shari. Who does he think he's talking to? I am the prince, and I will not tolerate being treated like this.

"Look at me when you talk to me, old man."

When he looks up, I flinch: his eyes are golden.

"Something wrong, Luca?" he asks knowingly.

Until now, he has not used my name, and now that I told him to look at me, he does not take his eyes off me. Why are his eyes the same as my mother's? No, they are the same color, but his have more gravity behind them. I've not been around a lot of people, but gold is not a common eye color. Something is going on, and I'm out of the loop.

"Do I know you?" I ask, looking for somewhere else to start this conversation.

"No, but I know you," he says in that mystic tone.

His responses infuriate me, and I don't know why. But just like he said, anger will get me nowhere. Even with Certus, I couldn't beat this man, and my bow is nowhere to be found. Honestly, I'm not sure I could win with that; his presence alone is frightening. For now, I will play his game.

"You said you will not answer my questions, so—"

He cuts me off with a raised finger. "No, I did not. I said I would not answer all your questions. I was led to believe you were smarter than this."

He looks up to the sky and shouts, "Yuna, are you sure this is your get?"

Yuna is my mother's name. The way he said it leads me to believe they are familiar. So I'm probably safe. My body untenses. What's a "get"? I'll figure it out later. I doubt he'd tell me anyway.

"How did I get here?" I choose to ask.

Another sigh. He is visibly annoyed. "You know how you got here. You were kidnapped, or did you forget? Again, wrong question."

"Why am I here?" I ask the question in question. At this, he

smiles.

"Finally! To save your life, of course." All kinds of questions run through my mind now. Let's keep it slow and steady.

"From who?" I ask, concerned.

"Not my story to tell, but you will find out soon enough."

I refuse to let his nonchalance frustrate me. Besides, he feels familiar somehow.

"Who are you?"

"Nope," he says quickly.

"Why are you?" He falls over laughing, holding his stomach.

"I do not know why I am; that is too philosophical, even for me. I just meant I wasn't going to answer that question. You should figure it out soon enough anyway," he replies, through a serious bout of laughter.

I am already tired of this old man.

"How long do I have to stay here?" I ask, annoyed. He grows serious at this question.

"I will not hold you against your will. But know this: there is a world beyond this forest that you are not ready for. You were left here for me to teach, and that is what I intend to do. Like I said, I will not stop you from leaving. But if you leave, know I will not be here should you decide to come back."

I do not trust this man, but I trust my mother, and he knows her. Also, setting me up with a teacher definitely sounds like something my mother would do. This is why I chose not to leave.

"What will you be teaching me?" I ask after a moment.

"Things you do not know, obviously. You're bad at asking questions, so let me just give you answers. I will educate you on proper manners, because you cannot be a prince when you leave here. And by educate, I mean humble you. I will teach you about society, the best I know anyway; it's been a while, you see." He flashes his wolf cloak at me. "I will help you hone your power—"

I interrupt, "Wait, you can touch Certus too?" I ask excitedly.

"No, I can't, but you can. Now stop talking and listen. I will give you books in a dead language—the one you saw upon the walls of the hut—and you will learn to read it. I will teach you to hunt and live in the wild. Lastly, I will help you master whichever weapon you choose. Now, eat." He gestures to the cooked deer. "And explore your environment, then get some rest. Lessons begin tomorrow." He stands and then walks toward the hut.

"Wait."

He doesn't slow. He just looks over his shoulder

"What's your name?" I ask, needing to know.

"I believe you called me old man. That will suffice," he says before disappearing into the hut.

I can't figure this man out, and it's driving me crazy. What does he mean I can't be a prince when I leave here? What else am I supposed to be? Way too many questions bombard my mind right now. I don't even want to bother trying to make sense of them. I notice he left his quarterstaff on the ground. Not able to help myself, I pick it up, grunting with the effort. This thing weighs about eighty pounds. What is it made of? Does he actually fight with this? Can anyone fight with this? With both hands placed on the staff firmly, I give it an experimental swing and lose my balance, nearly falling flat on my face. There's no way. This thing is just for show, or for walking. But he walked to the hut just fine. I place the staff back on the ground, grab some dear meat, and then go explore my environment.

Old redwood trees climb high into the sky, making it almost impossible to see the sun. There's no trail telling you where to walk or which way is safe. This forest is wild and ancient. I doubt it has been disturbed by any people recently besides me and the old man. Oddly, I find it peaceful; the sounds of unrefined nature are soothing. I decide not to venture out too far, lest some wild animal attack me while I am alone. Exploring my environment quickly turns into thinking about unanswered questions and what tomorrow will bring. Tomorrow will be a long day.

***

I'm awakened at dawn by the old man kicking my pallet on the floor of his hut.

"Get up and see to your necessities. It is time."

I get up and grumble something incomprehensible about water. My body is stiff from sleeping on the hard floor, far from the comfort of my bed in the castle.

"The water is in the well around back. Had you checked your environment, you would know that," he says disapprovingly.

Without responding, I go to the well and attend to my hygiene. As I splash my face with the ice-cold water, inhaling a sharp breath in shock, I recall Alrick saying Shari was up before the sun and out after it went down, training. Why? This is miserable, Shari. I wonder what happened to her. I hope she is okay. I make up my mind to ask the old man about her. I finish up, then move around to the front of the hut where I find the old man waiting.

"Do you know what happened to Shari?" I ask, concern clear in my voice.

"Who?" he asks indifferently.

"Never mind." He clearly doesn't know who I'm talking about.

"Enough distractions. First things first. You must change the color of your eyes and your hair. For someone of your supposed caliber, it should be a simple thing. "

"Why?" I ask simply.

"Now he wants to ask why, but you already know the answer. Someone is trying to kill you. That is why you are hiding in this forest with me. The first thing someone looking for you will see is your all-too-noticeable eyes. The hair is just for good measure."

He's just jealous. "But I love my eyes," I protest.

"Well, learn to miss them. Whatever you do with the power to change your appearance will not be permanent, so make sure you redo it every couple of days or so. Now go back to the well so you can see your reflection. Do not come back till it is done. I will be waiting."

I start walking to the well, then stop. "What will you be doing?"

"Waiting. Now, go."

This training better not last longer than a week, or I'm sure this old man will drive me insane. I approach the well and just stare at my reflection for a moment. I honestly have no clue how to do what he wants me to do. Why must I change my eye color? Who is trying to kill me? Why have my parents not dealt with my would-be assassin swiftly? Anger, confusion, and anxiety war inside me right now. This is the exact opposite of how I need to feel when working with Certus.

"Calm your anger. It will get you nowhere fast." I replay Shari's voice over and over in my head until my anger fades.

Now I'm just confused and anxious. Breathe. In. Out. In. Out. I close my eyes and call to mind a memory of my mother teaching me the basics about Certus.

"Certus is certain, sure, definite, decided, specific, and precise." Her voice repeats over and over again in my head. "You need to feel this way when working with it. Your end result just is; there is no other option." In my thoughts, I am certain. Sure. Definite. Decided. Specific. And precise. I focus on my eyes and feel them begin to tingle from the trickle of power that flows into them.

Now, what color? My mind immediately goes to my mother, but gold, or black, for that matter, is too close to what they are now. My mind wanders to Shari, and I smile. Green it is. I close my eyes and know they will be green when I open them. I'm not giving them a choice.

I open my eyes and laugh despite myself. One eye is green, and the other is still a golden-black vortex. Focusing on the power still behind my eyes, I wink the one unchanged eye, and it becomes green as well. Now, what color for the hair? I can't do gold for the same reason I couldn't do gold eyes, and red is a little too much. Strawberry blonde it is. I just picture my hair this color, and it changes instantly. Strawberry blonde with green eyes; this is the new me. I accept it, then walk back to the front of the hut. Is it colder, or is that just me?

Standing in the same exact spot I left him, the old man is doing just what he said he would: waiting.

"Took you long enough," he says, opening his eyes just as I enter the reach of his quarterstaff, which he so casually holds up to his right. He's not even leaning on it.

"That only took—"

"Hours," he says, cutting me off. "Look at the sun." He's right.

The sun is harder to see through the tree line, but it has moved quite a ways. It must have been harder than I thought to change the color of my eyes.

"Since you've wasted the best reading hours by playing with appearances—"

I cut him off, "You told me to," I say, frustrated.

"Shut up. Now, have you decided on a weapon?"

I really haven't even thought about it. If it isn't my bow, I could not care less. I stare at him for a moment before I'm stricken with an idea. Just to see if I can catch him off guard, I point to his staff.

"That one," I say, pleased with myself.

If he feels any type of way about my choice, he doesn't let it show. He merely tells me to hold the weapon as he goes to get another one. I shift with the weight of the staff as he tosses it to me effortlessly. How many of these staffs does he own? What is this even made out of? It's metallic for sure, but beyond that, I haven't the slightest idea. I wonder if I'll ever actually get good with this thing.

Snapping me out of my thoughts, the old man yells something at me.

"What?" I ask, turning to face him.

For the third time all too recently, the oxygen leaves my body as something hits me hard enough in the chest to knock me on my back.

"I said, duck. Did that hurt?" comes the old man's gratified voice.

"Of course it hurt. Didn't you just berate me for dumb questions?" I snap. "What possessed you to do that? I think you fractured something." Painfully, I sit up as he walks closer.

"Then heal yourself. Why is your shield not up like your mother instructed you?"

I squint my eyes at him. How does he know that? "How do you . . . you . . . you're . . . you're my grandfather!" I slowly piece together.

He smiles a genuine smile, letting me know I'm right. I don't recall ever meeting him, but that is the only reason I can think of that explains his gold eyes, age, and familiarity with my mother, and the way he makes me second-guess everything I do. Clearly, my mother learned from a master. However, she is graceful, and he is . . . maddening.

"Like I said, 'old man' will suffice. Now stand and heal yourself."

I stand and place a hand over the fracture in my ribs and attempt to heal myself. He swats my hand away.

"You do not need to touch your injury to heal it. In a fight, the extra movement could cost you your life. Focus on the pain and will the injury to restore to its proper form. Don't take forever like you did with your eyes either."

It's harder to grab Certus through the pain, but after a few minutes, I manage. Certain. Sure. Definite. Decided. Specific. Precise. The bones mend, causing me to exhale in relief.

"Good, now why did you pick that weapon?" the old man asks me, amused.

"Honestly?"

"I have little time for anything else," he replies.

Okay, you asked for it.

"Just to spite you. I saw you with it yesterday and again today. You have been getting on my nerves since we met, and I saw an opportunity to return the favor," I say, feeling righteous.

He just smiles.

"You are definitely my Yuna's get. Not as bright, but more controlled."

Okay, so "get" must mean "child." One more question off the seemingly endless list.

"You did not irritate me with your decision, child, but do not get into the habit of making decisions based upon emotion. That will not solve your problems. However, you are a man, at least in age, so I will not let you go back on that decision," he explains, then smiles mischievously.

"Pick it up." As I bend down to pick it up, I notice another quarterstaff just beyond mine. The difference is the silver color, opposed to this black one. It also has the same ringed circles that adorn my bow, wrapped around its center. There are three ringed circles in total. That must be what he threw at me. I go to pick that one up instead. Surprised by the weight, I chose to let it lie there.

"How much does that thing weigh?" I ask.

"Seventy-five pounds," he replies, chuckling, then walks over to pick up both staffs and hands me his black one.

"Really? Well then how much does this one weigh?" I ask, gesturing to the black staff.

"Fifty pounds," he answers. "I only use this one to train, so I can use the one you hold faster and with more finesse. While I train you, I will use this." He holds up the silver staff. "And you will use that." He points his staff at mine.

"How do I get one of those?" I ask, looking at his silver staff in wonder.

"You want one of these?" he asks, looking doubtful. "Tell you what, if you can touch me once with the quarterstaff you now hold, I will make you a staff personally that will put both to shame. Now step back."

Now excited, I do as I am told.

"Further, further, a little to the left, and stop. Okay, close your eyes."

Again, I do as I am told. Now that I know this is my grandfather, I'm a little more comfortable following his directions.

"Are you shielded?"

"Yes," I say right away. I hear his staff tap the ground twice and realize just before it happens, I'm about to be hit. Shit. Heart racing, I open my eyes only to realize I'm already flying through the air. I land on my back and roll backward to finish on my feet. Unhurt.

"I'm alive!" I shout excitedly. "And I didn't feel a thing."

"I would hope not. You said you were shielded. Now what did you learn?"

"Not to listen to you," I say lightly, but meaning every word.

"I do recall saying trust will get you killed, but seriously, what did you learn?" he asks, studying me.

"I . . . I learned . . . " I mumble, unsure what to say. What would my mother want me to learn from this? Think. "I learned that even though shielding protects me from external harm, the force and momentum from the blow can't be stopped." I grin, then nod my head, satisfied, more to myself than him.

"Good. Very good. Another thing you should know is that if someone shoots fire at you while you are shielded, you will be fine as long as you don't sit there and let it cook you. However, if someone shoots blue fire at you, it will cook you instantly, shield or no."

I nod in thanks at the new information.

"To make sure you truly understand the lesson you learned and are not spouting nonsense from a book, I will put you in a scenario."

I nod for him to continue.

"You are on a cliff's edge, the sea is behind you, but jagged peaks jut up from the water below for quite a ways out. The person you are currently fighting can touch the power like you, except he uses Potentia. Suddenly he hurls a giant boulder at you. Do you shield yourself?"

"Yes," I answer immediately. "My mother told me to always have myself shielded as if it were akin to breathing."

"Then you will die," he says matter-of-factly. "Be practical, boy, and stop saying what you believe people want to hear. If you are shielded when that boulder hits you, the force will knock you off the cliff. Shield or no shield, the impact on the jagged peaks will kill you," he reprimands.

I gulp as the consequence of my choice settles in.

"So, what should I do then?" I ask curiously.

"I don't know. You're the one who can touch the power, not me. Figure it out. I just wanted to point out that knowledge alone will not help you if you don't know how to use it."

I stand staring at the ground, already feeling defeated before the training has even begun.

"Tell you what, kid. Take the rest of the day off. You've got enough to ponder for now. Sun's going down anyway."

I think that's the first hint of compassion I've heard from him. "Don't think I'm taking it easy on you. I just need your mind ready by tomorrow before I beat you with this silver stick," he says, jovial-like, as he walks back to the hut.

So much for compassion. Tomorrow is going to be a long day.

5 A LONG DAY

The sounds of footsteps awaken me from a dream about a childhood memory of Shari and me. I shield myself instantly without moving a muscle.

"Good," my grandfather says in a deep, bone-chilling voice from above.

I open my eyes and look at him, then out of the hut.

"It's not even sunrise yet. I can't read in the dark," I complain. "Why are you waking me up?"

"Because we're going on a run," he says coldly.

I bolt upright. "On the run? On the run from who?" I ask, fear clear in my voice.

He places a hand firmly on my shoulder and kneels to talk to me. His eyes have a calming effect as they dissect my own.

"Listen, Luca, I know you're stressed out about your new living arrangements and maybe even a little scared. It's understandable. But you need to listen. I said we are going on a run, not going on the run."

I exhale a breath I didn't realize I was holding, and he smiles at me. With everything that has happened in the last few days, I've just been wound super tight. My birthday came and went without me even realizing it.

My grandfather stands and steps back. I rise to my feet as well. When did he get so tall? I guess I've never realized because he's never been this close. That alone proves my mental fatigue.

"Besides, you are with me now. If people happen to stumble across us, I assure you, we are not the prey," he says lightly. "They are," he says wickedly.

Well, that's a very comforting thought.

"Now hurry up and meet me outside," he says, then walks out of the hut.

That man is more frightening and more irritating than Shari, but nowhere near as pleasurable to look at. How did my mother put up with him?

Thinking of Shari causes a surge of worry to well up in me at not knowing what has happened to her. Could I possibly miss the vexation that is Shari? At the thought, my face heats. I quickly abandon that line of thinking and follow the old man outside.

He waits, barefoot, next to a dense area in the forest, looking as impassive as the nature around him. As I approach, he motions me to take off my boots. I didn't even realize they were on. I must have fallen asleep in them. I sit down and do as I'm told. It's too early to be rebellious.

"We will run the course I am about to take you on every morning until you can move like a ghost through the forest, unseen and unheard until it is too late," he tells me passively.

I look up. What course? All I see is raw and untamed nature.

However, that is not what I ask. "You believe in ghosts, old man?" I ask mockingly as I stand.

"Have you ever encountered one, Prince?" he asks, cocking his head to the side while his eyes dissect me.

I'm sure there is a lesson in this. "No, I have not."

"My point exactly."

I wince at the light stabbing in my feet from the undergrowth.

"Do not stand like that," he scolds.

"Like what?" I ask, having no idea what he is talking about.

"Flatfooted," he says through an annoyed sigh. "Walk on the balls of your feet. It will work your calves, but you will make less noise."

I transition my weight to the balls of my feet and wince at the light stabbing once again.

"You better walk lightly and get used to the pain, because for every twig you break or bush you rustle, there will be consequences. Do not heal your feet either. Embrace the forest. Now follow," he lectures, then takes off.

Watching him move makes me feel like my mind is playing tricks on me. If I couldn't see him, I would never know he was moving through a forest. Hell, I wouldn't even know he was moving at all.

I take off after him, and on my third step, I hear a twig break under my foot. He doesn't look back, but I know he heard. Today is going to be a long day.

After about thirty excruciating minutes and double the number of unwanted noise, I lose him. I looked down at the snapping noise under my foot from the most recent broken twig, then back up again, and he was gone. Another test, surely.

I stand completely still and shield myself . . . on second thought —. No, no, I'm not on a cliff; I stay shielded. Remembering his earlier trick, I crouch. Seconds later, I feel three light projectiles hit my shield where my spine is. I turn and find three darts on the floor behind me. Looking up, following what I guess to be their trajectory, I find the old man, kneeling on a branch in a tree with a dart blower in his hand, looking pleased.

"Proud of me, old man?" I ask arrogantly.

"Not really, I'm just glad I don't have to carry you back to the hut and waste another day of training," he says, indeed sounding relieved.

As I begin to walk over to him, my ears catch the sound of running water. Passing the tree in which he sits, I find a big creek. The water is so clear I can see the fish and plants beneath the surface, as well as the bottom of the creek itself. Now that I'm this close to the creek, the water is deafening compared to the quiet of the forest. There is no way I shouldn't have heard this. My eyes are one thing, but I'm starting to realize that I need to work on listening, in and out of combat.

"Drink, you have five minutes to gather yourself for the run back," the old man says from behind me, nearly causing me to jump out of my skin.

When did he jump down from the tree? I really didn't notice until now, so focused on trying not to lose the old man, but I'm breathing hard and sweating harder. My lungs feel like they are on fire, but this, all of this outdoors in nature, running, not knowing where I am and what's next, is refreshing. If only someone wasn't trying to kill me.

"Your mother told me your sight is . . . exceptional. Why is it, then, you make so much noise when you move?" the old man asked seriously.

Grudgingly, I raise my head from where I was drinking water from the creek.

"Excuse me for not being able to follow you, who moves like a wraith, through the forest; focus on breathing and shielding myself; and concentrate on everything I see at the same time.

"You can't even touch the power, so you don't know how hard it is to maintain a shield at all times. I'm exhausted, mentally and physically," I complain.

"All I heard is that you are weak, but that is okay. That is why you are here," he says, sounding as if this is what he expected. "Now, get up, sheep. The sun is almost up, and you have reading to do."

"Who are you calling sheep?" I ask, offended while standing.

"Again with the stupid questions. You are supposed to improve," he says chuckling.

I sigh with frustration.

"Why. Are. You. Calling. Me. A. Sheep,?" I ask, drawing out every word.

"Because you are soft and loud, just like a sheep. Now let's go." He takes off, leaving no room for argument.

Now irritated, I follow, trying to focus on the path ahead of me, shielding myself, breathing evenly, and not losing sight of the wolf in front of me. If I am the sheep, he is most assuredly the wolf. It is impossible. I don't lose him on the way back, but that's only because I somewhat remember the way we traveled to get here. I'm certain I made more noise on our return trip than on the way there, but I'm too tired to care.

I drop to my knees, body heaving for air, as I enter the clearing containing our hut. The sun broke through the tree line about five minutes ago, the day only just started. Already, I am entertaining thoughts about how I can't do this as I struggle to recuperate when the old man shouts from the hut.

"Get up, sheep. Go to the well and freshen up. You have reading to do."

Reading. I'm so happy that I don't have to run anymore that I don't care that he just called me a sheep. A sheep I will gladly be—just no more running, or I will be a dead sheep.

I head to the hut after freshening up at the well. The old man is standing over the table, which he has placed a couple of books on, thumbing through a book himself. Without looking up at me, he motions me to sit.

"Do you know what language this is?" he asks me, showing me a page in the book he holds as I sit.

I look at the page, and while I have never seen this writing style before, I'm drawn in by the symbols. It's almost like I can feel the symbols. Bold, delicate strokes mark the pages in patterns I've never seen before. What interests me most is where the strokes intersect one another. It looks like no layer of the writing wants to give, like the joints of the symbols are at war. Like . . . like my eyes.

"What . . . what language is this, old man?" I ask with no small amount of amazement in my voice. I turn the pages in a trance-like state, admiring symbols I can't read when he replies.

"It is the language of power."

I look up at his words, which held his characteristic mysticism.

"What is the language of power?" I ask, not caring how eager I sound right now.

The old man places his hands behind his back and looks me dead in the eyes. His gold eyes burrow into my own. He's so theatrical. That being said, I cannot deny that he does strike a frightening presence.

"The language of power is said to be the first language ever recorded in the world. Before there were different words for individual things, there were only concepts and relations. As you can imagine, that makes it extremely difficult to read and interpret these books properly . . . for those who can read them."

"Wait, everyone can't read these books?" I ask curiously.

"Still as bright as ever, I see," he reproaches.

"Why can't everyone read these books?" I correct.

He smiles. "Because only those who can touch the power can read this language."

I'm taken aback. Growing up as I did in the castle, books were my only escape to the outside world. I can't help but be offended. Everyone should be able to read everything. My brain begins to piece things together.

"So you can't—" Of course he can't, he can't touch the power. "How are you going to teach me to read this if you can't read it yourself?" The faintest hint of a smile touches his lips.

"I know the basic symbols, but when you line them up and begin entwining them together, the meanings simply elude me, as they do everyone who doesn't have the ability to touch the power. So I will teach you what I know, and the rest is up to you," he explains.

Well, that's both liberating and intimidating. I've always had a teacher.

"It is rumored that there is some type of ultimate concept to these books, but it is something like a riddle. Those who discover this concept or answer to the riddle are supposed to receive ultimate power or unity. The people who spend their lives collecting and reading these books cannot agree on which."

My curiosity has been piqued, and I can't wait to dive into these lessons, but something has been bothering me since I figured out he couldn't read these books.

"If you can't read the language of power, then why do you have all these books?" I ask, very interested in his answer.

"They belong to your mother, who is of the opinion that the ultimate concept will bring one unity, something she feels you need. No more questions. It's time to get started."

The next few hours are spent going over the basic symbols of the language of power, which are called elements. Not because they relate to fire or water, but because in them is supposed to be the composition of all reality. Whatever that means. If I could not feel the power radiating behind these symbols, I would not believe it. But I can, and undeniably so. If there is an ultimate concept to be gleaned or a riddle to be solved, I will do it. I take these books as a personal challenge. I think my mother knew I would before she found a way to get these books here. Sadly, I will not do it anytime soon. There are over 150 elements to remember and interpreting them is beyond me for now. Although, at the beginning of one of the books I saw a fairly simple combination of symbols which I interpreted to mean, "Everything Is Everything." I wonder what that is supposed to mean.

Eventually, my mind wanders, as it is prone to do, to thoughts on my mother. What were she and my father talking about the day I was kidnapped? It almost sounded like she wanted me away from my father. No, that's exactly what it sounded like, but why? Then he said he would kill her. I love my father. All I've ever wanted was his approval. But if he hurt my mother . . . I flee the thought to better things.

Shari, where are you? Damn it, I have no better thoughts. How did things just go from perfect to what they are now? I'm broken out of my ill reverie by the old man's voice.

"Enough, there are six hours of sunlight left in which to break your body. Put on your boots, grab your staff, and then meet me out front." He grabs his silver staff from its resting place by the entrance and heads out.

"Break my body?" He sounded a little too excited for my liking.

I do not relish the idea of finding out what he means by that. My muscles already plague me from the run. No point in stalling. I put on my boots and grab the staff before heading out front. The staff feels no lighter in my hands than the first day I picked it up by the fire. Why did I choose this weapon again?

The old man stares at me with that all-knowing gaze of his as I approach. We stand in an area encircled by giant oak trees as if the forest made its own training circle for us. It's really quite ominous. Even the wind has grown quiet awaiting what's about to happen.

"Twirl it," the old man says abruptly.

I'm about to ask, "What?" but I catch myself. He's referring to the staff. I do as I'm told, or pitifully try, anyway. I cannot keep my balance or footing, and I need to use two hands due to the staff's weight.

"Stop," he complains, seemingly frustrated.

I look to him, confused.

"Like this," he says, bending his knees slightly and over-emphasizing his erect posture. He then begins to twirl the staff slowly with two hands, side to side, as if he is a lone man rowing a boat, except he twirls the staff twice on each side, and once as he crosses over to switch sides. Quite the opposite of my demonstration, no muscle in his body moves or even twitches to betray his balance. He then picks up speed and begins to use only one hand, transitioning it to the other when he crosses sides. Is his staff really seventy-five pounds? There's no way. The strength that must take is staggering—show-off. The staff becomes a blur, and I can no longer tell how many times he spins the staff on each side. Then, as if what he was already doing wasn't impossible enough, he adds another rotation to his cycle. He starts spinning the staff above his head single-handedly to transition it from side to side—above, right side, right hand above, left side, left hand. Abruptly, he stops, jabbing the staff into the ground so hard it supports itself standing straight up. He then begins walking over to me slowly. Shit.

"Begin!" he shouts.

I know I just watched him do it, but I wouldn't know the first place to start.

"I can't ..."

He cuts me off, "Just the first part, Sheep," he says smoothly. "The slow, two-handed twirl," he says for good measure.

I bend my knees and straighten my back as I saw him do, then begin a slow, very slow twirl. Believe it or not, just the posture alone—.

Faster than I can see, the old man punches me in the stomach.

Gasping for air, I double over, dropping my staff in the process. Had I been shielded I would not have felt that. I catch my breath surprisingly quickly and straighten myself. He could have hit me a lot harder, so there is obviously a lesson in this.

"Why?" I ask.

"Had you been shielded, you would not have felt that," he says my thoughts exactly.

"But I'm glad you weren't, because that brings me to my next point. This—"

He kicks me in the stomach. I take a couple of steps back from the force of the blow, but I was shielded, so I felt nothing.

"Squeeze your stomach tight when you do . . . everything, really. Do not make me have to tell you again. Now, again." He smiles and steps back.

Ha ha, not funny. I pick up my staff and begin again. Slight bend to my legs, back straight, stomach tight. After about a minute, I stop. My body is on fire. All of it.

"Why did you stop?" he asks, honestly curious. "It burns," I whine like it's obvious.

He shakes his head in disbelief. "This is going to take longer than I thought," he says to himself.

"You are supposed to be teaching me how to fight, not . . . not whatever this is," I say, flustered.

"I told you I would teach you to master the weapon you choose. You cannot fight with a weapon if you are not strong enough to wield it," he says like it's common sense.

"Alrick is a better teacher and fighter than you. He could break you like this," I say with childlike frustration as I snap my fingers.

I don't really mean it. I really like the old man. I'm just sick of him always being so calm and in control. Besides, after that demonstration with the staff, I don't think anyone living could beat him in a fight.

"There are those who came before Alrick," he says cryptically.

Suddenly, I'm reminded of the scars that dance across his body, his physique, and his age. There is so much I don't know about this man, my grandfather, I feel dumb for lashing out.

"But believe what you will, Sheep. Just stop letting your emotions dictate your actions. Nothing good will come of it."

I know he's right, so I add it to the steadily growing list of things I need to work on.

"Do you know what chest-ups and leg bends are?"

I am eager to pass up my moment of child-like behavior, so speak hurriedly. "A chest-up is a simple motion where you flatten your body against the ground, belly down, palms pressed into the ground just below your chest, and push through your chest until your arms are almost all the way extended, before lowering yourself just shy of touching the ground. Leg-bends are even simpler. Keeping your weight on your heels, you squat until your thighs are even with the ground and push back up to standing position. Did enough of both, training with Alrick."

Well, looking at my grandfather's body, maybe not enough. "Good," he says simply. "This," he says, grabbing his silver staff out of the ground before walking over to an oak with lowered branches, jumping, placing the staff horizontally atop two branches evenly so they support his weight along with the staff's, with his feet off the ground, and pulling himself up with a wide grip until his chest touches the staff, then lowering himself, "is a pull-up." He drops down and jumps back up, this time facing me, holding the staff with an underhand grip as opposed to an overhand grip. "And this," he says, pulling himself up until his chin goes over the staff and lowering himself before dropping down to the ground, "is a chin-up." He walks over to where I wait.

"You will twirl the staff with proper form until you can't. Then you will do leg bends until you can't. Next, you will do chest-ups until you can't. Lastly, you will alternate between pull-ups and chin-ups, each round, until you can't." I stand dumbfounded. He's serious.

"How many rounds?" I ask, exasperated.

"Until you no longer see the sun coming through the tree line." I stare at him in shock.

"That's a little more than six hours from now!" I complain.

He gives me an ultimatum of sorts. "Will you be sheep forever?" he asks playfully before walking off.

I just look back and forth between his receding form and the silver staff he left in the tree branches, still not accepting this.

"Remember," he calls out, "stay shielded and keep your stomach tight. If you stop doing either, I will know." With the last, he disappears into the forest.

Grudgingly, I shield myself and squeeze my stomach, then begin. My staff twirling is as slow as—no, I don't think I've seen anything slower, but it burns deep. The staff pulls at my shoulders and is as heavy as a war hammer, heavier perhaps, on my forearms. Tightening my stomach helps my balance, but before long, that, too, begins to ignite. I drop the staff when my forearms decide they want to give out on me, and take that as my cue to begin leg bends.

I am only able to make it to fifty before the burn is unbearable. Keeping my stomach tight through all of this for six hours is going to be impossible.

Chest-ups, I get to thirty before my chest and shoulders cramp with displeasure, dropping me to the ground. Despite what my body is going through, I rise.

Time for pull-ups. They seem simple enough. I walk over to the old oak still supporting the silver staff in its branches, taking my staff with me so I don't have to keep walking back and forth. This is tiring enough as it is.

Dropping my staff to the ground, I jump and grab the silver staff in an overhand grip. I quickly realize this is going to be a lot harder than he made it look. Go figure. It takes all I am to do two, and when I drop from the bar, I feel every stitching of muscle in my back pulled tight, as if someone is using Certus to try to rearrange something back there.

My shield flickers. Focus. I stabilize it, but that does nothing for my muscle pains.

Again. I go through the circuit, and it feels worse than the first time. The only saving grace is that chin-ups are slightly easier than pull-ups. I got to four before I dropped back down.

By the end of the third round, I am ready to quit. This is stupid. My whole body is cramping and on fire. "Will you be a sheep forever?" I can't tell if that is really the old man talking from some hidden vantage point or his voice in my head, but it lights a different type of fire in me—the same type I felt when Shari said I was scared of her, but bigger.

I pick up the staff and begin to twirl it, legs bent, back straight, stomach tight, and shielded. I hear my mother's voice telling me what Certus is. Certain. Sure. Definite. Decided. Specific. Precise. I begin the chant in my own mind, using it as a focus point. Certain. Sure. Definite. Decided. Specific. Precise. It hones my thoughts and strengthens my shielding, but is far from enough. My body still hurts. What am I certain about? What is it I need right now, and why? I drop my staff and immediately start leg bends, too focused on my questions to acknowledge the burn.

Energy. I need energy and a lot of it. Certain. Sure. Definite. Decided. Specific. Precise. A Storm. A storm has near-endless energy as it tears across the earth and back out to the sea. I drop down and begin chest-ups. Numbers are no longer of concern; my body will stop whenever it stops. A storm is definitely powerful, but is it… Certain? Sure? Definite? Decided? Specific? Precise? Yes, I determine, and I jump and grab the staff, pulling into a chin-up with the motion. It is all of those things when it is on its course through the world, going exactly where it should. Men might not know where the wind blows, but the storm does. Will it work with Certus? Where am I going? And why? I am going to get to the end of this workout, and why? So I can break my body and rebuild, so the old man will stop talking down to me. But my biggest reason of all is simple: I am not a sheep.

Thunder rumbles in my head. Before I know it, the staff is in my hand. I close my eyes and envision a storm. Not a gentle rain, but a hard, cold rain that drops just as much ice as it does water. Lightning crackles across the sky of my mind, and the wind is strong enough that no man can stand outside. I hold this vision in my mind as I chant. Certain. Sure. Definite. Decided. Specific. Precise. Nothing is relevant but the storm and its path. Somehow, I know nothing can pierce my shield and my stomach will not untighten. I know this as fact, just as surely as I know the sun will set and rise again tomorrow. It just is. I feel my body move through the motions of the workout, twirl the staff, legs, chest, back, twirl the staff, legs, chest, biceps. But not the burn. I don't really know how I'm doing this with my eyes closed, but I guess it really doesn't matter. My body feels as if I'm moving in a pool and the water is extra thick, causing me to fight for movement, inch by inch. I will not be a sheep.

The sun sets through the tree line. I do not see it with my eyes closed, but rather feel it in the storm. The storm has run its course. I let it go, then open my eyes and collapse.

Pain, the likes of which I have never known, lances through every fiber of my being—mind, body, and spirit, if there is such a thing. If you've ever seen a piece of glass shatter, you know how I feel, visually, at least. I convulse on the ground, helpless to stop it for about a minute. Soon, I lie still, but the pain has not receded. I beg for death, but it doesn't come.

"Will you be a sheep forever?" I hear. Imagined or not, I don't know, but I force myself to stand. It is far from easy. My limbs feel like they will fall off, and my mind just wants to up and quit, but I will not be denied. However, forget tightening my stomach and shielding myself. The energy to do that left with the storm. If the old man is going to pop out and hit me, then I'll just die exhausted and not care.

I walk over to the front of the hut and see a plate with enough deer meat on it to feed five people. How did I not smell that? Well, I smell it now, and I'm starving. Have I ever been this hungry before? When did I even—it doesn't matter. I sit down and tear into the deer meat like a wild animal. I can't even think right now; existence is primal. Food is life, and I feel devoid of anything resembling life. By the time I finish, I feel a little better, but I still have not seen any sign of the old man. Who cares? I'm going to sleep. I start to rise to go in the hut, but stop myself. For what? That requires too much energy. I can sleep right here. And that's exactly what I do.

6 RISE RINSE REPEAT

After about four weeks of this grueling routine the strain on my body and mind finally begins to lessen. I also stop collapsing after releasing what I have taken to calling the storm. The old man has become no less irritating, but then again, I didn't expect him to. I also have memorized 150 elements in the language of power. I'm still no better at interpreting meanings. If anything, it's become more confusing because the combinations of elements are endless. Oftentimes, I find myself overwhelmed, but I refuse to give up. Running through the forest is also easier, but I am a long way from being able to move like my grandfather. He still calls me Sheep. I will prove him wrong. Lightning crackles as I summon the storm in my mind and pick up the staff.

***

After four months of the routine, I have expanded the distance I can run in the forest twice over. I do not require a break or a guide, and the old man stopped coming a while back—probably because not even ants wake when I move. But as good as I've become, he somehow always still knows where I'm at. I've made a game with myself of trying to sneak up on him. It never works.

I can now glance meanings from the elements but not the truth. I know what some things mean, but the power dwelling in me tells me there is more than just what's on the surface. I've also noticed reading and interpreting the elements takes a concentration of power. Oftentimes, I find my mind tired after reading. Like right now. I shut the book I'm reading, which is titled, Water, Together, Force, Fluid, or something to that effect, and stand.

Leaving the hut barefoot, I gave up the boots a while back. Nature feels good under my feet now. I walk over to my staff on the ground, pick it up, and look up to see the two branches of the oak tree, which still hold my grandfather's silver staff in the same position it's been for the last four months. Thinking about how far I've come, I smile to myself. I've gained twenty pounds in pure muscle, no doubt from all the deer meat, and I'd bet my father's kingdom you'd find a soft spot on a rock before you'd find one on me.

I no longer need the storm to get me through the workout. Really, I figured out a while back that I could just twirl the staff until the sunset and not have to do anything else. When I first started this, he said, "Twirl the staff until you can't." Well, that me no longer exists. I can twirl this thing indefinitely.

But that defeats the purpose, so I twirl it for ten minutes, do 150 leg bends, 150 chest-ups, and 50 chin-ups or pull-ups, then start over till the sun sets. This is not how I pictured my life outside the castle, but it is peaceful. I also enjoy the transformation my body is going through. I am about to begin when I feel three darts hit my shield right where my nose is. I watch them fall lifelessly to the ground and look up to see the old man shrugging his shoulders as if saying, "You can't fault me for checking." He's put me to sleep a couple of times like that in the middle of my sets. Once I let him do it because I was tired. The time that happened was well over a month ago though.

The old man walks right up to me so we're almost nose to nose.

"Drop your shield," he says.

This is clearly some type of lesson. I do as I'm told. I don't know if he knew I'd listen or just guessed, but quicker than a wind breeze, he punches me in the stomach, hard. His fist feels like a hammer. Four months ago, he would have broken something or I would have wet myself, but now . . . Now, I don't even flinch. If his fists are hammers, my stomach is the anvil—neither give.

Smiling, he says, "It seems you are a sheep no longer." I can't help but feel good at the compliment, and my face gives me away as I smirk.

"But what can you do with that staff you hold, boy?" he asks, pointing to the staff. Still a boy, am I? No, he just wants to see how I will react. I say nothing as I step back.

Using the proper form, I begin to twirl my staff, slowly at first, just like he showed me four months ago. Gradually, I pick up speed and the staff becomes a blur. I let go with one hand and begin to rotate between the two. I even add the overhead twirl into my rotation. I am about to stop when an idea hits me. In transition from left hand, left side to left hand, overhead, I spin the staff hard, then release it with an upward thrust over my head. Still spinning, it rises then falls, and I catch it with my right hand, continuing to spin it overhead, then abruptly jam it in the ground so it supports itself standing straight up. I look him in the eyes, and we just stand staring at each other for a moment. He breaks the silence.

"It seems you are ready for the next step."

"Victory," I shout, childish glee dancing across my face.

"But first, fix your eyes and hair," he reprimands.

Just couldn't let me have my moment. I should have known: there is no such thing as winning with this man. I grab Certus and will my eyes and hair to change color. Gone are the days it took hours; now it is just a simple thought.

"So, what now?" I ask eagerly, knowing my eyes are green and my hair is strawberry blonde.

"Now you learn to dance," he says knowingly.

Did he just say dance? I must have misunderstood what he said. No, I heard correctly.

"Why?" I ask, knowing that is the only question that will gain me an explanation.

"Because twirling a stick does nothing to help you fight with it."

"And dancing does?" I say, frustrated. Here we go again.

"You just made me twirl that staff every day for four months, and you're telling me it was all for nothing?" Anger plays in my voice.

"Yes, and nothing is for nothing," he says plainly, somehow managing to sound cryptic as well.

I know this game, and I am losing. I take a deep breath to calm myself, allowing my mind to relax and my anger to fade.

"Explain," is all I trust myself to say. He smiles a smile that lets me know he's enjoying himself at my expense, then speaks.

"I will teach you the quarterstaff master's dance, which is called the Water Dragon. Why, you ask? Because you will learn to give like water when you need to and strike like a dragon when the opportunity presents itself. I do not know if dragons truly exist, so don't ask. The dance is a compilation of one hundred positions and transitions from position to position. There is no order to the dance, only transitions from one position to the next, depending on your opponent's movements, fighting style, and weapon. I will teach you the positions, but you must learn the transitions on your own. Your body is your own, and no one knows it better than you do. For this reason, no two Water Dragon dancers are the same."

I think that is the most I've ever heard him say all at once, possibly even more words than he's spoken since we met. I'm amazed.

"And the staff twirling?" I ask, pushing my luck.

"You could hardly learn the dance if you could not wield the weapon properly. Now prepare yourself."

He moves to retrieve his silver staff from its resting place of four months. I snatch mine back from the ground and follow him to nature's training circle. When I reach him, he takes the staff from my hands and replaces it with his silver one. It's a lot heavier than the one I was just using and is about to complicate my balance and strain my body.

"Not going to complain?" he asks, surprised.

"I am not a sheep," I reply, seething.

He laughs. "So it seems. So it seems."

We line up shoulder to shoulder. Then he moves to my left a good enough distance to give both of our staffs room to move freely.

"Copy my pose exactly," he says seriously.

He drops his left foot back, bends at the knees, and extends his staff in a two-handed grip lower than the right. I do as he does, and the new staff strains my muscles, but it is nothing compared to what the other staff felt like when I first started out.

"Good," he says. "This is 1, do not forget it. I have no desire to teach you the Water Dragon beyond a week. In fact, I won't. If you cannot memorize these positions in a week, you will pick a new weapon, and all that twirling will have been for nothing," he says smugly.

I look at him and swallow. I am not a sheep. I am not a sheep. I repeat it over and over again as I go through the positions with the old man, one by one. I did not just waste the last four months of my life. I will learn these positions in a week. It just is.

∗∗∗

What follows is a week of nothing but learning the Water Dragon, from sunup to sundown—and the old man's annoying voice constantly saying, "Head up. Bend your knees more. Keep your back straight. Your grip is wrong." Running, reading, and working out have been temporarily halted and replaced so that I can burn this dance into my mind and muscles in a week. The silver staff only complicates things, but I refuse to complain. I am not a sheep.

Even though I have not actually begun to transition from position to position, the stances themselves feel like a type of meditation; they bring me peace. Before I know it, the week is over, and all one hundred positions of the Water Dragon have been committed to my mind and body. They are, to me, what wings are to a bird. I'm feeling surprisingly good about myself for having met the one-week deadline, but I can't help but be nervous about what comes next.

The old man stopped showing up around day five. I assume it's because I started doing fine without his pestering voice. Speaking of which, here he comes.

"What's next, old man? It's been a week already, and I have your dance perfected," I say confidently.

"No you don't. You merely have the positions memorized. Now you will learn how to transition from position to position, whichever way suits you best. Your normal routine continues, with one exception," he replies, downplaying my achievements. I had a sneaking suspicion he was going to say that.

"Let me guess, instead of working out, I will work on my transitions until sunset instead," I say knowingly.

"No, you will split your time after running and reading, between working out and transitions. Now get started. I have deer to catch." Having said the last, he walks off into the forest without another word.

Even though he walked away, somehow, I feel dismissed. I just sigh. I'm going to be here forever. Well, at least I'm able to read again.

Without further delay, I begin my workout. No time like the present, right? The new staff is still straining my muscles, and if that weren't already enough, he took the other staff back, so now I have to place this staff up in the branches, then take it back down every round. He knows what he did too. He's too smart not to.

I think about summoning the storm to get me through the workout, but it seems like cheating to me now that my body can handle the pain without it. I leave the storm wherever it comes from and endure. I am not a sheep. Three hours pass and it feels like time to work on my transitions, so I stop spinning the staff over my head, then fall into position 1. So used to always having a teacher, I just stand there for a moment, not knowing what to do next. What position to transition to next? How about 17? It's a position where I hold the staff out with my left hand extended out in front of me, chest to the sky, leaning back on my right foot so that my body is even with the ground. But how? With absolutely no clue as to how I should transition from 1 to 17, I just go for it. And like an idiot, I fall flat on my back. What was I thinking? That wasn't going to work. I recover and assume position 1 again.

Okay, what about this? Again, I fall flat on my back. And again. And again. And again. Finally, I conclude that I'm missing something, something important too. But what is it? The storm! How could I forget? I jump to my feet, get in position 1, and begin to summon the storm. I feel it waiting right behind my eyes. All I need to do is seize it. I hesitate; it feels wrong. Not the storm—the storm feels right as ever—but the need. The storm is not what I need right now. Well then, what do I need? "Certain. Sure. Definite. Decided. Specific. Precise," I think, closing my eyes. I need to get from position 1 to position 17. But how do I get there? Certain. Sure. Definite. Decided. Specific. Precise. What flows from one position to the next? Water! I feel like an idiot. It must be called the Water Dragon for a reason. Maybe I'm not Yuna's get . . . no, no, I must be; where else would the gold in my eyes come from?

Water flows from the sky to the mountains, from the mountains to the rivers, and from the rivers to the oceans. It goes whichever way it is thrown but stays on the path toward its destination, one way or another.

I picture a flowing river in my mind, nothing violent like the storm, but gently and smoothly flowing—the type I've read about in books that people travel to to have an enjoyable time with their families. Certain. Sure. Definite. Decided. Specific. Precise. I fall into position 1, then picture position 17 in my mind simultaneously with the river. Suddenly, without warning, my body shifts of its own accord, just like a river going from one place to the next. Surprised, I open my eyes and see myself in position 17. Then I fall. I'm not sure why I fell, but I laugh, despite myself, then stand. I know what I must do.

Over the next four months, my routine continues. The distance I run in the morning steadily increases, and my knowledge of the language of power continues to grow. The latter doesn't really mean much because the more I learn, the more I become confused. I once read something about being loudly silent. What does that even mean? How can one be loudly silent? It makes no sense. I swear, the more I learn to interpret this crap, the more it frustrates me. Things that make me feel like this remind me of my mom and Shari. I miss them something terrible. I would never admit that to Shari though. It's been eight months, and I still don't know how they are doing, or in Shari's case, where she's even at. I assume my mother is okay, or my grandfather would have told me. Well, I hope he would have told me. That old man is irritating, infuriating, vexing, irksome, but most of all, exhausting.

I haven't seen him in four months, and somehow, that's just as annoying as him being here. The only reason I know he hasn't abandoned me is because I find the deer meat he now leaves on a plate inside the hut, due to the snow from the cold season, and the sleeping darts that randomly hit my shield days apart. Every time I look up to find him after he shoots darts at me, he's already gone.

I've probably put on another ten to fifteen pounds in muscle, and my hair is a curly mop that reaches down to just past my shoulders when I don't have it up in a bun. I thought about cutting it, but it keeps my head warm at night, especially now that it's snowing. Training with the heavier staff and learning my transitions, learning how to flow, as I call it, was harder than I originally thought. I like the word flow instead of transition because it's less formal and that's what water does. When I would picture the river in my head, coupled with the position that I wanted to flow to, my body would move of its own accord. However, I had to pay attention to the way my body moved inside the river and practice the flow on my own outside the river. Complicated doesn't cover it by half. After two weeks, I began to get the hang of it. After a month, I could flow from any of the one hundred positions to another without hesitation. I would do this for three hours straight. Surprisingly, it was my favorite part of the day. Now, I dance.

Despite my recent achievements, I'm sick of being here. I'm also sick of not knowing how my mother, father, and Shari are doing. I could go on endlessly, especially if you get me complaining about the old man. But what I'm sick of the most is deer meat. I want some real food and a warm, comfortable bed.

I understand being here is supposed to be saving my life from some unknown assailant. What I don't understand is why I need saving in the first place. My mother and father are the best in their respective domains, and my father is not only a king, but a warlord. He is feared so much that even though we are surrounded by neighboring kingdoms to the north and south, they dare not attack us, even together, fearing his wrath.

I do not fear my would-be assassin. But he should fear my family, and now fear me. I have the river, I have the storm, and I have a body a deity would kill for. I was promised I could leave the castle when I turned eighteen and experience the world. Here I am, almost nineteen, and I have yet to see anything except this forest. Don't get me wrong, I love this place and its natural beauty, but I want to experience the world. What if there are girls prettier than Shari out there . . . Wait, did I just call Shari pretty?

Grudgingly, I admit to myself that Shari is beautiful and that I want to see her if only so I can know she's alright. I . . . I . . . I'm leaving. I stand from my seat at the table in the hut, move to the entrance, put on my boots, and walk out.

I make it about thirty steps in a random direction, snow crunching beneath my boots and wind whipping snow around aimlessly, before I hear his voice.

"Where are you going?" the old man says, intrigued.

I turn to see him dragging a deer, silently, through the snow behind him. I say, "I'm leaving," believing myself.

"Like that?" he asks, cocking his head to the side.

Only then do I realize I left the wolf cloak he made me when the winds began to grow cold inside the hut.

"You will die before you make it anywhere worth going. Besides, your training is not complete," he says nonchalantly.

"I beg to differ. You've trained me, old man. I am not the boy I was eight months ago, nor am I a sheep. Whoever is trying to kill me doesn't know what they've gotten themselves into. Not only am I this," I say, pointing toward my body, then raising my arms as if in challenge to the world, "but my father is a king and a warlord. When he finds out who is trying to kill me, they will beg for death before he is done with them."

"X'avion," my grandfather spits when he says the name. That is the first time in a long time I have heard anyone say my father's name. People usually call him the king, His Majesty, or some such. That is also the only time I have ever seen my grandfather angry.

"You don't like my father?" I ask, not understanding his anger, especially when he always lectured me about mine.

"It is not my story to tell," he says, offering no further hints on the subject. "But your training is not done; you are not leaving."

I'm about to remind him that he said he would not stop me from leaving, but I decide to ask a question instead. "Why?"

"Because the next and final part of your training will be to your liking," he says knowingly, giving me a wicked smile.

"I doubt it. Humor me," I say, sounding like a prince, even in my own ears.

He walks over to the outside of the hut where both staffs lean upright against it. He takes them both, one in each hand, and walks back over to me. Handing me the fifty-pound quarterstaff and keeping the seventy-five-pound one for himself, he says, "You can leave when you can land a hit on me." His wicked smile returns.

I want to leave so bad, but the idea of paying this man back for the hell he put me through is so tempting. I bite.

"You're going to use that?" I ask, gesturing to his silver staff. He nods. "Wouldn't that give me a speed advantage?" I ask, grinning at my odds.

"If I did not use this, you would never leave," he says smugly before walking back a couple of steps and falling into position 1.

I don't know if I was waiting on a ready, set, go or a 1, 2, 3, but it never came. The old man rushes me, and I panic. I didn't know it was physically possible to move that fast. One moment he is in position 1, and the next, he is in my face. My feet leave from under me with violent force, placing my body sideways in the air. Then his staff hits my shield right in the center of my stomach. I fly through the air and crash against a tree, causing the air to leave my lungs as I slide down it.

Never have I appreciated my mother more. If I weren't shielded, I'd be dead. I am on my knees, coughing, when I hear it. Without looking, I dive forward into the snow as the staff passes through the space my head was just in. If I didn't know any better, I'd think he was trying to kill me. I find my feet fast, but there is no sign of the old man. Sleeping darts fall from my shield, and I follow their trajectory, but he comes from the opposite direction. I feel no pain, but my head tilts right and my body follows it as I cartwheel through the air. I land, roll, then skid to a stop, turning to face the direction of the blow. I see him. But I have never seen him like this. He looks no different, but the way he moves his body is like a lion stalking a gazelle, a killer in his element. I'm reminded of Shari, but I do not back away from him; I run away.

Bolting through the trees, making just as much sound as the first day I ran through the forest, I try to gather myself, and fail. I don't even know where I'm going. I just need to get away from—

"You cannot run or hide from me, Sheep." That stops me dead in my tracks.

I didn't go through all this training just to run. I will not let this man demean me any further. I am not a sheep. I will not run. I close my eyes, then fall into position 1 and listen.

"There you are," he whispers. I turn to the sound of his voice as he lunges. I drop my shield for an instant so I can feel the air from his strike, and just before he makes contact, I flow. Side-stepping his attack, doing an inward 180-degree spin, and swinging both ends of my quarterstaff, I do one position at a time—position 13, followed by 64—then open my eyes. He blocks both, our staffs still pushing against each other.

"Good," he says, smiling. I don't have time to feel good because next he comes at me with a seven-step transition: 61, 53, 52, 78, 81, 84, 96. I flow and dodge them all: 3, 7, 16, 5, 32, 50, 24. That was not easy. I am starting to see a pattern in this dance. I put that thought away for later, lest I accidentally die.

"Faster," the old man growls. We exchange several more times, and I'm hit at least ten times. I cannot keep up with this man. Did I really like my odds when he handed me the lighter staff? How much worse would this be if our staffs were evenly weighted? Or if I had the heavier one? He was right, I would never leave. In the middle of our next exchange, I believe I see an opportunity. I take it. He thrusts his staff at me right-handed, extending his body too far. Flow. Spinning and lowering my body at the same time, picking up my left leg while leaning back on my right so my body is even with the ground, chest up, I strike right-handed. Position 17. I miss because he jumps and flattens his body over mine. I can't help but wonder what position that is as he grabs his staff in a two-handed grip and brings it down on my nose so hard the force breaks it even though I am shielded. My body, already in an awkward position, slams down on the ground hard. I am still conscious, but all I see are stars. I am laid out, limbs extended, when my vision finally clears. I raise my body to rest on my elbows at the same time his silver staff slams into the ground just between my legs, supporting itself upright into the air.

I follow the length of the staff with my eyes to find my grandfather. His right heel is balanced atop the pole, with his left foot resting on his right. His legs and arms are crossed, and he is standing straight up, staring down at me. He looks like some long-forgotten deity you pray to before you go to war.

"Not bad for your first dance," he calls down to me. I can't tell if he is mocking me or giving me a compliment.

"What position was that? I don't recall you teaching it to me?" I ask, recalling him floating over me just before he broke my nose.

"This," he bows from his position atop the pole, then straightens and crosses his arms again, "is position 101. I invented it, you see. Extra credit, you could say. I don't believe you can do it, so I didn't bother wasting my time teaching it to you."

Challenge accepted.

"No, not that. I'm talking about . . . never mind, you were right. I am not done."

Standing, I heal my nose, suck air through it, and spit blood into the snow. The contrast of my blood on the snow somehow fits my current mood. I look for my staff and find it to my right. I grab it and head back in the direction of the hut. I will not go out like this. In fact, I will die training before I let the old man embarrass me like that again. One day, old man. One day.

7 ONE DAY

I now firmly believe the old man has to be the fastest being in existence. Four months have passed, making my time in this forest a year, and I still have not been able to hit this man. I feel myself getting faster and becoming more fluid by the day, but as fast as I become, he is always faster.

2, 15, 19, 30, 99. I weave his four strikes and counter with one of my own. The pattern in the dance is a simple one: the first fifty positions are designed to be defensive maneuvers, the last fifty offensive. That is why there is no order to the dance, only what feels right next. 10, 12, 87, 100, 54, 62. Shit, he's fast. Most of the time he doesn't even bother with blocking. Although I have never hit him before, gone are the days when I was an easy target. Even with his lightning-like speed, I am only hit once every other day or so. That's the only proof I've gotten any faster. 3, 4, 6, 40, 32, 12, that hurt, 21, 6, 49.

I no longer run or read. I no longer need to run, but I have nowhere near mastered the language of power. The ultimate concept, which I will find, has been placed on hold. Sparring with my grandfather has awakened something in me I never knew existed. 69, 70, 100, 92, 53, 67, 10. Growing up in the castle, I abhorred violence and confrontation; that's why I chose a bow. Archery is peaceful and allows me to concentrate. I'm not going to lie—I do miss my bow, but . . . 14, 98, 30, 54, 54, 7 . . . this is amazing. The strain on your body, reading your opponent's movements, knowing their mind, and feeling your heart thunder in your chest. Shari, if only you could see me now. The bow will most assuredly always be my favorite; this is just . . . new. Speaking of new, I have something I've been meaning to try. My body learned to flow without the river a while ago, so . . . thunder rumbles in my head as I summon the storm. I hold it at bay for now.

For now, I will give like water until the opportunity presents itself. 12, 20, 40 . . . I know what he is going to do next. He will feint high and go low with a sweep of his staff, then roll. As soon as the feint comes, I backflip, and his low sweep meets with no resistance, causing him to lose balance. That's not to say he stumbled—losing balance for him is more like a simple twitch. Even so, I notice it. I land and allow the storm to pour its devastation into me, then rush. 91, 86, 53, 98, 61, 62. I do not relent. With the storm's energy flowing through me, I become reckless. 51, 100, 75, 57, 82. He blocks them all, but still I don't let up. 76, 84, 99. I feint high, and as he goes to block, instead of a low sweep, I strike at his silver staff hard. Stepping back with my left hand on the top back end of my staff and my right hand in an underhanded grip just past the middle of my staff, I swing upward. Pushing down with my left and pushing up with my right, his staff goes flying, and his eyes follow in disbelief.

It's now or never.

I hurl my staff at him with all the strength of the storm like a javelin. And because I let all the energy from the storm go with my throw, the staff is as quick as a lightning bolt. I half expected him to dodge it. The crunch from the impact on his chest is sickening. The staff carries him off his feet and into an old, immovable oak.

It's my turn to stare in disbelief as he and my staff fall to the floor, blood leaking from his mouth. Panicking, I rush over to him. "Talk to me, what's wrong?" I ask, sounding like a child on the verge of tears.

"You threw a fifty-pound staff at my chest like you meant to kill me. What do you think is wrong?" he shouts. "I can't shield myself like you, boy. Now shut up and heal me already."

I smile despite his rude behavior and heal the man. The bones heal, but the bruise does not.

"Get off me," he says, sounding normal once again.

I back off and stand up. He gathers himself, wiping the blood from his mouth, and stands. His eyes lock on mine; I don't know why, but I feel no small amount of fear.

"Congratulations," he says, elated. "Your training is complete."

I've been waiting to hear those words, but when I finally hear them, they don't register. "Why?" I ask, thinking this is another test or something.

He laughs and clasps me on the shoulder. "Because now that you have finally hit me, I have nothing left to teach you." He starts walking back to the hut. Confused, I follow like a lost puppy. We head inside the hut just before the sun sets and sit across the table from each other.

"So, what's next?" I ask, not knowing what I'm supposed to do now.

"Well, that depends on you, grandson." That is the first time he has ever called me that.

"What do you mean?"

"The world you know or thought you knew is a lie," he states, no hint of a joke in his voice. "You will soon find out for yourself. When you leave here, you can't be a prince, and people will not be kind to you." He pulls out three purple bags and sets them on the table. Thunk. Thunk. Thunk. Judging by the noise they made against the table, the bags are a decent weight.

"What's in them?" I ask, unable to contain my curiosity.

"One of them is full of copper," he says, sliding a bag to me.

"One is full of silver," he says, sliding another bag.

"And one is full of gold." He holds on to the last bag. "Use the copper for your daily needs. Silver if you need something special. Gold—" he tosses the bag to me "—gold only if your life depends on it. Where you're going, it will attract too much attention. Some you'll like; most you won't."

"That's all fine and great, but where exactly am I to use this?" I ask, curiosity building. I have never had money before because until a year ago, all I had to do was go ask and it was mine. My family might not have been perfect, but I didn't want for anything, besides leaving.

"We are in a forest on the southern border of Dragonrock."

Dragonrock is what my father renamed the kingdom after he took it. Stupid name if you ask me, but I won't be the one to tell him.

"The Ironlance kingdom is about a full day's travel to the south."

I know exactly where we are, thanks to all the books my mother forced me to study years ago. That explains why no one has wandered across us; we are on the edge of nowhere.

"When you leave here," he continues, "you will need to head north into your father's territory. The first town you will come across will be Last Stop. Nothing good resides in Last Stop, but that is your first destination."

I don't remember any town called Last Stop on any of the maps I've seen. As if knowing this, my grandfather moves to the bookshelf and grabs a map of his own. Placing it on the table so I can see, he points out my destination.

"Experience is the best teacher, so I will not tell you what to do when you get where you are going," he says like it makes the most sense in the world.

"And besides Last Stop, where exactly am I going?" I ask.

"I wish I knew," he says, sounding worried. "But you will find out soon enough. I will give you some advice though. Always have a plan; don't act on emotions."

This is too much too fast. He knows something that he's not telling me.

"Spit it out, old man; what are you not telling me?" I say.

There is a pause, and I can see that he is contemplating it.

"It would be best to hear it from those who don't know you or your situation. Only then will the truth really set in," he says, then walks out of the hut.

I sit for a moment and listen. It sounds like he's starting a fire outside. Alone with my thoughts, I realize I am a lot less ready to leave than I thought I was. I don't even own a shirt, just this wolf cloak that covers my shoulders and my back. The next couple of hours fly by without me noticing. Lost, deep in thoughts about not knowing where my life is about to go from here, the smell of deer meat begins to bring me back to the present. The sun has fallen, and I still don't know . . . I don't even know what I don't know.

What I do know is that I'm hungry, and the smell of cooked meat, even if it is deer meat, is making it worse. I head out and join the old man at the fire. I sit across from him, and he hands me a slab of meat. Wait. There's a plate underneath it; this slab of meat is just enormous. The old man looks kind of sad. I try to reach out to him.

"You know I've been here a year already and know nothing about you except for the fact that you definitely raised my mother."

He smiles at that. "It is best that way, at least for now. No one knows I'm alive right now besides you and your mother, my daughter," he says, looking up at me seriously. "Keep it that way."

I nod, then try again. "Do I have to keep this ridiculous hair color? It's gotten long enough that no one will suspect who I really am, even if I leave it brown."

He laughs. "I was actually going to tell you that a while back but thought better of it when I realized if you changed it back, I would have nothing to laugh at anymore."

For some reason I believe I know how a kicked dog feels. I let my hair change back to its original brown.

"Next time we meet, I will tell you everything you wish to know about me," he says cheerfully, then smiles. "For now, let's go over everything that will keep you alive. And not the prince. First—" he waves his hand dramatically and holds up one finger "—you will redo the power that keeps your eyes green every night before you fall asleep. Make sure it never comes undone." I nod.

"Second," he says, raising a finger, "do not get caught using your power. Keep yourself shielded at all times, but if you must come in skin-to-skin contact with someone, let it drop. And if you get into a fight, if necessary, act like the blow from a weapon hurts."

Makes sense. I nod again to let him know I still follow.

"Third," he says, raising another finger, "you can't be a prince." He lowers two fingers on his hand and flips his hand around so its back faces me and only his middle finger is still pointing upward.

"So you are a farmer's son whose wife left him five years ago. He can no longer afford to feed a grown man, so he kicked you out."

Harsh.

"What's your name?" he asks.

"Lu—Beau. My name will be Beau." It's the first name I thought of.

"Lastly," he says, dropping his hand altogether, "if you don't want to be robbed blind, keep your gold pouch tied inside your trousers by your manhood. Keep your silver tied inside your trousers on the waistband. Tie your copper on the outside of your waistband; if someone steals it, let them. One gold is one hundred copper, and ten silver is one gold. You can figure out the rest. There are one hundred coins in each bag. Use them wisely." With the last, he stands, then disappears into the darkness.

"Wait here," he calls back. A few minutes later he returns holding a new staff. When he gets closer, I can tell the staff is made of the same white wood my bow back in the castle is made of.

"Where—?" I begin as I stand, but he cuts me off.

"Irrelevant. I made you a deal. Touch me and I would make you a staff better than my own. You succeeded, and I've kept my word," he says, handing me the staff.

It's a fifty-pound staff, judging by how it feels as I twirl it, feeling it out, but it's way more beautiful than the staffs I used for training. Otherworldly even. The wood is polished and unblemished. "You could hit the trunk of the most ancient oak you can find in this forest as hard as you can, and it wouldn't even scratch that. Nor can the sharpest blade you know of cut it."

I look at him, feeling every bit the child who just got the birthday present they always wanted. "I will guard it with my life," I say, meaning every word.

"Well, the point is for it to protect you, but okay," he mocks. He smiles, so I know it's in good spirits. "You've come a long way, Luca. I'm proud of you," he says, not hiding the approval in his voice.

Finally, after a year of hell, I have his approval. My father has never even given me his approval. I don't trust myself to speak without crying or my voice cracking, so I just sit back down by the fire and place the staff across my lap.

"Be sure to get some sleep, young man," he says, walking back to the hut. "You're going to need your wits about you tomorrow, because come sunrise tomorrow, you will be among the wolves."

We depart before sunrise the next day. It is no different so far from my early morning runs, except for the coins jiggling at my waist with every step, the white staff strapped on my back inside its oak holder, and this backpack the old man gave me that smells like deer meat. I'm eager to finally be able to explore the world outside the castle and depart from that forest. But why am I so nervous? My grandfather is of the belief that I am not going to like what I discover. I disagree, but I also know the man is no fool. We'll just have to see how things go when I get there.

After a few more minutes of our light run, the forest begins to turn into a clearing. No, not a clearing: the end of the forest. I stop at the edge of the forest and am excited at what I see. About a mile beyond the forest is what I assume to be Last Stop. It doesn't look great by any measure, but it is big enough to hold at least ten of my father's castles.

From my vantage point, I can see stone and wood buildings, some with thatched roofs, others with roofs made of stronger wood. A few buildings even have chimneys. None of the buildings are over two stories high. The smell of smoke fills my nose as people light their chimneys as the day begins. As it's springtime, the morning air is not really cold, but I did just get done running for about three hours. There are about another three hours until high rise.

Dirt roads intersect each other between buildings, wide enough for one person to travel on a horse in each direction comfortably. Further inspection reveals a rocky terrain to the west; I wonder what that is. Not too many people appear to be out this early. I guess that makes it the perfect time to—shit. I still don't have a shirt. I look around for my grandfather, and he is nowhere to be seen, as usual. Shaking my head, I take two steps toward the town and hear him whisper.

"Find a tailor. Tell them you need farming clothes. Hurry up so you don't attract too much attention."

With that, I head to town, not bothering to look back because I have never met a ghost before.

I make my way into Last Stop and smell firewood, something that smells like the ale my servants used to drink but far less sweet, and piss. Buildings eventually swallow me, and I have no idea what I'm looking for, so I decide to ask one of the few people out this morning for help. Spotting a decent-looking gentleman, I approach.

"Excuse me, sir, could you—" I stop as he sniffs the air and, with disdain, turns his head, continuing to walk right past me.

So much for that. At a loss for what to do next, I turn and spot a woman in a blue dress sitting on a pile of boxes outside a building. She is white complexioned with black hair and appears to be maybe a little older than me. She either has not noticed me yet or chooses not to notice me.

I decide to walk over to her and try asking for help again, but before I can, my feet sink into the dirt, ankle deep. What the—? A sinkhole? No, because the dirt hardens, and then someone comes from behind me and snatches the copper pouch off my waist. Darting out in front of me is a kid maybe ten years old. He or she, too scraggly-looking for me to tell, wears a tattered white shirt plagued with dirt stains, brown shorts in no better shape, and no shoes. That is all the detail I can make out before the young thief, demon spawn really, bends the corner with its prize and disappears. I'm left standing ankle-deep in a patch of hardened dirt. Is this what I was so keen on leaving the castle for?

Despite my current predicament, I smile. That child earned his keep; he or she was not a sheep.

I hear a light feminine chuckle and look up at the woman I planned to ask for help. She's laughing at me. "Funny, was it?" I ask, smiling myself.

"Not from around here, are you?" she says, still giggling.

I did not notice at first, but she is rather pretty. Nothing compared to Shari, but her blue eyes are just as piercing as Shari's green, but friendly instead of intimidating.

"How'd you guess?" I ask sarcastically.

She flicks her left hand and the dirt loosens, allowing me to step free.

"How'd you—"

She cuts me off. "Can't touch the power either, can you?" she asks, standing and then walking toward me.

"I . . . No, I can't. It appears I'm not as fortunate as you and our little thief," I lie.

"Oh my God, what is that smell? Is . . . is that you?" she asks, stopping five feet away from me.

Personally, I can't smell a thing, but I can imagine what I must smell like after spending a year in the forest with nothing but a creek to bathe in.

"I guess," I say innocently, shrugging my shoulders, not knowing how I should proceed.

"You're lucky you're muscular and handsome. Name's Latrice; this is my inn," she says, gesturing behind her. "Blue Sky Inn," she says at the same time I read the sign, which is a simple wooden post above the door with the same color writing as her dress. And her eyes.

"Come on, come in," she waves me over, looking distraught by the smell. "You need a bath, on the house."

I follow her into the inn to find a modest-looking establishment. A long wooden counter with no one behind it separates the kitchen from the dining area, in which sit six tables that can hold two people each and three booths over on the far-left side of the inn that are for bigger or private parties of people. There is a wooden staircase to my immediate right that climbs to the second floor. Two giant windows on the wooden wall behind us allow in light in generous amounts.

"Up you go," she says, ushering me up the staircase impatiently. "Last door on the left is empty and has a tub. Bathe yourself, and then we can make proper introductions. I'll see if I can find something that will fit you, because it doesn't look like you brought a change of clothes or you'd be wearing a shirt," she says, clearly in charge.

"Thank you," I stammer out, confused.

No one hears me; she's gone. She might not be Shari, but she knows how to take control of the situation. I go down the hallway on the second floor to the room she indicated, the last door on the left, and enter.

A bed for two with sky-blue and white sheets is pushed up against the back wall centered in the room. Behind it, just above the headrest, sits a decent-sized window through which light enters the room. To the left behind the bed is a simple dresser and a face mirror, and to the right, a door, presumably the bathroom.

Done with the inspection of the room, I close the door behind me and head into the bathroom. Inside, there is nothing but a toilet, a sink, and an undersized tub. I turn one of the handles on the tub. Nothing happens. I turn the other one, and water comes rushing out. I stick my hand in it. Cold. Somehow, I knew it would be. Cold bath it is then. It really isn't much different than the creek. I stop up the tub with the plug that was already there and then look for soap, which I find in the soap tray built into the side of the tub. When the water gets about halfway full, I cut it off. I strip, carefully setting my staff beside the tub, and leave the backpack and trousers in a pile on the floor. I should probably wash the backpack too; it smells just as bad as me, if not worse. I step into the water and lower myself into the tub. This is way better than the creek. For starters, there are no fish in here. In no hurry, I allow my thoughts to drift.

I can't believe I won't be waking up in the forest anymore. No more going on early morning runs through the forest, no more language of power, and no more old man. I might be crazy, but I am going to miss the old man—even if he was a pain in my backside mentally and physically. He taught me how to use my brain, use my ears, and ask the right questions.

He also taught me how to dance. I think about the first day I summoned the storm, the day I found the river, and yesterday when I gave like water and struck my grandfather like a dragon. A smile works its way across my face. I am no longer a sheep.

Besides the tailor, I have no destination.

"Always have a plan," the old man said.

To form a plan, I need information. I hurry up and bathe myself, wash my hair, rinse off, and get out. My hair plastered to my back feels weird. Shit, there's no towel. Peeking out the bathroom door into the bedroom, I see a towel and a set of clothes on the bed. I dry off with the sky-blue towel and put on the clothes, making sure to tie the coin bags to the inside of the trousers, which are black cotton and rather loose. The shirt is even worse. The length is doable, but the size . . . Who wore this? A bear? No, because a bear would not put on a sky-blue shirt. My hair is still damp, so I decide to leave it down so it can fully dry; it grows curlier and curlier by the minute. I feel too noticeable; I need to hurry up and get to the tailor.

Grabbing my staff and placing it in the holder now across my back, I head downstairs, deciding to leave my smelly backpack for a later time.

Latrice is sitting at a table by herself, and her eyes are on me when I come down the stairs.

"Wow, your hair is long, and pretty . . . you look so cute," she says, the last beaming.

"I'm sure that's up for debate. Do you know where I can find a tailor?" I ask.

"Yes, but first, sit." I do as I'm told. Like I said, this woman knows how to command a room.

"I can smell your hair; it's nowhere near as bad as it was, but it still needs to be cared for. I'll wash it for you later," she reproaches, then continues. "You know my name, but I do not know yours. I have given you a free bath and clothes, no matter how they look, and I just offered to wash your hair."

Was that an offer? I thought she was demanding.

"The least you could do is tell me your name and a little bit about yourself," she says, looking at me interestedly.

"My name is Beau. My father and I are farmers, and my mother left us five years ago. My father recently kicked me out. He said he could no longer afford to feed another grown man," I say, willing her to believe the lie.

"Awe, you poor thing," she says, reaching across the table to put her hands on top of mine.

I drop my shield and let her. There is a moment of silence, then, giving up the act, she erupts into a fit of laughter.

"Ha . . . ha ha. Did you practice that?" she asks hysterically.

"It . . . it's the truth," I lie again without understanding what's so funny. She stops laughing.

"What's your mother's name?" she demands.

Just before I give her my real mother's name, I freeze, not having thought that far.

"I thought so. You're not a farmer's son, not with a body like that. You're built for war, so I'd wager you're some type of warrior," she states, eyeing me up and down. She's not far off. Are all people as smart as her? I remain quiet, not knowing what to say.

"Oh, don't look like that. I don't care who you are as long as I get to see that delicious-looking body again," she says, licking her top lip playfully.

I blush at her compliment and am at even more of a loss for what to say. She grins, then saves me from having to reply.

"But you should come up with a better story than that. Or at least be prepared to lie about the details."

My false persona is seen through by the first person I met.

This is bad.

"What do you want?" I ask hesitantly, trying to figure out her end game.

"Want?" she repeats, playing with the word. "Good conversation and company. Today the inn is closed so I can do a thorough cleaning. I don't know why you came to Last Stop, but it's clear to me that you are going to need some help. Especially since you can't touch the power."

At least she bought that part of it. Slowly, I nod in acceptance.

"Come," she demands, moving over to one of the booths and

pointing out a map on the wall of Last Stop. I follow. "We are here," she points to the location on the map marking her inn. "The tailor is here," her finger glides across the map, coming to a stop on a small shop in the southwest corner of town. I memorize the quickest route to the tailor. "Do you think you can handle getting there on your own, farmer boy?" she jokes.

"Do you think I can't?" I choose to reply, thinking about my grandfather. She chuckles.

"Go," she waves me off, and I move to oblige. When I get to the door, she shouts, "Hey!" I turn to see what I have done wrong. "Come back, we are not done here," she says, blowing me a kiss.

My face reddens again, and I make a hurried exit, soft laughter echoing behind me as I do.

There are more people outside right now than before, but not by much. By the time I go and come back, it should be high rise. Did I just say I was coming back? When did I make that decision? Latrice seems nice enough, I guess. I'm about to take off running by force of habit but catch myself. I'm not supposed to attract attention to myself, and this sky-blue shirt is already doing just that. I settle for a fast walk.

My walk to the tailor reveals the town to be in worse shape than I originally suspected. Trash and broken pieces of wood litter the dirt road, and the buildings made from wood all have holes in them. Broken glass windows seem to be a theme around here. Latrice's establishment is the nicest place I've seen so far.

I make it to the tailor without incident, a couple of awkward glances, at my staff, but nothing major. "Brenda's Tailor," the sign reads in simple black writing. There is a display of clothing to the right of the sign above the door behind a broken glass window. Why is this place so run down? People should have pride in where they live. Then again, maybe that's why they call this place Last Stop. So far, it's definitely the last place I'd ever want to visit.

"Hi, how may I help you?" comes an old woman's tired voice as I enter the shop.

Standing in the middle of the shop, sorting clothes, is the owner of the voice, dressed in a nice brown dress that has white trim along the edges coupled with brown sandals on her feet. Gray plagues her black hair, or maybe black plagues her gray hair; either way, she doesn't seem as old as she does tired.

"I am looking for some clothes that would be suitable for a farmer, two pairs if you have them," I say.

"Anything would do you better justice than what you have on right now, child," she snickers.

I just shake my head and curse Shari under my breath. Wait.

That wasn't Shari. That was Latrice.

"Color?" she asks, bringing me out of my thoughts.

I don't really care. "Brown and white will be fine," I say, giving her dress another look. She smiles at that.

"Do you have a type of material you prefer?" she asks. "We don't carry anything too expensive though."

"Something soft and comfortable," I say, thinking about the exact opposite of the rough animal hides my grandfather gave me.

"Stay here, I'll be back," she says, disappearing into the back.

I look around. Nothing noteworthy is lying about, just clothes on shelves and clothes in boxes. I notice a picture frame hanging above the door she just went through. In it is a family: a mother, father, and daughter. The mother is most certainly the younger version of the woman I just spoke with, Brenda, I'm guessing. The other two are her family, I presume.

Before I can guess too much, she comes back through the door holding a bundle of clothes.

"The curtain behind which you will change is over there." She points to my left. "Try these on and tell me how they fit."

I take the clothes and move to the changing area, raising the curtain as I pass its area of protection. The trousers are not trousers; they are sweats. They fit my waist snugly but loosen soon after to allow for freedom of movement, then taper into a cuff around my ankles. They are brown, and I like them. The shirt is a white T-shirt that collars with a V-shape in the front. Does that make it a V-shirt? It fits but exposes the top of my chest slightly and shows off my muscles a little more than I would like.

"Do you have a slightly bigger size shirt?" I ask.

"Like the one you came in with?" she jokes.

"No, please no . . . not that big, just slightly bigger than this one," I say, still on the other side of the curtain.

"Lavender!" she yells. "Two of the same shirts but in a slightly bigger size, please, love."

Who is Lavender? I wonder.

"Here," she says after a couple of moments.

I come around the curtain, sweats on, chest bare. There is a girl staggered behind Brenda to the left, the same girl from the photo, except she's older now. She looks to be around sixteen, and she is blushing.

"Enough with making my daughter blush. Finish changing," Brenda says, handing me the shirts, then turning her daughter's shoulders in the opposite direction so she can steer her back into the back.

As I move back behind the curtain to finish changing, I can't help but be gratified with myself. Not in a conceited way, I'm simply happy with the reaction my body gets from girls. What can I say? The old man did his job. I also can't help but feel like I'm still getting too much attention. If the old man didn't want me to make a scene, why did he train me so and feed me like a hog? He may have done his job too well.

I finish changing, then place my staff on my back and come from behind the curtain holding the second set of clothes. This shirt is better, still tight around the arms, but better. Brenda stands there waiting.

"How much do I owe you for the trouble?" I ask.

"Trouble?" she repeats, questioningly. "Please, you are far from trouble. Besides, any paying customer is a good customer. For both sets of clothes and a bag to carry your second set in," she lifts a bag up in her hand, "five copper."

I finger the bag tied inside my waistband and toss her a silver piece. She looks at me suspiciously.

"This is my first day in town, and some little kid robbed me of copper using the power. That's all I have," I explain.

She accepts the story and goes to get change.

"Is that man in the photo your husband? Where is he? Why has he not fixed that broken glass window in the front of the shop?" I ask her in rapid-fire fashion.

She stops counting coins and gives me a look that lets me know I said something I shouldn't have.

"I'm sorry—"

"No, it's quite alright," she says, cutting me off. "You really are not from around here," she says, coming to some realization.

I am, but I just shake my head no, playing my role, so I can find out what happened to her husband.

"My husband was a man who could touch the power. Not Certus, like the free people you will meet in this kingdom, but Potentia, like the king. He was nowhere near as powerful as the king, mind you, but regardless of that fact, the king recruits anyone who can touch Potentia in his kingdom into his army. Those he cannot bring to heel, he kills. Most choose to leave for a different kingdom rather than work for our king. My husband would not abandon us or our life here, so they came for him. When they came, he could not be brought to heel. Ten years ago, his body was found chopped into tiny pieces in a random alley. Those who found him knew of me and brought the news to me two days later." She pauses, gathering herself. "He only wanted to be able to raise his little girl," she says, looking at the picture above the door in the back. "I will never forgive the king for my husband's death," she spits with venom, then comes around to give me my change.

"Is that all you will be needing?" she asks, saddened by her own story.

"Yes, I believe it is. Thank you."

8 WOLVES & BEES

Exiting the shop in a daze, I walk aimlessly for ten steps. There are even more people on the roads now—a lot more. I look around slowly, trying to watch everyone at the same time. I've already been robbed once today and hardly anyone was outside then.

This town is a lot busier than the forest. However, even though it is busier, it is less alive. The people move with no joy or excitement; they just go. Whatever their day holds, it just is, like Certus. That's an odd but seemingly factual comparison.

A cool wind blows through the town as the sun starts to deliver its heat. As I begin the walk back to the Blue Sky Inn, my eyes take note of the sun's position in the sky—there is about an hour until high rise. With thoughts of the old woman's story, Brenda's story, fresh in my mind, I do the best I can to fit in with the crowd. Would my father really order a man's death because he wanted to stay with his family and raise his daughter? I knew he was a hard man—you must be to rule a kingdom the way he does—but that doesn't justify killing an innocent man for loving his family. I don't want to believe my father would do something like that, but Brenda doesn't even know who I am; she would have no reason to lie to me.

"It would be best to hear it from those who do not know you or your situation," my grandfather's voice echoes in my head.

No, that couldn't have been what he was talking about. I refuse to believe it.

"I will kill you," my father's words to my mother replay in my mind.

No, there is a rational explanation for all of this. I just need to—

"Hey, you!" a rough-sounding voice shouts, saving me from a headache.

"You with the white staff, stop!"

I turn to find three unruly men, wading their way through the crowd approaching me. So much for blending in. They all wear black, though none of their shades match, and they all have a white handprint on their shirts. As they continuously move toward me, I can't help but notice how clumsy they all look. There is no balance to their gait whatsoever.

"What's a low-life like you doing with a staff like that?" the one in the middle asks when they get within arm's reach of me. The other two flank him to either side; he must be their leader.

"It's a family heirloom," I answer, not knowing what this is about.

"Yeah, well, today it leaves your family. Come on now, hand it over," he says, holding his hand out expectantly.

Not knowing enough about these men, I choose to ask the right question.

"Why?" I see the annoyance dance across his face, like it does mine when my grandfather speaks. See, I learn, old man. People are openly staring now, okay, maybe not.

"Do you not know the King's Hand when you see them, lad? Now be a good boy and fork it over," the leader says impatiently.

They are nervous now; I can see it in the way they shift from side to side. They came over thinking I was just going to give up my staff. They thought I was a sheep.

"If you can take it, you can have it," comes my even reply.

More people stop to watch our altercation—we have a crowd now. So much for not attracting attention.

"Wrong move, boy," the leader says. He then motions to two others in the crowd before walking to the opposite edge of the circle the crowd has now formed. "Kill him," he says unsympathetically.

The crowd begins to go on about its business again after my death sentence from the leader is passed, as if this is an everyday occurrence. The two men surround me, then rush. The one in front of me throws a punch aimed straight for my face. Instead of moving, I just tilt my head to the left, and he misses. I hear the one behind me grunt as he, too, throws a punch. Not even facing him, I step to the left, and he, too, misses.

"Stop messing around, or you'll make us look bad," the leader yells at them.

I note that he has not moved. My two would-be killers pull out daggers the size of their forearms. There comes a sharp intake from the crowd, which for some reason has returned. It's my turn to be annoyed. If you are too slow to hit me, it doesn't matter what weapon you hold. I cross my arms and feign indifference. The two men rush at me again, but this time they are side by side. They both stab at my chest at the same time. Flow. 3. I dip underneath both blades and come head-level with their stomachs. I pass on the opportunity to rob them of all their breath, all too familiar with the horrible feeling, and instead pat them both on the stomach twice to let them know I could have. Quicker than they can react, I jump out of their reach and walk over to their leader. Too scared to continue, they don't follow, which I know because I was listening for their footsteps.

"Why do you not fight your own battles? You wanted my staff, so why do they have to take it? Are you a sheep?" I ask mockingly, knowing the answer.

He draws a longsword from a sheath across his back. "Was that your idea of an insult?" he asks, irritated. "Did you grow up on a farm or something?"

If only he knew. I smile. "Yes, I did. Do you have a problem with that?"

That enrages him. He rushes me with wild abandon, recklessly swinging his sword. He is quicker than the others but still slow, boringly slow: 3, 17, 12, 15. Compared to the old man, these people appear to be standing still. Curiously, I wonder what kind of life my grandfather lived to be able to move the way he does: 3, 17, 12, 15. The leader is throwing the same couple of strikes repeatedly—how dull. Soon he begins to tire. Out of breath, he motions to the other two.

"Let's go. This farm animal is not worth our time." The crowd makes a hole for them as they leave. Still in the middle of the circle, I look around at everyone with uncertainty. Coming to a unanimous but unspoken decision, the crowd disperses, all going back to what they were doing before I caused a scene.

Now, all of a sudden, I just don't exist again. That's fine, suits me. I look at the sun—it's two hours past high rise. Shit. I'm late. Why do I even care? I don't know, but I do, so I make my way back to the Blue Sky Inn. The rest of the trip is uninterrupted.

Going into the front door of the Blue Sky Inn, the smell of vanilla creeps into my nose. I look up and find candles lit on every table; she did say she was going to do a thorough cleaning.

"There you are, handsome. New clothes, new bag . . . what took you so long? I was beginning to think you ditched me," Latrice says playfully.

I follow the sound of her voice and find Latrice coming from the back of the kitchen with a plate of food in her hand. She looks different, more beautiful than before. Her black hair is groomed in a bun with some sort of stick through it, and a few loose strands dangle freely in front of her face. She wears a tight blue dress that shows enough cleavage that I can't help but blush.

She goes to sit at the last booth in the back, away from the window, then motions me over. I sit across from her in the booth, which has one of the vanilla candles lit on the table. As my eyes move from the table to her face, I can't help but glance at her cleavage, then her delicate neck, and finally her beautiful face. I notice for the first time that she has really small, beautiful freckles. Sky-blue eyes stare back at me as she pushes the plate of food across the table to me. She might not be as pretty as Shari, but she is not far off, at all. I feel my face redden again.

"Don't be shy now. Eat, so we can talk. And tell me how the food tastes."

She knows I'm still wary around her, and yet she just goes with it. I look at the food for the first time, and my mouth begins to water. Steak, not deer, fills half the plate next to cheesy potatoes and a huge biscuit. Awestruck, I look back up at her in disbelief.

"Go on, I didn't give you a bath and get all dressed up just to poison you. I promise."

That's all the encouragement I needed. I tear into the food.

"How is it?" she asks after about my tenth bite. I swallow a mouthful of potatoes before I speak.

"Wonderful," I say, not just because it's the first real food I've had in a year. That's probably why she runs an inn—being a good cook is sure to draw in business.

"Thank you," she says, sounding pleased. "Is it good enough for you to tell me your name?"

I stop eating and look at her.

"Okay, Beau . . . let's start with easier questions. What took you so long to get back?"

I feel bad, especially after all the kindness she has shown me, but there is absolutely no way I can tell her my name.

"Three men in all black, with white hands on their shirts, tried to take my staff from me," I answer, more focused on my steak.

"What happened?" The tone in her voice causes me to look up at her.

I just told her what happened. I think the old man has rubbed off on me too much, but I will not repay Latrice's kindness with rudeness. I tell her how my encounter with the King's Hand went down, downplaying my own actions.

"Ha! I wish I could have seen the look on his face. Stupid King's Hand, taking whatever they want from whoever they want. Serves them right . . . You should be careful though. Now you'll have a target on your back," she finishes.

Based on what I have seen, I am not concerned. But that is not what I say.

"How do you feel about the king?" I ask, maybe a little too interested. If she finds it suspicious, she doesn't let on, but maybe that's because she knows I'm hiding things.

"Hate is a strong word," she pauses, thinking. "I do not want to hate anyone, but he comes as close as it probably gets. You see how I am the sole proprietor of this inn," she waves her hand around in an encompassing manner. "It's because of him. Both my parents were gifted with the ability to touch Potentia. They would have died before serving him—"

"He killed them?" I interrupt dramatically.

She taps her ear with one finger twice.

"I said *would* have died before serving him," she places extra emphasis on the word *would*. "But, no, they fled the kingdom together on my sixteenth birthday after they were sure I could run the inn on my own." She pauses for a moment, then continues. "I don't understand why they all run. I understand no single person could overpower the king, but if they just stood together, maybe, just maybe families wouldn't be torn apart."

There are tears in her eyes. I don't want to believe her words, just like I didn't want to believe Brenda's, but the tears in her eyes, coupled with Brenda's sadness, make a convincing case. I drop my shield and move a hand to wipe her tears away.

"Stop," she laughs playfully, swatting my hand away. "That was nine years ago. I'm over it. Sometimes I just . . . still get emotional. It can be rough on a girl when she's alone." She pauses in thought. "I know how to fix it," she declares, standing and then disappearing into the kitchen.

Not even a minute later, she returns with a pink bottle and two glasses. Multihued oranges and reds stream through the window, indicating the sun will be setting soon. She sets the two glasses on the table and—pop. The top of the bottle shoots off, followed by the smell of sangria. The only reason I know the smell is because my mother used to drink it when I was younger, much younger.

"Never had wine before?" Latrice asks, noticing the amazement in my eyes.

"No, I've never had wine or ale before," I say uneasily.

"Oh, ho, a virgin. Tonight is going to be fun." Her tone is jovial.

She decants the wine into the two glasses with a practiced hand, then returns to her seat across from me.

"So what do I get to know about you?" she asks abruptly, picking up her glass and sipping from it.

I resist the urge to tell her that I am not a sheep, but not the urge to joke. "I am not a farmer's son, and my name isn't Beau," I say, thinking myself funny.

Thankfully, she does too. Latrice almost spits up her wine as she laughs.

"You're an ass," she says, wiping her mouth delicately.

"I am good with a bow. You could say it's a passion of mine," I say, taking a sip of the wine.

She giggles at the face I make. It tastes bitter and sweet at the same time.

"Really?" she asks, sounding like she doesn't believe me. "You don't look like you have the finesse to shoot a bow. You look too . . . hard," she says, examining me.

"Looks can be deceiving," I reply knowingly.

"Sometimes," she says, unperturbed. "Your body may be hard, but your face is still soft. You don't look like you're a day over twenty—tell me I'm wrong."

I don't.

"Why are you trying to figure me out? Why did you help me when the kid robbed me? Why are you being so nice to me?" I ask in rapid succession, then sip my wine.

She raises her eyebrow at me.

"Not trusting, are you? Good, around here that will get you killed."

Hearing her repeat my grandfather's wisdom, I decide to like her.

"When the kid took your money, you just watched him go, no anger or wrath present in your demeanor. In fact, you smiled." She smiles at the memory. "There aren't too many nice people around here. Your looks played no small part in my decision either. Most of all, though, I know the look on your face: you're lost. I don't know where you're headed, but I've felt the same exact way every day since my parents left me," she finishes.

A heavy silence hangs between us. This woman is not malicious.

"A toast then, to the lost," I say, shattering the silence.

She looks up into my eyes and smiles. "To the lost," she repeats. We clink glasses, then proceed to down the wine. She moves to refill our glasses.

"I wish I could tell you more," I say, staring into her sky-blue eyes. I feel weird, loose, relaxed. I can tell her lovely face slowly begins to turn downcast. "But you can tell me about you," I finish.

At this, she tilts her head ponderously to the side. First, her face becomes thoughtful, then accepting, and then she just launches into telling me stories about her childhood. We laugh the hours away as she tells me about the first time she rode a horse and when she first learned she could use Certus. She made her dad's pants fall in the middle of the road accidentally while they were carrying a cask of ale one day; he never figured out it was her.

I miss this innocence, not having a care in the world because someone else has it figured out. I know she does, too, and by the look in her eyes, I know we share more than just that. Maybe it's just the wine, but without warning, Latrice leans across the table and kisses me.

I have never kissed a girl before; it's soft and wet. A new hunger lances through my body like a fire, and my body stiffens, causing her to pull away.

"Are you okay?" she asks worriedly.

I feel my entire face heat through the influence of the wine.

"Yeah, I just . . . I've never kissed a girl before."

Her worry transforms into a devilish smile. She stands and moves to my side of the booth. I stand, not knowing why she is smiling like that. My balance is off, way off. I feel like how those King's Hand men looked. Latrice reaches up to touch my face; I am too late to release my shield. Her hand touches my face anyway, delicately.

My concentration must be shot. It must be the wine.

Her hand rubs my cheek and then goes into my long, curly hair. She then grips it roughly but delicately at the same time. I still don't understand "loudly silent," but the conflicting way in which she grips my hair lets me know it's possible. She then pulls me down to her and kisses me again. However, this time she puts her tongue in my mouth. My knees buckle when she does, and we fall into the booth on the cushions.

She has not let go of my hair, nor has her tongue left my mouth; I have no idea what I'm doing.

The river! I think out of nowhere. I just relax and let her tongue guide mine. Noticing my boldness, she puts her other hand in my hair and mounts me, still not breaking our kiss. I feel my manhood stiffen, and I know she can feel it through her dress, but unlike Shari, she does not move. We kiss like this for a couple more seconds until, sadly, she raises her head from mine. She does not move from atop me though.

"That was a real kiss," she says, breathing every bit as hard as me.

"That was . . . that was amazing," I stutter out.

She looks down at me sweetly. "That is only the beginning. Do you want more?" she asks seductively.

I nod my consent eagerly, feeling like a child again. She laughs a cute laugh, then stands, pulling me after her and leading me through the dining area, up the stairs, and down the hallway to the last door on the left. She pulls me in, then throws me down on the bed and locks the door behind her.

Moonlight shines through the window, illuminating us both. I am sitting on the edge of the bed when she walks straight up to me, sky-blue eyes never leaving mine, turns around, and sits in my lap.

"Unzip me, please," she asks and commands at the same time. I reach up to the neckline of her dress and do as I'm told. The zipper whines as I slide it down to the bottom of its track. Slowly, Latrice stands, dropping her dress to the floor, still turned away from me. She has on only a thin pair of light blue underwear, strings, really, that don't really cover her bottom. She reaches up and takes the stick out of her hair, letting it fall down her back, then turns to face me.

She is definitely beautiful; however, my eyes keep falling down to her full breasts. The moonlight does her skin justice. I hear Latrice laugh, and I look up from her breasts to her eyes. Then she comes to me. She slowly pushes me back until my back touches the bed. Suddenly, I am scared. I slide backward until my head hits the headboard. Thunk.

"Careful," she says, pulling my shirt over my head and then kissing me deeply. Her hands explore, no, caress, my upper body, and I let them. Her touch is soft, soothing, and welcoming after a year in the wilderness. I relax and allow my hands to explore her body. She then lowers herself to take off my sweats. She kisses my lower stomach once before doing so, giving me the chills. We are both in our underwear at this point, chests bare, kissing like we have no care in the world. But I do.

"We can't do this . . . I can't do this," I mumble.

"Yes we can. I'll take good care of you, I promise," she teases.

"It's not that . . . It's just . . . I—"

She jumps back away from me, quick as a cat.

"There's someone else," she says disbelievingly, looking into my eyes for askance.

"I don't really know, honestly. There could be, or I could be mistaken. We never really talked about it, and I haven't seen her in a year," I say, confused, among other things. I see her body go from tense to relaxed as she moves to sit down on the edge of the bed.

"See, that is why I like you. I knew you were different. Most men wouldn't have even thought twice about that," she says.

"May I sleep next to you tonight?" she asks sheepishly. "It has been a long time since I have trusted someone enough to be able to do that."

"It would be my pleasure," I say kindly, and honestly meaning it.

The sexual tension leaves the room just like that. She climbs up next to me, rests her head on my chest, and then pulls the blankets over us.

"What is her name?" she asks after a moment.

"Shari," I answer, deciding telling her couldn't hurt.

"Shari," she repeats, tasting the name. "Shari is one lucky girl. Well, goodnight," she whispers.

Soon after, she is breathing the deep, even breath of sleep.

"Goodnight," I whisper.

9 INFORMATION

I awake from sunlight beaming in my face, coming in from the window. It's been a while since that happened. The sun is already up; it appears I've slept in rather late. Latrice is gone. Bolting into an upright position, I see my sweats still on the floor where she threw them last night. I move them aside for my pouches, which I find just as full as they were last night. I feel ashamed for allowing myself to entertain the thought that she would do something like that, especially after all the kindness she has shown me.

I head to the bathroom to wash up, and this time the hot water works. The heat on my muscles is pure joy. I'll be sure to thank her when I go downstairs. I take the time to wash my hair extra well this time, fearing her washing might lead to another intimate encounter. Remembering the way her body felt, I don't know if I'll be able to hold myself back again. I hope things aren't awkward between us now. Finishing quickly, I dry myself, get dressed, and head out.

I hear noise coming from downstairs as soon as I enter the hallway. Cautiously, I begin the descent down the stairs. Latrice is as kind as they come, but the rest of this town is either lawless or lacks courage, besides Brenda. And maybe her daughter. As I reach the bottom of the stairs, I see a few people sitting around eating. Nothing special, until my eyes fall upon a man sitting at the front counter: he is massive. He wears a simple green shirt that squeezes against his muscles, and dark blue trousers. The hair atop his head, which resembles a bulldog's, is short and brown. He turns to stare at me when he hears me coming down the stairs, revealing brown eyes and a face that resembles that of an old grizzly bear.

"Who are you?" he says protectively for some reason.

"My friend," Latrice answers for me, coming from the back of the kitchen with a few plates stacked in her arms. "And you will treat him with every kindness," she finishes, setting a plate on the counter next to the big man and waving me over to come sit next to him.

"Good morning," she says cheerily.

"Sit, eat, and introduce yourselves. I'll help. Bron, Beau . . . Beau, Bron," she says, pointing to each of us in turn. "Bron, be nice. Beau isn't much of a talker." She winks at me, then moves off to continue attending to her customers.

Bron stares after her in either disbelief or shock, I can't tell. Seeing the look on his face makes me happy—I'm not the only one she gives commands to.

"You're a new face around here," Bron says, turning to face me.

"I just arrived yesterday. Latrice kind of just took me in."

"Sounds about right. You must have a good heart or something resembling one, then. She's a good judge of character, that one." He pauses for a moment, visibly thinking. "Any friend of Latrice's is a friend of mine. I know she just told you my name, but . . ." he extends a massive forearm for a handshake ". . . Bron."

I shake his hand.

"Beau."

"Well met," he says.

"How do you know Latrice, if you don't mind me asking?" I ask, wanting to know the circumstances that led to their friendship so I can compare them to my own. He looks way too old for her, and she just doesn't seem like the type of girl to just give herself to anyone. But then again, what do I know? It doesn't hurt to ask.

"I've been coming to this inn since she was a wee lass. I was good friends with her mom and dad, Aluara and Randy. Randy worked with me at the smithy when he could spare the time. Good man, if I ever knew one. When they decided to leave, he asked me to watch over her the best I could. I've been finding reasons to drop by twice a week ever since. Though the way she cooks is reason enough," he explains, laughing with the last.

"She is a fantastic cook," I agree readily. "So you were close with her parents. Do you know why they left?" I ask.

"Of course, they fled the all-powerful, good-for-nothing king. They would rather live free than serve him. And they most certainly got that right. It just sucks for Latrice, but she'd have a better life here than she would've had if she started over in a new kingdom with them."

Well, that answers my next question. Everyone seems to dislike my father. I'm not even sure if I can blame them after everything I've heard.

"Have you any news on the king and queen?" I choose to ask instead.

"Not since the flaming pillar in the sky about a year ago; the castle's been strangely quiet ever since."

"Flaming pillar in the sky?" I repeat, squinting my eyes questioningly.

"You're telling me you didn't see it! Where have you been, under a rock?" Not knowing how to reply to that, I choose to stay silent.

"Not much of a talker indeed," he says to my suspicious silence, then pauses. Not wanting to come up with a lie, I just wait for him to continue. "Anyhow, just about a year ago a pillar of fire shot down from the heavens into the castle. Never seen anything like it in my entire life. It wasn't much from here, but for us to have seen it from so far away, it must have been of truly monstrous proportions. No doubt the only one with that kind of power is the king. No one knows what happened, but rumor is he lost something. It's also rumored that the pillar of fire was someone's, or a few someones', by the size of it, cremation."

109

I feel like I have been punched in my gut, before my grandfather's training, as the last thing I remember while I was being kidnapped plays through my mind. Everything is black again. "Where's the boy?" my father's voice asks belligerently. "Far away from you by now," my mother's voice taunts. "I'll kill you," my father's voice roars. Everything is black again—No, everything wasn't black; everything was red in a pillar of flame while I was unconscious. I am brought back to reality by Bron's voice.

"Are you alright, lad?" he's asking me, concerned.

No, I am not alright, I am hyperventilating. I can't even answer him. I am spared the need to as Latrice comes from somewhere, takes my hand, and quickly pulls me up the stairs. "Hold down the fort for a minute, Bron," she yells back down the stairs before taking me into a room, sitting me down on the bed, and kneeling so I can see her face.

"Beau," she calls my fake name, worried. "Beau, talk to me, what's wrong?"

"My mother . . . He," I start, but then catch myself.

She can't know. Tears fill my eyes, and my body shakes in rage and fear as I look at her. She knows I will say nothing else. Standing slowly, she pulls my head to her stomach and holds me tight. "It's okay," she says caringly. "I don't know what's wrong, but I am here."

That's all it takes for me to break down and start crying. I'm sobbing so hard I can barely breathe. I haven't cried like this since—ever. My mother, he killed my mother. How could he? Why would she let him? She doesn't have the power like him, but I've seen her do some incredible things with Certus; she could have stopped him, right? She did not have to die. He did not have to kill her. What is going on? No, not *what—why*? Why was my mother trying to get me away from my father? I force myself to stop crying even though the wound is raw and bloody.

"Better?" Latrice asks hopefully, looking down at me. I didn't realize I was holding her.

"No," I reply, dropping my arms from around her and trying to cut myself off from the world.

I want to be cold, angry. Something stirs inside me that I've never felt before. It is—"Stop that," Latrice commands softly, swatting at me lightly. I look up at her. "I don't know what's wrong, but this—" she makes a circling motion with her hand over my cold, dead, and angry face "—this is not you, and I am not your enemy." She pulls me into her and kisses my forehead as a sister would a younger brother.

"It's going to be alright. I'm here for you. You're not alone. But right now, I must go attend to my inn, and you must get a breath of fresh air. You said shooting the bow is a passion of yours, correct?" I nod. "I will tell Bron. Be downstairs in five minutes," she commands, then departs.

She has calmed my anger, but all the other emotions war inside me right now, frustration dominating them all. This must be why my grandfather said, "Always have a plan, never act out of emotion." In fact, I'm sure of it. He must have already known my father killed my mother, his daughter. It most certainly explains his distaste for my father, which I now share.

That . . . that . . . that sheep. How could the old man know and do nothing? I recall what I did to him while I was holding the storm; if one hit from me did that, then my father would obliterate him. He knows it too. That's what this is all about. The training, he wants me to avenge my mother. But for that, I need to grow stronger. Immensely stronger doesn't even cover it. I also need to get better control of my power so I can bend Certus to my will for anything I need when the time comes. I need to learn about my father's operations throughout the kingdom as well, so I can disrupt them in any way possible. I need a plan, and what better way to plan than from the shadows?

Deciding there is nothing I can do right now, I slide back from my mental retreat. The room is foreign; well, at least it's not the one she gave me. The sky-blue sheets are made of fine silk, the bed is way more comfortable than my own, and the walls are painted sky blue. The setup is the same, if not larger.

My eyes explore the room, which, from the looks of it, definitely belongs to a girl, until they fall on a picture sitting atop the dresser. Standing, I move over to the dresser and pick up the picture. In it is a much younger-looking Latrice and presumably her parents. She looks just like her mother; the resemblance is eerie. They all look so happy, but my father has taken that from them, from her, just as he stole my mother from me.

"I will see to vengeance for the both of us," I promise Latrice to myself.

Setting down the photo, I prepare myself to be Beau again. Once the mask is in place, I walk out into the hallway, briefly note that Latrice's room is the first door on the left, and go down the stairs. Bron and Latrice are talking quietly by the front door when I get down there and go silent as I approach. Latrice eyes me warily.

"Better?" she asks again, just as hopefully as the first time.

"Yes, thank you," I lie, but I really mean the "thank you."

"Good, because you and Bron are going to spend some time together doing target practice," she says excitedly.

Bron opens the door, then walks about halfway through. "You ready, lad?" he asks enthusiastically.

I can't help but appreciate the extra effort these people are going through for me. It does make me feel better.

"Yes," I say simply, making my way over to him. Latrice still watches me worriedly.

"Wait," I say, stopping in my tracks, giving Bron pause.

I turn to Latrice, drop my shield, and hug her. "Thank you," I say, stepping back. "For everything."

She smiles brightly. "You're welcome, but please fix that." Her hand does the circular motion thing over my face again. I smile, a sincere smile, for her, despite how I feel on the inside for both of us.

"Much better. Now off you two go," she says, ushering us out the door.

Bron chuckles. "Women," he says.

"No, I believe that is just her," I respond. It's not like I would know, but I feel like I'm right anyway.

"You're absolutely right, lad," he says after a moment, then pauses again, no doubt remembering some past time involving Latrice. "Well, no point in wasting daylight. It's already past high rise. Let's go."

As we move through the town heading east, Bron takes it upon himself to give me a tour of sorts, pointing out notable taverns, different shops, and inns. He even shows me a brothel that has a pink sign depicting a woman . . . Wait, what is she doing? I don't know, but just outside the brothel, two half-naked women try to lure people in with very vulgar sexual advances. Men, women, it doesn't seem to matter much to them. I am not interested. Having seen Latrice's naked body atop my own, their state of undress doesn't make me blush. But the memory of Latrice on top of me does.

"What's the matter, lad? Never had a woman?" Bron asks brotherly.

"No . . . but I could've," I retort, trying to sound smoother than I feel.

"Then why didn't you?" he asks with a raised eyebrow.

"It just didn't feel right," I reply, thinking about Shari.

"So, it's men then?"

"What? No!" I shout. "What makes you think—"

He holds a hand up, cutting me off. "Whoa, whoa. Just asking, lad. Times are changing, that's all. I wouldn't judge you," he explains.

"There is a girl who is somewhat special to me. I would like to figure things out with her first," I confide in him, somewhat embarrassed.

"Young love, is it? I remember those days."

"Maybe. If I'm being honest, I'm not sure."

"You're a curious young lad, you know that?" he says, unable to figure me out.

If only he knew.

"What's that?" I ask, pointing to a section walled off from the rest of the town.

"That is the King's Hand's barracks. It isn't really different from the rest of the town. They just made a fort so they could feel special about themselves. You familiar with them?"

Just as he finishes his question, I see some men dressed in the same uniforms as the ones who tried to take my staff come around the corner of the barracks on what appears to be a patrol.

"Three of them, anyway," I say.

Bron looks at me questioningly. Sighing, I begin to tell Bron about my run-in with the King's Hand regarding my staff.

"Really?" he laughs when I finish. "I would have loved to see that." He eyes my staff interestedly. "She looks to be a beauty. May I?" he asks pleadingly.

I remove the staff from its holster on my back.

"Careful, it's heavier than it looks," I warn, tossing it over to him one-handed.

"I am no—" he begins, and is pulled up short when he catches the staff two-handedly.

"Whoa," he continues, smiling then looking up at me. "This staff must weigh at least forty pounds; you could do some real damage to a man with this," he evaluates aloud.

"Fifty, and believe me, I know," I say, recalling the sickening crunch my grandfather's chest made before he flew into a tree.

"What kind of wood is this?" Bron asks inquisitively.

"To be honest, I don't know. Why do you ask?"

"Well, I'm a smith, s'all, and I've never seen anything like this. Ahhh, here we are," he finishes, coming to a stop and handing me back my staff.

"This is my smithy," he says proudly.

"You make weapons?" I ask excitedly.

"Think I got this big sitting around and doing nothing my whole life? Been hammering iron since I was fifteen. I'm forty-seven now."

Yeah, I suppose that would turn any man into a bear like Bron.

The smithy is a one-story stone building, not quite as big as Latrice's inn. Windows line the building, two on each wall, and there is a chimney currently not in use coming out of the middle of the building. No signs hang on or over the building; there is only the emblem of a hammer atop a shield etched into the front door.

"We can explore the smithy later. The archery course is around back. Latrice said you like to shoot the bow. When's the last time you got a chance to shoot?" he asks, grinning.

"It's been far too long," I reply, missing my bow.

"Well, come on then. Let's go relieve some stress," he says, walking around to the back of the building. I follow, feeling no small amount of excitement. We reach the back of the building, and my eyes take in the clearing, which is about five hundred yards or so. Over one hundred targets decorate the field, some low, some high, some close, and some far. Well, far for everyone else. A few are angled, and there are three hanging on the stone wall all the way at the end of the clearing. Bron walks over to a cabinet attached to the back of the smithy.

"Choose your bow," he says dramatically, opening the cabinet and bowing before me. I can't help but laugh.

"Grab me one, too, along with a couple of quivers of arrows, and meet me over there," he says, pointing behind me to a red line painted in the dirt that marks the do-not-cross point.

He then boastfully walks over there, swinging his arms behind his back. He's too big to do whatever he's trying to do, and the sight causes me to burst out in a fit of laughter. He's a good man.

Turning back to the cabinet, I notice all the bows are the same—not mine. I just grab two at random, along with three quivers of arrows, and head over to join Bron. After handing Bron his equipment, I survey the field, trying to decide where I want to begin. Bron is nowhere near as caring; he fires at a target around 250 feet away. Thunk, almost dead center. His aim is decent, but even Shari would have hit that right in the middle.

"Do you and Latrice have something going on?" he asks abruptly, without taking his eyes off the targets. Thunk.

"You just thought I liked men. Now you think I have something going on with Latrice?" I respond, not understanding his logic.

"Hey, I know some men who like men. Doesn't mean they won't take a woman every now and again. Usually, they take someone else's woman for making fun of them."

Well, there's a thought—never would have guessed. The world is strange.

"No," I reply quickly.

"You don't have to lie to me, lad. I've seen the way she looks at you."

I just got here yesterday. Does everything have to happen so fast? I step up, nock an arrow, then begin to fire.

"We had a moment," I begin. Bullseye. "She is a beautiful girl with a beautiful heart. But as I said earlier, my heart belongs to another." Bullseye. Bullseye. So much has happened in a day. Bullseye. Bullseye. Bullseye. "Everything happened so fast, I didn't know it would be like this." Bullseye.

"What would be like what?" Bron asks, astonished.

Why would he be amazed at that? What did I say? I look at him and continue to fire. "My first trip into this town…." Bullseye. Bullseye. "…I just saw everything happening so differently. People were supposed to be here that aren't. I shouldn't have to, Arrrrrghhhh!" I yell in frustration. Shooting the bow has made my mind and mouth careless. I should not be talking to Bron so freely.

I close my eyes and sight the farthest target on the wall, 500 feet away. I fire five arrows in quick succession. Fwip. Fwip. Fwip. Fwip. Fwip. I open my eyes. They all hit dead center, the second arrow splitting the first, the third arrow splitting the second, and so on—as I knew they would.

"That's quite some aim you got there, lad," Bron says, astonished. Oh, that's why he sounded like that. He can't decide if he wants to look at me or the target on the far back wall I just hit five times dead center. "Where did you learn how to shoot like that?"

I remember my lessons and my most recent showing off in front of Alrick. "Nowhere special, I've just been practicing since I was six," I casually lie.

"Is that so?" he asks, clearly unconvinced.

I hate lying to good people, but I must, right? I move to put the equipment back into the cabinet to end the moment. "Should we go back?" I ask, trying to bypass my obvious lie.

"Go back?" he repeats. "You may be a perfect shot, but you have not seen me swing my hammer," he says matter-of-factly.

I don't really want to fi—Oh, he means to craft weapons. "I would love to see that," I say, not having to feign interest.

There is no back door, so we must walk back to the front after he puts up his equipment. "Welcome to my domain, lad," he says proudly, opening the door for me. I know Bron just told me he was good at making weapons, but I didn't think he did it on this scale. It looks as if someone is preparing for war here. All kinds of weapons line the walls, from axes to morning stars to javelins and everything else you can think of. Bron closes the door behind me, which does nothing to dim the light because of all the windows, and moves to walk the length of the smithy.

I follow and admire the craftsmanship of the weapons—Bron is good, really good. I drop my shield to feel the edge on one of the short swords; it cuts me deep. I heal myself before Bron notices.

There's a loud whooshing noise from behind me. I turn to find that Bron has lit a fire in something that looks like a giant oven located in the middle of his shop. Is it just me, or did it get hot in here rather quickly?

"Come on over, Beau. Let me show you a thing or two," Bron says, waving me over.

All the studying my mother had me do does no justice here. I feel like I am in an entirely different world as I walk over to him.

"See, getting the fire hot enough is a big part of making weapons, but knowing which metals act best under different amounts of heat is key." Bron takes a black blade that looks like it will be a rapier when it's done in between some tongs and places it in the giant oven. I don't want to ask questions because I don't want to sound stupid. Suddenly, I feel something, and the flames flare up and turn blue inside the oven. It's so hot I feel like I might suffocate. A moment later, they die back down to their original reddish-orange color, and Bron pulls the blade back out of the oven. It's glowing a bright yellow, almost white color. I can't help but be amazed and consumed by the glow. Bron moves the blade so that it's dangerously close to his face, then turns to me.

"You best get out of here. Now, I have some real man's work to do," he says, grinning at me wickedly.

Something about the way he looks at me right now makes me want to do just that. I head to the door without another word, quickly.

"Careful on the way back now," he says brightly, as if he didn't just try to frighten me. "And do me a favor, be another pair of eyes to look after Latrice."

He didn't even have to ask that, but I appreciate his care for the girl.

"Of course," I say before going through the door and beginning the walk back to the inn.

I arrive just before the sun sets. Going through the door, I am pleased to find that the dining area is empty. With my grandfather's voice constantly in my head telling me to avoid drawing attention, the emptiness of the inn is comforting. I move to the same booth where Latrice first kissed me and sit.

"I thought I heard the door. How was target practice?" Latrice asks, coming from the kitchen, drying off a plate.

"It helped a little bit. I still don't know what I'm supposed to be doing though," I say, mentally drained.

"Well, that makes two of us," she says playfully, eyeing me.

"Your mother is beautiful," I abruptly change the subject.

"Thank you, but remind me how you know what my mother looks like."

"The picture on your dresser," I answer nonchalantly before another thought occurs to me. "I didn't look at anything else, I promise."

She sets the plate down on the table and sits across from me. "If I didn't trust you, I wouldn't have brought you in there in the first place," she responds reassuringly.

"How long can I stay here?" I ask, concerned.

"As long as you need. You'll always have a bed here, even if you must share mine," she says kindly.

"How much is this going to cost me?"

"You know what I just noticed? When you get nervous or upset, you start asking a lot of questions. Why is that?"

I blush, not knowing I did that. When I don't answer, she lazily backhands the air, then speaks. "We're the lost, remember. Don't worry about paying for your room. On second thought, if it's not too much to ask, do you mind sleeping in my room so I can continue to rent yours out? Taxes don't pay themselves, you know."

I know, alright. You pay them to my family, well, my father.

"Honestly, I hate sleeping alone, so I'll enjoy the company. Just don't try anything you're not ready to finish—I do bite," she says, then chomps her teeth.

My eyes widen and my face reddens.

"I'm kidding," she laughs. "I know you're Shari's man, but until you find her again, you can be my teddy bear," she says a little too happily.

"Bron already thinks we have something going on," I say.

"And? Bron is just an overprotective mother grizzly. If I am happy, then so is he."

I laugh, thinking about Bron as a mother grizzly. It's surprisingly fitting.

"But—" I start.

"But nothing. You worry too much, and I can't worry with you because you won't tell me anything. Come on, up." She stands, leaving the plate on the table, and heads upstairs.

"It's bedtime. I have to get up early, and I want to make use of my new teddy bear," she commands.

I follow her upstairs into her room, wondering what I just got myself into. As soon as I close the door behind us, she drops her dress onto the floor in front of me. Blushing, I look down.

"Don't be shy now. You've seen more than just my underwear. Besides, I've already put on my nightdress," she says humorously. I look back up and see that she has indeed put on her nightdress. However, it is a see-through pink color and stops entirely too high. In my head, I thank whichever gods exist for her still having on her underwear. She hurriedly climbs into her bed.

"Keep the sweats, lose the shirt. Hurry up. I'm tired," she commands, snapping her fingers to press her point.

First, I drop my shield, then take off my shirt, and finally go to the opposite side of the bed and lie down. A lot of good it does me. She slides right up next to me and puts her head on my chest and her hand on my stomach.

"Goodnight, teddy bear," she says softly.

"Goodnight," I mumble.

Gods, she's soft. Eventually, I hear her begin to breathe the even breath of sleep, and I relax. She's not Shari, but if this doesn't go too far, I could get used to this. With that thought, I fall asleep.

Two weeks passed before we knew it. I've not forgotten to redo the power that keeps my false eye color every night, except the first. I'm also sure to drop my shielding every night before I go to bed with Latrice. At first, it was awkward, but after about the fourth day, her body became a welcome comfort to me. Not in a sexual way, more like being glad I'm not alone anymore. What was it she said? "I hate sleeping alone." Yes, I find that statement appropriate. Especially considering I haven't done much else lately. Latrice did make good on her demanding offer to wash my hair. Despite my earlier concerns, the experience did not lead to an intimate encounter, and my hair is better for it. I've frequented a couple of taverns Bron has shown me, asking people at random how they feel about the king and if there's any news to be had. Of course, they all hate him, and just like Bron, no one's heard anything new since the pillar of fire. It's like the castle has been locked down since that day. My grandfather said, "Always have a plan." How am I supposed to plan if I can't find out any information?

Today is Latrice's weekly cleaning day, so the tavern is closed. She is already downstairs cleaning for the day while I am remembering how lovely it is to sleep in. I hear something break downstairs. I jump up quickly and grab my staff. Sweats on, shirt off, I fly out of the room. Latrice let me put my coin bags in her dresser weeks ago, so I don't jingle when I walk anymore. I'm down the stairs as quick as lightning. Latrice stands just in front of the counter, staring at the door. A plate is shattered at her feet.

"Are you alright?" I ask with no small amount of concern in my voice.

"Yeah, someone kicked the door and scared me. Probably ju—" She is cut off by the sound the door makes as it is broken off its hinges. In come nine men in all black with white handprints on their shirts, one of whom is the leader I met before. However, he is not the leader this time. I move to position Latrice behind me as nine men form a half circle around us with the counter at our backs. In walks another man, bringing the total count to ten. On height with me but dark complected, almost as dark as the clothes they wear, this man walks with the grace of a jungle cat. Two short swords crisscross on his back, and there is a wicked long dagger on his hip. He moves behind his men, then pulls a chair out and sits like he owns the place. He smiles at me, revealing pearl-white teeth before he speaks. "It has been said that a man with a white quarterstaff has been going around asking questions about the king. You wouldn't happen to know who that is, would you?" he asks as if we were best friends or something.

"I have no desire to hurt you or your friends. Please, leave me and my friend alone," I plead, if a wolf can do such a thing.

"I would, but there is a bounty on your head, and it seems you've already embarrassed a few of us once before. You will not do it again," he explains kindly before passing my second death sentence.

"Kill him."

The nine men move as one to tighten the half circle around us. To keep them focused on me, I step up to meet them.

"Beau," Latrice calls my name, frightened. I turn my head to look her in the eyes.

"I'll be fine, don't worry. Just stay back," I say, then smile reassuringly. That's when I hear a man grunt from throwing a punch. I pivot on my left foot and spin around him; he nearly falls. The inn erupts in chaos. The next few moments are spent dodging all nine men's blows. Not only do they move terribly slowly, but I can dance terribly well: 16, 34, 12, 2, 49, 27, 25, 10. I dip, duck, dodge, and jump around the inn. They couldn't land a blow on me to save their lives. They are so enraged by this that they begin to break chairs and tables around the inn to get to me.

"I don't want to hurt you, but if you keep—" I stop talking as the dark man who has been sitting quietly in his chair up to this point pulls his dagger and throws it. But I am not his target, Latrice is. Shit. 13, I slide underneath a kick and place myself in front of Latrice. I let my shield flicker so I can push her backward, then reactivate it, just in time. Had I not, I would be dead. I never took my eyes off the dagger, but I was a fraction of a second too slow. The dagger hit my shield, and I caught it with my fingertips the split second after. Only a trained eye would be able to tell. Fortunately, they don't appear to notice.

"You made a mistake," I say, anger beginning to stir within me. I've had no choice in the way my life has played out in the last year. It's been hard, but my grandfather prepared me to deal with men like this. Latrice is powerless here. She is just a simple inn owner who chose to show me kindness. He would have killed her. I don't summon the storm; it comes unbidden in response to my rage.

I hurl the knife so hard at the closest man to my left it goes through his kneecap and out the other side, sticking into the wooden floor at an angle. He will never walk the same again.

When he falls, the other eight charge. I do not bother dodging; I just move faster than they can keep up with. 94, 73, 51, 82. I step inside a man's punch, so we are face-to-face, while simultaneously punching him in the throat. He drops. Another one tries to kick me; I catch his leg and kick back. The leg he was balanced on bends in the wrong direction, followed by a sickening snap—another one who will never walk the same. The other six are more hesitant now. However, it's too late to be scared. Two more come at me, one punching high and the other going for a low sweep, trying to take out my legs. I jump slightly to the side, evading the punch and the leg sweep, then kick the one who punched high in the face. Bones break. Landing on one leg, I pivot and bring my foot down in a stomp on the extended leg of the man who tried to sweep my feet from under me.

"Enough!" the dark-skinned man yells while standing. The remaining four men stop advancing on me, looking relieved. "It seems this one is worthy," he says, drawing his short swords as his men make a path. I casually twirl my staff. He approaches slowly, confident in himself. He is about to lose that confidence. The storm focuses itself, having found its destination.

He swings both his blades at me overhanded. 14, I swing my staff underhanded, blocking both his strikes and holding them up. 68, I lean back and bring my left heel to his chin, raising him up so my legs are almost perfectly vertical. His arms drop to his sides, and he releases his swords. I let him fall but catch his chin with the tip of my staff and support his body weight so that we are eye level. I lean in and whisper, "You are not." Then I spin my staff, releasing the hold on his chin, and slam it into his side, making him fly over by the door they ruined. I heard his ribs break. In fact, everyone still conscious did. The remaining four stand in awe but quiver in fear.

"Leave," I say, the storm's energy gone with the wind. The four uninjured men grab their leader and their wounded and begin to head out the door.

One man lingers. He is the leader of the first group of three I danced with. "The assassin will come," he warns timidly. "Our captain wanted to collect the bounty on your head before the assassin came. I do not know who you are, but if you value your life—" he hesitates, not wanting to threaten me. After what I just did, I don't blame him.

"They say the assassin wears a mask and no one living knows what their face looks like," he pauses, "because if you see it, you will die." With that, he is gone.

I survey the destruction of Latrice's inn. This is all because of me. If I just—

"You lied to me," Latrice says plainly.

"What?" I ask, turning to Latrice.

"You lied to me," she repeats, looking hurt.

"I did not lie to you. I simply didn't tell you anything."

"You said you couldn't touch the power," she says accusingly.

"I can't," I lie matter-of-factly.

"And you continue to lie to me." She laughs in disbelief. She looks wounded beyond measure, and tears begin to form in her eyes.

"Latrice, what are you—?"

"What am I talking about?" she snaps. "When you pushed me away from the knife, I tried to grab your hand, knowing you wouldn't make it in time, so I could take you with me to the ground, so you did not die. I could not feel your skin and you didn't even notice because you were shielded . . . and that was the second time."

"The second time?" I ask, not understanding that I messed up not once but twice.

"The first time was when you freaked out talking to Bron. When I grabbed you and took you to my room, I felt it, and when you were crying, it began to flicker in and out. I didn't mention it because you were going through something; it wasn't the right time. Then I just decided you would tell me on your own time. Shielding is a high-level use of Certus that only very few people alive know how to do. I was alarmed then, but now . . . now you have a bounty on your head and an assassin on your trail, and my shop is in ruins. Now you are a dangerous man. I have no wish to die, but I also have no desire to put you out. I need you to tell me the truth about everything. Whatever it is. I must know what I'm getting myself into so I can be prepared," she explains, then looks down at the floor, hurt and confused.

There is no preparation for this, Latrice.

"Have you told anyone else?" I ask after a moment.

"No," she answers without looking up from the floor.

"You said trust will get you killed around here," I say, firmer than I meant to.

She looks up pleadingly. "Yes, and I meant that. However, I no doubt know, as well as you do, that I couldn't kill you if I tried, and I have no desire to try."

My grandfather also said trust will get you killed. I want to heed his warning, if not hers, but . . . This woman has known about me for a little over two weeks now and has not told a soul. I've slept beside her every night since I've come to Last Stop. I'm sure if she meant me harm, it would've happened by now. She opened herself to me, yet I remained closed. If I can't trust her, then who can I trust? We are the lost.

"Are you sure you want to know everything?" I ask her playfully. Her face brightens and she nods.

"Why do you look so happy all of a sudden?" I ask, stalling for no reason.

"Because I was going to kick you out if you didn't tell me, and I didn't want to. You saved me the heartache," she explains.

"You know I still haven't made up my mind on whether I will tell you or not, right?" I jest. She just rolls her eyes at me.

"Do you remember the pillar of fire that came down from the heavens into the king's castle?" I ask her.

"Yes, who doesn't," she answers, sounding unsure about where I'm going with this.

"The king lost something that day. Do you know what it was?" I ask.

"No, no one does," she replies, now curious.

I hesitate. Once I cross the line, there is no going back.

"Me . . . his son," I say seriously.

She just laughs. "You expect me to believe you, who are so kind, are the son of the all-powerful tyrant king, a person no one has ever seen before?" she states sarcastically. "No, I will not believe that. Besides, rumor has it that his eyes look like—"

She stops short when I let my eyes turn back into their original color.

"This," I finish her sentence.

Her mouth drops open slowly as she stares in amazement into my eyes.

"You . . . You're . . . the king's son," she says, having trouble breathing. "The man who is the reason my parents left me is . . . your father?" she questions, knowing the answer and slowly beginning to back away from me.

Tears trickle down her face. This is not something she was prepared for.

"Latrice," I call her name pleadingly, "I am not my father."

She is not listening to me, but she is steadily backing away. I close the distance in the blink of an eye and grab her arm softly. She gasps in fear. I look into her eyes before I speak.

"My father killed my mother. That pillar of fire everyone saw was her execution. I will never forgive him. I am more lost right now than you can imagine," I say, feeling defeated, then let her go.

Those words register; she collapses on my chest, heaving deep breaths as she cries. If the tears are for me or for her, I don't know, but I stand and hold her, as she did for me, while she cries. She manages to get herself together rather quickly. Abruptly, she jumps back from me.

"I'm sorry, Your Highness, I—"

"Don't," I cut her off. "My name is Luca, but you must continue to call me Beau," I say, using Certus to change my eye color back to green.

There is a moment of silence in which I entertain the thought that she will still tell me to leave—I wouldn't blame her.

"I know I said I wanted to know everything, but this—"

"I have not told you everything, but if you don't kick me out, I will," I say, the last part tinged with worry.

"Beau, I wouldn't do that," she says, rushing up to me and taking my hands in hers.

She eyes me differently, then turns to her inn, which is in shambles. Broken tables and chairs litter the floor, along with wood splinters everywhere. The door is off its hinges in a way that lets me know the whole frame will need to be replaced.

"What am I going to do?" Latrice asks out loud, clearly dismayed.

A thought occurs to me.

"I will fix this."

"How?" she asks slowly.

"You haven't looked in the coin bags you allow me to keep in your dresser?" I ask in shock.

She just shakes her head no.

I laugh out loud. Who is this girl?

"Copper will not be enough to fix this place up," she says, letting me know my thoughts are appreciated.

"The kid stole the copper. The other two bags are silver and gold."

10 THE LOST

For the rest of the day, we spend our time in Latrice's room as I tell her about the events that led up to my kidnapping, where I've been, and what I've been doing for the last year. I also tell her why I believe my father killed my mother.

"But you said yourself there was a bag over your head and you lost consciousness," Latrice says, trying to give me hope.

"No, I don't know for sure, but who else could the pillar of fire have been for? I mean, he said, 'I'll kill you,' after she told him I was gone," I explain again.

"That doesn't mean anything. You said yourself your mother is a master with Certus. Why do you believe she would die so easily?"

I would hardly call dying from being incinerated by a pillar of fire easy. I sigh. "You're right," I admit. "I just don't want to give myself false hope." I recall a random memory. "You can touch Certus. You helped me when the kid stole my copper," I say eagerly.

"Yes, but not like you or your mother. I can barely access it to do the smallest of things."

I look at her with my mind made up.

"What?" she asks, seeing the decision on my face.

"I will teach you to shield yourself," I tell her confidently.

"You can't—I mean, I can't. That is only for people who are adept with Certus," she whines.

"Have you tried?" I ask smoothly.

"No," she answers defiantly. I can't help but laugh. "That settles it. You have shown me a kindness that is immaterial. I can't repay you, but maybe I can teach you something that might one day save your life." I smile, then grab her hands, one in each of mine, and sit us on the bed, leaning forward so our foreheads touch. "Close your eyes," I command.

She does.

"Repeat after me: 'Certain. Sure. Definite. Decided. Specific. Precise.' This is what Certus is, so this is what you are. Don't stop repeating it. Now, visualize little lines of air around your body moving freely. Make them yours. You are certain, sure, and definite that they are yours. Now decide that they will specifically intertwine in such a way that forms a barrier of force around you through which there are no gaps."

Nothing happens for a moment.

"Certain. Sure. Definite. Decided. Specific. Precise," I repeat aloud, willing her to focus.

Slowly, very slowly, our hands and heads begin to separate. She's so focused on trying to concentrate she doesn't even notice. I smile.

"Open your eyes."

When she does and sees our hands and heads separated, her eyes widen.

From excitement or on purpose, I don't know which, her shield drops and her head slams into mine. We fall back on the bed, her on top of me.

"Sorry. Thank you. Sorry. Thank you. Sorry. Thank you," she repeats, excited and embarrassed at the same time.

She raises herself so that she is pinning my arms to the bed and looks into my eyes.

"Shari is truly lucky. I respect your feelings for her."

Latrice once told me she bites, then she said she was kidding. If she were to bite right now, I would bite back, and I'm not kidding. Instead, she pushes herself off me and returns to the sitting position.

"Again," she says enthusiastically.

We spend the next few hours going over shielding exercises. Try as she might, Latrice can't hold her shield longer than three seconds, but it's a start. Those three seconds may save her life one day.

"I'm mentally exhausted," she complains, throwing herself back on the bed.

"You've done well," I compliment.

"How long could you hold it when you first learned?"

I could shield myself for over half an hour my first time when I was six, but I dare not tell her that.

"Doesn't matter. What does matter is my friend can now shield herself," I say, smiling.

"Thank you. I think this is the kindest thing anyone has ever done for me," she confides.

"No need to thank me, especially after all you've done. Are doing," I correct. "There is an assassin hunting me, and that may put you in harm's way. My hope is that if you end up in a bad way, shielding yourself will save your life. After all, we are the lost, not the dead."

She reaches over and hugs me, and I hug her back. Eventually, she lets go and stands to walk over to her dresser.

"You said your grandfather was making you read the language of power during your training," she asks and states at the same time, as is her way, while looking in her drawer for something.

"I did. Why?" I ask.

"Why?" she repeats, laughing.

After I told her the whole story about my grandfather and the

131

question why, I think she's taken a fancy to the question.

"Found it," she shouts. "It's not a library but—" She hands me a blue book with a gold three-ringed concentric circle on the cover. There is no title. "Some old man left this in his room when he left and never came back for it. I can read it, but it's too confusing for me. I want you to have it." I can feel the power radiating from this book.

"Do you not feel that?" I ask curiously.

"Feel what?" she asks, confused.

"Nothing."

I open the book to a page at random. There are combinations of symbols and elements I've never seen before. Some of the ones I have seen say very specific things like, "All is one, from one comes two, and three springs from two. One, two, and three make all. All hangs between does and doesn't, which is harmonized by all."

"What?" Latrice asks.

"I didn't even realize I was reading aloud. I was just reading this here." I point out the elements I was just reading on the page.

"All that says is 'Everything Is Everything.' Where did you get numbers from?"

"Everything is everything?" I repeat questioningly. Where have I heard that? I didn't. I read it in another book containing the language of power. "That's all this says to you?" I ask, thinking about how far my understanding must have come. She just nods. It's confusing, but "Everything Is Everything" can be broken down into what I just read. What's even scarier is I get the feeling that I haven't even interpreted it all the way yet.

"Bron has the power too," Latrice says, snapping me out of my thoughts.

"Bron can touch Certus too? Good, I will teach him to shield himself as well." This is good, I think to myself, I can—

"No," Latrice says, cutting me out of my thoughts again. "He can touch Potentia like . . . like my parents. Like the king," she admits timidly. Of course—that explains the blue flame. Silence hangs between us for a moment. "He says that he's got it under control. He can only use it to heat fires in his forge to extreme temperatures and strengthen his hammer blows while making weapons," she explains. A forge must be the giant oven.

"Why . . . why did you tell me this?" I ask, not knowing her end game.

"When the king started making a mess of things, Bron ended it with his lover. He told her only an unhappy ending awaited him and that she should be free to enjoy life. As far as I know, he has been alone since. He's lost, too. I just thought that you should know."

"Latrice, I can't—"

She holds up a hand to stop me from talking. "I will not tell Bron about you, nor do I think you should, I just . . . It's just sad." I don't know what I can say that will comfort her, so I just decide to change the subject.

"How do you propose we start on fixing the shop up?" I ask.

"I know a carpenter," she says immediately. "I will go and see Amy while you stay here and make sure no one comes in to steal anything while the place is a wreck."

I know why the ability to touch Certus is in her: it didn't have a choice. I swear, every time she says something, it just is. She grabs a few things from her dresser and turns to leave.

"Hurry," I say before she exits the room, causing her to stop. "With the impending threat of the assassin, I'm really not comfortable with you out of my sight," I say more harshly than I intend.

She just smiles at me appreciatively.

"Yes, Daddy," she jokes as she walks out the door.

My face is on fire right now. Stupid woman. I grab the blue book

133

and head downstairs to see what I can easily make to eat in the kitchen.

The kitchen is well stocked, and as I am trying to decide what to eat, I come across a pink bottle of wine, the same kind Latrice poured for us the night we met.

I grab it, foregoing the food, and move to the same booth Latrice kissed me in to see what else I can interpret from this book. Before I sit, however, I notice the cork still in the bottle. I don't know how Latrice made it pop open like that. I set the book on the table, walk over to the knife I threw through the man's kneecap, which is still sticking out of the floor at an angle, and pick it up. I stick the knife in the cork and push upward until—

Pop.

The cork flies off. I am pleased with myself . . . until I realize I could have just done that with Certus . . . whatever. Keeping the knife and sipping the wine, I head back over to the booth. Time to see what this book says.

It's interesting, really. There are a lot of concepts in here that seem like they require meditation or something. It's almost as if they are designed to bring something out of you. Here, it says, "Goodness begets goodness, but to true goodness, even evil is good."

What does that mean? I ponder as I continue to sip wine, already feeling good. Does it mean if my intentions are well, it is okay to do evil? Or does it mean that if evil is presented to me and I am truly good, I will be able to use the opportunity to turn evil into good? I don't know why, but I think my mother would favor the second one. If everyone followed the first, then the world would be a way more chaotic place than it is now.

More elements catch my eye. Here it says, "Seek and find. Continue to seek and continue to find." I know I'm probably misinterpreting its meaning because it sounds so simple, but through the power, I can feel its meaning, and it's deep. It feels like it means people find on the surface answers to their problems and assume they have things under control.

But if one would just continue the search for the root of the problem, they would find understanding instead of temporary answers.

This book is so deep, I can't even understand all the symbols. I wish my mother could have read this. The pain I feel at her loss is deep. I know Latrice said I don't know for sure, but somewhere deep in my mind, I know. I take another swallow of wine. The bottle is half gone, and so am I.

What am I supposed to do, Grandfather? I know why, because my father believes himself to be the one true God and must be stopped before it is too late. But what can I do? If only I had the power to wield Potentia like him, then I would challenge and defeat him.

"Amy said she would help, but the process will take about a month," Latrice says, walking over toward me. Shit. I'm supposed to be watching for thieves, and I didn't even hear her come in. I'm wasted.

"Amy?" comes my late reply. Damn. The sun is already down.

"You know," she says, squinting her eyes at me, "the carpenter I went to see." She approaches the booth and picks up the bottle of wine. "Oh my, it appears I need to play catch-up," she says, then downs the rest of the wine and sits across from me. "So what did you learn?" she asks, eyeing the book in front of me.

"That evil might be good or a chance for good, and I need to keep looking," I say with liquid confidence.

"What?" Latrice laughs.

"It's complicated," I say, trying not to slur my words.

"You're complicated," she says, laughing again. I don't see what's so funny.

"You know everything about me now—simplify me."

"There is only one way to truly simplify a man," she says seductively.

"How?" I demand the answer, not catching on.

She stands then comes to sit next to me. "Show him the power of a woman," she bites.

I want a distraction from the weight of my life right now, and the wine has emboldened me. "Simplify me," I bite back.

"I shall enjoy this," she says, taking my hand and pulling me through the dining area toward the stairs. "Grab a chair that isn't broken and put it behind the front door so it doesn't open," she commands teasingly.

I stumble drunkenly to do as I'm told.

"Come," she whispers in my ear as soon as I finish. I follow her up the stairs to her room and close that door too. Nothing is on my mind but relief from the weight of the world on my shoulders, relief from my mother's death. She unzips her dress, dropping it to the floor, to reveal her underwear. She then unhooks something behind her, and her bra comes off, too, revealing her moonlit breasts. Not in any mood to be outdone, I strip down to my underwear too. She climbs into bed and bids me to come to her with her pointer finger. I don't shy away.

As soon as I reach her, she grabs me and places me on the bed, mounting me in the process. Her hand slides through my hair as she leans down to kiss me. I do not wait for her this time: my tongue enters her mouth and begins to flow. I also reach up and grab her breasts roughly but delicately at the same time as she does my hair.

A surprised gasp escapes her lips, followed by a naughty laugh.

She moves her mouth past mine to my ear and begins to flick the lobe with her tongue. I don't know what that did, but I feel my manhood stiffen instantly. She then starts kissing on my neck and chest, working her way down to my stomach before retracing her way back up to my lips.

I caress her, a moan escapes her lips as I let out a drunken laugh.

She rolls off the top of me to lie next me. I position myself so that we are face-to-face. She kisses me deeply, passionately for a moment, two, then stops.

I go to kiss her back but she stops me by placing a finger on my lips, pushing me backwards.

"I gave you the distraction you need because I have been where you are. But for Shari's sake, do not ask me to simplify you again. Because the next time you do, I will not hold myself back. No matter who your heart belongs to, Luca," she finishes, rolling over to face away.

This is not a threat, but a silent promise. Next, she reaches over, grabs my hand, and places it on her waist, then slides back into me so her back touches my chest.

"Do not move or let me go. Hold me tonight, Luca, please."

Is she crying?

We are already close together, but I scoot even closer so I can comfort her.

Shit. Maybe I got a little too close, as her body tenses for a second as my manhood bumps up against her.

But she does not move, and I am too scared to.

So that is how we sleep.

I wake up to something soft in my hand. It is really soft. I finesse it in my hand.

A soft moan escapes Latrice's mouth, and my eyes shoot open. The events of last night replay through my mind quick as lightning, I also realize we are still in the same position we fell asleep in.

"Enjoying yourself?" she asks testily.

I can barely think enough to speak. My liquid courage is gone, replaced by . . . me

"You told me not to move." That's all I can come up with.

She laughs.

"So I did. So I did."

She slides away from me and then stands up and turns to face me. The sunlight shines on her bare breasts. She yawns while stretching like a cat.

She sees me looking and smiles smugly.

"I am going to wash off this heat I feel for you. I suggest you heed my warning, for Shari."

Having said that, she leans down and slides off her underwear in a very seductive manner. I don't know why, but I can't look away. She then tosses her underwear at me, which lands on my face, and walks into the bathroom without bothering to close the door.

Why are her underwear so wet? I wonder as I remove the underwear from my face and toss it onto the floor. The mystery is driving me crazy.

I hear splashing water coming from the bathroom, breaking that line of thought. Something has been bothering me about her promiscuity since the day we first met. I haven't given my thoughts voice out of respect, but now, since she is so comfortable with me . . .

"Why are you so comfortable with your sexuality?" I ask through the open door.

No reply.

"Do you do this often?"

"I have only been with one other man," she fires back immediately.

"Really?" I reply disbelievingly. "You sure have a lot of confidence in yourself for only having slept with one man."

She is silent for a moment as if trying to decide if she wants to tell me something or not.

"It was six years ago," she begins, voice devoid of emotion. "I was nineteen when he came. Justin, if that's what his real name is. He wandered into my inn one night and pulled out a lute. He spotted me out quickly and looked at me in askance. I gave him a slight nod, music being something of a delicacy around here, and he began to play. But he was not your average musician; I can still see the music he played for us in my head. Soon, the entirety of my inn was on their feet dancing, food forgotten about. All anybody wanted to do was drink ale and dance.

"Justin was your typical pretty boy—you know the type—blond hair, blue eyes, and a devilish smile. The smile got me the most though. Whatever he was so happy about, I wanted to experience it. He played until everyone left and we were alone. I will save you the boring details. Just know that night I lost my maiden's head. He stayed for a week, and for that week, every night, we had each other.

"He was not very well endowed, if you catch my meaning, but he could last forever. It didn't matter much to me. I thought we were in love. During that week I thought my luck had changed and I would never be alone again. Then one morning when I woke up, he was gone. No explanation, no letter, absolutely nothing. Now that I look back on it, it was really silly of me to believe he actually loved me. He was almost perfect, if only he had your—"

She abruptly stops talking.

"If only he had my what?" I press.

"Nothing, it doesn't matter."

I have absolutely no idea what she is talking about, but I am enjoying getting under her skin for a change. "Not so confident after all," I say smugly.

Water splashes loudly, and I look up to see Latrice walking out the bathroom naked, dripping water with her hair sticking to her body. I feel my face redden.

"I thought so," she says, walking over to her dresser, looking at me the whole way.

I feel like if I look away from her, I will lose whatever game she is playing, so I force my eyes to drink in her body. She goes into her dresser and then looks back to me as she bends over really slowly, exposing herself to me while going through her clothes.

My manhood, which only just recently started to relax, shoots back to attention.

"Why do you do this to me!" I yell.

"Because you lack confidence in your body," she says teasingly.

"What!" I challenge. Does she really believe that?

I stand and move to face her naked form. "I am confident in my body," I tell her seriously.

We stare at each other for a moment while she is still naked and dripping wet.

"Your underwear is still on, Mr. Confident."

I blush again. I'm tired of her making me feel this way. I quickly pull off my underwear, manhood still stiff as a board.

She looks down at it then back up at me. She's blushing.

Yes! Victory! Finally.

"Didn't anyone ever teach you to control your emotions? I wonder what else you would give me if only I knew how to ask," she says while stepping so close to me my stiff member pokes her in the belly.

I look into her sky-blue eyes for a moment, then fold. I step around her and walk to the tub, but not before she smacks my bottom rather hard. I jump and yell, at the same time running to the bathroom. Unlike her, I close the door.

The water is still hot and clean, so I decide to re-use it. I wrap my hair in a man bun before I get in, so I don't get it wet. Sitting in the hot water, I finally allow myself to relax. Latrice is really beautiful and has a good heart. I don't know if I can continue like this.

Shari, I don't know where you are, but if you're alive, hurry.

I bathe myself before the water grows cold and get out.

Shit, I don't have any clothes or a towel to dry off with. I poke my head out the door, Latrice is still in here, but she is clothed now, in her normal attire. Without looking back, she tosses a towel at the door. It just falls in front of the door, where I notice she has placed my folded clean set of clothes.

She continues to amaze me. Are all women like this?

"I'm sorry," she says when I come out after drying off and getting dressed.

"For?" I ask, making her sigh.

"I'm sorry for making you feel uncomfortable. It's a part of this whole commander role I've adopted. I know your heart belongs to Shari. It's just, last night was so hard for me. I was so ready, but despite your actions, I know you were not."

That's when I realize for the first time that Latrice has fallen in love with me, and had she taken me last night or pressed a little harder this morning, I would be wrapped around her finger right now. No matter what or who I am in love with, I will always appreciate Latrice. She has a special place with me now.

"You are not the only person to blame," I say forgivingly. "I could have made better decisions as well. And I admit, when you got in the tub, I was just trying to make you feel as uncomfortable as you make me feel," I explain. "So do you forgive me?" I ask.

"Only if you forgive me," she says shyly.

"Lost," I say, moving over to her and extending my hand so she can shake it.

She looks down at it and then back up at me. She jumps up and hugs me. "Lost," she echoes.

There is a knock on the door—not hers, the one downstairs that the chair is holding shut. We separate and then go downstairs to see who it is. Latrice is standing behind me, slightly to the right, when I remove the chair. The door falls inward and to the left, barely hanging onto its hinge, to reveal Bron.

"Whoa!" he shouts, eyeing us. "I heard about what happened," he says, looking past us to the destroyed inn.

"Whoa," he repeats a little less excitedly. "So it's true then," he asks.

"What's true?" Latrice and I ask at the same time.

"What do you mean, what's true? Talk is all over town about how the boy with the white staff beat the stuffing out of the captain of the King's Hand here in Last Stop for destroying the Blue Sky Inn," he rambles off quickly. "And nine of his men," he adds as an afterthought.

"That's not true," I retort.

Both Bron and Latrice look at me.

"I beat him up because he threw a knife at Latrice. Five of his men just happened to be in my way. I didn't even touch the other four."

Bron just stares at me for a moment, then tilts his head back and roars with laughter.

"Get inside, Bron, before you cause a scene," Latrice demands worriedly.

He comes in, and Latrice walks us over to sit in a booth, not the same one she kissed me in. Latrice takes a seat next to me, and Bron sits across from us.

"Much as I like the fact that you beat the snot out of those King's Hand idiots, we have a problem," Bron warns us.

"Yes, we know, the assassin," I say knowingly.

"No . . . wait, what? The assassin is after you? How do you know that?" he asks in a mix of confusion and worry.

I quickly tell him about everything that happened after the King's Hand stormed in here.

"And that was the message given to me after the last man stormed out," I finish my story.

"Damn, that's a problem," Bron says, rubbing his chin.

"Wait, what problem were you talking about, Bron?" Latrice asks.

"Oh, that's right, the town is singing your praises, lad. They go on and on about how you're here to liberate Last Stop from the king's power. This is obviously going to put a target on your back, and Latrice's by association."

"Shit, that is a bigger problem," I say.

"I wouldn't be too sure, lad. I believe in you, I do, but the way I hear it, the assassin has had over a hundred targets and has not failed once."

"I'm not too worried about anything the King's Hand has to throw at me. So far, they have been nothing but a disappointment," I say, crossing my arms.

Latrice and Bron just stare at me wide-eyed.

"You should have seen him, Bron," Latrice says. "He can fight, but the way he fights is so . . . peaceful looking. But the damage he does is . . . I've never seen anything like it."

"If you two say so."

"I do. Now, you said 'the King's Hand in Last Stop,' as if there are more out there. Is that the case?" I ask, needing to know.

"The King's Hand is in every major city and town; they even patrol some major roads going to and from cities. The ones here in Last Stop are the bottom of the barrel; most of them were born and raised here. Everywhere else, they are soldiers of the king's army and fight as such. Here, they are nothing more than thugs and wannabes. That's why this place is so run down," he explains.

Hmmm.

"What if we took them down?" I ask, wheels turning in my head.

"Lad, they are over a hundred strong. There is no way. First, we would need to infiltrate their barracks at night . . . No, no, first, we need a *map* of their barracks—" he trails off as he notices me grinning from ear to ear.

"Always have a plan," my grandfather's voice echoes in my head.

"You can't be serious," Bron says, seeing the determination in my eyes.

"Blueprints, we'll start with that. Can you find me blueprints, Bron? Beau is now the center of attention, so it would do him no good to look for them, lest he tip someone off, alerting the King's Hand," Latrice pipes up from beside me.

The trust she has in me is . . . it feels good.

"I have a guy, but it will take some time if you want me to avoid being suspicious about it."

I nod.

"What will you do about the shop in the meantime?" he asks Latrice.

"It is already taken care of," Latrice and I answer together.

Bron flinches.

"Do you two . . . do you have something going between you?"

"No," we answer together again.

"Just asking, just asking. So how long will it take till this place is up and running? And how much gold will it cost?" he asks, shaking his head at the price before he hears it.

"A month and twenty gold," Latrice answers evenly.

"Twenty gold!" Bron shouts. "Where are you going to get twenty gold from?"

"Already got it." Latrice smiles.

"How?" he asks, flabbergasted.

"Savings," she lies.

He squints his eyes at her and then looks to me. He knows she is lying.

"Well, I best be off then. Weapons to be made and blueprints to acquire. Just wanted to check on you and fill you in," he says, standing.

We walk him over to the door.

"Thanks, Bron," I say.

"Thanks, Bron, love you a bunch," Latrice says playfully.

"Don't mention it. Stay safe, you two."

"Always," we say together.

He just looks at us, then shakes his head and heads off.

I set the door back up and put the chair behind it to keep it in place. After doing that, I turn around and find Latrice laughing softly.

"What?" I ask, wanting to be privy to her reason for amusement.

"You would think we practiced that!" she laughs excitedly.

Her infectious laughter causes me to laugh right alongside her.

"Spend enough time around someone, and you really get to know them," she says, smiling at me.

I can't help but admire her beauty.

"So . . . so what's next?" she asks me, calming her laughter.

Hmmm, I visibly think, then snap my fingers.

"Up for working on your shielding?"

"Of course," she says, grabbing my hand and pulling me up the stairs.

11 THE ASSASSIN

With not much to do but eat, sleep, and work on Latrice's shielding, that is what we do. After three weeks, she can hold her shield for thirty seconds. Nothing amazing, but progress, nonetheless. We still sleep next to each other every night, but she has taken to sleeping with her back against my chest in her underwear, with me spooning her while I wear nothing but underwear—her silent promise to me. I can't help but like it, and I believe she knows that. The boundary that keeps us apart is beginning to fade, and I'm beginning not to care.

I awake next to Latrice today, manhood relaxed, which it has been for the last week and a half, a feat that took no small amount of willpower. I just lie there, unmoving, enjoying how good she feels in front of me.

"Good morning, Luca," she says, not moving.

"Good morning," I respond, squeezing her tightly in greeting.

She lets me for a moment, then sits up to stretch, always cat-like. She then stands and moves to the bathroom, closing the door behind her.

"One of these days," I tell myself.

I stand and grab the blue book off her dresser and sit on the floor with my back against the bed, legs spread wide, and set the blue book between them. Looking at the blue book, I can't help but wonder if Bron has had any luck obtaining the blueprints. We haven't heard from him since he left, but he did say to give him some time. I am patient, so I can wait.

The inn should be up and running in the next week or so. It's all clean downstairs. Now we're just waiting on some new chairs and one more table.

I flip open the book in-between my legs. I've been reading it every day but have not been able to interpret any new elements as clearly as the first two times I opened it. I flip another page, then stop.

What's this?

Anger bad understand? Anger animal understand? I focus the power behind my eyes, then in my mind, and feel the elements.

"Anger is animalistic. Do not suffer frustration; seek understanding." Wow. That's deep. But still, it's more because the way the elements are written implies they are opposites. So it's like you're only angry because you lack understanding, or you understand, therefore you are not angry.

I feel like that's something my grandfather would say.

Actually, I feel like it somehow relates to his advice, "Always have a plan, never act on emotion."

The bathroom door opens, revealing Latrice, who comes out wrapped in a towel and wet and walks over to her dresser to grab clothes. She bends over and her towel raises up her legs. I could see everything if I wanted to, but I don't look up. She does not look back to see if I look up either. We are that comfortable around each other now. She sits above me on the bed to my right and begins to dress herself.

"What did you learn?" she asks, sliding on her underwear.

"That anger is animalistic and the opposite of understanding. You are only angry because you lack understanding, or you are not angry because you have understanding," I explain.

"That's deep," she says, standing in front of me. "Zip up my dress please."

I close the book and then stand and do as I'm told, careful not to bump into her on the way up.

"So, what's on the agenda today?" I ask.

"I am going to take this money to Amy, and you are going to stay here out of sight."

She is worried about the assassin no matter how much I try to reassure her. *Thanks, Bron.*

"Why do you get to go out and I don't?" I complain.

"Because the assassin is after you, not me," she states.

"And what if the assassin decides to get to me by hurting you?"

She takes a moment to think about that and then smiles.

"I will shield myself!" she says with childlike glee. "Also, you remember what happened to the last person who did that, don't you?" she finishes, smiling.

How can I not, I did it.

"But I'm way better—"

She silences me with a shushing noise coupled with a finger to the lips.

"I will be back before dark," she says, then walks over to her dresser and counts out twenty gold coins from my bag. "Thanks," she says, but looks back at me in askance one more time before she leaves to spend it.

I simply nod, and with that, she is gone.

If she can be out and about, then so can I. I wait about fifteen minutes to be sure she is gone, then get dressed and grab my quarterstaff.

I need to remain mostly unseen, so I leave the inn and head south, back outside of town, toward the edge of the forest where my grandfather left me. I then begin to walk the perimeter of the town, heading west and then up north.

The day is beautiful and gives the cooling warmth only late spring can bring. Days like this make me wonder how my father can be so evil when life is just so beautiful. I haven't been to the northern part of Last Stop yet—not that I expect much, but I am rather interested in seeing what it holds.

As I head west through the forest, the terrain behind me gives way to rocky ground. I remember wondering about that when I first saw the town. The rocky walls are slightly higher than the trees, and in them are dozens of passageways that lead deep into the stone environment, none of which look safe. I wonder where they lead.

As I continue my westerly trek, my ears catch the sound of running water. I stop.

That can't be what I think it is. The north can wait, I tell myself, turning toward the rock valley. I walk further away from town and close in on the treacherous stone maze. The closer I get, the louder the sound of running water becomes. No, it is not running, it is rushing or crashing.

I scout for a path through, but most of the openings end in dead ends or steep climbs. I did see one earlier that looked like it went rather deep into the valley, but it wasn't safe at all.

Needing to satisfy my curiosity, that is where I go. When I make it to the beginning of the path, I stretch in preparation for my run. Yes, run—I have not been on one since I parted ways with the old man, and now is the perfect time because I do not fancy being caught between a fallen boulder and the wall or the floor. I look behind me to make sure no one is watching—not that it matters because no one in their right mind would attempt this path—and no one is.

I take off down the pathway and am swallowed by stone. As I sprint through the miniature canyon, I notice the stone walls are not smooth, but jagged and sharp as if the stone is a predator itself. It might be. Abruptly, the path turns left at a ninety-degree angle, but it is so narrow I can barely fit running. If I lose my balance, this will hurt.

For the first time in a while, I summon the river to my mind and dive in. I jump up in mid-run and kick the right wall, projecting myself to the left down the ninety-degree turn.

I made it, but my achievement is short-lived. As soon as I complete the turn, I am greeted by a wickedly jagged-looking wall that I'm heading face-first into. The path narrows even further, and I have no way to stop. At the last second, I see a path that banks right. I quickly kick off the left wall, projecting myself upward and to the right. The strain in my legs is a possible death sentence right now. Shit, to make things even worse, there is another wall in front of me now, with more jagged edges than the last and nowhere to turn. I prepare for impact, by which I mean I accept that this is about to hurt.

A ledge.

I notice it right before I crash into the wall and reach.

I feel my nose break when I hit the wall, but I catch the ledge. Hanging there for a moment to slow my . . . everything, I take the time to heal myself, then do a pull-up to see what's beyond this ledge. I stand once I pull myself up, then over, and look at a sheer drop of about fifty feet or so, followed by a trail a little less wide than the length of my staff.

"At least the stone walls are smooth," I tell myself.

The sound of rushing water is accompanied by the sound of crashing water. I have an idea.

I jump, then pull my staff out and place it perfectly horizontally above my head so it will catch the walls on either side of me and slow my descent. It works. True to my grandfather's word, the staff holds its own and remains unblemished. I could go all the way down like this, but another bright idea comes to mind.

Remembering the way the old man stood atop his pole in position 101, extra credit, about fifteen feet from the ground, I decide to turn my staff vertical and hurl it like a javelin into the ground.

If the old man can do this, so can I.

I place my heel on the exposed end of the staff, but when I do, the staff tilts forward, and I lose my balance. Arms flailing helplessly through the air, I fall backward and land on the ground hard enough that the air leaves my lungs. I do not miss this feeling. I was shielded, so I avoided the worst of the damage, but God, this sucks.

Slowly, very slowly, air returns to my lungs, easing my discomfort. I sit up, then check my surroundings. The path widens out a little way down and is no longer dangerous. If anything, it has become gentle.

Well, I guess I'm done running.

I get up, remove my staff from the ground, and follow the path down a little way where it bends to the right. The sound of rapidly moving water is steadily growing louder as I approach the bend; the water is definitely crashing into something. I round the corner and stop dead in my tracks, amazed at what I see. This is why I came here.

In front of me lies a waterfall, which holds more majesty than my father could ever hope to match, that empties into a small body of crystal clear water about the size of Bron's archery range, maybe a little smaller. I move to look into the water and find I can see all the way down to the bottom. I can even see small fish in there.

The way the sun shines down upon the water, coupled with the refreshing mist from the water, makes this place feel like a paradise. Latrice would love to see this place, and so would Shari.

My mind wanders to thoughts of Shari exiting the pool the last time I saw her. I never really appreciated Shari like I should have. I think it's because she was all I knew. But while Latrice is beautiful, Shari is perfect. My face reddens, remembering the way her hips swayed when she walked, the way her curves bounced. Her red curls.

I quickly strip down to my underwear and jump into the water to cool the fire in my veins. My body tenses in shock. The water is as cold as ice and almost causes me to panic. It takes a moment to adjust, but when I do, I swim freely just like I did in the palace. The palace . . . seems like it was another life entirely.

Suddenly remembering seeing the bottom of the water, I dive, eyes open. It's beautiful down here. All types of fish swim about, and there are a lot of plants as well as corals that I haven't seen before in my mother's books. I swim over to where the water from the fall crashes into the body of water. Looking around in pure fascination, I spot an underwater cave that leads into the rock bed. I surface for air, then dive back down to investigate.

The cave is dark. If I go in, I won't be able to see. Oh well, if it feels like it goes too far, I'll just swim back. What a waste that would be. I enter the cave and begin pulling myself across the cave floor with my hands since I can't see, so I don't run into a wall. It's a short swim. The cave structure goes about twenty feet inward, then begins to incline upward. I can start to see light penetrating the water from up above, so I swim toward it and find the surface.

What awaits me is breathtaking. Sunlight filters through the cracks and openings in the roof of the cave to reveal a cove embedded with small crystals that make the cove sparkle with sunlight. I swim to the ledge where the water meets the floor of the cove and pull myself out. It's not very big, but the sunlight is mesmerizing; who knew such things existed? I have to show Latrice.

Shit, Latrice.

Judging by the light, the sun will go down soon; I need to hurry back. I gather my things, then leave the miniature paradise and head for the inn.

The sun is nearly down by the time I arrive at the inn. Man, I hope I beat Latrice here; I really don't want to argue. I walk up to the door, which has been replaced by the carpenter, and suddenly every fiber of my being is set on edge.

"Where are you coming from?" Latrice asks, coming up from behind me.

It's not her setting me off.

"Get in the inn and do not come out until I get back," I tell her, opening the door for her.

"What's going—" She's cut off by me closing the door in her face.

I'm being watched. I look around as the last bit of the sunlight leaves the sky and see no one. I take off running into the town in a random direction to see if my watcher follows.

They do—I can feel it.

Recalling some of the streets Bron took me through, I come to a dead end. My watcher will have no choice but to show themselves if they want to keep an eye on me. I wait at the back of the dead end no longer than fifteen seconds before a short person in an all-white kimono with a black hand imprinted on his chest walks around the corner. On his face is a white mask depicting a fox spirit with red swirls on the cheeks.

"I've been waiting for you," I say playfully. "The others were a disappointment. Will you entertain me?"

There is no response.

Instead, he pulls two swords, one long and one short, from sheathes on his back, then begins walking toward me slowly, dragging his long sword in the dirt behind him as he walks.

"You're one for theatrics, I'll give you that," I say, pulling out my quarterstaff.

As he approaches, I fall into position 1. The assassin reaches into his sleeve with the same hand that is holding the short sword, then flicks his arm at me. Off the end of the sword fly three small metal star-like projectiles. I bat them to the floor with my staff. When I look back up, the assassin is gone.

Behind me, flow. 17.

I barely manage to avoid what would have been a killing blow aimed at my neck, if I weren't shielded, by leaning forward and then turning inward and bringing my staff up to block both blades.

This guy is dangerous.

The assassin jumps back, hurling more star-like projectiles at me. I twirl my staff without taking my eyes off my opponent, blocking them all. He charges, swinging both blades in a calculated and controlled rhythm. 15, 42, 33, 37, 49, 2. God, he's fast, but he can't touch me because I'm faster. Thanks, old man. 79, 80, 51, 66. I land a blow across his back, driving him into the ground, but he goes with the motion into a roll, then extends his foot to skid to a stop, throwing more star knives at me. They come at me seemingly endlessly. I could have broken his back when I hit him, but he hasn't done anything to wrong me personally, and he's a good fighter—even if he can't dance.

I might be crazy, but I'm enjoying myself. It's been a while since I've sparred with the old man, and while this is nothing compared to that, this will do.

I end up blocking all forty-four star knives—I counted—flowing from position to position.

"No more stars?" I mock when no more appear to be forthcoming.

He charges me again, and I let him. I let him attack well into the night, only lightly tapping him with my staff to let him know he left me an opening, which is a lot. To his credit, he learns fast. I don't think I should let this go on this long, but I have no desire to hurt this man; I also want to see how deep his resolve is to kill me. I used to spar all day long with the old man, and I want to see how long the assassin can keep this up.

"Seek and find. Continue to seek and continue to find." The quote from the book randomly comes to mind. I know for a fact that he can't beat me, but what else will I learn, understanding maybe? Either way, when the sun comes up, he will know he's lost, and it isn't far off.

"Give up," I say, swinging my staff to correct him again.

That's when he does something that makes me feel like I've seen a ghost. He ducks, sliding to the side as if he were dancing, under my corrective strike. I've only seen two people do that before, and he is too small to be my grandfather. It can't be . . .

He notices my slight lapse in concentration and swings his blade six times, connecting once with the pommel of his long sword. I back up and pretend I'm hurt, even though I'm shielded. The old man said to play the part. Thinking it his chance at victory, he rushes me, not accustomed to the superior reach of my staff. I extend my staff as quick as lightning, but only enough to hit the mask. He is too late to react.

The mask shatters, revealing his face. I continued to seek, but what I found has not granted me understanding.

He is a she. And she is . . . Shari.

I stumble in confusion.

"Sha . . . Shari, it's me," I mumble.

The sun breaks the horizon, causing her to look up then back to me.

"This isn't over," she says, snarling, then disappears around the corner.

I chase after her, but when I come out of the alley, she is nowhere to be seen. I do all I can do: walk back to the Blue Sky Inn, unable to think.

The sun is up when I walk through the door of the inn looking as if I am hollow.

"Beau," Latrice shouts, coming up to hug me.

I just close the door behind myself.

"You're alive," she says, grabbing my face in both hands, forcing me to look at her. "Does that mean the assassin is dead? Or at least defeated?"

"No, I'm lost," I say, going to sit in our booth.

"You, lost?" she asks disbelievingly, sitting across from me.

I don't correct her.

"It's okay, you're still alive, so we can figure something else out," she says, trying to cheer me up.

"Latrice, I need to be alone with my thoughts right now," I say, standing up and going up the stairs to the room.

She doesn't follow.

I sit on the bed all day dealing with mixed emotions. I am happy that Shari is alive, but why is she working for my father? Surely she knows what happened a year ago. Why would she align herself with the person who killed my mother? My mother brought her into our family.

The door opens, bringing me to. The sun has gone down, and Latrice has come to lie down. Have I really been thinking all day? I will not keep her out of her own room at night.

"I will not talk," she says before I can do anything.

I see her looking at the tears in my eyes. She strips down to her underwear and climbs into the bed. Instead of lying down, she moves to sit behind me, wrapping her legs around me and pulling me into her so the back of my head lies atop her chest. I resist at first, not wanting my anger, among other emotions, to be pacified, but she just pulls harder. I give in and lean into her. My head is atop her breasts as angry tears stream down my face. She runs her hands through my hair. Surprisingly, it soothes me.

Why did Shari start working for my father, and why did she try to kill me? She couldn't have known the bounty was for me, but when she saw my face—

My eyes!

Latrice runs her hand through my hair again. And my hair!

I jump up, and Latrice jumps beside me, half naked.

"What?" she exclaims.

I look at her excitedly, then hug her tight and kiss her right on the mouth. "Thank you," I say, then move to grab my things.

"For what?" she says, clueless and blushing.

I don't even know where to start. "Everything," I say before I exit the room and run down the stairs and right out the front door. If it wasn't for her soothing my anger, I wouldn't have been able to think straight. This is the second time she's held me when I cried—what would I do without her?

I stand in front of the inn and wait, and it doesn't take long.

I feel her presence out there watching me. I bolt to the southern edge of town, and she follows me. Good. Time to go for a run. I hope you're in shape, Shari.

I head straight for the rock trail that leads to the waterfall. It's dark outside, and with nothing more than moonlight to guide the way, the trail will be a lot more dangerous to navigate this time. When we come to the entrance, I increase my pace. What happens here will tell me if the rumors about Shari are true.

She does not disappoint on the initial passageway, matching me step for step. When I come to the fifty-foot drop off the ledge, I decide not to make a show of things and just use my staff to slide all the way down to the ground. I walk to just before the path bends, turning into paradise, then stop. Curious to see how Shari will choose to get down the fifty-foot drop, I turn around.

I see her pull herself to the top of the ledge, and then without hesitating, she jumps off the edge at the left wall. My heart drops into my stomach. She pulls both of her blades out and rams them into the rock wall, slowing her fall. Then she pushes off that wall and jumps to the opposite wall, doing the same thing. She jumps back to the other wall one more time in this same fashion before she is delivered safely to the ground.

So the rumors are true. Show-off.

I bend the corner to paradise and wait fifteen feet away from the entrance. She follows around the bend after me.

"Shari, take off the mask," I yell.

She pauses, then slowly takes off her mask and sets it on the ground. "I don't know how you know me, but my secret will die with you," she yells back.

God, I miss her voice, even if she is threatening to kill me.

"You will kill your prince?" I ask playfully.

"Enough of your games. It is time to fight. The prince doesn't have green eyes, long hair, and the body of a warrior."

I chuckle. "The body of a warrior, you say?" I comment smugly. "The green eyes reminded me of you," I say while staring at the floor and wrapping my hair into a man bun. I allow my eyes to change back to their original golden-black vortex, then look up at Shari.

There is a sharp intake of breath as she drops her blades and covers her mouth with both hands.

I reply by setting my staff on the ground and then motioning for her to follow as I jump into the water. It's even colder at night, but after the long run from town, it feels nice. I dive, not bothering to check to see if Shari is following. I find the underwater cave and swim through it, surfacing in the cove. Pulling myself out of the water, I notice this place is even more beautiful at night with the moonlight reflecting off the crystals instead of the sunlight.

I hear the water part as Shari surfaces behind me, and I turn to watch her get out of the water. She is still stunning, her kimono clinging tightly to her voluptuous, drenched form. Her hips still sway in that hypnotizing rhythm when she walks, more so in fact. Her red curls bounce, full of water, when she steps. But her eyes, as beautiful and penetrating as ever, are full of hope and confusion. She stops five feet away from me.

"Where are your blades, assassin?" I joke, not knowing when I'll have the upper hand again.

"Next to your staff, Princeling," she says sheepishly, blushing and looking at the ground.

Her voice is music to my heart—now I feel bad.

"You are late," I say, thinking about how long the year apart from her felt.

"Fashionably, something about relevance," she says, finding the courage to look up.

"By the gods, you don't know how much I've missed you," I say, running up and hugging her.

Did I just say that out loud? She is even softer than Latrice, but at the same time, her body is hard—she is a killer. I remember putting her down after spinning her in circles through the air. She is blushing furiously but smiling nevertheless. We stare at each other for a moment, and I can't help but blush too. She laughs eventually, passing the silent moment between us, and I am the first to speak.

"Why are you working for my father?" I ask, pointing to the hand on her kimono.

"I have been trying to work my way up in his ranks without my face being seen so I could kill important people around him. I didn't know what else to do."

At that moment, I realize she is lost too.

"You don't need to be working for him like this, no matter your intentions. You could get hurt," I reprimand, concerned.

"I can take care of myself, Princeling," she counters, offended.

"Clearly, demonstrated by how I beat you," I say smugly.

"That remains to be seen," she whispers defiantly.

"Shari, I let you—" I start in anger, then quickly remind myself that she has been on her own for a year, too, and is just as lost as me. At least I had the old man.

"He killed my mother, Shari," I say, expecting her to—

"Your mother is not dead," she says knowingly.

"What?" Did I hear her right?

"I said your mother is not dead. Who do you think got me out of the castle before your father thought to look for me, hmm? It wasn't Alrick. She . . . she told me it would take a while, but I should try to find you. It's been over a year. I gave—" She stops, rubbing tears from her eyes.

"It doesn't matter—what does is that you found me. Even if you *were* trying to kill me," I say, smiling. I recall our training session with Alrick. "Again," I add.

She laughs, still wiping tears from her eyes. I move to hug her.

"I thought you were dead," she says, barely holding back tears.

"Well, I am very much alive, thank you." I grab her chin and tilt her head up so she can stare into the golden-black vortexes my eyes create. She wraps her arms around me, my cue to lean down, and she leans up. We almost kiss, but she shoves me back with force instead.

"You smell of vanilla and another woman. Where have you been?" she yells.

Do I hear jealousy in her voice?

"I am currently staying at the Blue Sky Inn owned by a woman named Latrice. She lights vanilla candles all over," I explain.

She eyes me searchingly. "That's not what I meant. Where have you been for the last year, Luca?" The venom in her voice is gone.

I look around and motion for her to come sit with me—this is going to take a while.

I tell her everything, starting from being kidnapped, which turns out was arranged by my mother, to training with my grandfather and beating him, and ending up with Latrice. Well, almost everything; I conveniently leave out the things that lead up to Latrice's silent promise.

"So that's why I couldn't best you," she says out of nowhere.

"What's that supposed to mean?" I ask, confused.

"Your mother told me stories of your grandfather, her father. He is a Precursor."

"What is that?" I ask, intrigued.

"It means to come before. They are said to be of the old blood. Marked by their golden eyes, they are the world's mightiest warriors. Beyond that, your guess is as good as mine."

"There are those who came before Alrick," the old man's voice echoes in my head. Yes, he has a lot of explaining to do the next time I see him. "The last time I saw you, you were mad at me for backing away from you and for using the power to silence you. I apologize for both."

She sighs. "You were forgiven long ago." She smiles.

"Why were you so upset?" I ask.

"Do I have to answer?" she says emotionally.

"I would like to understand so I don't make the same mistake twice."

She loses herself in my eyes for a moment, or maybe I lose myself in hers.

"As for using the power to silence me, I was scared. I can't reach the power, and being so helpless to defend myself after what happened to my parents is nightmarish. That, and it was the first time anyone ever used the power on me," she explains.

"I'm sorry about yo—"

"Sshhh," she cuts me off. "As for you backing away from me, " she takes a deep breath and begins again, "I didn't like you when I first came to live with you. You were rich, spoiled, and had things I never even dreamed of. When I arrived at your castle, all the servants pitied me. No one saw me for the person I truly was except your mother and you. You were my age and easier to relate to than your mother. Over time, I got used to you, and then I realized I couldn't blame you for your upbringing and began to open myself up to you. At first, you were like the little brother I never had. As we got older, that began to change. Many nights, I lay sleepless thinking about what your mother would do if she found out how I felt, so I never told you. You saw me for me and treated me like a normal person. I would never have seriously hurt you then, nor will I now. So, when you backed away from me that day in fear, it hurt like I can't explain."

She stops being lost in memory. I take her hand in mine and intertwine our fingers.

"I will never back away from you again," I say, looking into her eyes.

Moonlit crystals sparkle all around us. She leans forward as do I, and I bring my hand to the side of her face. She kisses me experimentally. I smile. I softly lock her hair into my hands and kiss her back. I part her lips with my tongue, then maneuver it into her mouth. Flow.

She is timid at first, but in this, too, she learns quickly. I pull her closer, and a moan escapes her lips. She opens her eyes after a second, smiling.

"Why are you so good at that?" she asks.

I'm busy feeling proud about myself when her smile suddenly drops.

"Latrice," she says, scooting away from me, anger and jealousy clear in her every expression. "I thought you said Latrice is just the owner of the inn you are staying at," she explodes.

"She is!" I say defensively.

"No! She is more than that. Explain yourself."

No good is going to come from this, but I will not lie to Shari.

"I didn't even know if you were alive," I begin.

I proceed to tell her everything that happened between Latrice and me, all of it. I can't know how Shari is taking all of this because she is staring at the ground with no emotions, just listening. Finally, I end the story with Latrice's silent promise.

Please don't hate me, Shari.

She just continues to stare at the ground for a minute. I'm on edge, willing to do anything so I don't lose her after having only so recently found her alive and well. She scoots back closer to me, then intertwines our fingers once more and looks up at me. My heart jumps for joy. Her green eyes, reflecting the sparkles from the crystals embedded in the cove, pierce my own.

"You said you would never back away from me again," she states.

"Never," I say, meaning it in my heart.

"I was living in my own fantasy when I started thinking of you as mine. But now, I will ask. Are you sure this is . . . I am who you want, Luca? Because I am not—"

I kiss her before she can continue, and I feel her smile through the kiss after a moment.

"Good, because now that I have found you again, I don't plan to lose you . . . to anybody."

Standing, she releases my hand. I hurry to stand with her and pull her into my embrace.

"Where are you going?"

She brings her face close to mine, and I try to kiss her. She stalls me with a finger to my lips. "Not yet," she says, pushing me off her. "We are going to the Blue Sky Inn so I can meet this Latrice," she says with jealousy thick in her voice.

"You . . . you can't go into town dressed like that," I say, pointing to her kimono with the King's Hand emblem on it, trying to stall her.

"Then I will go like this." She loosens the kimono and drops it to the ground.

My eyes drink in her body. A perfect caramel skin tone adorns a frame every bit as curvy as I remember, covered only by a red bra and underwear. The two pieces complement her red curls. My eyes make their way back to her face; she is smiling because I am blushing. I take off my shirt and throw it at her, and her mouth falls open. I almost forgot I look like this; I only threw my shirt to her because I don't want anyone staring at what is mine alone on our way back.

"How about that kiss now?" I test my luck.

She looks tempted but just says, "Not yet," again before putting on my shirt.

The night is about half over, and it is a long walk back. We swim to the spot where we left our weapons and grab them, along with her mask. After she conceals her swords underneath my shirt on her back, she grabs my hand. This does little to comfort me on the walk back because I know she is about to confront Latrice.

Gods help me.

We arrive with about four hours left until sunrise. Shari's grip tightens on my hand as we approach the front door of the Blue Sky Inn. I open the door.

"Beau!" Latrice shouts, standing from her chair and rushing over to me.

Shit. She has been worried sick about me all night, and I am about to break her heart. She stops as she sees me pull in Shari from behind me.

"Who is she, and why is she wearing your shirt?" Latrice asks with jealousy dripping from her voice.

"My name is Shari, Latrice," Shari spits Latrice's name like it's poison.

I close the door.

"Turns out Shari was the assassin," I say, trying to lighten the mood.

Realization dawns on Latrice's face, and a cold calm comes over her, which I have never seen from her before.

"Congratulations, I'm glad you found her," Latrice says evenly.

"You should be," Shari says aggressively. She doesn't want congratulations—she wants to fight.

Latrice is not slow by any means. "Shari, is it? May I have a word in private?" Latrice asks.

Shari releases my hand and walks straight up to Latrice so their noses almost touch. Latrice leans forward so her mouth is by Shari's ear and begins to whisper. Her sky-blue eyes lock on mine, which are green again, and don't look anywhere else. My mother taught me a trick with Certus that enhances voices, but only to my ears, for spying, really. I use it now.

". . . not love me. He loves you. Do not act like a child and do what you want to right now. If it comes to that, we both know he will choose you. However, he has a good heart, so the decision will hurt him more than you know. I will not lie to you, I do want him and could have had him twice now if I didn't care about the way he feels. I don't even know you, but I know that he loves you fiercely. I can't beat you physically or for his heart; I am not your enemy. Don't mistake me, though, should he find you lacking in any way . . . I will be here—"

I don't listen to the rest. Instead, I walk over to the booth and sit down. As I pass Shari, I notice her eyes are wide with shock. I don't even want to know what Latrice is telling her; I do wonder if this encounter turned out how Shari thought it would. The thought causes me to chuckle. We all have our ways, but Latrice has courage neither Shari nor I can match. Yeah, Shari lost her parents at an early age, but she had me and my mother. Latrice has been on her own since she was sixteen, and the way she carries herself shows it.

They finish talking, and Shari comes over to sit next to me, while Latrice disappears into the back. Shari grabs my hand under the table.

"Latrice is a strong woman," Shari states in wonder.

"Yeah, no kidding," I agree.

Latrice returns with three glasses and two bottles. Pop. Pop. Yeah, she definitely used Certus.

"It is time for a celebration, no? Two lovers reunited after a year. I, for one, will drink to that," she says, filling the glasses to the top and then sliding them to us without spilling a drop. She takes her seat across from us.

"To the lost," Latrice says, raising her glass.

"To the lost," I repeat.

Shari raises her glass. "What's the lost?"

Latrice and I share a laugh.

"Shari, my dear," Latrice says, twirling her empty hand in a circle to point at each of us, "*we* are the lost." Then she downs her glass.

As the wine does its job, we spend the next two hours telling stories of us growing up in the castle together to Latrice, who is riddled with laughter at the back-and-forth that took place between Shari and me.

"Sounds like you two were closer to enemies than lovers," Latrice jokes.

"I had some growing up to do. I did not appreciate her then as I do now. When I was in the woods for a year with the old man, it was the first time I realized that I . . . I loved her." I turn to Shari. "I love you," I say with liquid courage.

She kisses me on the nose.

Both bottles are gone at this point. Shari is definitely feeling the effects of the wine, because her cheeks are a permanent rosy red.

"I've known I loved Luca since I was fourteen. I just didn't know how much until he vanished. And then when I found him again, I was so happy. Then I realized he smelled like you," Shari says, looking at Latrice.

So many emotions ran through Shari just now: love, confusion, fear, and jealousy. Again, Latrice is not slow.

"Shari, do me a favor and come sit by me, please," Latrice asks politely.

Shari looks at me, and I shrug my shoulders, just as clueless as she is. She lets go of my hand and moves to sit by Latrice.

"What do you want?" Shari asks nervously.

"A lot, but right now, just you."

Latrice leans over to kiss Shari, who tries to flee but fails when Latrice grips her hair. Eventually, Shari relaxes and goes with it. Across from me sit two beautiful women sharing a kiss—wow. On the left is the one who took me in and fell in love with me, and on the right, the love of my life who I thought I lost. Right now, I am loudly silent.

Latrice pulls Shari's hair down, forcing her to look up, and kisses her on the neck while staring at me with fire in her eyes. At that moment, I know Latrice is hurt, but this is her telling me she will make it through this.

"I'm sorry," I mouth silently to her, knowing words will never be enough.

She releases Shari's hair and looks at her. Shari opens her eyes, and green meets sky blue.

"That was . . . that was amazing," Shari says excitedly.

Latrice just laughs at the irony.

"She is a better kisser than you," Shari tells me, causing Latrice to laugh even harder. "I think . . . I think that makes us even," Shari finishes, jealousy sated.

"Not quite," Latrice says, climbing over Shari seductively and then standing.

Latrice lowers a hand to Shari, who looks at me and then back to Latrice and takes it. They move to the stairs. *What's going on?*

The sun is not far off but has yet to rise, but I do, and follow.

I trail them upstairs and into Latrice's room in a daze. When I enter, Latrice has taken my shirt off Shari and is staring at her curvy body approvingly. Shari looks at me and then turns even redder than the wine already has made her.

"This is not for him," Latrice whispers loudly and seductively in Shari's ear, dropping down to her underwear so she can match Shari.

Shari then turns back to Latrice and smiles. Latrice unsnaps her bra and then pulls Shari down atop her on the bed. My manhood stands at attention through my sweats, not that either of them notices. Shari and Latrice are moaning between kisses as their hands explore each other's bodies with wild abandon.

I approach the bottom of the bed and stroke Shari's leg softly with my hand. Her leg rises slowly, as if in loving response to my touch, then kicks me softly but hard enough to send me back to the door.

She raises off of Latrice for a split second to say, "This is not for you, Princeling," before Latrice pulls her back down and they pick up where they left off.

I back out the door and close it, realizing I am unwanted. I do not understand what is happening through the influence of the wine.

However, I do know the sun is coming up and I'm tired. I do the only thing left that makes any type of sense to me: I walk down the hallway to the last door on the left.

12 PLANS

By the time I awake, it is nearly high rise. I am still shirtless but do not stop by Latrice's room to retrieve my shirt when I walk down the hall, scared of what I might find. I go down the stairs to find Latrice sitting in the booth, clothed in her normal blue dress, drinking coffee. I move to sit across from her, and when I sit, she stands and leaves, leaving the cup of coffee. Okay. She's not even gone thirty seconds before she returns with a second cup of coffee, which she hands to me, then takes her original position at the table. She still has not said a word.

"So, if you cannot have me, you will have my girl?" I break the silence.

"You don't even mean that," she says like she's talking to a child.

And she's right, I don't.

"I could no more take that girl's heart from you than I could take yours from her. That was an act, albeit an act I enjoyed, but an act nonetheless and a relationship fixer," she explains.

"What?" I all but shout, not understanding.

"Did you not hear her say, 'I think that makes us even,'?" Latrice says, like that's supposed to clarify everything.

When she sees I am still none the wiser, she sighs. "Men! As soon as you closed that door, Shari fell beside me and started crying. She didn't even want to do what she did, but she knew she would be jealous of me forever because I was your first experience, so I became her first experience too. Now I am no longer foreign to either of you, and you guys are, as she said, 'even.' There is nothing in the way of your love for each other now."

Stunned, I sit in silence. Do women really think this much?

"You're welcome," she says as she sees the realization dawn in my eyes.

"Are you going to be okay with this?" I ask hesitantly.

She eyes me from across her coffee, sips it, and then sighs, setting it down.

"It appears I am hopelessly in love with you," she says grudgingly. "So if you are happy, then I will find a way to be happy. Just do me one favor: try to keep it down in the bedroom when you make it that far. And be gentle with her. You are endowed very nicely between your legs."

My face heats. I am sure it is the color of a tomato.

Latrice giggles. "Don't be shy. Now it belongs to another."

Her eyes cut to the top of the stairs before she gets up and walks to the back again. I look to the top of the stairs and see Shari coming down the stairs wrapped in Latrice's sky-blue sheet. We eye each other warily before she comes to sit next to me, grabbing my hand and placing it on her lap.

"I am sorry," she begins before I can cut her off with a finger to her lips.

"I understand." I smile, with Latrice's words fresh on my mind.

"You do?" she asks excitedly, perking up.

"I do. Nothing else will come between us now?" I ask nervously.

"Not even the gods," she says, extending her neck to kiss me.

Latrice chooses this moment to return and hand Shari a cup of coffee, which she takes gratefully.

"I am going to the tailor to buy you clothes, Shari, because you cannot walk around like that, and your body is blessed with curves a ball would envy, so my clothes will not fit you. May I borrow some money, Luca?"

"You may *have*," I stress the word, "as much as you need, and buy some clothes for yourself too." She tenses for a second, then relaxes.

"Thank you," she says, turning to go up the stairs and get the coins.

"You have money?" Shari asks, her head leaning on my shoulder.

"I do," I say. Then I tell her about how I got robbed my first day here.

We are both laughing when Latrice comes back down the stairs.

"I will be gone most of the day now, seeing as how I have shopping to do for the both of us. Do me a favor: This young love wildfire thing you two have going on—" she wags a finger back and forth between us "—get it out now, because the inn opens in a few days, and I do not have a room to spare after a month of being out of business. So you two will be sleeping in my bed with me," she explains in her commanding way before heading to the door.

"Wait!" Shari shouts.

"Don't you need to know my sizes?" she asks curiously.

"I figured that out last night," Latrice says, smiling devilishly before disappearing through the front door.

"That woman can be scary," I say absentmindedly.

Shari stands and then turns to face me.

"Latrice has awakened a hunger inside me I did not know existed. I

171

do not want to talk, Princeling."

She says the last seductively, then drops the sheet from around her body. I do not look away from her eyes and let mine change back to their true form as I stand, picking her up in the process. She wraps her legs around me, undoes my man bun, and runs her hands through my hair wildly while we kiss passionately. She has gotten better than me in her one night with Latrice. Shari is just a quick learner in general.

I carry her up the stairs slowly, savoring every moment. When we enter Latrice's bedroom, Shari kicks the door closed behind us, after which I lie her down on the bed softly and take off my trousers.

I lift her back up and try to unsnap her bra. It is a puzzle I don't have the patience for right now. When she laughs at my difficulties, I decide to use Certus, and the clasp breaks. I push her back down and then kiss her neck and down her stomach.

We kiss like this for what seems like forever, since neither of us knows what to do.

Then she separates her mouth from mine. "What's next?" she asks, green eyes piercing my own.

"I don't know, I haven't been this far."

She smiles at that. "Me either," she says. Slowly, we figure it out together as our bodies become one.

"Are you okay?" I ask, sensing she is in discomfort.

"Do not back away from me, Luca," she says with a feigned boldness, placing her hands on my back, and drawing me closer, to which I oblige.

If there is a heaven, this is it for me.

Several minutes later, we lie side by side, panting, blissful. So this is what I'd been missing out on.

"That was heaven on earth," she tells me with love and adoration on her face as her green eyes search mine. We make love all day until the sun sets.

Latrice walks in the room while Shari and I are still in the act, and I stop, not knowing what to do.

"Oh!" Latrice says, averting her eyes out of respect.

"When you are done here, I have gifts for you, Shari. Take your time; don't rush. If you are going to do it, do it right." She backs out and closes the door.

Shari looks back at me. "She said to finish, Princeling. What are you waiting for?" she says cravingly. Love and lust war for my being as we finish.

I find my shirt that was left in here the night before and get dressed. Shari just puts back on her underwear, since her bra is completely broken, and wraps a sheet around herself again. By the time we make it down the stairs, Latrice has prepared a hot meal for us.

"Hungry?" Latrice asks when she sees us coming down the stairs. "I highly doubt you two have eaten anything but each other the whole time I was gone." We both blush and look down.

"Stop that!" Latrice reprimands. "Here are your clothes, missy. Go upstairs and put something on unless you want to eat naked; it won't bother me." Latrice says, walking over to us and handing Shari three full bags of clothes.

"Thank you," Shari mumbles before kissing me and running back upstairs with the bags, no doubt happy to be out of Latrice's line of fire.

Latrice chuckles. "So, what did you learn?" she asks me as the door upstairs closes behind Shari. Her tone carries the same seriousness as it does when she asks me the same after I finish reading the blue book.

"That a woman is truly the only thing that can simplify a man."

She erupts in laughter. "And don't you forget it. Now come eat." She motions for me to follow her as she moves to the booth, which has enough food on its table for five.

There is chicken, roast duck, cheesy noodles, salad with dressing, and a couple of different desserts, one of which is a white cake that looks to be made of cream.

"I call it . . . cheesecake. Try it," she says proudly.

"You can make a cake out of cheese?" I ask disgusted.

"Uh," she groans, offended, and then puts a piece of cake in my hand.

"Try it!" she commands.

Well, she hasn't killed me yet. I bite it, and a rich, delicate cream fills my mouth, the likes of which I have never experienced.

"If life would have just taken its time with my father—" I begin, still working the bite of cake around in my mouth "—like you did with this cheesecake—" I swallow it "—if life would have handled him as delicately as this cake just handled me, he would have turned out an altruistic and righteous man."

I finish, meaning every word.

"I knooowww ittttt," comes Latrice's drawn-out, cocky reply. Then she registers what I said and doubles over, holding her stomach in crying laughter.

"Why is she laughing like that, and what is that?" Shari asks, having crept up behind me.

Still as good as ever at that, I see. Before I can answer either question, she bites the cake in my hand. I turn to find her dressed in a brown button-down shirt, the two top buttons undone, with a white T-shirt underneath and skintight blue jeans that make her bottom look bigger than it already is. She is also wearing simple brown boots that come to just below her knees.

"Oh my, by the one true God," she says, chewing the cheesecake. "Luca, I think I lied to you," she says, appearing to seriously think it over.

"Our time alone upstairs was not heaven on earth, this is."

She says, taking the cake from me.

Latrice laughs harder.

"You still did not answer my questions," Shari tells me enjoying the cake.

Latrice replies for me between still calming laughter. "That is cheesecake, and I was laughing at his reaction to the cake."

"Did he say something about me?" Shari asks, concerned for some reason.

"No, he mentioned his father." Latrice fully calms herself.

"And out of all the outfits I bought you, you picked the one that wasn't a dress," Latrice complains.

"Yeah, well, I'm not a dress type of girl."

"Yeah, yeah, yeah. Well, you two sit and eat so we can talk."

We do just that, at least I do. I eat a little of everything and enough roast duck for three. Shari only eats a piece of chicken and some salad, and she grabs another slice of cheesecake after she finishes the first. When we are finished, Latrice speaks up.

"So, before you made your way here and started trying to kill Luca, speaking of which, Luca, you have been Luca enough. Go back to being Beau."

Shit, being reunited with Shari has made me careless. I touch Certus and change my eye color to match Shari's.

"Who is Beau?" Shari asks, confused.

"Beau is what you must call me in public. Since I am trying to keep my identity a secret."

Shari hisses at me when she notices my eyes are green, but grabs my hand under the table and gives it a squeeze.

"As I was saying, before you showed up trying to kill Beau, he was planning on trying to take down the King's Hand here in Last Stop." Shari looks at me wide-eyed.

"Does the plan stop because you have found her?" Latrice points to Shari, yielding no signs as to how she feels about the subject.

"No, I will not leave these people to suffer. We must stop my father somehow, and even though this is a small start, it is still a start," I explain.

"This is dangerous," Shari says from my side, eyeing Latrice and me.

"How is it any more dangerous than what you were doing taking out individuals?" I ask her. "By yourself," I add for good measure.

"I was taking out individuals for your father and those loyal to him while wearing a mask. You look to take out a group of his militia. No matter how small or undisciplined they are, there will be consequences," she warns us gravely.

"So you won't help?" Latrice asks Shari skeptically.

"I didn't say that. I just said it will be dangerous." Shari smiles at Latrice.

"Wait, why does she need to help at all? I can do this all by myself," I question, not too eager to put Shari in harm's way after I just so recently got her back.

"Because no matter how good you are, two is still better than one. They are still one hundred in number, and I have no desire to see you killed," Latrice explains.

"Am I so helpless now . . . Beau?" Shari asks in anger, tightening her grip on my hand underneath the table. "No, but I am still the assassin. Remember, I will be able to do things and get information you can't. You'd be amazed at what people tell you when they believe it will save their lives."

The direct manner in which Shari so casually speaks of killing people makes me sad.

"She is right, Beau, and you know it."

At first, I was just hopeful, but with her to help, I believe we can do this!

Latrice tilts her head to Shari. I know these women, and no matter what I say, I will not win this argument.

"Fine, but I don't have to like it." Shari loosens her grip on my hand and then kisses me on the cheek.

"Do not worry, I will be careful. I will not lose you after only just finding you, Princeling."

Her feelings reflect my own.

"That settles it. We are still waiting on blueprints from Bron . . ."

"Who is Bron?" Shari cuts off Latrice.

"A friend," Latrice continues. "He will be providing us with blueprints of the King's Hand's barracks soon so we can know where and how to strike. How will you factor into this, Shari?"

Shari is thoughtful for a moment before speaking. "I know of a couple of important people in town who may or may not have valuable information we can use. The assassin will pay them a visit. It will most likely take them a couple of days though."

"Don't kill them," I say, looking to Shari.

"That is unwise," she replies quickly.

"I don't care what is wise or unwise. . If you are as good as they say, you will get what you need without killing people," I tell her. "And I know you are," I add.

She looks at me—Is that concern I see in her eyes?—then nods.

"You cannot be seen coming and going from this inn dressed as the assassin," Latrice states fact.

"I know this, Beau has shown me a hiding place among the rocks to the west of town I can use as a safe point until I gather the information we need."

Latrice looks back and forth between the two of us, wondering when we had the time to do that.

"This is all fine and dandy, but where do I come in, what do I get to do?" I ask, feeling useless.

"Nothing," they both answer at the same time.

I now know how Bron felt.

"You are too noticeable to move around, with or without changing your eye color," Latrice explains. "You will wait until it is time to attack and then do what it is you do best." Shari nods in agreement.

"So what now?" I ask, slightly irritated.

"Now we relax, because tomorrow everything gets set into motion." Latrice leans back into the cushion behind her.

The rest of the day flies by in a blur. I try to show Shari the blue book and tell her about the things I've learned in it, but even though she is interested in it, she isn't as enthusiastic about it as I am because, not being able to touch the power, she can't read it.

She and Latrice seem to be doing some bonding as Latrice shows her all around the kitchen while they discuss, at length, which spices and seasonings bring out certain food the best. I've been in the blue book the majority of the day even though I haven't learned anything new today—it still vexes me.

The sun is down, and I am worn out from the continued concentration I must maintain on Certus to try to interpret the language of power. Shari and Latrice make their way back over to the booth, where I sit, from the back of the kitchen.

Latrice yawns loudly and stretches like a cat. "I'm tired, and it will be a busy day for us all tomorrow, so it is time for bed. Let's go." She commands, walking toward the stairs.

I am tired, too, and understand where she is coming from. What I don't understand is why she gets to decide when everyone is going to sleep.

"Why do you get to decide when we are going to sleep?" I can't help myself.

She makes a clicking noise with her mouth. "This will be the second time I've told you this," she says, slowly walking up the stairs. "Shari, it will be the first time you've heard, but . . . I simply hate sleeping alone," she says, disappearing up the stairs.

Shari and I stare wide-eyed at each other, neither of us knowing what Latrice has planned. Shari is the first to recover. She grabs my hand then looks me in the eyes.

"Together," she says, determined green eyes probing my own.

I nod, unable to think quite right just yet, and she leads me up the stairs after Latrice. She can pretend she's calm and in control all she wants, but my heart is hammering in my chest because I know better. We are both afraid of Latrice in the bedroom, and rightfully so.

We enter the room and find Latrice lying down on the right side of the bed in her underwear.

"Strip to your unders." Latrice smiles.

Shari and I exchange looks, upon which she nods. Then we do as we are told.

"Oh, don't look like that," Latrice whines. "This is hardly a death sentence." After we are done stripping, Latrice continues, "Okay, this is how this is going to work. Shari, you come lie behind me, and, Beau, you come lie behind Shari."

When we get into the bed, Shari is holding Latrice from behind as I hold Shari from behind. Latrice speaks again, "Good, now get comfortable and do not try anything nasty. I will know. Courtesy of you two not opening a window, I know exactly what you smell like down there, girl, and how delicious it is. Goodnight."

I can see Shari blushing profusely in the moonlight. At least I'm not the only one. I lean in and kiss her on the neck, and she calms. Under Latrice's new promise, we sleep comfortably and quietly, too scared to move.

I awake to a space between Latrice and me. Shari is gone. It saddens me that I didn't get to say goodbye, but it is probably for the best. I no doubt would have held her up, trying to talk her out of going.

I move carefully and quietly out of the bed, trying not to wake Latrice, then get dressed. After grabbing the blue book from its typical place on the dresser, I head downstairs and sit in the booth. I think I've sat in this booth every time since coming here, except for when Bron sat and talked with Latrice and me.

It's strange to think that this is the same booth Latrice gave me my first kiss in. It feels like such a long time ago and yesterday, all in one. I feel bad for Latrice. She's been robbed of love twice now. Once by "Justin" and once by me. But the feeling is overshadowed by everything I now feel with Shari back in my life. She is really here, and she is really mine. My mother isn't dead—another heavy burden removed from my heart. Even though Shari knew my mother wasn't dead, she does not know where she is currently or how she fares. If my mother survived the pillar of fire, then she is alright now. *Just hang in there a bit longer, Mom. I don't know how yet, but I will find you.*

"Something on your mind?" Latrice says from above me, walking down the stairs. She moves so quietly that if I did not know any better, I would swear she knew my grandfather.

"Just thinking about my good fortune," I say as she sits across from me.

"Care to share your good fortune with me?" she asks, smiling.

"Shari is back in my life, I get to help the people of this town push back against my father, and my mother is alive." I smile with the last.

"I told you your mother is alive first," Latrice says in defeat, dropping her eyes to the table.

She did not know, but she tried to get me to hold onto hope when I was in all but ruins. I wish I could do more for her.

"I also met a girl who owns an inn who took me in out of the kindness of her heart, made sure I was bathed, and fed me. She also shared the charms of a woman with me, not just any woman, mind you . . . Latrice is one of a kind and is a true friend."

She blushes and looks away. "Yeah, well it was nothing." She composes herself. "I would have done it for anyone."

"You don't even mean that," I mock her with a smile.

She laughs.

"Are you ready to work on your shielding?" I ask her, standing.

"Of course," comes her enthusiastic reply.

We spend the next few hours practicing her shielding until she is too tired to leave the bed. Try as she might, she cannot hold her shield longer than thirty seconds, but her control grows, making her shield stronger and stronger. She is now sleeping on the bed, exhausted.

I move to the floor, lean my back against the bed, and place the blue book between my legs in hope of learning something today. Some of the newer elements are beginning to make sense, or at least I think they are—there's no telling.

Wait, what's this?

"Mind. Over. Space. You."

"What!" I shout out loud, confused. Whoops, I turn to see if I've woken Latrice . . . Nope. She's still passed out.

Returning my focus to the book, I concentrate on Certus while trying to interpret these elements. Certain. Sure. Definite. Decide—

Mind exists apart from space. You

I have not uncovered the meaning of the "You" part, but this seems to imply that there is a realm where my mind exists apart from my body. Spiritual? Maybe, but I have never seen a spirit or a god, so it is unlikely.

I look back up to Latrice. She is still sleeping soundly, but now moonlight replaces sunlight. How long did it take me to interpret that? I notice off-handedly that my mind is tired. With nothing better to do, I climb up on the bed with Latrice, careful not to wake her. I leave a space between us for Shari even though I know she won't be returning tonight.

Latrice and I carry on this routine for three days, her working on her shielding till exhaustion and me reading the book. I have been stuck on the same interpretation the whole time and have not been able to interpret the "You" part, no matter how hard I try. It is maddening, but I feel like this is something I need to know.

I step out of the tub, grab a towel, dry myself off, and get dressed. When I awoke this morning, Latrice was already gone downstairs. The inn opens tomorrow, so she is probably making last-minute preparations right now. She has yet to mention the distance I keep between us for Shari at night. I hope that is a good thing. Thinking about Shari, she should be back soon. I grab the blue book off the dresser, as has become my custom, and head downstairs.

The inn has been fully repaired and looks better than before, thanks to the carpenter using unblemished wood. Latrice is indeed in the kitchen making last-minute preparations. It smells delightful.

"Did you teach Shari some of your recipes?" I ask hopefully.

"No, believe it or not, from what we've discussed, I can tell she already knows how to cook. She said she learned from your mother and her own before she was killed."

Wow, Shari must really be taking a liking to Latrice for her to have told her about her parents.

"Did she tell you how her parents died?" I ask curiously.

"No, and I could see the hurt on her face when she said what she did, so I did not ask."

Latrice is busy doing three things at once, so I cannot see the look on her face.

"I never knew Shari could cook." I bring the conversation back to lighter things.

"There is a lot you don't know about Shari that you will soon find out now that your eyes are open."

I eye the back of her head, "Such as," I ask, refusing to believe Latrice knows things about Shari that I don't.

"Shari is a beautiful girl, inside and out. If you are going to turn me down for anyone, I'm glad it's her. But there is hate and violence living in her that if left unchecked will get her killed at worst, seriously hurt at best. I don't know what has happened to her or what is causing those negative emotions to run through her, but she must not let them consume her."

I stare in awe and confusion as she continues to multitask. How does she know this?

"Have you told her this?" I ask, seriously doubting it.

"No, it is not my place. It is yours. She wouldn't listen to me anyway. Love and hate are two sides of the same coin, I don't know who or what she hates, but she loves you. Only love can beat hate; only you can fix what is broken inside her." She finishes.

I'm too stunned to speak. I definitely don't wan't to know what else she knows that I don't about Shari.

"Come," she demands, motioning me to come around the corner. "Help me while you sort your thoughts."

And so, I begin to help Latrice prepare the kitchen for tomorrow while I sort my thoughts, and they do require sorting. I know what Shari hates: the loss of her parents and my father. The latter we are at the beginning of dealing with, and the former we can do nothing about. How am I supposed to help Shari deal with the hate she has? Her parents are never coming back.

These are the thoughts that plague my mind as the sun passes from the sky, leaving it in darkness.

There comes a knock at the door, and Latrice and I leave the kitchen to—

"Sit," Latrice demands, pushing me into the booth.

"The last thing a girl wants when she has not bathed properly in three days is her man in her face."

I guess I see the wisdom in that. Reluctantly, I do what I'm told. Latrice opens the door, but Shari does not come in. Instead, Latrice bends down, picks up a box, and then closes the door.

"No name on it," she says, walking over to me.

She places it on the table, then sits it across from me.

"Maybe it's from the carpenter. She might have forgotten to give you something," I guess.

"Highly unlikely. She isn't a lazy one. She would have just brought it to me herself," she says, opening the box so I can't see its contents.

She screams in horror, throwing her hands over her mouth.

"What! What is it?" I shout, still held in suspense.

She slides the box away from her, turning it in the process so we can both see its contents.

My mind shuts off, and thunder rumbles in its place. Resting in the box is a head with its mouth frozen in a scream. *Bron.*

Next to it is the set of blueprints containing the layout of the King's Hand barracks we so desperately wanted. But neither of these holds my attention right now. What does is the note attached to the inside of the lid. It reads: "We have the assassin."

"Beau . . ." Latrice calls. I do not hear her. "Luca . . ." she tries again.

Nothing. I stand.

"Luca, calm down and listen to me, w—"

I don't hear her because I am already out the door running into the night. Shit. I forgot my staff. Recalling the blueprints to mind, I don't stop running. I will just run to the back of Bron's smithy and grab a bow and some arrows. They think I will come from the ground. I will not. But arrows will rain down from above. Somebody is going to die tonight, and they better pray to whoever they believe in. It's not the assassin, because if Shari dies . . . they will all die tonight.

13 MISTAKES

Stepping away from the cabinet, I place two quivers of arrows on my back. I shoved five extra arrows into each so they both now contain twenty-five arrows total.

If Shari is dead, the other fifty will die by my bare hands. The storm is so violent within my mind, it is hard to think, but thinking is the last thing I want to do right now, so I embrace it. I have yet to kill a man, but there is a first time for everything. I pick up the bow and move.

According to the blueprints, the barracks has four buildings housing twenty-five men each, with a large clearing between them that serves as a command post. The top of the easternmost building serves as a sentry point at night. That is where I'm headed now.

Bron's smithy is just a block away from the barracks, so it doesn't take long before I am in the shadow of a building watching the lone sentry walk back and forth on a rooftop behind the wall that encompasses the entire barracks.

He has a rope on his hip. Good. I can use that. I am right under his nose, so I can only see him when he comes to this edge of his patrol on top of the building as he does now. I nock an arrow, he looks over the edge of the wall.

Fwip.

The arrow hits him between the eyes and sticks out the back of his head. He falls off the building onto my side of the wall. I catch him so his body doesn't make a loud noise against the ground. Setting him down, I take the rope off his hip. I need to hurry up before someone finds his body. I tie the rope to the end of an arrow and shoot it at the wood sentry post, then use the dangling rope to scale the wall. As I take the sentry's place, I unstick the arrow with the rope attached to it and fire it into the night. Lightning crackles in my mind, growing in intensity. I drop down prone and crawl over the edge of the rooftop facing the barracks to see what I can find.

There!

I see Shari bound to a chair in her kimono, white fox mask still covering her face, guarded by two men dressed in King's Hand garb. Thunder booms.

"So, this is the famous assassin, huh?" one of the men says while I scout my environment.

"Funny, I have seen your mask, and I am still alive." He cocks his hand back and slaps Shari hard.

He doesn't know it yet, but he just forfeited his and his partner's lives.

"Hey, cut that out. Boss says he wants her alive, even if the kid with the white staff doesn't show," the other guard says.

"Just having a little fun, Tim," the one who slapped Shari replies.

Oh, I am here, but I did not bring my staff. I brought death. Fwip. Fwip.

Both men fall dead, with arrows protruding through their eye sockets—fwip, fwip, fwip, fwip, fwip—as do the ten others who hid in the shadows and thought they could not be seen. I drop from the roof to the floor, then rush over to Shari. Using the tip of an arrow, I cut her restraints, but she does not rise.

"Shari," I whisper her name. "Shari, we have to go now," I say a little louder, taking off her mask.

She is blindfolded and gagged. I remove both. Shari's eyes go wide with recognition, but I can tell she is drugged.

"Nnnnmmmr," she slurs, looking sad even through the drugs.

"It's Okay, I'm here now."

Suddenly the entrance to the barracks opens from behind me. I turn to see around forty men fill the way out.

Shit.

They must have been searching for me on the ground outside of the barracks. They are about eighty yards away from me, and they all start unsheathing their weapons, laughing. That's Okay; I suppose it's good to die laughing. I pull my bow. The storm has gone nowhere, and they will never close the distance. Shari is still alive, so this is for Bron.

Fwip.

One man goes down, and the rest all stop laughing and just stand there staring, uncomprehendingly.

Fwip. Fwip.

Two more go down; the rest charge me.

I let the storm pour its wrath into me, accepting every ounce of power it gives me. I begin to shoot arrows so fast my hands begin to hurt as if burned.

Fwip.

The second-to-last man falls fifteen yards away from me as I run out of arrows. The last man stops, realizing he is alone.

"You have run out of arrows, boy. Now what?"

The answer is simple really. My bow back at the palace does not have a string because I can create one using the power. This one does, so I will reverse the process.

I pull the string off the bow and create an arrow of power using Certus. The man's jaw drops in disbelief. Fwip. Then his head explodes.

At least he didn't die choking on his own blood like the others. I shot them all in the throat for laughing. I turn to Shari.

"Can you walk?" I ask, concerned.

"Nnrgh." She makes the same noise she did the first time and swings her arms clumsily around my neck.

I will take that as a no.

I pick her up and begin to walk through the sea of dead bodies to the entrance of the barracks, which is still open. I only make it halfway before—

"Ahem," a deep voice clears its throat from behind me.

I turn around and look up. Atop the northwestern building stand two men. One is dressed like everyone I just killed and raises a horn to his lips about to blow. The other stops him. This man is yellow complected with long, straight black hair that falls to his shoulders and a face that reminds me of a snake. He wears a black robe that is trimmed red along its edges and has a red hand imprinted on its front. I can feel the power coming from him through the storm.

"Where do you think you are going?" he asks me in an unnervingly deep voice.

"I will be right back," I promise him with venom in my voice.

"No, you will not leave here alive." He raises a hand, and a ball of fire begins to grow until it is three times my size. Then he hurls it at me.

I will not be able to outrun it with Shari in my arms, but I'm shielded, so I will be fine. Shari, however, will not. I set her down and wrap myself protectively around her, hoping my shield will blunt the worst of it, but I am no fool. I can't cover enough of her. She will die, but I will try anyway out of love.

"I love you," I whisper to her, closing my eyes and waiting for the flames to engulf us.

Right before they do, I feel a hand wrap around my shoulder and another knee touch mine. Shari's body is pulled in tighter. The ball of fire reaches us and erupts, engulfing us in scorching flames for a full ten seconds before it dissipates. I open my eyes and find Latrice joining her body with mine to protect Shari from the flames.

Not knowing what to expect, I look down at Shari, she is unharmed.

Latrice looks up from Shari to me, then smiles, but behind the smile I see frustration. I know we must talk later. I stand and turn to the man in the black-and-red robes.

"I will kill you," I promise him.

The storm's energy is beginning to cause me pain because it has run its course, yet I refuse to release it. There is a new target for my wrath now and he must —

"No," Latrice says, placing her hand on my shoulder. "Let's go." She points a finger at the defenseless Shari lying on the ground where I left her.

I don't want to leave this man alive, but Latrice is right. I move back to Shari, then pick her up off the ground and turn to face the man who just hurled flames at us. He smiles a knowing smile, then waves farewell to us and departs, despite what he just said, letting us leave.

I set off at a light jog so Latrice can keep up as we head back to the inn. By the time we arrive, Latrice is out of breath. I open the door and go straight to Latrice's room and lay Shari down on the bed. I'm just standing there staring at her by the time Latrice makes it to the room.

"Are you Okay," Latrice asks me, no doubt worried out of her mind.

Deciding that Shari is alive and back under my protection I calm.

"Yes," I sigh, releasing the storm.

I fall, convulsing so violently it feels like my bones are breaking and then rebreaking. Pain is my body, and my body is pain. My vision goes white, and then I lose consciousness.

I awake to the sound of light snoring in my ear. My body feels like it has been ground to dust and only recently been made whole again, barely. I am lying on my back and there is a light pressure on my chest. Opening my eyes, I find Shari, who is also the source of the light snoring, sleeping on my chest. Then I see Latrice sitting in a chair at the end of the bed, staring at me, with teary bloodshot eyes. She holds a finger to her lips and points to Shari, then pauses for a moment and points to herself, then the floor. She wants to talk to me but wants me to be careful not to wake Shari up.

Got it.

Latrice rises from the chair and silently exits the room. With my muscles in agonizing pain, it requires every bit of effort I can muster, but I succeed in leaving the room without waking Shari. I move down the stairs slowly and carefully, arriving at the bottom to find Latrice sitting on the counter with her arms crossed over her chest, pouting. Anger and worry war on her face. I approach slowly, stopping about five feet from her.

"We thought you were dying," she says, frustrated with me.

"I don't believe I've been shown how to properly yet," I joke.

She laughs sarcastically, then continues to stare at me. "May I?" she asks. I nod, and she jumps down from the counter and runs up to me.

I extend my arms for a hug, but she slaps me, and it stings. Then she hugs me hard, releasing quiet sobs.

Had I been shielded, I wouldn't have felt that, but my everything is exhausted. I just hold her for a minute. When she's done, she backs away and returns to her perch on the counter.

"Why did you slap me?" I ask, confused.

"Why did you leave without me?" she counters.

"Without you?" I repeat questioningly.

"Yes, without me. I tried to tell you to calm down so we could plan because I wanted to help you rescue Shari." Anger coats her voice.

"I could not hear you through the storm," I reply softly.

"What storm? The sky was clear last night just like it has been since you've come to stay with me," she hisses.

"No, the storm is . . . Shari." My brain skips.

"The storm is Shari?" Latrice repeats, confused.

"No, you helped me save Shari." It is my turn to rush to her and hug her. I am hugging between her legs as she sits on the counter, when, "Luca," Shari's voice whispers my name as she walks down the stairs.

She wears Latrice's pink see-through nightgown with nothing on underneath.

I quickly back away from Latrice.

"Shari, this isn't what it —" I begin, but she walks straight past me and fills the void I just left.

She reaches up and grabs Latrice's chin, then softly kisses her on the lips, lingering for a second. With that done, she walks over to me, then turns with her back facing me and presses herself into me.

"Hold me," is her simple request.

I wrap both of my arms around her and pull her further into me. My manhood swells at the feeling of her bottom through my sweats atop of it. For my part, I look up to Latrice in confusion. She shrugs her shoulders.

"She has been doing that for three days now. I'm used to it," Latrice says casually.

"Were it not for her, I would be dead, and we all know it. My body could not function properly through the drugs, but I was fully aware. There is not much of me to give, and you already hold my heart, Luca. She saved my life. I owe her." Shari goes silent after this.

"Wait. Three days?" I question, late on the uptake.

"Yes, you have been unconscious for three days. I told you we thought you were dying. And, Shari, you owe me nothing. If you feel you owe a debt to me, then pay it by loving that man and keeping him alive." She points to me.

Shari nods but remains silent. We all remain silent for moment.

"What is the storm?" Shari asks abruptly.

She must have been standing at the top of the stairs listening for a moment before she came down.

"The storm is a state of mind I discovered training with my grandfather. My mind develops a storm as violent as my desire needs it to be. Lightning crackles, thunder booms, wind blows, and clouds roll inside my head, making it hard to think. In return, I am granted a surplus of energy equivalent to that of the storm. Whether it is my own energy or borrowed from elsewhere, I don't know. The storm usually runs its course and dies down. Last night . . . well, three nights ago, I did not allow it to die down."

"Pain wracked my entire body, but I would not let the storm go until I knew Shari was safe. The last time I collapsed from the storm was shortly after I discovered it. Even then, I would only convulse for a minute at most, and I never lost consciousness. Eventually, I gained control over the storm and the negative side effects stopped, or so I believed."

It's quiet for a long moment as Shari and Latrice digest my words.

"Do not summon this storm anymore," Shari whispers, breaking the silence

"I agree with her," Latrice says, hopping down from the counter.

"I will give you two a moment." She walks up the stairs. "On second thought, moments. I'm going to take a bath." With that, she disappears up the stairs.

When Shari hears the door close behind Latrice, she turns to face me. She stares at me with those penetrating green eyes. I know what she wants, but I know what I must tell her first. I pull her close to me so she can feel me and the seriousness in everything I'm about to say.

"Shari, if you get yourself killed, how do you expect me to feel?"

She looks down and away from me, embarrassed.

"Can we—" she starts before I interrupt her.

"No, we can't. This must be discussed," I say, feeling anger dominated by love.

I pull her chin up so she is looking at me and let my eyes turn back to their black-and-gold vortexes.

"You have hate in here"—I poke her left breast—"but you also have love. I know this because you love me. I know you hate what happened to your parents and I know you hate my father, but do not let that hate control you. Would your parents want you living like this? Holding on to a pain you cannot fix? No, they would want you to move on and be happy. Moving on does not mean forgetting; it means embracing. Don't embrace the pain or the hate. Embrace the love they showed you and the lessons they taught you. There is nothing you can do to change the fact that they are gone. And as for my father, we are working on that. You said you hated it when the servants pitied you and treated you like you were not a person; then act like one. Let go of the pain you so desperately hold on to and be the person that you are. Because you are all I need."

She stays quiet for a moment after I finish.

"If . . . if I let go of the pain . . . and hate . . . there will be a hole in me," she says grudgingly.

"Then I will fill you," I say, taking her hand in mine.

"Will you?" she asks.

"Yes," I have never told a stronger truth in my life.

"No, I mean right now," she says, smiling. Her look of need does not escape me.

She needs this right now. I am not content with our conversation by any means, but I have a job that needs to be done, and it is a job I love.

I smile back at Shari and pick her up. She kisses me slowly, experimentally at first, as if she is coming to terms with the fact that I am still alive. While we kiss, I carry her over to the booth so we can't be seen through the windows. I lay her back on the table, and she slides the see-through nightgown over and off her head, throwing it into a seat.

God, her body is amazing. I slide myself on top of her, and we make love until I know she is satisfied. Then, right before my release, I pull my sweats back up, sit down in the booth, and toss Shari the night gown. She puts it on hurriedly and comes to sit by my side.

"I did not feel you erupt. What's wrong?" she sounds offended.

Trying to pretend making love to her is not the best thing I've ever felt is hard, but I act because I need to prove a point.

"I gave you what you needed, but what good will that"—I point between her thighs—"do me if you are dead, Shari. I love you, not that." I love both, really.

She is quiet for a moment, then, as tears begin to build in her eyes, she speaks, "I will try to do as you've asked me, but I can't promise it because it's not that easy. I don't want to die. I don't want to leave you. Four days ago, when they captured me, I thought they were going to kill me. I accepted death. But through that acceptance, I could not stop thinking about you. Then you showed up and saved me after I had already accepted death." She is crying freely now. "Then after you saved me, I spent the next three days believing you were dying and it was all my fault. Then I awoke and you were not by my side, and I was terrified. I exited the room in an emotional wreck but froze when I heard your voice. I walked down the stairs and saw your face but could not believe it. I even had you hold me, but it wasn't enough. So forgive me if I needed a little more proof you were alive after all of that . . . I needed to feel you . . . inside of me. There is no faking that."

She looks down as she finishes, and remains quiet except for her sniffling. Now I feel dumb, insensitive, and even dumber. How do women do that?

"I'm sorry, Shari. I just don't want you to die. I don't want to live a life without you," she's quiet for a moment, and her expression becomes thoughtful.

"I told you not to run from me and you did . . . for three days." I'm caught off guard by her words.

"Aaah . . . On the contrary, I was running to you. That is why I ended up collapsing." She giggles.

"I will give my best effort to rid myself of the pain and hate, but don't worry about me throwing my life away recklessly. You are reason enough for me to live, my love."

Raising a hand to touch my face, she leans over and kisses me softly, passionately. After a few moments, a thought occurs to her and she pulls away from me.

"Do you still not desire release, my love?"

Again, I am caught off guard.

"Aaah—"

"You do," she exclaims with childish glee.

Quicker than lightning, she is on top of me.

"You will not deny me your explosion ever again. It is a part of my pleasure. Do you understand me, my love?"

"My love," what happened to Princeling.

I take too long to answer her, so she bounces atop me causing herself to squeal as she stifles a moan.

"Do. You. Under. Stand. Me. My. Love," she repeats,

bouncing atop me with every syllable.

It feels so good, I don't want to answer so she continues, "Yes ma'am," I say playfully.

"Good. Now relax."

***

"Better, my love?"

"I love you," I say simply.

Thought is beyond me right now. We sit like this, still one, while she kisses my neck, until we hear Latrice's bedroom door open. Shari rises up off me, allowing me to pull up my sweats before sitting next to me.

Latrice walks downstairs, then heads over to us. She looks back and forth between Shari and me. She knows.

"Shari, the smell of you is turning me on. Please go bathe and put on some real clothes," Latrice commands.

Shari turns red and runs up the stairs, holding the night gown down at her sides. Then the door closes behind her.

"Can you really smell her?" I ask intrigued.

"Mhm," she affirms, sitting across from me.

"What does she smell like?"

"Good," is all she says. I breathe deeply getting a soft smell of strawberries mixed with the vanilla that permeates the inn.

"That girl is loud. I heard her all the way in the tub with both doors closed."

I blush. "We're sorry."

"No you're not, but it's okay. You provided me with some entertainment of my own." She winks.

I cock my head to the side like a dog, not understanding.

197

Latrice giggles. "Do not think about it too hard. What you should be thinking about is if you're ready to be a father. At the rate you guys are going, you will be one, and very soon."

I gulp. "I haven't thought about that," I admit worriedly.

"Young love never does. Don't worry, I'll talk to Shari and show her how to brew some tea that will keep her from becoming with child."

I just nod to her in thanks.

"Till then, you know there are other ways to please a woman, right?" she asks, knowing I don't.

"Really?" I fall for the bait.

"Yes!" she says excitedly. She begins telling me all the ways in great detail. Right now, Latrice is some all-knowing mystic guru I hold in higher esteem than my grandfather.

"Thank you. I don't know what I would do without you," I concede.

"Stink," she says simply, referring to the day we met.

We share a laugh.

"After Shari comes back down, you should bathe too. The three of us have more talking to do. With Bron dead and the appearance of the man who can throw fire, we need a new plan."

"I agree," I say seriously.

"Always have a plan. Never act on emotion," the old man's voice echoes through my head.

I definitely acted on emotion when they kidnapped Shari and killed Bron. It almost got Shari killed and then me.

"Did you talk to her about what we spoke about?" Latrice asks.

"I did."

"And?" she says expectantly.

"She said it won't be easy but she will try. She also said not to worry about her recklessly throwing her life away because I am enough reason for her to live." I sigh.

"That is a good thing, so why do you look sad?" she questions.

"Because I want her to live for herself, not for me."

"That will come. She said she would try. Till then, be the man that she needs," she says, laying a hand on my shoulder.

Forty-five minutes go by as we sit there and idly banter back and forth before I decide to go check on Shari.

"I'm telling you, she's fine," Latrice yells up the stairs from the booth.

I walk to Latrice's bedroom, then open it to find Shari standing there looking like she was about to come out. My mouth slowly falls open as my eyes take her in. She wears a tight black dress with extra cut-up layers attached to it, and her red curly hair bounces dripping water, still slightly wet from her bath.

"Well, hi," I say, admiring the dress.

"Do you like it?" she asks nervously.

I make a show of inspecting the dress some more.

"Well, it does look rather ravishing on you, but, no, I love it."

She smiles, then hugs me.

"Look, about what you saw when you came downstairs—" I start, but she shushes me.

"I told you I froze when I heard your voice. I stood listening to you long enough that I knew the context of what I saw. I'm happy she saved my life too. I trust her. But more importantly, I trust you."

She leans up and pecks me on the lips with her own before moving around me and going downstairs.

"Well, that went well," I tell myself out loud.

***

I bathe myself quickly and soon find myself walking across the dining area to sit in the booth with Shari, who sits across from Latrice. I notice Shari is sipping a cup of tea. Her thoughts must have been the same as mine; right now is no time to raise a child. As I take my seat, Shari rests her hand on my thigh underneath the table.

"So, mistakes," Latrice says the second after I sit. "What were they? Shari, let's start with you."

"Usually, I do not let those I hunt live," Shari begins, setting her cup of tea down. "However, Luca desired that I not kill anyone because we only needed information. So I let them live. And just for the record, I would have killed a lot less people than you if you'd let me handle business my way—" she looks my way "—not that I'm complaining. I thought the fear of my legend would keep them silent. I was wrong. One of them went to the King's Hand and told them about me and the information I sought. That is why they called Ki'ra in, and it was he who captured me."

"Who is Ki'ra?" Latrice interrupts.

"Ki'ra is the man in black and red who threw the fire. I know this is obvious, but I will say it anyway: He can touch Potentia and works for Luca's father as one of the ten generals. He is actually the tenth and last general, so he's not very high in rank or skill from what I've heard, as far as those things are determined."

"Well, he sure did know how to hurl fire," I interrupt.

"I'm just telling you what I've heard," Shari continues, "but now he knows my face and will no doubt relay this information to the king, as well as the story of the boy who brought death with arrows and rescued me." She cuts her eyes to Latrice. "You will have your part in that story too."

I stand.

"I must stop him from relaying this information," I say, about to go do just that.

"Sit down, Luca! That was your mistake. Something you don't like happens and you're all go, no stop. It almost got Shari killed!" Latrice yells at me.

Feeling ashamed, I sit. She continues,

"I don't mean to be mean, but I can't do what the two of you can, and when you leave me behind, I worry that I will not see you again. I almost lost you"—she looks at me—"both of you," she corrects, looking at Shari as well. "If I cannot help you physically, then you will let me help you plan so I can at least factor your safety into things because you two won't," Latrice states.

Shari nor I argue.

"What do you want us to do?" Shari asks Latrice.

Latrice is thoughtful for a moment before she speaks.

"Wait here while I go gather information, the normal way, since it is the only thing I can do. Right now, Luca is too high profile, and they now know your face." She points to Shari, saying the last, then stands to leave.

"But what about the inn? Who will run it?" I ask, concerned.

"I trust Shari enough to cook, but I do not trust the crowd you two would gather right now, so it will remain closed for now. I will be back before sundown, hopefully. Be good while I am gone, and please open the bedroom window." Latrice shuts the door behind her and is gone.

"The nerve of her. Why does she just assume she knows what we will be doing?" I complain, amused.

"Well, is she wrong, my love?" Shari asks, downing the rest of her tea.

"Why did you suddenly start calling me 'my love'?" I ask, the question having been on my mind since earlier.

She sighs. "Do you always have to know everything?" she complains. I want to say no, but then I'd be lying, so instead, I smile.

"You are not the same boy I lived with in the castle," she begins.

"I mean, you are him, but you have grown. When I accepted death, my love for you was the only thing I could still feel. So you have ceased to be Princeling and became my love," she explains.

I was not expecting an answer so deep.

"Well, no, my love," I say, taking her hand, intertwining our fingers, and pulling her out of the booth. "She is not wrong."

I take Shari up to Latrice's room, and after opening the window, we do what we do best: each other.

The sun is down, as are Shari and I, sleeping naked under the cover, when Latrice bursts through the door. "This is bad, this is bad, this is bad," she says, sitting at the foot of the bed not even bothering to look up at us.

Shari and I both sit up. "What's wrong?" we both ask at the same time as Shari pulls the blanket up to cover her chest.

"He's gone!" Latrice shouts frustratedly.

"Gone where?" I ask quickly.

"To Altissia. He left sometime while you were unconscious. From what I have heard, he left in quite a hurry."

Latrice's head is in her hands.

"What and where is Altissia?" I ask, not recalling the name from any of my mother's books; I should have studied harder.

"Altissia is the next town—city, rather—north of here, about two weeks travel on horseback," Shari answers, distaste clear in her voice.

"Then we follow and try to catch him," I say, not understanding why Latrice is so upset.

"And leave my people to suffer for the death of the King's Hands you caused for her?" She turns and points to Shari, not in accusation, but just stating facts. Her words strike me like lightning. I hadn't even considered that until just now. I have a job to finish.

"I will not leave your people to suffer the consequences of my actions. I will destroy the remainder of the King's Hand here in Last Stop before I leave."

Shari slips one of her hands under the blanket to grab mine. "We," she says boldly. "We will destroy the King's Hand in Last Stop."

"I'm glad you two are willing to help, because that is not all the news I've brought. Ten of the King's Hands men from Altissia have been brought here to strengthen and discipline what remains. They are not thugs; they are soldiers trained for war."

This doesn't particularly bother me, but my confidence is not what Latrice needs right now. She needs hope.

"We will find a way through this, Latrice, for Bron and for the rest of the lost we don't know," I comfort.

She picks her head up out of her hands and then looks to me. I nod. Shari reaches to tug at Latrice's hand while keeping one close to her chest holding up the blanket.

"We cannot change what has happened, but we can do better in the future. We will need a plan, and you are the brains, so you need to rest. So strip, and then come lie with us."

Latrice nods her head passively as she walks around to Shari's side of the bed, then strips, revealing a bra and underwear that match Shari's hair.

"All of it," Shari adds when Latrice grabs the blanket. "Unless you want to be the only one with clothes on."

Latrice looks back and forth between Shari and me, then blushes—a rare sight. She did not know because we opened the window.

Latrice suddenly begins to laugh, "You two sure know how to make a lady comfortable." She loses her bra and underwear, then lies next to Shari under the blanket. Shari moves to embrace her, and then I move to embrace Shari. We sleep well that night.

14 PREPARATIONS

We've been trying to come up with plans to take out those who remain at the barracks for two days now. One of the main problems is surprise is no longer on our side. We also don't know what makes these ten special soldiers from Altissia so special. Shari is of the mind that between the two of us, with Ki'ra gone, we can just go in at night and kill them all while they sleep. Latrice, however, doesn't believe it's going to be that easy anymore because of my daring rescue. "They will be more prepared for something of that nature in the future." She thinks we should pick them off slowly, two or three a day, but we don't have that kind of time. Who's to say they won't send for reinforcements? And besides all that, we still don't know what these ten men can do. I just want to do something, anything, and now.

So that is why I am jumping from roof to roof, in the middle of the night, on my way to the barracks to see if I can catch and corner one of the ten and find out what they're all about. I land silently on a rooftop next to the western wall of the barracks, crouch down, and tiptoe slowly to the edge of the roof. From my vantage point, I can see one of the ten.

I know he is one of the ten because he is wearing a tight, all-black chain mail suit with a gold handprint on the front. The only thing that remains uncovered is his face. He wields a longsword in one hand and dons a shield in the other. It looks like he is moving in a patrol route.

As soon as he bends a corner, exiting my range of sight, another man outfitted exactly the same comes around the corner closest to me, walking the same route. I watch for a while to make sure nothing changes. When I am satisfied and the next soldier comes around the corner closest to me, I nock an arrow. Latrice wouldn't approve of this, but if it is this easy, I will kill them all tonight. As soon as he turns his back to me, I release the arrow.

Fwip.

The arrow sails on track to enter the back of his head and come out his mouth. I know this because I don't miss. Inches from the back of his head, the arrow freezes and drops to the ground. He stops to turn around, but I am already gone, hopping from roof to roof, on my way back to the inn.

Shit. They can touch the power. That is going to make our jobs here a lot harder, and to make things worse, they know they are being watched. I don't look forward to explaining this to Shari and Latrice, especially Latrice.

"Why did you fire an arrow at him?" Latrice shouts at me after I finish telling them what I discovered on my trip.

We are currently downstairs in the booth, and they both sip coffee and have just been woken up.

"You were supposed to catch and corner one of them quietly so they didn't know what we were up to! And had you managed to take him out, which I'm sure you could have, they would be none the wiser for at least a day or two."

I feel like a child again underneath Latrice's scrutiny, and Shari comes to my rescue.

"There was no way he could have known, and if he had done as you said, the fight would not have been short, nor quiet. They would have known either way. At least this way, he has returned to us alive and well." Shari possessively grabs my arm and intertwines our fingers.

"Of course you are right, Shari, but that doesn't mean I have to like it." Latrice looks down at the table, shaking her head in frustration.

"I'm sorry," I say to Latrice, face downcast.

"You have nothing to be sorry for. You did the best you could," comes her discouraged reply.

"So where do we go from here?" Shari asks.

"For starters, it would be safe to assume all ten men can touch the power," Latrice states.

"That one touched Certus, but do you think some can touch Potentia? Five and five, maybe?" I ask.

"Probably not. More than likely, they can all only touch Certus, or they would be more than simple foot soldiers. But I like where your mind is, so do not rule out the possibility."

I nod, seeing the reason in what she said.

"How long can you shield yourself, Luca?" Latrice asks calculatingly.

"Indefinitely," I answer. She gives a frustrated sigh as her calculations stop.

"They are not him," Shari speaks up quickly. "He gets his talents from his mother, and there are none better than her at wielding Certus. For soldiers of their caliber, I'd say they can hold their shield for five minutes max, and that's being generous. Even then, it still requires extreme concentration. Break their concentration, then break them," Shari says knowingly.

Latrice sits quietly, processing the information through that head of hers. I did not realize it until Shari mentioned it a few nights ago, but Latrice really is the brains of the operation.

"You two will need to take them out together, one by one, so they can't concentrate on shielding. I've no doubt in my mind the two of you will overwhelm one of them."

Shari beams with pride.

"But it will not be at night," Latrice finishes. Shari and I just stare at Latrice, not understanding, awaiting an explanation. "It will be at sunrise, when they believe they are the safest, three days from now."

"Why three days from now?" Shari asks.

"To let the tension die down from Luca's mishap." She waves a hand through the air.

For the second time and for a totally different reason, I believe that Latrice is a scary woman.

"What will we do until then?" Shari questions.

"You will go out every night come high moon and watch their every move until thirty minutes after the sun first kisses the sky. You will not be seen or heard, and you will report the details back to me. I will continue to plan from there."

Scary woman indeed.

"I need weapons. They took mine when they captured me," Shari concedes grudgingly, blushing from embarrassment.

"The night is still young. Luca, take her to Bron's smithy and see what you can find."

"Won't it be locked?" I ask, thinking of Bron's head in the box.

"He gave me a key of my own in case I ever needed anything in there." Latrice pulls a key on a chain from around her neck. "I never thought I'd actually need it."

I see the sadness in her eyes at the loss of Bron. I wish I could help.

She tosses the key to me but looks at Shari. "Hurry up and come back. Restrain your hunger for each other until you get back. Don't come back without him." Her eyes slide to me. "And don't come back without her. I want you both back alive and healthy for my own selfish reasons. Now, go."

Latrice stands, then walks up the stairs to her room. I know it kills her that she can't help us, protect us, but we will be fine.

"Are you ready?" I ask, standing, then looking over to Shari.

She stands after me, then complains, "In this?" waving to the black dress she still has on.

"Are you saying you can't?" I challenge.

"No, but I would rather—"

I run to the door and smile back to her as I open it. "I've already got a head start on you," I say, then disappear into the night.

"Shit," she yells, but I hear nothing more over the sound of the wind in my ears.

I arrive at the smithy before Shari, unlock the door, and go in, leaving the door slightly ajar so Shari knows I'm here. I turn to the smithy and find it much the same as the last time I came, loaded down with weapons like Bron was preparing for war. I walk the length of the smithy, admiring the weapons, until my eye catches something that was not here before. A black pair of feminine boots sits on a counter. They look like they might fit Shari. I wonder why they are on display like weapons. I pick up one of the boots and rotate it sideways so I can see the bottom. A small blade shoots out from underneath the tip of the boot. It's about a finger length and three inches wide. With my curiosity piqued, I continue to investigate the boot. Further inspection causes another black blade to shoot from underneath the first. However, this one is the size of a dagger, almost as big as the boot itself. I set the boot back down, making a mental note to show Shari when she gets here.

"I want those," Shari's voice whispers from the back of the smithy.

I see she is just as annoyingly quiet as ever. What happened to the dangerous aura I felt from before? I move over to the back of the smithy so I can see what she is talking about.

Upon the wall, mounted on a plaque, are two fat black swords. One is long, the other is short, and both have perfectly serrated edges. They appear to be made of the same type of metal as the blade in the boots. Now that I can see more of it, I know it is a metal I have never seen before. The weapon's hilts are also black, making it look like you could easily lose them in a shadow were it not for the small white three-ringed concentric circles on the grips.

"Get them for me," she demands, too short to reach.

"I know you can get up there easily," I protest, earning a half-hearted swat.

I guess that is my fault. Reaching up, I grab the swords carefully by their hilts, and as soon as I touch them, my hands begin to tingle. What is that? It doesn't hurt, so I hand the weapons to Shari to see if she feels it. She takes them from me, masterfully, and swings them a couple times in practice.

"They are heavy," she says, "but if I would have had these during our battle, I would have bested you," she brags, continuing to swing the blades. Does she really believe that?

"You don't feel that?" I ask, surprised.

"Feel what?" she asks in return. There is my answer.

"You could not have beaten me with those or any other weapons," I jest.

"Care to put that to the test, my love?" she challenges, pointing one of the blades my way.

I pull my staff in answer.

The smithy is not big and has islands placed randomly inside it with weapons atop them. We must be very careful.

Shari comes at me, feet not making a sound. She stabs low and high at the same time, forcing me to spin my staff to block both. Then she spins, lifting her leg high so I can see her white underwear between her thighs inside her dress, and kicks me in the face. I was shielded, but the force of the blow still hurt. She smiles at me knowingly as I recover.

Okay, time to dance. As hard as she tries, she cannot hit me again. She is fast and moves with a grace most would envy, but I can tell the blades are heavy for her and will take some getting used to. I use my staff to show her the openings she leaves me, just like I did when she was behind the mask, but I do not strike her. Ducking under the next correction she knew was coming, she swings the longsword horizontally at my stomach, then reverses her grip and slashes back the other way while trying to impale me with a straight thrust from the short sword. Were I not faster than her, she would have succeeded.

She is learning the way I move, but I have not attacked yet. Spinning, I lock the arm holding the extended short sword between my arm and the staff. She tries to stab backward at me with the longsword, as I knew she would. I twist the staff, forcing the arm I have locked up behind her back, also blocking her stab at me. Another twist of the staff, after I grab her free wrist and place it atop her other one, locks both hands behind her back, which still hold both swords, respectively. I let go of the staff, the lock holds, and then I spin Shari around to face me.

"I told you, you could not best me, my love," I joke.

"Take me," she says, breathless but full of desire.

"What?" I heard her but —

"I said *take me*," she says louder.

She is turned on right now, but I don't know why, "Latrice said to restrain ourselves," I protest, trying to be responsible.

"I am restrained," she counters lustfully. The black swords clatter to the ground.

"We do not have time for this—" I am cut off by the sound of my staff hitting the ground after she figures out and undoes the hold it has on her.

"I have on a dress." She slides her white underwear off from underneath her dress seductively and walks over to me.

She begins to kiss me, and I undo the top of her dress. As soon as I pull her dress down and my hands find her breasts, there comes a noise from the front door.

Ducking, I turn to look as I attempt to pull Shari down with me, but she is already gone. I turn back to look in front of me. She is nowhere to be seen and neither are her new black swords. I pick up my staff. If she plays the shadows, then I will play the front.

I stand so the intruder can see me. Shit. He is one of the ten.

"Aaahhh . . . if it isn't the boy with the white staff." He eyes me, then my still stiff manhood poking through my sweats, slightly twisting his head in confusion.

I don't have time to be embarrassed; I must focus.

"I don't know what you were doing by yourself in here that was so pleasuring, but the greater fortune is mine. You are the reason I was sent to this shithole from Altissia, correct?" He pauses dramatically, knowing the answer. "The sooner I kill you, the sooner I can return home. Any last words?"

"Can you actually fight, or are you all talk?" I provoke.

He dons his shield, then pulls his longsword in response.

I rush him to try and break his concentration. 97, 55, 82. My last strike is a blow to the back of his head with the bottom of my staff, which is the only one that connects. But he is shielded, so it doesn't affect him in any way that would give me some type of advantage.

"You will die for that, boy," he says like he didn't just tell me he was about to kill me so he could return home.

He swings his sword at me, and I move to block, then counter with my staff, but before I connect, weapons rip themselves free of the walls, flying my way driven by some unseen force. This forces me to forego my counter and dodge. One of the blades knicks my shield, causing me to lose sight of the soldier amidst the weapons flying at me from different directions. Suddenly he appears behind, ramming me with his shield hard. I fall forward and roll with the blow, then quickly find my feet. The soldier stands across from me in the moonlight, smiling.

"Do you still believe you will survive the night, boy?" he calls to me as if he is the predator and I am the prey.

"Belief can waver, so, no, I don't believe. I know it as fact." It's my turn to smile.

More weapons rip free of the walls and fly at me; that will not work again. I flow. 16, 17, 44, 37, 2. I dodge them all while slowly making my way to him. When he is within my reach, I feint with the top of my staff, causing him to raise his shield, then reverse the swing and use the bottom of my staff to whack his manhood twice. If that doesn't make him lose concentration, nothing will.

"Now!" I shout.

Shari drops from the ceiling like a wraith, breasts and bottom still exposed. She lands on the soldier's back while he is reaching down at his manhood, and plunges both black blades deep into his neck. He falls to his knees, but Shari is not done. She removes her hands from the blades and replaces them, gripping the blades differently, then pulls her arms outward until she decapitates the man, showering us in blood as he falls lifelessly to the ground.

"Now!" Shari yells, approaching me.

213

"It was all I could think of to say," I defend.

"No, now," she says, dropping her blades and reaching for the waistband of my sweats again.

"Now?" I question, confused, pushing her off me.

Why would she want to take me after we just killed a man?

"I . . . I don't know," she says, fanning her face and taking deep breaths. "My heart is racing and the adrenaline . . . and the . . . please," she whines, not quite able to explain herself.

"Shari . . ." I start, walking over to her.

She jumps on the island counter behind her and then spreads her legs wide. Her bare skin is splattered red, and blood drips off her already red hair as her green eyes snatch at my soul. She looks like a goddess of death. I realize as I walk over and place my hands on her waist that I am excited too.

She can't wait for me and grabs me to her forcefully. We make love right there while a man's body leaks blood from his headless neck.

***

"What took you so long?" Latrice yells as soon as Shari and I walk back into the inn, close to sunrise, covered in blood.

"One of the ten walked in on us," I say hurriedly. Latrice cocks her head and raises an eyebrow.

"While we were grabbing weapons for Shari," I add.

"Is he dead?" Latrice asks in suspense.

"Yes, I made sure of that," Shari says, presenting her new black blades to Latrice from behind her back.

"Unless he can live without a head," I joke.

"So those are the weapons you chose, I presume," Latrice asks.

"And these," Shari kicks her foot out twice, showing off her new boots and the black blades concealed within the tip. She said the boots were a little heavy but fit perfectly.

"Catch me up," Latrice commands, walking over to the booth.

We spend the next couple of minutes explaining what happened in Bron's shop, leaving out nothing, except for Shari's need after the fight.

"So you killed him with those?" Latrice asks skeptically, pointing at Shari's black blades.

"Yes, why? Do you not believe I could kill a man who could touch the power?" Shari asks, offended.

"No, of that I have no doubt. It's just that he was also a soldier. A hit to his manhood should not have been enough to break his concentration," she explains, eyeing the black blades warily. "May I?" she asks.

Shari nods, not knowing where this is going. Neither do I. Latrice picks up the smaller of the two swords with effort.

"Why does it tingle like that when you hold it?"

"It doesn't tingle when I hold it," Shari replies, confused.

"No, but it did when I held them," I inform them both.

Shari eyes me, but Latrice just nods, already in deep thought.

"Shari, take this." Latrice hands her back the blade. "Luca, hold out your arm and make sure you're shielded.

"What is this about?" I ask, but do as I am told.

"Ssshhh . . . Shari, cut him lightly."

Shari doesn't even hesitate.

"Shit!" I curse. "Why'd you do that?" I ask, healing myself.

"Why were you not shielded as Latrice told you?" Shari panics.

"I was," I retort. Then realization dawns on us both. "I was," I repeat.

Shari and I both look over to Latrice, who is sitting there smiling like the gods have been cruel to her all her life and she's just figured out how to make them mortal.

"How is this possible?" Shari asks in fear or excitement, I can't tell which.

"I don't know, nor do I care, but I do know three days from now, the King's Hand won't know what hit them. Thank you, Bron," Latrice says coldly.

We run a couple more tests with the blades and figure out three more important pieces of information. 1. I cannot heal while the blade is in contact with my skin. 2. When I hold the blades, I cannot touch the power. 3. Shari cannot be affected by the power while she holds the blades. For the last, I am grateful. The blades will keep her safe from things I can't. The sun is high in the sky by the time we finish.

"So how does this change the plan?" I ask, doing my best to stifle a yawn and failing miserably.

Shari is already half asleep, leaning on my shoulder.

"It doesn't. You said you locked the door to the smithy back when you left, correct?" Latrice states, earning a tired nod from me. "Then they will not find his body before you two send them to join their companion. However, for now, you two need to get some sleep. Come high moon, you will both be out scouting for the night, so go wash the blood from your bodies and then rest."

"And what will you do?" I ask.

"I will do what I do best. Be the unwatched, unfeared innkeeper and gather information."

I can hear the hurt in her voice; she wants to be able to do more.

"Well, be careful. We couldn't do this without you," I try to comfort while standing and pulling Shari after me.

"Yes you could," she says, not swayed.

"You're probably right, but we don't want to," Shari says before leaning down to kiss Latrice on the lips.

Either the kiss or the statement, perhaps both, brings a smile to Latrice's face. With that we head upstairs to bathe, then sleep, and for the first time in a while, when we lie beside each other, we just sleep.

We don't sleep for more than four hours before Latrice comes rushing through the door, falling to her knees. Shari and I wake with a start.

"They're beheading people!" Latrice shouts, tears pouring down her face.

"What!" Shari and I shout at the same time.

"They found his body and are beheading people outside the smithy to try to scare people into revealing his killer," she cries.

"They don't know who killed him!" I shout in frustration. "How can they tell something no one saw?" I stand and prepare myself to go put a stop to—

"Luca, sit down," Latrice whispers, face downcast, disbelieving the words coming out of her own mouth.

"No, I will not—"

"Sit down, Luca!" Latrice shouts ferally, cutting me off. "You will do nothing because we have a plan that we will follow. These were my people before you decided to fight for them, so believe me, I feel the loss way more than you . . ." she balls her fists and looks up to Shari and me from her knees, tears rolling freely down her face. "...two days," she cries. "Two days."

The next two days take forever to pass. In total they ended up beheading sixteen people. I can't help but feel like this is all my fault. No one saw me, but the people of Last Stop know who killed that man or at least suspect. They know I stay at the Blue Sky Inn with Latrice. Hell, even the King's Hand knows I stay here. But they continue to spill innocent blood as a declaration: Serve the king, give up the rebel, and live, or harbor him and die. So far, the people have said nothing, and I know it is because they tire of living like this, but sooner or later, "living like this" will be better than not living at all.

There is so much pressure on me. I don't fear winning or losing this fight. I fear that when I win, these people are going to want more. I am no leader or king, nor do I desire to be one after realizing what my father has become. Would they still want me in that position if they knew I was the king's son?

Being able to protect or not protect someone is a weight no one should have to bear. However, as Shari tightens her new black boots on her feet and I pick my staff up off the floor, I know today their faith in me is not misplaced. Perhaps some other day, but not today. Today is Liberation Day.

15 LIBERATION DAY

Latrice's plan is fairly simple and straightforward. Since they want me, me they shall have; I will be the decoy. When the remaining nine men finish their patrol routes around the outer wall of the barracks at sunrise, I will follow the last one inside the open gates. I will take him out quickly, if possible, but I know they will be shielded, too, so that is unlikely. Regardless of the outcome, the commotion will catch the attention of the other eight and anyone else who is up. They want me dead, so they will charge me, and I will put up a fight but keep my focus on evasion; after all, I am the decoy. Shari will scale the wall opposite the entrance and sneak in while everyone's attention is on me, bringing death from behind to the nine remaining soldiers who can touch Certus.

The only thing that makes this plan possible is the black blades we found in Bron's smithy. I wonder what they're made of, to be able to counteract the power like that. Did Bron make them? While the fighting is taking place, Latrice will try to stir up the town, preaching the time to fight back against the King's Hand is now.

Overall, they will be of no use, but there will still be around fifty King's Hand members to deal with after we kill those who can touch the power. Latrice says they only joined to be able to live more comfortably and have no real devotion to the king. Nevertheless, it is still wrong to take freedom by suppressing the liberty of others. So if they don't surrender when they see not only Shari and me oppose them, but the entirety of Last Stop as well, they, too, must die. This is a better plan than I could have come up with. It utilizes our strengths, and if I do my job of distracting everyone, it keeps our weaknesses to a minimum. I am not a sheep, but today I will act like one to draw the wolves so a wraith with two scythes can move unseen among them.

Minutes before sunrise, I stand with Shari in the shadows of a building directly across from the entrance to the barracks. The soldiers from Altissia have begun turning in from their nightly sentry duty; the last man will turn in soon. I grab Shari and pull her close to me.

"Please be careful. I will be surrounded and unable to help you," I say softly.

"I don't need your help so long as I have these." She smiles up at me, gripping the hilts of the black blades on her back.

"You might not need me—"

She silences me with a look, loudly silent. "I didn't say I don't need you. I said I don't need your help. I will always need you." She leans up and kisses me.

"Shari—" I start, but the sun chooses this moment to kiss the horizon to the east.

"I must go," she says, melding further into the shadow, then disappearing.

"I love you," her voice whispers, body nowhere to be seen.

"I love you too," I say back, turning to face the entrance to the barracks.

As soon as the last man walks through the entrance, I dash, as silent as my morning runs with the old man, to follow, entering the open gates just behind him. He is looking to the dirt, for what I don't know, when he takes a deep breath. The moment he exhales, I throw my staff as hard as I can, like a javelin, at the back of his head, so when it hits his shield, he will fall forward.

The idiot must have let go of his shield when he exhaled because my staff caves in the back of his skull. He falls forward alright—dead. Planning is everything.

A horn sounds. I've been spotted. The remaining eight men who can touch Certus turn to find me. There is a silence between us, an understanding: Death is the only way out now. One of the men hurls his sword at me; that won't wor— The dirt beneath my feet begins to grow soft. I backflip over the sword, kicking up sand as I do, which would have turned back into solid ground, rooting me to the spot, causing me to be impaled by the blade were I not shielded.

The kid who robbed me the first day I came to Last Stop probably just saved my life.

As I land picking up my staff, two things happen. One, I see Shari drop down from the far wall and blend in with the shadows, and, two, something hits my shield from behind. Sparing a glance down behind me, I see the thrown blade facing me on the ground.

I need to be more careful.

The remaining eight men share a laugh together. They don't know what I did to the last group of men who laughed at me.

"We have one who can touch the power, boys. Let's show him what we can do," the one closest to me yells.

What they don't notice is one of their number fall as Shari impales the furthest man from me from behind. One of her blades goes in his back, through his heart, and out of his chest. The other goes through his neck and out his throat so he can't scream out. Why was I so worried about her again?

Seven men left. Six charge me, and one stays back, choosing instead to bend his knees and begin throwing wild punches at the air.

Okay, maybe they're dumber than we thought. As the six men rush at me, I prepare my body to flow. The first one reaches me and sideswipes his sword at my head. 3. I move to duck but am hit with something unseen right in my chin, bringing me back up to get sideswiped by the first man's blade. I am shielded, so he doesn't slice my head in two like a melon, but the force of the blow sends me cartwheeling to the left. I land flat on my back.

What just happened? No time to think.

I roll right as one of them tries to impale me to the ground, causing him to hit nothing but dirt. I'm about to stand when the dirt goes soft beneath me. Instead, I begin to sink. Shit. This is bad, really bad. Suddenly, it stops, and my body is back on solid ground. That can only mean one thing.

Six left. Thank you, Shari.

Two can play this game. Now how did—ah, yes, like this.

Five men sink knee-deep in the dirt as I do to them what they were trying to do to me. I admit, it was a bit of an experiment, but what can I say? I am my mother's son.

I walk over to the closest man to me, who is trying to rectify his situation. I wonder, can he concentrate on his problem and maintain his shield at the same time? I swing my staff at him in a two-handed grip, like I'm trying to swat something out of the air. His jaw shatters and he is stuck, rooted knee-deep in the dirt, asleep.

Nope, guess not. Five left.

All of a sudden, I'm bombarded by punches to the gut, causing me to lean forward. Then a punch to the chin drops me to my knees. I look up. All the soldiers are still rooted knee-deep in the dirt, except one. He was never punching the air; he was sending punches of force through the air to strike me from a distance. Shit. I need to get to him, but of course, the rest of the soldiers choose now to figure out how to free themselves. I look back to the man throwing punches: His head is gone—four.

"There's another one!" one of the normal King's Hand members shouts, seeing Shari as he exits their barracks to see what is going on.

Two of the soldiers break off to go deal with Shari. The other two circle me.

Shit. Shit. Shit.

The only upside is the normal men seem content to watch, no doubt not wanting to end up a casualty.

Shari hurls her short sword at one of the soldiers; why would she— he doesn't know. Believing his shield will protect him, he doesn't dodge; the blade pierces the front of his skull and comes out the other side.

Three soldiers left.

The men circling me both rush at the same time. 9, 7, 15, 19, 40, 36. I just dodge, trying to keep my eye on Shari. She is doing well so far, even though she has yet to hit the last soldier facing her. The two fighting me decide to change their tactics.

One of them continues to circle me while the other plants his feet firmly in the ground, drops his sword and shield, and bends his knees. He is about to start throwing punches of force. I'm game.

At least, I am until I see Shari's feet sink into the dirt, rooting her to the spot. Shit. I can't get there fast enough; the soldier is walking up to her stuck form like a wolf. That wasn't supposed to be able to happen. The power shouldn't be able to affect her as long as she wields the blades, which she does.

Realization dawns. Shit.

The power didn't affect her; it affected the dirt she was standing on.

223

The soldier is about to behead Shari.

Think. Think. Think.

Three punches of force drop me to my stomach. I can feel the other soldier swinging his blade into my back repeatedly, but he can't break through my shield. My eyes never leave Shari. The man swings to behead her.

"Noooo!" I scream.

As I scream, something instinctual inside me acts where I am unable. My hand reaches for Shari, and she is pulled from her ankle-deep in the dirt, further, to knee-deep. Her would-be killer misses, and she doesn't give him the opportunity to correct himself. She thrusts her longsword through his chin and out the top of his head.

Two soldiers left: the two beating me.

I lost concentration on my shield when I saved Shari, and the man hacking wildly at my back chopped into me three times. It hurts. I bet he didn't even realize he was actually cutting into me, because if he did, all it would have taken was a stab through the heart or head and I'd be dead. I force my shield back into place through the pain so he doesn't kill me, but that is all I can manage. If I attempt to heal myself right now, my shield will fail, and I will die. If I don't, then I will bleed out and die anyway.

It was a good run.

I roll onto my back so I can see my killer's face. He has not stopped trying to hack into me. As he brings his blade down for another strike, it stops short, blocked by a thrown blade. Was it black? Am I imagining things from blood loss, or is there really a black sword sticking out his throat?

One soldier left?

I roll back onto my stomach and see the man in his stance hurling punches of force at Shari as she runs at him; she doesn't have the blades to protect her anymore. She doesn't run in a straight line, though, jumping left, then right, and back again while she closes in until she finally rolls within his reach. How will she defeat him with no way to hit him? Finding her feet, she kicks the side of his knee, and it buckles, dropping him to his other knee. Is he bleeding?

How?

She then kicks him in the ribs and retracts the kick, bringing her foot back to his head. When it connects, a black blade exits the opposite side of his head she kicked.

Oh yeah.

She pulls her boot blade out of his head, and he falls down to the ground, already dead.

"Luca!" Shari cries, rushing over to me and dropping to the ground so she can hold me. I am not Luca right now. I am Beau, but I do not have the energy to tell her that right now.

"Heal yourself, now!" she demands, crying.

"Can't . . . What about them?" I flick my eyes to the fifty men slowly surrounding us. She looks up and cries harder.

"Go," I say. She can still get away.

"I won't leave you, my love, and you will not die. Now heal yourself so we can fight."

I would give her anything in the world, but right now she's asking for something I don't have the energy to do. If I heal myself, I will not be able to fight, my vision beginning to blur. The men are formed in a tight circle around us now. Shari will no longer be able to escape.

"I love you," she whispers to me through tears, still holding me.

"I love you too," I say as we accept death together.

A voice cuts through the barracks. "If you value your lives, you will walk away from them. Your superiors are dead, and there are only fifty of you. There are hundreds of us."

The circle parts, allowing me to see Latrice walking toward us through the entrance of the barracks, hundreds of people at her back. They are not soldiers or warriors; they are the people of Last Stop. Some hold swords, some hold daggers, but most hold rakes, hoes, pitchforks, cudgels, or hammers. They have come.

"If you want to live to see high rise, on your knees and hands behind your back until we figure out what to do with you. Try anything, and, yeah, high rise and all of that," Latrice says, steadily approaching, the entirety of Last Stop on her heels.

Grudgingly, they comply, and the stronger-looking people of Last Stop move to detain them as Latrice walks over to us.

"Heal yourself, now! Please, my love," Shari pleads.

I let my shield fall and slowly, painfully, find the energy to heal and close my wounds. Shari cries in joy as she feels the wounds on my back begin to close. Latrice finally arrives, kneeling opposite of Shari.

"I told you we couldn't do it without you," I joke, looking up to her.

She just stares at me for a moment, then leans down to hug me tightly, causing me to cough from my all-too-weak back muscles being squeezed.

"And I told you I wanted you back alive and healthy for my own selfish reasons," Latrice says to me loud enough for Shari to hear. Then she raises herself from me and looks to Shari, wipes the tears from Shari's face, and kisses her on the lips. "Both of you," she finishes.

"We are alive," I jest, earning a tight swat from Shari, who doesn't find it funny.

Latrice just shakes her head at me.

"Beau, you need to address the people. You fought for them, and they came for you. You owe them a speech of some sort," Latrice commands while I have one foot in the grave.

"Almost dying isn't enough?" I complain.

"She's right, my love," Shari agrees.

I move to stand, but pain causes my back to spasm, robbing me of my breath.

"Beau!" they both shout in concern. The name sounds weird coming from Shari's lips.

"I'm fine . . . Hand me my staff, please, Latrice."

She does as I tell her—I could get used to that—and I place my weight on the staff as Shari and Latrice help me to my feet. I look up, and the entirety of Last Stop is staring at me—at *me*, awkward. I wobble, still dizzy from the blood loss. The ground slowly turns soft beneath my feet, causing me to sink, but solidifies a moment later, helping my balance. I look to Latrice, and she just smiles at me. I still don't know what I'd do without her. Looking back to the people, I don't know what to say. This is not me. I am not a leader . . . so I decide to tell them the truth, as much of it as I can anyway.

"Those who pretend to be leaders in your town have been broken, but I am no leader either. Where you go from here is your choice, but I suggest you build. Build so that next time they come to break you, you don't even bend. You are already a tough people. Believe it or not, you won your freedom yourselves. How, you ask? When they began beheading people, looking for me, you could have given me up. But you didn't. Instead, you chose to place your wrath in me and suffer for a just cause. This allowed me to do the easier part and swing my stick."

A few people laugh at this.

"If they want to live," I point to the returned King's Hand members. "Then they will teach you what they know and help you defend Last Stop with their lives."

Some of the returned men nod in agreement and thanks.

"This is not a new beginning. This is growth from which you came. Beginnings are soft, but growth is characterized by overcoming challenge," I say, thinking about my own experience. "You definitely overcame a challenge this day. So today, you are free to celebrate . . . because today . . . today is your liberation day."

The crowd erupts in a cheer allowing me to release a breath I didn't realize I was holding as I motion to Latrice to unroot my feet so I can sit. She does so, grinning wildly. With Shari's help, I sit while everyone moves to some unknown task.

"What are you grinning for?" I ask Latrice.

She comes to kneel next to Shari and me so we can hear her over the gathered crowd.

"You are very charismatic when you want to be. I'd even feel moved if I didn't already know you," she jokes.

"Yeah, yeah. Can you two just help me get to the inn please?" I ask, still in pain.

"See, I would, but I must help these people plan and organize this mess you've made. I should also help establish some sort of town council or something . . . Shari will no doubt want some time with you to herself as well, so, ta ta . . ." Latrice begins to back away from us.

"Shari, make sure he doesn't die on the way to the inn please."

"He will not get away from me so easily," Shari whispers to an already departed Latrice, then kisses me.

"Come on, my love, let's go." Shari helps me to my feet.

I smile to a few random people who thank me on our way to the entrance of the barracks, and we begin the long, painful journey to the inn.

Hours later, I lie in Latrice's bed on my stomach with my shirt off as Shari sits on my bottom, massaging the newly healed skin and muscles in my back. We didn't make love when we arrived. I think both of us are too busy thinking about how invincible we are not. Today was a narrow escape, and these were just ten foot soldiers. If I can barely survive them, how will I stop my father? What was I supposed to learn from this day—how impossible the task ahead is? No, no matter how true that may seem, it is unfair. I did learn how to use Certus in different ways today.

"Baby steps," I whisper to myself.

"Baby steps indeed," Shari agrees as if she is reading my mind, still kneading my muscles.

God that feels good. Abruptly she stops and lies down on me with her breasts pressing into my back.

She positions her head so she can whisper in my ear. "Last Stop may be free, but our work is not done, my love."

"I know, I know. I will rest the rest of the day and tomorrow. Then come sunrise two days from now, we will pursue Ki'ra. He's got a week head start on us, so we probably won't catch him." I say the last in frustration.

"All we can do is all we can do," Shari says, reaching for my hand and taking it in hers.

"What about Latrice?" she asks after a second.

"What do you want to do?" I ask, wanting to hear her answer first.

"I don't know, but if we leave her, I will miss her. She has become like family to me." At least we both agree on that part.

"Latrice stayed in Last Stop when both her parents fled my father.

229

This is her home, and it would be selfish of me to ask her to leave it. I won't even put her in that position."

I feel Shari nod her head in acceptance atop me.

"Do you have a girl crush on her or something?" I ask, trying to lighten the mood.

"No, you are all I need and more, but she saved my life. For that I will forever be grateful," she says seriously.

I just lie there in silence.

"Why? Do you grow jealous of the kisses I share with her?" she asks playfully, nibbling my ear.

I take a second to think before I answer.

"No. Maybe if it were someone else, perhaps. Actually, not perhaps; I'd be lividly jealous. But Latrice deserves more than either one of us can do for her. So the kisses you share, in a way, express my gratitude for her as well."

"You're sweet," Shari replies after a moment.

"Speaking of kisses," she tugs at me to roll over. I do.

"Shari, my back is —" she silences me with a finger to my lips. "If I wanted this . . . her hand finds my manhood and grabs it, I would not have asked."

She lets it go and brings her hand to my face. I kiss her deeply. Her tongue parts my lips and I let it. We kiss for what feels like a lifetime, tongues finessing each other's, playful lip bites, and long moments where our lips are just locked together. When I'm with Shari, time feels irrelevant. Randomly, while enjoying ourselves, I think to myself, "I must get stronger so I can protect her." Losing her is not an option.

Eventually, Latrice comes into the room.

"Oh, I'm sorry—"

I cut her off, "It's fine, we're decent," but Shari jumps from me, causing no small amount of pain to dance through my lower back, and runs over to Latrice, enveloping her in a hug.

They share a look with one another, then kiss. Shari has tears in her eyes.

"What did he do? What did you do to her?" Latrice yells at me angrily.

I chuckle at the ferocity of this woman. Wasn't she supposed to love me?

"We're leaving in two days," I tell Latrice. Realization calms her, and Shari moves back to the bed, sitting on my right.

Latrice doesn't look as devastated as I thought she would. If anything, she seems to be trying to figure out how to say something.

"Can . . . Can I . . . May I come with you?" she asks, face going red and falling toward the floor.

I'm so shell-shocked I don't answer. She wants to come with us.

Shari isn't so slow. "Yes! Yes, yes, yes, yes, yes!" she exclaims, running back to Latrice and hugging her harder this time.

Latrice is smiling but eyes me from where her head rests on Shari's shoulder.

"What about the inn? What about Last Stop? This is your home," I ask, disbelieving she will leave all of this to come with us on a journey that very well might get us killed.

Latrice sighs in relief, then pulls Shari over to the bedside so they can both sit by me. Did she think I was going to say no?

"This *was* my home, but then I met you." Latrice grabs one of my hands. "And then I met her." She grabs one of Shari's hands, then pulls both of our hands into her lap. "When Bron died, that was hard on me.

He was all I had when my parents left. Me, him, and the inn. When he died, sad as I was, I started thinking about how everything I have keeps getting taken away from me. Then I realized I was wrong because I still have you two. For me, home is not a place. It is wherever you feel most comfortable. I feel the most comfortable when I am around you two; therefore, you are my home," she finishes.

Shari is smiling from ear to ear.

"What about the inn? What about the town council? What abo—"

"Do you want me to stay?" Latrice cuts me off.

"Of course not . . . I—" I turn red and Latrice giggles, then shushes me.

"I know, I just wanted to see you blush, but I am the brains, am I not?"

"Yes," I say simply, not wanting to question her anymore.

"You said two days. In two days, I will have Brenda's daughter running the inn and put Brenda herself, along with Amy the carpenter, on the town council. They will see to it that Last Stop is taken care of. Amy will also make sure the town builds itself properly. Yes, I have work to do," Latrice says, standing.

She makes her way to the door, then pauses. "See to it that you are both well rested and well acquainted by the time it's time to leave, because you will not be this comfortable on the two-week journey." Having said that, she leaves.

"Well acquainted?" I repeat questioningly. "We already know each other. We've known each other for more than half of our lives." I look to Shari.

"That is not what she means by that, my love, but your back is too hurt to do much, so rest."

To do much? What's that supposed to—oh . . . I send a wave of healing through my back. It doesn't do much for tender muscles, but in two days I will not be alone again with Shari for at least two weeks. We will get acquainted very well in two days.

"Shari, my love," I say deviantly.

"Yes?" she looks over to me.

"Do me a favor please."

"Anything," she says seriously.

I smile. "Strip," I say.

Then she, too, smiles and strips. I take my trousers and underwear off, and Shari climbs on top of me. She will have to do all of the work because my back is hurt, but other parts of me are not, and Shari is up for the challenge. We make love until just before the sun goes down, then pass out.

***

Something is annoying my eyelids, so I open them. It is still night, but I have never seen night before quite like this, as everything is bathed in a red light. I stand from the bed, naked, careful not to wake Shari. My back doesn't hurt anymore.

Good.

I walk around the room in amazement, inspecting everything, including my own body, and then finally, I look out the window. I smile at what I see.

"Shari," I call, moving to the foot of the bed.

"Yes, my love?" she says sleepily without opening her eyes.

She is lying face down on the bed, also naked. Silently, I drop to my knees.

"Open your eyes," I whisper. She does, and when she does, I hear a sharp intake of breath.

"What is this?" she asks, frightened.

"Look out the window."

She lifts her head and stares directly into a blood-red moon, which paints everything in the room a deep red. "I've never—" she starts, but is interrupted by me softly pulling her by the legs toward my face.

"What are you doing?" she purrs, leaning up on her elbow.

"You did what you had to do in the smith's shop. I will do what I must while the moon paints the world red," I tease.

Even her normally penetrating green eyes match her hair, as well as the rest of her body right now.

"I am not dumb, my love, but why are you down there and not —"

Her body locks tight as she realizes my intentions. If I were not holding her thighs apart, she would have choked me with them. Her body is so tense, I stop, unsure if I've somehow hurt her.

"Are you alright?" I ask in concern.

I can't tell if she's blushing because right now we are both colored a blood red, but her eyes are wide.

"That felt good . . . a little too good," she says, embarrassed.

That's all I needed to hear. There is another sharp intake of breath in the tone of a moan as I resume what I was doing.

"Luca," she moans my name.

"Luca," she moans again, trying to get my attention. I don't want to talk.

"Luca!" she moans my name loudly, gripping my hair and pulling my head back. "You have to stop . . ." She looks embarrassed. "It is too sensitive down there to continue what you are doing."

I am so turned on, I don't want to stop, so her words come as a disappointment to me. She sees my downcast face and laughs. She raises herself to me, kisses me on the lips, and brings her mouth to my ear.

"I said you couldn't keep doing that with your mouth. I still want this." She grabs my waist, leans back on the bed, and rolls over onto her stomach, motioning for me to come to her.

I don't hesitate, and she softly pulls me into her, saying, "I am at your mercy, my love. Do not hurt me, but know I am no weakling either. There isn't a shadow of a doubt in my mind that you love me. Now prove me right."

Her words do something to me that I can't quite explain, and I take her with vigor until we are both left in a sweaty, panting heap on the bed, exhausted.

I can't take my eyes off of her beautiful form, and just before she closes her eyes and drifts off to a blissful sleep, she looks me in the eyes and says, "Luca, I thought I couldn't love you more than I already did. I was wrong."

16 THE JOURNEY

After the blood-red moon, Shari and I fell into a state of lust fueled by love. Two days, two weeks, two hours, two minutes, or two seconds, whatever it was, is gone. All we've done is each other in a state where time has no meaning.

Latrice's arrival this morning brought us back to the present and let us know that it is time. I don't think we even ate.

"Oh God, it smells delicious in here," Latrice says, walking into her room, going to the dresser and sitting on the far end of it.

We wake slowly and uncomprehendingly.

"Come on up, you two. It's time for an adventure." Shari stands, still naked, and walks over to the other end of the dresser to get clothes.

Latrice eyes her the whole way, smiling. Only when I stand does she turn her head toward the door, giving me privacy. If Shari notices the gesture, she doesn't let on. She just finishes grabbing her clothes, then walks over to Latrice, kisses her on the lips, and goes to the bathroom, closing the door behind her.

Just like that, she left me, her love, naked in the room with another woman, even if it is Latrice. I stand naked, trying to figure out the logic.

"Ahem," Latrice clears her throat. "Clothes, Luca." She continues to look away.

"I know you're not embarrassed, so what's the big deal?" I ask, sliding on my trousers, then shirt.

Noticing me dressed out of the corner of her eye, she turns to me. "Respect and restraint," she says simply.

"You respect Shari, I get that, but restraint?" I say the last questioningly.

She sighs, believing me clueless.

"I respect Shari and you, as well as the love you share. I exercise restraint in looking because I still want you more than I let show. I don't want to tempt myself, no matter how much you two trust me," she explains.

"We couldn't ask for a better person to be our friend, our home, because they don't exist," I say appreciatively.

She blushes. "Yeah, yeah. Come downstairs and help me cook. If I know you two, and I do, you haven't eaten anything in two days," she says, hopping down from the dresser and leaving the room.

"Shari, I'm—" I begin to yell, only to be cut off.

"Just because I'm bathing doesn't make me deaf, my love," she states plainly.

Okay, off to the kitchen I go.

When I make it into the kitchen, I find Latrice preparing eggs and toast. I move beside her and start helping. We cook in silence, just enjoying each other's company until Shari comes down the stairs. She's wearing her only outfit that isn't a dress again, with one exception. She has on the black boots that conceal the black blades instead of the brown boots. Shari enters the kitchen and is given a cup of tea by Latrice that I didn't even notice her make. Latrice then begins to take food from the kitchen into the booth. I can't help but wonder if this will be the last time we are here.

When we are all seated and about to eat, Latrice stalls us with a question, "Shall we pray?"

"To whom?" I question uncaringly.

"To the one true God, of course," she replies quickly.

I'm shaken. That is the God my mother believes in, and as far as I know, I have not discussed that fact with Latrice nor Shari.

"I would very much enjoy that," Shari concedes.

"What's the matter, Luca, do you not believe?" Latrice asks.

"I don't know. I've never really put too much thought into it. My mother's history books show that one of two things is likely to happen to people who believe in gods. Either they live in fear, or they become crazy people, 'prophets' I think they are called, who do all manner of immoral things in their god's name. They partake in absurd rituals, await deliverance to be given to them by some unknown source, and take free will out of the journey that is life," I state mater-of-factly.

"Is your mother one of these people?" Latrice asks, somehow knowingly.

"No," I concede grudgingly. She smiles.

"I will pray, and you will listen," she commands, taking one of my hands in her own and Shari's hand in the other and bowing her head.

Shari and I bow our heads as well, and Latrice begins to pray.

"Our Father who is in mystery, reveal to us your righteous character. Give your children on this earth this day, to see the way, the light, and the truth. Show us the pathway of eternal progress, and give us the will to walk therein. Establish us with your divine loving grace, and thereby bestow upon us the full mastery of self. Let us not stray into paths of darkness and death, lead us ever lastingly beside the waters of life, and be pleased to help us become more like you. Even so, not our will but yours be done. Guide us on this journey for increasing relative goodness, until we find the infinite goodness from which it came. Amen."

I look up and stare wide-eyed at Latrice, and she stares back, smiling. This is a form of prayer I've never heard before. The things she implies are . . .

"You called the one true God our Father," I accuse, not having the best of relationships with my own father.

"I did," she owns her words.

"Explain," I say critically. She has my complete attention.

"Your mind exists apart from your body and so, too, does your soul. God endowed you with both mind and soul, so he is your father, in a spiritual sense," she explains as if it's just common sense.

My mind goes further into shock; she said, "Mind exists apart from your body."

I read that in the blue book, but it made no mention of a soul.

"Did you read that in the blue book?" I ask Latrice.

She squints her eyes at me. "You know as well as I do, I can't interpret the elements like you do, so are you suggesting I am a liar?" She's offended.

"No, no, it's just . . . that concept took me a while to interpret, and you not only understand it, but allude to it in common prayer as well."

I look at Shari, but she doesn't seem to be as shocked as me.

"You understand this too?" I ask her.

"Yes, your mother took it upon herself to enlighten me when she took me in. I believe in the one true God."

I stare at Shari, feeling offended and jealous.

"Why did she not teach me?" I ask, hoping she knows the answer.

"I asked the same question once. She told me that because of the things I had been through, I needed the one true God, so he would reveal himself to me. But you, her son, believed that you had everything you needed. So the one true God's infinite goodness and love would not appeal to you until such a time when you found yourself desperately in need of him."

There is a silence as I try to gather my thoughts.

"Your mother is wise," Latrice starts. She pauses, then continues, "My mother taught me of the one true God, but I didn't seek him until my parents left me alone."

"Seek and find," I recall the words from the blue book in my head.

"What did you find when you found him?" I ask curiously. She chuckles before she replies, "I have not found him yet, Luca. I am still on that journey and don't know how long it will take. But seeking him and learning of his ways has thus far granted me peace—" she makes a thinking face "—and understanding in some areas of life," she adds after a moment. There is another pause. "I will not stop until I find him," Latrice declares in finality.

"Continue to seek, continue to find." The concepts from the book continue to smack me in the face as she talks.

My mother believes, Shari believes, Latrice believes, and the wisdom I have been able to discern from the blue book agrees. Not only that, but I don't think there's ever been a time when I've wanted for anything. And now, I want and need help, desperately. I see the relevance of the elements in my life, how could I be so ignorant? The one true God exists, and he and the blue book are somehow related. I promised myself I would find the answer to the ultimate concept and now I will add to that. I will find the one true God.

"I want to learn, I want to believe," I say, feeling conviction.

Shari places her hand on top of mine and smiles like that's the best news she's ever heard. Latrice smiles wide too.

"We will help you, but you must open yourself and seek him with your whole heart," she says.

"I am willing," I reaffirm.

"Good. The fact that you are willing means our Father has already found you. So today, your journey begins to find him," Shari says from beside me.

We eat our food in a cheery mood. Shari is sure to finish her tea. By

240

the time we are done, it is nearly high rise.

"So, besides the obvious, trying to catch Ki'ra, what's the plan?" I ask Latrice.

Both Shari and I look at her expectantly. She smiles at us and takes her time to answer, basking in our dependence upon her.

"I have procured the necessary supplies for the journey to Altissia. Rations, a tent, water skins, horses, etcetera." She waves her hand dismissively. "I have also pillaged some not-so-necessary supplies." She grins madly at us.

"Such as?" I ask, playing into her game.

"You can shield yourself indefinitely, but we can't, so I took the liberty of taking the chain mail suits off of our would-be leaders and had them fitted for us so we can use them for protection, possibly even disguises. They might even stop you from being chopped in the back." She raises her eyebrow at me.

Do I even want to ask how she got our measurements? Recalling her conversation with Shari about buying her clothes, probably not.

"I also bought you and her a bow with one hundred arrows each and some extra weapons. Everything is awaiting our arrival at the northernmost point of town," she adds.

Why can't she be the leader? I wonder.

"Also," she says, looking down.

"Yesss?" Shari and I both question at the same time.

"I realize this will slow our progress and lessen our chances at catching Ki'ra, but can you teach me how to fight or at least defend myself along the way? You two will not always be here to protect me, and I don't fancy dying," she asks in shame.

Shari speaks before I can. "Don't look like that. Ki'ra is a week, perhaps more ahead of us by now. We were never going to catch him. I will teach you all you can learn in two weeks, and in return, you will promise me not to die, and keep that promise," Shari says with compassion, giving voice to my feelings as well.

"I don't know if I can keep that promise, but I will try," Latrice smiles unconfidently.

"I don't think you understood Shari, so let me be blunt. You. Are. Not. Allowed. To. Die," I say seriously.

Tears threaten to leave Latrice's eyes, but she blinks them away.

"Okay, okay, I get it. I promise I won't die. I promise I won't leave my home." She laughs her fear away.

"Good. Now that the boundaries are set, do not cross them," I joke. Latrice, Shari, and me all burst into laughter at a joke only we could understand.

With breakfast finished, we head out to the tailor so Latrice can give the keys to the inn to Brenda's daughter before we leave. I make sure to grab the blue book before we go. I will have plenty of time to read as they train over the course of our two-week-long journey.

Turns out, Brenda's daughter's name is Lavender. After we give her the keys to the inn, we head north through Last Stop, for the last time. As we walk through the town, people begin to follow. First, it is one, then two, and so on, until we have a tide at our heels. They don't speak to me or the two women on either side of me, nor do we speak to them.

We reach the northernmost edge of Last Stop, where our things for the trip are located, and I turn around. It looks much the same as it did when they showed up to stop the fifty men from hacking Shari and me into pieces. Minus their weapons, the entirety of Last Stop has turned out to see us off. The crowd parts, and Brenda walks through the rift with what appears to be a key. She comes straight up to me and holds out the wooden key for me to take.

"We don't have much, so we made you this," Brenda begins, "as a symbol. Whenever you find yourself or your friends . . . our friends," she amends, eyeing Shari and Latrice, "in need, remember this key. This key is from all of us here in Last Stop and is to remind you that Last Stop is always open to you and yours. If you need it and we have it, it is yours."

I reach for the key, but she swats my hand, and the crowd laughs lightly as I look at her in confusion. She smiles, then reaches up and places the key around my neck. Only then am I allowed to touch it.

Amy made this key—I can tell by the master craftmanship of the wood—and while it is only a piece of wood, it means a lot. I find Amy's smiling face just behind Brenda, smile back in thanks, and then eye the crowd.

"I need you to be alive when I get back," I shout. "Can you do that?" I ask them all, not knowing if I'll ever return. Farmers, butchers, tavern keepers, mothers, fathers, and normal people all look to me for a moment. Then there is a roar so loud, for a second, I believe I have summoned the storm to my mind. But this is no storm. It's louder. It's the people of Last Stop's will to live.

I turn to the open grassland that separates us from our destination and look to the three horses already saddled, ready to go. They are nothing special, just normal brown steeds, but they will do. I go to the biggest one and slowly raise my hand toward his nose, allowing him to sniff it. He hesitates for a moment, then does, after which he nuzzles his head against me. I take that as his acceptance and mount him. I learned that from one of my mother's books. Shari and Latrice do the same. With a wave of my staff back at the crowd, I nudge the horse forward, then set him to a gallop. We're off.

Shari takes the lead, knowing exactly where we are headed. Hours blow by as we travel through the vast sea of grass. The sun blesses us with its warmth while the air refreshes us with its cool touch. Not a cloud can be seen in the sky.

The one true God is real, and I am on a journey to find him or understand him, maybe even both. My mother says the one true God is a combination of every good quality I've ever known and more. Infinite goodness basically. If that's the case, how will I ever find or understand him? How does one find and understand infinity? The thought is intimidating as well as invigorating.

"A journey for increasing relative goodness until we find the infinite goodness from which it came." I do believe that is what Latrice said in her prayer. That definitely sounds like an adventure worth going on. Shari breaks me away from my thoughts by slowing her horse to a stop. Latrice and I follow suit, but there are hours of daylight left—

"Why have we stopped?" I ask Shari.

"Because you can't ride horses endlessly without letting them rest or drink water. Also, we must set a schedule where I can train Latrice, and while she practices, you can train me. Today we got a good enough start, so now we will train, but tomorrow, come sunrise, we will do so again, and then travel till sunset, resting ourselves and our mounts at night."

Seems she's done some thinking of her own on our ride. Latrice dismounts her horse and begins to set up camp. I dismount my horse as well, but walk instead to Shari, who is already off her horse as well complaining about something.

"Oh God, I'm sore," she grumbles.

I don't think she meant to be heard.

"What's wrong? Horse riding got you a little sore between the legs?" I jest, really voicing my own discomfort.

"Oh no, I'm not sore from riding the horse . . . At least not this one." She pats her mare.

I blush, discerning her meaning. She just giggles and kisses me.

"When did we decide I was going to train you?" I ask, desperate to get the heat from my face.

"I decided Latrice would need time to practice what I teach her. While she does this, I will learn from you. Since you are mine, your vote belongs to me as well. So even if you did disagree, you are outnumbered," she says with an air of finality.

"Will you two stop flirting and help me set up!" Latrice hollers.

Shari walks past me to oblige, with a grin plastered on her face.

I suppose that makes it final, not that I have a reason to object. Actually, I like this thought process of hers, but she better not complain when I use it on her. I move to help the girls set up camp. It doesn't take long. I unload the horses, Shari and Latrice set up the tent, and we each tend to our own horse's needs.

Before long, Shari is showing Latrice the basics with a short sword. It really looks no different from what Alrick taught us, except Shari is not teaching Latrice to move like a soldier. She teaches her to move like an assassin. The main focus seems to be watching the opponents' movements for the openings they leave so you can exploit them, big and small. She's also showing her the best way to hold the short sword and how to use a person's weight against them. With both of them being girls and weighing little compared to men in armor, this is probably for the best. I don't fool myself though. Shari is a killer, and she is training Latrice to be one as well.

Well, it's time for me to pull out the blue book. I move to grab it from inside the tent, then return to my spot in the grass near their training.

"Before you read that, meditate on this. If God is your spiritual father because he gifted you with mind and soul, what does that make the people around you who are also gifted with mind and soul?" Latrice shouts in between movements with Shari.

I think for a moment.

"Are you saying you two are my spiritual siblings?" I ask.

Latrice is breathing hard at this point. "Go deeper," she yells, clearly distressed. "And I said meditate, not ask me questions."

Whatever. Okay, so the one true God is my spiritual father because I possess mind and soul. I close my eyes, which transcend material space. This is proven by thoughts; they exist, yet they are not contained in space.

Mind and soul are gifted to me by God, but I am not the only one who possesses these things. As far as I know, everyone has a mind, regardless of how they choose to use it, so that makes them God's spiritual children as well. So am I to understand that every person in existence is God's spiritual child? But then we'd be family, all of us. That's a big family. What about those who don't know or don't accept him? They are still his children because I did not accept him at first, but I was still endowed with a mind to be able to make my own choices, and now, now I am here. We are all God's children, no matter how lost, we are God's family. But what about my father? If God is everything good, how could he permit an evil such as my father to exist and roam free?

I open my eyes.

That's as far as I make it in that meditation session. Thoughts of my father disrupt any further progressive revelations. Now I open the blue book to a page at random, hoping it can distract me from the negative. I land on the page that has "Seek. Find. Continue to see. Continue to f—"

Wait, no. This is different.

"Seek. First. High Shadows Move."

What could that possibly mean? Having not had any luck with the second part of the other interpretation, I decide to spend some time with this one: "Mind exists outside of space. You."

Focus, I begin the chant. *Certain. Sure. Definite. Decided. Specific. Precise.* The elements reveal their deeper meaning to me.

"Seek first higher realities, and the shadows of the material realm will have no choice but to follow."

Is it me, or am I getting better at this? But what does it mean?

Shadows of the material realm?

"Luca," Shari interrupts my concentration.

"Yes?" I look up from the book to her. Hours have passed. I can tell by the position of the sun. It will set soon.

"Latrice is practicing. Now it is your turn to teach me" She looks way too eager.

I close the book, stand, and then stretch.

"What do you want to learn?" I ask, unsure of what exactly I'm supposed to teach her.

"Everything," comes her immediate reply.

I chuckle. "I don't know everything, and if I did, two weeks would hardly be enough time to teach it. Try to be more specific."

She brings her hand to her chin and thinks for a moment. "I want to learn how to move the way you do. You always seem to glide from one position to the next—from attacking to defending and back again, effortlessly," she concludes.

This time I don't chuckle, I laugh.

She wants to learn how to dance. But the quarterstaff is not her weapon. That's okay, I'll improvise.

"What I'm about to show you is a dance meant for the quarterstaff, so we have to freestyle a little bit," I say, moving five feet away from her and assuming position 1.

"I don't wish to dance. I want to learn to move the way you do," she reprimands.

"I know this, and when I fight, I dance," I say, just to irritate her.

To my surprise, she nods, then pulls both of her black short swords out, placing them hilt to hilt so she can mimic my movements with the quarterstaff, and positions her body like mine.

So it begins, me teaching Shari the first fifty positions of the Water Dragon because that's all we have time for before the sun sets.

"I like this," Shari says, breathing hard.

"Like what?" I ask for more detail.

"This . . . dancing you do. I know it's for killing, but it somehow feels peaceful," she says in a trance-like state, moving from position to position.

"Ha, killing? Everything I just showed you was for defense, evasion," I enlighten.

She looks to me wide-eyed, and at the same time, I notice she is moving from position to position in order.

"They do not go in order. You must learn how to move from one to the next as the need arises," I explain.

She's thoughtful for a moment.

"Then we need to spar, my love," she beams as if she has just had a wish granted. "But not tonight. It is time to sleep. We will be up before the sun, so let's rest."

She walks over to me, then kisses me before walking over to where Latrice is still practicing, breathing hard, and tells her the same.

Shari picked up the positions a lot quicker than I did, and I only had a week. Maybe it's because the year we were apart was a lot harder on her than it was on me. Who knows? What I do know is, whenever she does perfect the Water Dragon, she is going to be a very scary individual.

Soon we find ourselves drinking from water skins outside the tent in starlight. Latrice decided we didn't need to start fires out here. One miss-step and we would have a raging wildfire we could not stop. Besides, the stars are beautiful and give off more than enough light.

"So what did you learn in your earlier meditation?" Latrice asks out of the blue.

"That we are all the one true God's children, which makes us all, every single person on the planet, spiritual brethren," I answer, recalling my earlier thoughts.

"Good, very good," Latrice says happily.

"But if we are all his children, all his family, why does he allow evil such as my father to exist? I thought the one true God was only good?"

It's Shari's turn to speak.

"Don't say such things. Without your father, you would not be here. Even evil can produce good. But as far as your question about good and evil, your mother explained it to me like this: The one true God does not crave slaves; he desires children who love him. For that, they must be given the power of decision, free will. The one true God is infinitely good, and, therefore, evil can't possibly exist inside him. But by choosing to give you free will, he made it possible to choose that which is not of him, evil. However, evil itself doesn't need to exist. Character growth results from choosing goodness, even when other evil or erroneous paths exist. You choose to be good, God-like, and your soul progresses closer to the one true God."

I nod my head in understanding.

She continues, "For example, Latrice could have had you while you knew not what had become of me, but she knew your heart and instead chose to do good in place of what she desired. And from that choice grew a home." She takes Latrice's hand in her own. "People choose evil or error because they lack understanding of the one true God's ways or simply reject him. So even though evil only need be potential, through our choices and decisions as people, we give it life."

Wow, I sit in amazement. I had no idea Shari believed to the point of gaining this understanding. I also had no idea my mother was so adept in her belief. Lacking doesn't quite describe how I feel. It's much worse.

"I see the look on your face. It's never too late. Your desire to seek the one true God is proof enough that your journey is under way. Don't be deterred by fear or anything else. Eventually you will find him. Eventually we all will," Latrice comforts.

We sit in silence for a few moments before Shari says it's time for bed. Latrice and Shari crawl into the tent. I stand and then look to the stars. They light the sky in numbers that have no rival, truly making a single person feel insignificant

"God, are we your only creation? Why are we so lost? If you are

249

infinitely good and we are . . . what are we?" I question the sky.

When no answer is forthcoming, I decide to save myself the headache and crawl into the tent. Poking my head in, I notice that Shari and Latrice lying down under the blanket takes up almost the entirety of the tent. Outside it is, then.

"And where do you think you are going, my love?" Shari asks when I move to leave.

"There is not enough room in here for three. I will sleep out—"

"You two may be lovers, but you are also my family now, and I will not allow anyone in my family to sleep in the cold," Latrice interjects. "So take your position behind Shari. Don't make me tell you twice."

I laugh, despite her seriousness. I love these women. I climb behind Shari, who kisses Latrice goodnight on the cheek, then kisses me on the lips. And after our first day of travel, this is how we sleep, cramped tight in a tent, Shari holding Latrice as I hold Shari. Home indeed.

I'm awakened by a kick to the foot. Opening my eyes, I see Latrice's sleeping form. Shari is gone. She must have been the one to kick my foot. I silently exit the tent to find her waiting for me. The sun is still a long way off. I breathe deeply and embrace the cool night air.

"What?" I whisper, trying not to wake Latrice.

"Latrice is new to this, so she will require more sleep for her muscles to recover. We, however, are not. You will spar with me while she sleeps and teach me while she practices," she motions me to follow, moving a good enough distance from the tent so our noise will not disturb Latrice.

"I haven't taught you anything but defense, and you need to memorize those stances first," I reply.

"Then when we spar. You attack, I'll defend, and please don't insult me again."

Insult? Does she already have the first fifty memorized after practicing only once?

Damn.

"Shari, I am a lot faster than you—" I begin, but get cut off.

"I know, but it is not you I am trying to save myself from. Sparring against you, no matter how bad I do, will only help me," she says, eyes downcast.

How can I say no to that? I walk to her, then take her chin in my hand, lifting her face, and kiss her before stepping back again.

"Prepare yourself, Shari. I will not go light on you if it means possibly saving your life."

She smiles, then pulls her black blades from their sheathes on her back, and assumes position 1.

"I would have it no other way, my love," she says boldly.

Shari is about to have a very rude awakening. I pull my staff and attack.

Even though I said I would not take it light on her, I still hold back power in my strikes. For now, she can barely keep up, but she will not give up. Her battle instincts are on point. The positions she chooses are the correct ones, but I am just too fast. She's better than I was when I first started, that's for sure, but her anger is distracting her.

When the sun touches the horizon, she signals me to stop. By this time, she has a busted lip, a swollen knee, and countless bruises that decorate her skin. Anger is clearly the dominant emotion on her face. I knew she wasn't going to like this.

"Are you alright?" I ask in concern.

"I don't require your sympathy, Princeling," she spits in frustration. She called me *Princeling* and not *my love*.

"So, I am back to Princeling now, huh?" I say, attempting to mask my hurt.

She flinches. "No, I . . . I'm sorry, I just didn't realize the gap in our skill was so vast. It frustrates me," she concedes, then adds, "my love."

I walk up to her and put one hand on her waist. "It's not a gap in skill. It's a gap in speed. I did this for a year, and you just started yesterday," I explain.

"Yeah, that too. You're really fast. I can barely see you when you move."

"Ha!" I laugh. "Me? You should have seen my grandfather."

"Are you saying he is faster than you?" she asks, not quite believing my words.

"Leagues faster. I hit him one time in four months, and I had to summon the storm to do that." She just continues to stare at me in disbelief.

"The sun is up. I do believe that means it's my turn." We both turn at the voice to see Latrice walking to us, wincing with every step.

"Are you okay?" I ask.

"I'm fine. My muscles just hurt everywhere," she replies.

"I told you her body wouldn't be used to this, but as you told me, if it will possibly save her life, I will not take it lightly," Shari tells me.

"I don't want you to. Now let's go," Latrice shouts the command.

The girls move off to the side and begin more of Latrice's assassin-type training. With the sun barely up, I will—

"Latrice, what should I meditate on today?" I ask excitedly.

"Build off of what Shari started explaining last night about good and evil," she says after a moment of thought then diverts all of her attention back to her training.

Good and evil, huh? I think as I sit, then close my eyes. The one true God is infinite goodness, and evil is . . . evil is my father, but why is he so evil? Should I seek understanding? But if I understood why he was doing evil, would that also make me evil? . . . No, because I understand good, and he does not or does not wish to. So in substance, Shari said the possibility of evil is necessary to moral choosing but not to the actuality thereof. Evil is as a shadow, only relatively real. Actual evil is not necessary as a personal experience. Potential evil acts equally well as a decision stimulus in the realms of moral progress and spiritual development, becoming Godlike. Evil becomes a reality of personal experience when a mortal mind makes an evil choice. But if you factor relativity into this, all the choices we make are evil, or at least error, because this journey is for progressive relative goodness. What is relatively good is still not actually good. So how do we know what's good and what's evil with our relative understanding? To us, good and evil are merely words that symbolize relative levels of mortal comprehension of what we observe. I guess we could take the standard of good of the current social order in a normal society, but that seems lazy. My father runs the current social order anyway, and he is far from good. So then, what should be my standard of good? Hmm? If the one true God is real, and my journey is one for progressive relative goodness until I find the source of infinite goodness from which it came, the one true God, then to emerge into his infinity, I must make a living and personal choice between good and evil as they are determined by the true values of the spiritual standards established by my soul, which was gifted to me by the one true God . . .

My head hurts.

I'm done meditating for the day. I quickly eye Shari and Latrice. It seems like Latrice is taking quite a beating during this training session. Would Shari take out her own inner frustrations on Latrice? I hope not. I'll be sure to ask her before we start her training session today.

I grab the blue book from inside the tent and open it to another page at random. I like how things went when I did that yesterday. Nothing new comes to me today. Strange. That hasn't happened in a while. Latrice's meditation today has worn out my mind already though. That must be what it is. I close the book and watch Latrice struggle through her lessons. After a couple of hours, Shari leaves her to practice on her own and walks over to me.

"You wouldn't happen to be venting your own frustrations about the gap between you and me in combat on Latrice, would you?" I ask boldly.

"I would never, but I assure you, it's quite the opposite actually. She saw me all beat up and was determined to go even harder," Shari says caringly.

"You two are crazy," I say bluntly, really meaning it.

"That we may be, but you are wasting daylight, my love. It is time to teach me the next fifty positions," she counters.

I just shake my head. I grab my staff, standing as I do, then walk over to Shari and begin teaching her the last fifty positions of the Water Dragon. Hours pass and the sun begins to set. She's picked up these last fifty positions quicker than the first. It's like Shari was made for attacking.

"Who came up with this style? They must have been a truly fearsome person," Shari says to me.

"My grandfather taught me. Beyond that, your guess is as good as mine. You said my mother told you he was a Precursor. I'm sure that has something to do with it. He said he'd answer all my questions when we next meet. I'll be sure to ask," I reply thoughtfully.

Shari just nods, still moving from position to position.

"Do you not think we should get some rest now?" I ask loudly enough for Latrice to hear.

Shari sighs then straightens. "Yes, yes we should rest," she admits grudgingly. "Latrice!" she shouts. "Time to rest."

Latrice drops to her knees, exhausted, catching her breath. I realize this is necessary, but I can't help but feel bad for her. She has been nothing but an innkeeper since she was sixteen. Now she pushes her body in ways she never has before.

After we refresh ourselves, we pile into the tent to get some rest. Both women are tight-lipped tonight, too focused on becoming stronger, and are soon asleep. My last thoughts of the night are on whether everything we're doing is even going to matter. Will it be enough?

A week and a half pass as we hold tight to our schedule; we should arrive at Altissia in three days. It is hard to tell how much Latrice has improved because she is still going over form and technique. One thing I have noticed, though, is her body is beginning to lose soft tissue and become hard. Her womanly assets have not diminished in the slightest. They simply appear more toned. Shari, on the other hand, has improved rapidly. Both of her training sessions are sparring now, and although she still can't hit me, it has become a lot harder to hit her. Where I flow and dance like a calm river, she is a rushing current that knows exactly how to pull you under. She moves with so much grace, she doesn't even appear violent, but I know better. I feel sorry for the next opponent she faces in serious combat.

I quickly learned riding a horse at full gallop is just as hard as running, well, harder for me. You use different muscles than you do when you walk, and the strain on your back is almost unbearable. Shari seems to be used to it, but for Latrice's sake, we don't gallop the horses for too long each day, which I am happy about.

We pass a bunch of small streams running through the grassland which we allow the horses to rest at and drink from. Shari told Latrice and me that the streams we encountered, although they slowed us, were a good thing. Apparently, a lot of people fall prone to riding their horses to death when on a journey such as ours. A horse will run until it is half dead if you let it. Since we have quite a distance to cover, we allow the horses to warm themselves up at a slow jog for a while before setting them to a full gallop, which we are now doing.

The wind is rushing in my ears when out of the corner of my eye, I notice Latrice's horse suddenly slow to a stop. Shari and I slow and turn our mounts to see what the holdup is. Latrice stares off to the west and is clearly contemplating something. Shari looks to the west as well to try to see what Latrice is looking at . . . or for. Then her eyes go wide.

"What would be the point?" Shari asks Latrice.

"He . . . We need to see what we face," Latrice says, sounding remorseful, looking to me.

"What is it I need to see?" I question curiously, looking back and forth between the two of them.

"It would be much easier to show you," Shari tells me. "This will not take long. Let's go," Shari prods her horse west, and Latrice and I follow.

I'm nervous.

Whatever they are about to show me is bad. I saw it in their faces. We ride for about thirty minutes in this new direction before Shari reins in her horse and forces it to walk up a grassland hill, stopping at the top. Latrice follows her lead, stopping at the top, and they both stare out at something. Whatever they are looking at is making me uncomfortable. I feel something—

"Hurry up, Luca. I have no desire to be here any longer than necessary," Latrice calls to me over her shoulder.

I trot my horse up the hill to where they are and see nothing, then stop abruptly, giving way to a massive hole in the earth, easily bigger than Last Stop. The hole is so deep you can't see the bottom. It looks like someone took a giant scoop out of the land with a serrated spoon then left. The shadows coming out of this pit feel—

"This used to be a town," Shari says coldly.

"Alterain," Latrice whispers its name.

"What happened to it . . . what happened to Alterain?" I ask, astonished.

"Your father," Shari answers simply.

It takes a second to process, and then I recall Latrice's earlier words, "He needs to see what we face."

"My father can't be this powerful," I say to myself in disbelief.

"Oh, he is, and do you know why he did this?" Latrice asks with hate in her voice.

I shake my head no, already dreading the answer.

"Because during the conquering of this land, he told them to surrender, and they took too long to find the proper leaders for an official surrender."

I can't believe what I just heard. I knew my father was an evil man, and I knew he was powerful, but to be able to do this . . . and just because . . . I can still feel his power in the shadows down—

"I am sorry, my love, but Latrice was right, you needed to—" Shari's voice is cut short when a massive black tentacle shoots up from out of the depths of the pit. The tentacle is so black . . . I've never seen anything darker. I take a step back, but the tentacle splits into three. One of them wraps around Shari's neck, and another around Latrice's, then pulls them into the blackness.

"Nooo!" I scream.

They never had a chance. The last tentacle sways side to side for a moment, as if thinking or looking at me without eyes, then wraps itself around my neck as well. I try to fight, but there's not much you can do to a shadow, even if it is as solid as steel. I am lifted off my horse and into the air, then pulled into the dark bottomless pit that used to be Alterain. My heart thunders as I am pulled deeper and deeper into the pit. Light vanishes. I can no longer see anything, and it is quite early. My only sense that seems to be working is touch, because I can feel this tentacle wrapped tightly around my neck and the wind on my face from being pulled down rapidly. My ears pop three times before the tentacle slows my descent, then releases me completely. I hit the ground hard.

I lie there for a moment trying to catch my breath and look up. There should be a light coming in from above me from the opening I was just pulled through, but there isn't. The bottom of this pit is pitch black.

"Shari!" I shout her name, hoping for a response.

The only reply I get is my echo. Latrice probably isn't here either. I stand, not knowing what else to do. I can't explain it, but the blackness is alive, just like the tentacle, and it is urging me to move forward toward . . . toward its source. Whatever its source is, is frighteningly powerful. I feel it in my . . . my soul. I don't want to move toward what must surely be my death, but I see no other option. I must also find Shari and Latrice, even though I don't see how I can help either of them.

I blindly step forward; nothing hinders my process. One step turns to two and two into four, until I begin to walk somewhat confidently into the blackness. Eventually my hand finds a wall, and I use it to guide me to wherever it is I'm walking, closer to the source. That's the only thing I know.

The wall feels like it is made of jagged, unworked rock, which makes sense, considering I'm underground. It starts to become difficult to move, like I am moving through water, but thicker. I know it sounds crazy, but it feels like I'm moving through the blackness itself. My heart feels like it stops when the presence of the source I was walking to is suddenly among me. I want to fall on my knees and beg for my life . . . but I am not a sheep.

"WHY HAVE YOU COME HERE X'AVION?" a voice booms from . . . everywhere, from the blackness itself, which serves to further terrify me.

"ANSWER ME." The voice does not sound pleased, but it called me my father.

"I . . . I am not X'avion," I stutter out.

The shadows around me seem curious. I don't know how I know that; I can just feel it. Two eyes easily bigger than my head spring into existence in front of me about fifteen feet in the air. They are feline.

"YOU ARE NOT," it confirms.

Suddenly the shadows become very still, watching my every move. The eyes never leave my face; they don't even blink.

"YOU ARE OF HIM. THAT I KNOW FOR CERTAIN. YOU REEK OF HIS POWER. WHO ARE YOU, AND WHY SHOULD I NOT KILL YOU WHERE YOU STAND?"

Kill me? Please don't. I get the feeling this thing does not like my father. That makes its question rather dangerous for me to answer truthfully, but I will not risk lying to . . . whatever this is.

"X'avion is my father," I say honestly.

The blackness around me becomes hostile; its intentions are to kill.

"YOU WILL DIE HERE," it lets me know calmly, despite the aura it emits; I believe it.

"I like my father no more than you," I say, accepting my death sentence.

I can feel this thing's power; there is no way I, nor anyone else, could beat it.

"Please don't kill the women. They have nothing to do with my father," I add pleadingly, hoping Shari and Latrice will be spared.

The blackness becomes curious once again. "YOU ARE OF X'AVION, BUT YOU ARE NOTHING LIKE HIM."

Did I just hear the voice soften?

"Are you . . . are you a god?" I ask.

Again, I don't know how, but I can feel the blackness laughing at me.

"NO, I AM OF GOD AS YOU ARE OF X'AVION," it explains.

Now, despite my impending death sentence, I am the curious one.

"I know you're about to kill me, but . . . what exactly are you?"

I feel the blackness laugh at me again. Suddenly, the blackness begins to pull in on itself centered on the giant feline eyes. I am who knows how many leagues under the earth, so there is no light, but the blackness continues to reel in on itself, and the rocky cave around me suddenly becomes visible. It is then that I know the blackness for what it is.

Shadow.

As the last of the shadows pull in on themselves, I am left standing in front of a giant panther, made entirely of shadow.

"DO YOU SERVE YOUR FATHER?" the giant panther asks without moving its mouth.

It's disorienting.

"I just told you I don't like my father any more than you do," I retort.

The panther cocks its head at me.

Okay, maybe I shouldn't tempt this thing.

"MANY MORTALS WHO DON'T LIKE X'AVION SERVE HIM. THEY FEAR HIS POWER. NOW ANSWER THE QUESTION."

This thing has a very good point, but how is it so informed about my father? I better answer this question first.

"No, I actually am at the very beginning of a journey to remove him from power." I feel it laugh at me again. "What's so funny?" I ask boldly.

It cocks its head again. "YOU FELT MY LAUGHTER?" it asks me.

"I felt everything, the curiosity, then intent to kill, the hate for my father, and your laughter," I reply, gaining confidence for no good reason.

"YOU ARE ABNORMALLY SENSITIVE TO POTENTIA FOR A MORTAL. YOU WILL NOT DIE BY MY POWER," it states.

I can tell this thing is intrigued by me now. The fact that I oppose my father must have saved my life.

"What are you?" I ask again.

"I AM A BEAST OF POWER, THE BEAST OF SHADOW. I AM UMBRA," Umbra says pridefully.

What is a beast of power? Are there more? And why does this one hate my father? One question at a time.

First, "What did you do with my companions?" I ask worriedly.

"THEY HAVE BEEN RETURNED TO THE SURFACE. THEY NOW SLEEP. WHEN THEY WAKE, THEY WILL REMEMBER NOTHING. YOU INTEREST ME, MORTAL, SO I WILL ANSWER THREE OF YOUR QUESTIONS. CHOOSE WISELY."

I don't even have to think about the first, "What is a beast of power?"

"WE WERE CREATED BY THE ONE YOU KNOW AS GOD WHEN HE BESTOWED POTENTIA UPON THIS WORLD. I AM THE POWER OF SHADOW IN ITS ENTIRETY MADE MANIFEST IN THIS FORM. IF I DID NOT EXIST, NEITHER WOULD THE ABILITY TO USE SHADOW BY WEILDING POTENTIA."

Umbra grows silent, waiting on my next question.

Shit. I want to think about what Umbra just told me, but I don't want to run out the beast's patience.

"Are there more beasts of power?"

"MORTALS . . ." it disapproves of my question.

"YES. YOU JUST WASTED A QUESTION. MAKE YOUR LAST WORTH IT."

Wasted a question? Ooooo . . . Shit. Umbra is the beast of shadow, so there is probably a beast for every category of Potentia. What about Certus? A good question maybe, but it is not the one I ask.

"Why do you hate my father?"

I feel Umbra laugh, but not at me, then grow serious.

"HE BESTED ME, AS WELL AS THE OTHER BEASTS OF POWER, IN BATTLE FOR COMPLETE MASTERY OF THE POWER

THAT IS US. I DON'T KNOW ABOUT THE OTHERS, BUT I DESPISE BEING ON EQUAL FOOTING WITH MORTALS."

My father beat Umbra in battle? No, that's impossible . . . but Umbra just said it was so, as well as all of the other beasts. Such power . . . can't . . . how—

"IT IS TIME FOR YOU TO DEPART. CAN YOU KEEP YOUR

KNOWLEDGE OF ME SECRET?" Umbra asks, walking, for the first time, toward me.

"Secret?" I repeat, thinking about Shari and Latrice.

"Ummm—"

"DON'T WORRY ABOUT IT. YOU WILL NEED TO SEE ME AGAIN IF YOU SERIOUSLY PLAN TO DEFEAT YOUR FATHER, BUT WHEN YOU WAKE YOU WILL REMEMBER NOTHING," Umbra says, still walking toward me.

"When I wa—"

A tentacle shoots out of the giant panther's back and wraps itself around my head.

"SLEEP."

I lose consciousness.

"Luca," I awake to Shari's voice calling my name.

"Why am I sleeping in the grass and not in the tent?" I ask sleepily.

"I only just woke myself, but—" Shari's voice cuts out as she snatches my leg while I am in midstretch.

She pulls me a couple of feet down the hill we are apparently on.

"Be careful, my love," she says, pointing behind me when I look up to her like she's crazy.

I stand and then look behind me. There is a massive hole in the earth. That's right, Alterain. Our commotion has awoken a sleeping

Latrice, who I just noticed.

"Latrice, don't move!" I shout.

Her body locks in fear as her eyes shoot open.

"Slowly back away from the edge," Shari says, more calmly than I.

Latrice is even closer to the edge than Shari and I were. She slowly scoots back, still on her belly, then stands.

"Why am I waking up in the grass?" Latrice asks us like it's our fault. "And so close to that," she adds, pointing to what used to be Alterain.

"We have no idea. We, too, just woke up in the same position as you," Shari answers her.

A horse neighs, interrupting our conversation. We all turn to stare down at the horses, which are still loaded with what looks like all of our things.

"So, we don't know why we were asleep by the bottomless pit, but we weren't robbed," Latrice says distastefully.

I can tell this is bothering her.

"Do either of you feel funny?" Latrice asks us both.

"No, I actually feel extremely well rested," I reply honestly.

"Me too," Shari adds.

"So do I . . . I don't like this. The last thing I remember is us all looking into the pit," Latrice says, attempting to piece things together.

"Well, let's not do it again. I don't like blacking out like that," Shari says, walking down the hill toward the horses.

She doesn't like this one bit either.

"Let's go. We still have a job to complete," Shari shouts back at Latrice and me.

"I don't like this, but she is right," Latrice agrees, walking down the hill after Shari.

I spare a glance back to the pit that used to be Alterain. How do we stop a man who can do something like that? I don't know, but when we find the answer, my father can't be allowed to live. With that thought, I turn away from the void and follow the girls back the way we came.

We travel as far as we're going to for the day and make camp. After getting everything set up, Shari and Latrice begin to stretch in preparation for training, but I stop them.

"We are three days out from Altissia, and despite our seemingly peaceful blackout, you two have been putting your bodies through a lot. The time for training is over. Take these next few days to let your bodies recover," I tell them both.

"Do you think we can't handle—"

Shari cuts Latrice off. "As much as I hate to admit it, he's right. You've worked hard, Latrice. Your body has developed muscles in places you never thought to put them. We need to rest while we have the chance. There is no telling what awaits us in Altissia."

"Speaking of Altissia, what can you two tell me of the town," I ask both women.

"Besides the fact that Altissia is a city, not a town, not much; I've never been," Latrice replies.

"I've been. It's actually where I was prior to hunting you," Shari says after Latrice.

"Well?" I ask, pressing for more.

"Altissia is huge, so I can't tell you much of value, but I do know that the rest of your father's generals should be elsewhere currently. At least that was the case when I left. I also know of a high-end tavern that has the tendency to host the worst people," Shari explains.

"What good does the second part do us?" I ask, not sure why she brought it up in the first place.

"Information," Latrice says, not as slow as me.

"I imagine at a place like that, you can find out anything you want to know, for the right price," she answers in Shari's place.

"Yes. Also, the King's Hand soldiers sometimes frequent the place for drinks. We might be able to learn something from them," Shari adds.

"Okay, it's a start," I say.

"What else?" I want as much information as possible. I'm sure Latrice does too.

"Nothing else of value, I'm afraid, but I will warn you, Altissia is not Last Stop. The city may be more grand, but the people can be far worse. You said you were pickpocketed in Last Stop. That will not happen here. Someone will befriend you in public, get to know your whole life story, and that same night slit your throat with no hesitation, then take what they desire. Trust no one."

I get the chills from Shari's warning. Why are people so cold? We're all supposed to be the one true God's children.

"What about your face?" Latrice asks Shari.

"Ki'ra is the only one who knows my identity. Everyone else is either dead or back in Last Stop. Aside from telling Luca's father, I have no idea what he will do with this information. I do know we must hurry if we wish to move freely. For all we know, it may already be too late; my description could be posted everywhere," Shari answers.

"You, my love, will have to keep that staff of yours hidden. The bounty I took was for a young man with a white staff. No one has turned in your head and staff, so it is sure to still be active. While there is not a picture, the staff is a dead giveaway," Shari says to me as an afterthought.

"Well, that sucks," I complain.

"I brought bows just for you. You will be fine," Latrice tells me, dismissing my complaint with a wave of her hand.

No longer feeling fangless, I smile. My smile fades rather quickly when I think of another rather important question.

"Where will we stay?" I ask Shari since she's the only one of us who has been here.

"As long as we stick to the edges of the city so we can avoid any unwanted attention, any inn will do. Also, we will stay at the same inn but rent three separate rooms. We will not be seen traveling to and from the inn together either. Groups attract more attention than individuals," she explains.

"What!" Latrice shouts. "But I hate sleeping alone," she complains.

"I believe I know the feeling, so I will alternate sneaking into your rooms every night so I don't have to and so I can pass information," Shari says, smiling at Latrice.

Well, it sounds like we got everything covered, as far as we can, anyway.

"Anything else you guys can think of?" I ask, just to be sure.

They both shake their heads no. Three days; Altissia, here we come.

17 ALTISSIA

We are a couple of hours out from Altissia, but I can see it from here. Well, not the city itself, but the three-story stone wall that encompasses the city. Shari said there would be soldiers watching the traffic entering and exiting the city, but as long as we don't draw attention to ourselves, we should be fine.

My mind is anything but calm. Will we be walking into a trap? There is really no telling what Ki'ra did with the knowledge he obtained. This will also be my first time in a city, so, as paranoid as I am right now, I can't help but be excited. Last Stop was alright, but the people were as broken as the small town itself. I hope with this fresh start, they build something to be proud of. Altissia, however, while not the best city my dad's kingdom has to offer, is far from the worst. I've read about it before, in my mother's books. They say there is a little of everything in Altissia, and you will find exactly what you're looking for if you know how to look. Let's just hope no one is looking for us.

Shari reins in her horse as we come to the back of the long line of travelers and merchants awaiting entry into the city. The stone wall I saw from afar is a lot larger up close.

Massive slabs of granite stacked upon each other climb at least one hundred feet in the air. How did they get such heavy rock that high? It must have involved the use of Potentia; I can think of no other way. Atop the wall, the King's Hand soldiers stand spread out as far as my eyes can see, ready for any disturbance. I count thirty before the wall wraps around the city on both sides. If they are spread so far apart, this must not be the only entrance into the city.

"Dismount, you two," Shari calls to Latrice and me while doing so herself.

"I didn't know a place could be so big," Latrice says to no one in particular after landing on the ground.

I stare at the massive wall in amazement, just as wide-eyed as Latrice. Shari leads her horse over to us, and we get in the back of the line. People from all walks of life are here today trying to get into Altissia. I see warriors, merchants, whores, families, and even a group of traveling performers.

One of the performers shoots an arrow through an apple on the head of another performer, thirty feet away; everyone watching applauds. He missed the center of the apple though; the arrow is slightly more to the left. I smile because my shot is better than his—

"What are you smiling at?" Latrice asks unexpectedly.

Caught off guard, I don't know what to say. "I uh . . . I'm just looking at all the people. They're so different from the ones in Last Stop," I stutter out.

"Yes . . . yes, they are," Latrice says untrustingly.

"However . . ." she drops her voice to a whisper so only Shari and I can hear her ". . . we are still on a mission, so remain focused and try not to get caught in the city's vices. Also . . ." she punches me in the shielded stomach ". . . slouch your back. Even without your staff, you still look imposing."

Shari nods in agreement.

Sighing, I slouch my back, effectively knocking a couple of inches off my height; it is extremely uncomfortable. My staff has been covered with dirt and has random articles of clothing tied to it.

Shari is currently tying the three horses to it by their reins using some extra rope we had, so they each have enough space to move. It's the best we could think of.

The line doesn't take long at all to move. The soldiers aren't really searching too many people, just a few suspicious-looking individuals here and there.

There is a commotion ahead of us. This was supposed to go smoothly. It appears the soldiers want to check the traveling performers' wagon for anything that might be a problem. The group and two soldiers move to the side to allow traffic to continue.

Not even a minute later, we come to the front of the line, and a tired looking soldier waves us through without a second glance. And just like that, we're inside the massive walls and their thick spike-studded iron gates.

As we clear the gates, Latrice and I slow to a stop and both look up. Shari takes my hand as if she's worried I will get lost. Buildings three- and four-stories high litter dirt roads which don't seem to have any order to them whatsoever. The city is a beast, full of people, buildings, horses, and more people. Neither the people nor the buildings resemble anything in Last Stop. Compared to this, Last Stop was devoid of life. There is an absurd amount of noise. People yell at other people to buy their goods, a man is being kicked out of a tavern for being drunk this early, and four women who all give Shari a run for her money wear next to nothing as they successfully lure people into what is surely a brothel. Even Latrice blushes at the sight of them. It's so loud; how does a place like this sleep?

Shari tugs at my hand, breaking me away from my overstimulation and pulling me through the maze that is Altissia. I reach back and grab Latrice; so much for not getting lost in the city's vices.

I don't know how Shari is finding her way right now, but I just saw a man open his black cloak to reveal all kinds of expensive-looking jewelry and trinkets.

Speaking of revealing, there is a blonde woman on the fourth story of a pink building to my right in a window, pulling her shirt up and revealing her breasts to all on this dirt road who chance to look.

What is going on right now? This is absolute chaos. Hearing a door open in front of me, I turn to look.

"Look after our horses," Shari tells a young girl inside the door, letting go of my hand and untying the reins from my staff, then handing them to the girl.

"Get in here," she commands Latrice and me, clearly agitated.

We enter the tavern and it is packed. The walls are green, the floor is wood, and there's a counter somewhere behind this crowd of people. That's all I can tell about the place as Shari leads us through the crowd and into the back.

"Three ales, please," she tells the tavern waitress in passing before finding us a corner of relative quiet.

She turns to face us as I pull Latrice in front of me to stand by her.

"What was that?" Shari asks, looking back and forth between the pair of us.

Both of us are stunned speechless and have no forthcoming answer. Shari just waits expectantly.

"Altissia is a lot bigger and has a lot more going on in its walls than I ever could have imagined," Latrice says, still somewhat awed, after she gathers her wits.

"You have only seen a small part of what this city has to offer, and it's already got you distracted. We came in here with a plan, remember," Shari scolds.

Oh yeah, she's right. We're not supposed to be seen traveling together or going in or out of buildings together. I completely lost sight of that when my eyes fell upon the city. I'm willing to bet the same happened to Latrice.

"It's okay . . ." Shari sighs. "I thought something like this might happen. At least it happened right at the beginning and not while we were deep in over our heads. Take a minute and get accustomed to the speed of life here."

Just as Shari finishes her last word, the waitress she ordered the ale from finds us and hands us our drinks.

"Will you be opening a tab, or just the three drinks?" she asks in a hurry, eyes everywhere else but on us.

"Not sure yet," I say, flipping a silver piece to her from out of my coin bag.

She catches it with practiced hands and walks away. Her job must be stressful. As soon as she leaves, a big man with a grotesque red beard and missing teeth fills her place. I step beside Shari and Latrice to give the man some space for whatever he is about to say.

"Hello, beautiful. Let's you and I disappear somewhere and get better acquainted, if you know what I mean," the man says drunkenly to Latrice, slapping her bottom, then giving it a full palmed squeeze.

The man's breath reeks of ale and uncared for teeth. I'm about to break the man's hand when Shari places a hand on my hip, stopping me. She wants Latrice to handle this on her own. To Latrice's credit, she didn't even flinch when the man grabbed her bottom, nor does she move to dislodge his hand.

"You have three seconds to remove your hand, or you will not like what follows," Latrice says calmly, staring straight into the big man's brown eyes.

"Oh, kitty has claws, does she?" he laughs.

"Two," Latrice continues her count.

"I like being rough anyway," he says, squeezing her bottom harder.

"One."

Latrice grabs the man's hand then turns her back to him while bending her knees and heaving forward. The man, carried by his own weight, is flipped over Latrice's shoulder and lands on his back. However, she is not finished. She twists his arm, forcing him to flip to his stomach, then moves to hover over him. She whispers something in his ear, then pushes his arm upward until there is a loud pop. I'm willing to bet his arm is dislocated. The man loses his breath from the pain, but Latrice is still not done. She then pushes the dislocated arm outward, causing a sickening crackling noise. Now his arm is dislocated and broken. At this, the man screams, but only for two seconds before he passes out from the pain.

I now realize the whole tavern has gone deathly silent at this point. All eyes are on Latrice and her would-be consort. Latrice stands, making sure she looks at everyone in the process.

"Does anyone else want to cop a feel?" she asks the tavern in challenge.

No one bites, and what follows eases my tension.

The whole tavern raises their drinks toward Latrice, gives a loud cheer, then goes back to doing whatever they were doing, as if this is an everyday occurrence.

Two men wade through the crowd, then pick the unconscious man up by his arms, not caring in the slightest that one is broken, and throw him out. One of them claps Latrice on the shoulder in passing on the return trip.

Latrice walks back over to us, but the confidence she displayed just a second ago is gone.

"How'd I do?" she asks Shari, doing her best not to sound nervous.

"Couldn't have done better myself," Shari says proudly.

"Please never do that to me. It looked quite painful," I say, laughing.

"Please . . . One, you are my home. Two, Shari would kill me. Three, I don't think I could catch you even if my life depended on it," Latrice jokes.

She did well, but I can tell her first experience harming someone to that degree has her shaken. He deserved worse. The waitress comes over to us with three more ales.

"On the house," she says, smiling at Latrice before walking off.

I'm not even sure what happened to the last ones. Latrice's hand shakes as she sips her ale. I'm about to speak to her, but Shari beats me to it.

"You did fine, truly, but you must calm yourself." Shari then kisses Latrice on the lips, letting it linger, until I see Latrice's body visibly relax.

"I'm sorry," Latrice sighs when Shari steps back. "I just, I've never actually hurt anyone like that. It was quite intense, but the rush was . . . is it wrong that I liked it?"

"Absolutely not. Remember when Shari and I went to Bron's Smithy? She—" Shari silences me with a back fist to the stomach.

Latrice just stares at us trying to figure out what I was about to say.

"He was just going to tell you that I am no stranger to the rush. And while it is okay, don't let it trick you into doing something you are not ready for," Shari explains.

Latrice looks thoughtful for a moment, then nods.

We stand in the corner of the tavern, making light talk as we drink our ale and become accustomed to the speed of life here.

We're basically people watching. Already, I've seen two men grope women's behinds, but instead of being beaten or embarrassed, they simply disappear out the front door with the women, presumably to get better acquainted. Who knows with this place though? Crazy doesn't cover it by half.

We've been served a couple more ales each. It is not as strong nor as sweet as wine, but I can still feel its influence upon my body. If Shari and Latrice feel it, they don't let on.

"Are you two ready to try this again?" Shari asks us. "There is still time to make it to the Pale Horse."

"What's the Pale Horse?" Latrice steals the words right out of my mouth.

Shari sighs in annoyance.

"I expected that question from Luca, but not you, Latrice. The Pale Horse is the high-end tavern I spoke of where we will go to gather information."

"Sorry, must be the ale," Latrice says, blushing.

"Yeah, we're ready," I say, the ale having calmed my nerves.

"Then let's go," Shari says, moving through the crowd.

I wait for a moment, then follow. Latrice mimics, following me.

Shari leads us through the city, which has not grown any calmer, with confidence that only one well acquainted with Altissia could muster. Thanks to the ale and my being focused on trying not to lose Shari, I don't notice much of the rabble going on around me.

The sun begins to set. When Shari stops, I spare a glance behind me to find Latrice patiently awaiting my next move. I look over in the direction Shari is staring and see two King's Hand soldiers leaving a white building that has a sign posted on the door which reads, "The Pale Horse," along with a silhouette of a white horse against a black background. The door is rather fancy as well, white gilded with gold. I just noticed this part of town looks way fancier and has fewer people.

Shari motions to me that she and I will follow the soldiers and Latrice will enter the tavern. I relay the message to Latrice, and then we all move. I continue to follow Shari, who is now trailing the two soldiers at a distance. I hope Latrice doesn't get into any trouble without us there. Should I really be worried about her after what she just showcased at the tavern earlier? I would be a fool not to be.

I bend the corner I just saw Shari go around moments earlier and find her standing twenty yards off in front of a three-story stone building that has no windows and a simple wooden door. She stands leaning on the wall with one foot. Catching my eye, she slightly nods at the wooden door, telling me this is indeed where the soldiers went. I nod back, and she goes in. Seconds later I am right behind her. We've entered a hallway that has stairs climbing up two stories, ending with another wooden door. Shari is waiting for me at the second door. I quickly close the door behind me, then move to Shari.

"There is noise beyond this door, my love. I also smell strong drink. I believe we might have caught them with their pants down, but I don't know how many there are," Shari whispers.

"There's more than two?" I ask in a whisper, concerned. "Yes, but don't worry, my love, we can do this," she whispers back before kissing me.

She doesn't give me time for another response, turning back to the door and drawing her black blades from underneath her shirt. That's not fair, I don't have a weapon. BOOM! Shari kicks in the door.

When we enter, there are eleven soldiers in a plain stone room. Three sit gambling, five are drinking strong-smelling alcohol from barrels, two have their pants down, taking turns with a naked woman, who, for her part, looks to be unwilling as well as terrified, and one is sitting in the back, watching it all with a smile, including us. Shari's eyes flick to the woman on the floor who clearly is not enjoying the man thrusting on top of her. She has tears in her eyes. I can feel Shari again as I once did when she hunted me outside of Latrice's tavern. I wonder what that is? Whatever it is, it is very unnerving.

"Do not interfere, Luca, my love," Shari says loud enough to be heard by everyone in the room.

The soldier still has not stopped thrusting the woman. No one else has the chance to speak. Shari is among them using her two black blades, hilt to hilt, like a quarterstaff, just like the dance I showed her, except . . . this is wrong. Not her movements. She performs the dance perfectly, better than me even. But the dance was meant for a staff, not blades. I have never seen so much blood.

Her first victim holds a cup with dice in it and, standing, turns to face her. 57, 87. He loses the hand with the cup and his head. The other two gamblers rise in a hurry, but they aren't quick enough. 81, 62, 99. Shari sweeps the end of her bladed staff through one man's legs; he loses them both, carrying over to slash at the other man's neck twice. He was dead from the first cut to the throat; I don't know what the second was for. Everyone in the room is panicking, except for two people—the soldier still thrusting the woman and the one all the way in the back who is watching in horror.

Shari moves to the five soldiers next, 17, ducking under a kick, placing herself in the center of their drinking circle. I don't know how to accurately explain what follows, but Shari begins to move her "bladed staff" like she is the lone passenger traveling in a small rowboat. The only difference is, instead of pushing water, she is cutting off limbs. 99, 97, 84, 72, 65, 53, 71, 100. The five men fall in more than fifteen pieces, and blood showers Shari. The soldier with his pants down awaiting his turn is still standing in disbelief. Shari just moves past him . . . wait, no, now he is missing his member; he faints.

"Where are you going, you stupid bitch?" the soldier who was thrusting the woman asks her as she flees Shari's path.

The man only makes it to his knees before 74, 78. She cuts off both of his arms but is not finished. 100. She chops off the man's still swollen member, then picks it up off the floor and shoves it in his mouth, which is open, screaming in pain. 51. She impales his throat with her short sword, leaving it there so he can choke on his own manhood as he dies. Shari turns to the last soldier, who has yet to move.

"Where is Ki'ra?" she asks him with no anger evident in her tone.

I think that somehow made the question scarier. She doesn't have time to ask twice.

"Where he is now, I don't know, but in a week's time he will be leaving. Ap . . . apparently, he has some information to share with the king that can't be passed through letter or messenger. He's headed to Dragon Rock and will be leaving via horse through the northern gate at high noon . . . in . . . in a week. That's all I know. Please let me live," the man says, quivering.

"Go," Shari tells him simply.

He bolts up, eager to flee Shari, but only makes it halfway before she throws her longsword at him. It pierces the back of his skull and comes out of his mouth.

"Why did you tell him to go if you were just going to kill him?" I shout; something about all the violence unnerves me.

"I was going to let him go, but then my eyes fell on her . . ." she points behind me to the naked woman hugging her knees in fear over in the corner ". . . and I got angry all over again. Besides, you and I both remember what happened the last time I let people live."

That takes the anger right out of me. I'm grateful she didn't mention the fact that it was me who told her not to kill anyone last time. I don't care how violent Shari is; I don't want to lose her.

"Everything is alright now," Shari says, approaching the woman.

No, she is no woman; she's probably only sixteen. Her body is developed for her age, any age really, but her baby face gives her away. The girl pushes herself farther back into the corner, trying to flee Shari. After what she just saw, I can't blame her.

"Shari, you're frightening her. Step back," I say softly.

"Frightening her? I just saved her from—" Her words fall short when she notices the girl is shedding tears but is too scared to make a sound.

Shari backs up like a wounded dog. She was just trying to help.

"It's alright," I tell the girl, approaching slowly. "We mean you no harm." I kneel before her to make myself seem less a threat.

That's when I notice the girl has no blood on her except that leaking from between her legs. These bastards, how could they? This girl was still a maiden. Shari did right. They got what they deserved. I do my best to rein in my anger.

"What's your name?" I ask her in my best soothing voice.

"Stacey," she answers in a voice that cracks my heart.

"Where is your family, Stacey? We will return you to them."

Stacey's tears stop, and her face grows cold. Did I do something wrong?

"My father was long gone before I was born, and my mother just sold my virginity to these men for a good fuck from one of their number. I have no family."

Shit. I turn to Shari for answers but instead find a look of jealousy. What did I do now?

"Shari, can you go find her some clothing, please?"

Shari's eyes go wide in disbelief before she goes down the stairs, slamming the door downstairs behind her.

"How would you like us to help you, Stacey?" I ask, directing the attention back her way. Instead of answering my question, she asks one of her own.

"Was that your woman you just sent to find clothes for me?"

"Yes, how'd you know?" I ask curiously.

She eyes me like the answer is obvious. "You saw the look of jealousy on her face as well as I did," she says, like that explains it all.

"Yes, but what I don't know is why," I say offhandedly.

"Uh," she utters in disbelief, "maybe because you're kneeling right in front of a naked eighteen-year-old girl and sent her off to go get some clothes after we both saw you look between my legs."

Stacey's explanation hits me like lightning. Only now do I realize how attractive Stacey really is. She is fair complected like Latrice, but has Shari's height and build. Her eyes are hazel, and her hair is golden like my mother's. Stacey's curvy figure is currently naked in front of me, even if it is curled up in a corner.

"I'm sorry, I did not realize," I fumble for words. "I only looked because you were bleeding," I say, averting my eyes from her and turning my body in a complete 180 while still remaining on a knee.

There is a moment of awkward silence before she speaks.

"I almost forgot, I've been bleeding down there since they began this morning. It hurt at first, but those two men you saw sharing me were the last to have me. You have no reason to apologize to me. I woke up a virgin, but now I am nothing but a common whore."

"You are not a whore!" I shout. "We do not let these people dictate what we are or what we are not! Your life is your own!" I continue to shout, standing and turning to face Stacey.

She cringes back from me in fear. Shit.

"I'm sorry, I didn't mean to scare you . . . I am just tired of the King's Hand abusing people's freedom. You have no reason to fear me and every reason to continue to pursue your dreams. We cannot let them win. You cannot let them win," I finish, spinning back to look away from her.

My head is in the palm of my hand when I feel a light tap on my shoulder from behind me, from Stacey.

"Yes?" I ask, hesitantly, turning to face her again. As soon as I complete the turn, she hugs me with what I imagine a bear's grip feels like. I barely managed to drop my shield before she hugged me.

"Thank you for your words. I've never been told something so kind," she says, crying harder than when Shari was approaching her, finally allowing the gravity of the situation to set in.

Her emotions swarm her and her crying intensifies. I am at a loss for what to do. There is a very attractive, naked blond girl hugging me, seeking comfort, who has just had her maiden hand stolen by eleven men. I settle her, simply patting her head. Her breasts are bulging into me, making me slightly uncomfort—

"I'm sure you just said something to make her fall head over heels for you, Princeling, but it is time we depart," Shari says, appearing out of nowhere behind me, causing Stacey to push off me and go back to the corner in fear, which serves to further aggravate Shari.

Shari tosses Stacey a brown traveler's cloak, then turns to leave again. I hope Shari knows I love her, because I am about to make her very angry.

"Shari, we can't just leave Stacey." Shari freezes in her tracks.

"And why not? . . . Princeling." She puts emphasis on the last word, spitting it with venom.

"Because Stacey is lost." The words ring true to Shari.

I can tell because compassion just replaced the anger on her face. But the compassion too is quickly replaced; hurt takes its place.

"It appears she is . . . very much like my heart right now," she says, sounding betrayed.

"Shari—"

She cuts me off. "Not now, Princeling, we have to go before it gets too late. Bring the stray."

With that, Shari disappears back down the stairs. Shit. She's calling me Princeling again. I hope I can fix this. I turn back to Stacey, who has put on the brown traveler's cloak, which comes just past her knees. The hood is up and her hair is tucked back into it.

"Are you sure about this?" Stacey asks, sounding worried about her safety.

"As sure as I'll ever be. Shari will not harm you, but she will not be happy with me either." Stacey nods, then abruptly takes my hand in hers.

I look confused at her hand in mine, then up to her.

"Please," she pleads. "It's not like that . . . you just . . . make me feel safe."

I surrender what fight I have left, allowing it. "Let's go," I say, knowing this will hurt Shari even more.

If Shari sees me holding Stacey's hand, which I'm sure she does, she doesn't let on. She just continues to lead us back through the night to the Pale Horse. It's a lot easier trailing her this time around, even with Stacey holding my hand, because there is a lot less traffic in Altissia at night. But even this would be considered a busy day in Last Stop.

We make it back to the Pale Horse, which I see Shari enter. About five seconds later, I follow with Stacey in hand. When I enter, I am shocked, yet again, by what I see. Straight ahead of me is a long marble counter centered in the room, behind which sit the biggest alcohol barrels I've ever seen. They are made of expensive-looking wood and are lined up, side by side, ten feet off the ground. There is a man cleaning glasses with a white cloth behind the counter. To either side of this main feature rest staircases which go to the next level where another drinking room is stationed. And all around the edges of both this floor and the second are stools and islands placed so people can drink and converse as they do. They even have booths, twice the size of the ones in Latrice's inn, in which parties may talk privately. And it is in one of these booths, on the second floor, I spot Latrice talking with someone.

From my vantage point, I can only see the person's silhouette. Shari is already en route to Latrice. Not knowing what else to do, I follow, pulling Stacey after me. As I walk up the stairs to my right, the man with Latrice gets up to take his leave, exiting on the opposite stairwell from Shari and me.

He is young, maybe five years my senior, and powerfully built. His skin is the color of mine, but his eyes are dark cold blue, like deep water. He has short curls, like my hair used to be, but they are blond. He wears a green-and-brown military-looking uniform of some sort with a farmer's hat hanging on his back from a string around his neck.

Our eyes meet for a split second, and when they do, I know fear. The power he radiates is terrifying. Ki'ra compared to this man is a drop of water in the ocean, and this man is the ocean. This is not the first time I've felt power like this, but I can't recall where or why I know this feeling. Shit. How can such power exist? To make things even worse, I realize that my father is still stronger. The man doesn't stop to talk to anyone on the way out; he just simply takes his leave. Why was Latrice talking to him? This can't be good.

I approach the booth with Stacey, moving to let her take the inside seat, and we sit across from Shari and Latrice. Their stares and silence are making things really awkward.

"You said that man bought us a room? What number?" Shari asks Latrice.

Why did that man buy us a room?

"214," Latrice answers.

"I will go buy one close to it. I need to be alone right now," Shari tells Latrice before kissing her on the lips and departing without so much as a glance my way.

"Who was that man?" I ask Latrice in anger, not at her but at Shari for acting the way she is.

I would never betray her love. She should know this.

"Who is the girl?" Latrice counters defensively, like hers is the more important question.

Stacey leans over to me, hood still on, and whispers a question of her own in my ear.

"You said the other one was your woman, so why does this one give off a jealous air as well?"

"What did she just say?" Latrice asks, ready to go off.

Stacey may fear Shari, but she does not fear Latrice.

"My name is Stacey, and I wanted to know, if Shari is his woman, why do you sound jealous?" Stacey asks, removing her hood in challenge.

Wrong move.

"I will answer that when you tell me why I can smell your sex from here and why it smells like a burning fire," Latrice shoots right back, not one to back down.

Stacey laughs once, the way someone hurt does, then licks the top row of her teeth, closing her eyes. Tears begin to roll freely behind her closed eyes, and she begins to shake.

"I will go. I appreciate your kindness," she says, looking to me, "but I can tell I am unwanted company," she finishes, standing and trying to leave.

I place my hand before her to bar her path. "Stacey, please sit. If we can't figure this out, I will leave with you until I can assure your safety," I say as politely as I can.

I can tell she doesn't want to, but something in my voice makes her sit. Shari and Latrice are being extremely rude. This is not who they are. I refuse to accept this.

"May I answer Latrice's question?" I ask Stacey for her permission.

She simply nods, uncaringly.

"Shari and I found Stacey being raped by eleven soldiers in a hideout of some sort. By the time we arrived, the last two were taking turns with her. Stacey's mother sold Stacey's virginity this morning for a good . . . what was the word? Oh yes, fuck . . . for a good fuck from one of the soldiers. Do you feel better knowing the answer now, Latrice?"

Latrice's eyes are wide with shock, then soften in compassion.

"Now answer her question, Latrice," I say coldly.

"I had no idea, Stacey, please forgive my rudeness," Latrice says, sounding truly sorry.

"All is forgiven. Please don't think about it," Stacey says, sounding defeated.

"Answer her question, Latrice," I push.

Stacey will not be the only one whose business is out there.

Latrice sighs. "I fell in love with the man sitting next to you at a time when Shari was not around. His heart still belonged to Shari, so I held myself back for a while, and just when things looked like they were about to go my way, Shari popped up out of thin air. He is a good man, as I am sure you no doubt already know, and although he is Shari's and Shari is his . . . he still holds my heart, so I can't help but be jealous, especially when he shows up with someone as beautiful as you," Latrice finishes, smiling at Stacey.

"Thank you, Latrice," Stacey says.

"Well, if that's the case, if you and Shari saved Stacey together, why is Shari so upset?" Latrice asks me, not understanding.

Stacey answers, "Shari did the saving, and because she probably had so much adrenaline rushing after killing eleven men, when her man here—" she flicks her head my way "—kneeled before my naked body, staring at the blood between my legs, and asked her to leave to find me clothes, she couldn't properly rationalize the situation. Also, when she came back, I was hugging him for telling me not to give up and let . . . let them win and for reminding me my life was my own. I'm sure that didn't help."

"Well you're an honest one . . ." Latrice says to Stacey. She continues, "And you may be a good man, but you're not a bright one, at least not when it comes to women."

"I kind of picked up on that about him too. That same innocence is why I feel safe around him," Stacey tells Latrice.

"Well, you're in line behind me," Latrice jokes.

"No, it's not like that. I don't think I ever want to be touched by a man or his member ever again," Stacey explains, sounding disgusted.

"Really?" Latrice asks, amused.

"Then why are you still holding his hand?" Latrice follows up.

Stacey blushes, quickly releasing my hand under the table. "He is different. It was comforting me through the pain," Stacey mumbles, embarrassed.

"I only kid, Stacey. If you are going to join us, you better get used to it. I do my best to make him and Shari blush at least once a day," Latrice informs Stacey.

"You can make Shari blush?" Stacey asks in wonder.

All she knows about Shari is the fact that she is a killer, a very good one at that.

"Like you wouldn't believe. Shari may be a little violent, but she is as good of a person as the man you sit next to," Latrice says lightly.

Stacey takes a moment to process that statement, then asks, "And who is the man I sit next to?" looking to me.

I look to Latrice, unsure how I should answer.

"His name is Luca, darling, but do us a favor and call him Beau in public please," Latrice answers for me, deciding we can trust this girl. Stacey simply nods.

"Now who was the man you were talking to? I'll have you know he is very dangerous. The power he gives off makes Ki'ra seem laughable by comparison," I tell Latrice, not having forgotten about the man.

"That's funny. He said the same thing about you. Except he said that even the king would fear your power if he found out," Latrice replies.

Stacey stares at me, wide-eyed, wondering what she just got herself into.

"He also called you a fool for not masking such power," she adds, cocking her head to the side.

What's that supposed to mean? Why would he say that about me? I couldn't best my father even if there was ten of me and one of him.

"Who is he?" I decide to ask again.

"His name is Donte, and he was kind enough to pay for the most expensive room here, not just for me, but us," Latrice informs me, which does little to satisfy me.

"Is that all you're going to tell him?" Stacey pipes up from beside me.

"What else is there to tell? He saw me break a man's arm at a tavern, then decided to pursue me and ask me on a date. He also warned me that you and Shari give off dangerous auras, but I knew that already, so—"

"So you don't know either," Stacey cuts Latrice off.

"Know what?" Latrice and I ask together in annoyance.

"That man, Donte also goes by the name of Storm, and he is the king's strongest general. Some say he can even summon dragons." Stacey's voice trails off with the last.

I eye Latrice, who eyes me back, looking conflicted, then drops her head to look at the table as she speaks. "He is a good man. When we talked, I felt like I was talking to another version of you."

"Latrice, he is my father's right hand," I say simply, like that clears everything up.

"I know, but he is not your father. He is kind and caring, and he listens," she argues softly.

"Latrice, what did you tell him?" I almost shout.

"Nothing!" she does shout. "Am I all of a sudden dumb?" she hisses at me, bringing her voice back down.

"That is not what I—"

She waves her hand at me, cutting me off. "I know, I'm just in my feelings a bit. Besides his warning, we talked about simple matters. I assure you, though, he is not a danger, at least not yet. When he warned me about you, I told him you were my home, my family, to which he replied, 'Then get him as far away from the king as possible.' He knows you can touch the power and did nothing."

While that is worth thinking on, it is not enough for me to risk our home.

"When are you supposed to go on this date?" I decide to ask.

"He never gave me a day. He just said he'd be sure to see me again. He has to leave Altissia soon. He also confirmed that there are no other generals aside from Ki'ra, who he seemed to dislike, currently here," Latrice replies.

"You play a dangerous game, getting information like that," I warn.

"Was I wrong about you?" Latrice asked me, tired of being second-guessed.

"No," I say, uncertain about what she is getting at.

"Then trust me, Luca, he is a good man." With that, she stands, irritated.

"I am going to find Shari and do some damage control for you. Take Stacey to our room, number 214, and get some rest. Stacey, behave yourself. Shari is a good woman, but if you attempt to do anything with Luca, even the one true God will not save you," Latrice enlightens Stacey and me.

Stacey gulps in fear and grabs my hand again, already terrified of Shari. Latrice takes her leave to go find Shari.

"Shall we?" I ask Stacey. She looks like it's the last thing she wants to do with that warning fresh on her mind, but she nods her consent.

We exit the booth and move back to where the stairs are located on the sides of the drinking area on the second floor. There are two hallways with purple carpets adorning the floor that leads to the back. I choose the hallway on the right, going with my intuition. We move down the hallway, passing doors with golden numbers on them, and I am rewarded for my choice. The first door we pass is numbered 208 and the next 209, steadily increasing the further we move down the hall, until we come upon the last door, which ends the hallway, numbered 214. I look at Stacey, shrug my shoulders, and then walk in, pulling her behind me.

A massive bed with see-through white drapes around it is the first thing I see. The bed is large enough for ten people to sleep in without touching each other. I look up because the room is well lit despite the fact that I don't see any lights above me. Embedded in the ceiling is a large glass panel which allows either sunlight or moonlight to filter in, never allowing the room to truly get dark. Right now, the room looks amazing in starlight. There is a fireplace to my left and walk-in pool to my far right, again, big enough for ten people. On the far side of the pool rests a door, presumably the bathroom, and over by the fireplace sit multiple cabinets and dressers. Oh yes, and the floor is white carpet. All in all, this is the fanciest room I've seen outside of my father's castle.

"A little bit of luxury after what you've been through is deserved, right?" I say, smiling at Stacey.

"I want to take a bath," is the first thing she says.

"I think that's the bathroom," I point to the door beyond the pool. She drops my hand and walks around the pool to the other door. I move to the bed so I can relax.

"Um, there's a toilet, a sink, and a huge mirror in here, but no bath," Stacey shouts.

I look around but do not see another door. Stacey must have already done the same because she simply says, "Oh well, it's not like you haven't already seen everything worth seeing," before removing her brown cloak, underneath which she is completely naked.

At second take, Shari's body is curvier and more defined, but Stacey's is still magnificent. Stacey walks into the pool until her head is the only thing above water.

"The water is heated," Stacey says, sounding surprised. "This feels nice."

I definitely want to try out the pool, but not today, or around Stacey. I told her I would assure her safety, but if Shari came in while a naked Stacey and I were bathing together, I don't believe Stacey would survive the experience.

"Take your time, enjoy yourself. I will not watch," I say, lying on the bed and looking up into the stars through the glass sheet.

"Are you a prince?" Stacey asks out of nowhere, somewhat alarming me.

"Why do you ask that?" I counter, on guard.

"Well, Shari called you Princeling quite a few times."

Shit, Shari needs to control her emotions better.

"Yeah, you could say that," I answer cryptically.

"So which of the kingdoms do you come from and why are you here?" Stacey asks curiously.

"What makes you believe I'm foreign?" I ask her, deciding this route is the easiest.

"Because if you were the prince of this kingdom, that would make you the king's son, and you're nothing like the evil bastard and . . ."

I know what she's about to add. I'm starting to enjoy what I'm about to do.

". . . I've heard a rumor that the prince's eyes look like—"

"Like this?" I cut her off, sitting up and allowing my eyes to return to their original vortex as I look at her. Stacey gasps in shock. Yep, it never gets old.

"You can't be—" Stacey begins, but loses her voice to tears.

Shit.

"I am, but I am not my father. You know me for who I am despite my eye colors," I tell Stacey, allowing my eyes to change back into green orbs.

I remain silent to give her time to process.

"You trust me?" she asks after a moment, like that wasn't already obvious.

"If I didn't, you wouldn't know my name or what my eyes truly look like," I explain. "Why?" I ask.

She is definitely contemplating something. "You trust me, so I will trust you," she says, backing out of the water so only her head, breasts, and stomach are exposed.

What can she possibly trust me with that is equivalent to what I just shared with her? I am about to turn my head away from her naked top half when I feel power begin to radiate in waves from Stacey. Wings of fire spring to life behind Stacey's back, but it is a golden fire, and the wings are large yet peaceful. They don't burn anything around them or rage like a normal fire. It almost looks as if the golden flame is liquid. Stacey stands there, golden hair clinging to her wet form, breasts bare, and large golden wings of fire at her back. She looks like a goddess. Abruptly, the wings go out, and she steps back into the pool, neck deep, her face a mask of fear. I stand from the bed, amazed, and walk over to the pool and kneel.

"Why are you scared, Stacey," I ask in concern, trying to hide my excitement.

If I was her, I would be bragging.

"I have never shown anyone that before, I know the king has people killed for that. I didn't know how you were going to respond," Stacey tells me with her head down, looking into the water.

"Stacey, that was amazing." I let my excitement overtake my voice. "Which power can you touch?" I ask, hoping I can learn how to do that too. She looks up, smiling.

"I don't know. I've never had a teacher to explain such things. All I know is I can do some stuff other people can't. It's not like I could have shown my mother because . . . well, you understand what type of person she is," Stacey explains.

"Can you fly?" I ask, still excited.

"Not sure. I've never had anywhere to try where I wouldn't be seen," she answers. So many mysteries.

"Can you shoot fire or lightning? Or make the earth quake beneath people?" I ask, trying to figure out which power she touches.

"Probably, if I tried, but I've never been fond of violence, so I've never tried," she says, honestly giving it thought.

"Did that make you tired?" I ask, trying to gauge her power since I can't feel it by simply looking at her, as with Storm or Donte, whatever you want to call him.

"Yes, as a matter of fact, it did," she says, having just realized it herself.

She turns from me, then walks out of the pool, bottom jiggling as she walks, and puts on her brown cloak. Now decent, Stacey walks past me and over to the bed. She stares at it for a moment before jumping into it like it is also water.

She is enjoying herself, or at least trying to. I can only imagine what it's like inside her head right now.

She crawls to the edge of the bed nearest me, then asks, "Will you hold my hand while I sleep?"

I would have said no, but the look on her face is not one of desire. It is a mixture of fear and embarrassment.

"Sure," I say lightly.

I walk over to her and sit on the floor near enough to where she can hold my hand and be comfortable. She takes my hand without looking at me, then lies on her side facing me; before I know it, she is sleeping. To fall asleep so fast, she must have been exhausted. I told myself I was going to stay awake in case Shari decided to come in, but I lied. I fall asleep minutes after Stacey, still sitting upright, holding her hand.

18 APOLOGIES

There is a barely audible click from the doorknob, causing my eyes to shoot open. Stacey is still asleep, but I watch the door swing open silently to reveal Shari. Shari takes in the situation. I had enough time to drop Stacey's hand but chose not to. If Shari is offended that I'm sitting on the floor holding this girl's hand while she sleeps, in comfort, after all that happened to her yesterday, then she can stay offended.

Through the ceiling glass, I can tell it is near sunrise. I can clearly see the hurt on Shari's face and tell that she is contemplating something. Eventually she nods her head to me asking to speak to me outside. Only then do I drop Stacey's hand, who remains sleeping, and follow Shari so we can talk.

She leads me down the hallway, down the stairs, and outside of the Pale Horse. When we make it outside, I stop so we can talk, but she doesn't; she just continues to walk, so I continue to follow her. Growing tired of her game quickly, I catch up to her and grab her hand, spinning her to face me.

"What do you want to talk about, Shari?" I ask in a low voice, even though there aren't many people out right now.

Shari hasn't let go of my hand even though she refuses to meet my eyes, choosing the ground as the more interesting view. Her grip tightening on my hand is my only clue she is about to speak.

"I am sorry, my love," she whispers with tears in her eyes.

Why do I suddenly feel bad? Shit. I don't want to say this but I must.

"My love? All of a sudden, I'm 'my love' again? What happened to Princeling? Either you love me or don't," I reply, feeling guilty for the last statement. I know she loves me.

Shari flinches and lets go of my hand. The tears in her eyes begin to flow as she stares at the ground, crying silently. She needed to hear that, at least that's what I tell myself as I grab her hand again. As she looks up into my eyes, I allow them to change back into their original colors.

"There is not a shadow of a doubt in my mind that you love me; now prove me right," I echo her own words back to her so she knows I feel the same. Her body tenses with recognition. "My love for you is unconditional, Shari. I would die before I betrayed you, so please stop being jealous," I say softly but seriously.

She nods her understanding. "It is not that simple," she whispers.

"And why is that?" I question.

"First of all, you've seen Stacey. She's drop-dead beautiful and has the body to match. Secondly, I love everything about you, so when I see you talking with any other female, no matter your intentions, I can't help but covet your attention. I even still feel that way about Latrice sometimes. Thirdly, you're so kind and honest-hearted that you don't even know when you're hurting me. Your pure intentions make my jealousy sting worse," Shari explains, then sighs deeply. "Latrice was right," Shari adds.

"Latrice was right?" I repeat questioningly. "Did she tell you I was in the right this time?" I ask hopefully, knowing it doesn't sound like something Latrice would say.

"No, she said you were stupid," Shari says, pausing, letting the statement linger.

Well damn, that hurt. As if reading my thoughts, she continues, "But stupid in a way that makes us love you for it, and you simply can't help it because it's who you are." She sounds defeated.

Backtracking in my head a little, "Yes, I have seen Stacey, and, yes, she is, as you say, drop-dead beautiful, but I have also seen you." I delicately grab her chin, then continue, "I have not only seen you, but I've fought you, listened to you, felt you, and been in you, and you know what all those things make clear, Shari? The fact that I am in love with you and no one else," I finish.

The tears are still in her eyes, but they have stopped flowing. Shari leans up and kisses me. It is a slow kiss that I allow her to guide, reacting to her need as she demands it.

She finally separates her lips from mine, then speaks. "I know it won't make much sense to you, but I only act this way because I love you," she concedes.

She's right: that makes no sense. Get mad at me for being the me you love? I don't comment on it. Instead, I ask another question.

"After all this time, you're still jealous of Latrice? Why? She has been nothing but respectful, and she is now our family," I say, not understanding.

"That is why, my love. You see how you just came to her defense? I want that for nobody from you except me. You're right, though, Latrice is different. She owns a piece of you I will never get back. However, I want her to keep it because she deserves it, even if it does sometimes still make me jealous," she explains.

"So did you used to get jealous of my mother?" I ask, honestly curious.

"Never, and for more than one reason. If it wasn't for her, I wouldn't have gotten a chance to experience you and your love. Also, that woman holds a piece of me always and is the only other person I love in equal measure to you, well, almost equal," she says, then pecks me on the lips.

Good answer, I think to myself. I don't know what I would do if Shari was jealous of my mother.

"I asked Latrice if you and I could go on a date and she said yes," Shari says so quietly that I almost don't hear her.

"A date?" I repeat.

"Yes, a date. Ever since we found each other, things have been wound tight and all we've had time to do is make love, train, and sleep together. Don't get me wrong, I love all of that, especially making love, but I just want to spend some time together like a normal couple," Shari explains to me, embarrassed but sounding in need.

"I would love to," I say the first thing that comes to mind.

Shari hugs me tight and lets out a squeal of joy. Shari is so dangerous, sometimes I forget she is really a soft person.

"Don't worry, Latrice will watch over Stacey, and we already have all the information we came for," Shari says, reading my mind.

Stacey. Shit.

"Shari, Stacey can use the power, and she's quite strong in it," I tell her. Shari's eyes widen and her face turns serious.

"Are you worried about it causing any problems?" she asks.

"No," I reply quickly.

"Good, then we will go on a date," she says happily, linking her arm in mine.

"Now where to?" she says, more to herself than to me.

The sun reveals itself over the city wall, and more people begin to flood the streets.

"Ah yes, the Crystal Gardens," Shari says, pulling me in some seemingly random direction.

"What is the Crystal Gardens?" I ask.

"Not sure, I've never been. But the name is enticing, no?"

She's right, the name is enticing, but more importantly, I feel like Shari is getting the chance to be the girl she never got to be, and I'm glad I could be here for it for her.

I stop, causing her to stop walking as well.

"What's wrong, my love?" she asks worriedly.

"You said we are going on a date, right?" I ask knowingly.

She just nods at the obvious question.

"Then we will find a tailor first so we can look the part on our first date."

I smile. I can see the love in her eyes. Shari wants me right now. She will just have to wait. Today is going to be a good day.

"I will pick your outfit and you will pick mine. That is not up for debate," I tell her.

She just smiles.

"What a wonderful idea; let's go." She pulls me off in a different, seemingly random, direction this time.

We move through the busy city of Altissia, nothing more than two people in love, about to go on their first date. The experience is freeing. I laugh with Shari about many of the same things I see now that at first had me overwhelmed. I am enjoying just spending time with Shari with no agenda to rush us. I can't wait until this becomes a permanent part of our daily lives.

"Did you know I like flowers?" Shari asks me. I didn't.

"I do now. Which is your favorite type? I want to know that too," I say.

"Daisies," she says simply.

"Is there a reason why?" I ask, wanting to know that too. "Your mother's eyes. Every time I see a daisy, it reminds me of her eyes, and I love that woman. Not like you. It is more and it is less. Hard to explain really," she explains.

"My eyes are partly yellow too," I jest. She hits me on the chest.

"Don't be selfish. I am already yours." . . . Did she just . . .

"Did you just tell me—?"

She cuts me off. "Sssshhh. If it makes you feel better, if I lost her, I would be hurt beyond words, but you, you I could not live without."

I ponder her words for a second before—

"We're here, my love," Shari says to me excitedly. I look in front of me to find an all-black building with no sign to give its name. Instead, there is only a picture of a white mask that only goes around the eyes above the door. There are also no windows. I don't like it.

"Are you sure this is the place?" I ask cautiously.

"Positive," she says joyfully before pulling me through the door.

Inside, we are greeted by a woman in a mask depicting some type of animal. Behind the mask rests straight, long blond hair and smooth skin that is the color of dark chocolate. Ice-blue eyes stare at us through the mask.

"How may this one have the pleasure of helping you today?" the mysterious woman asks mysteriously.

"This one?" I repeat, trying to figure out her game.

Shari swats at me. "She is in character for her job. Don't be rude," Shari says, like I was supposed to know that.

"Thank you, mistress. To what does the mask owe the pleasure of your experience?" the woman in the mask asks Shari and not me.

"Who or what is the mask?" I ask them both.

"I'm sorry, he can be quite slow at times," Shari apologizes for me.

"The mask is the shop we are currently in, and they call it so because . . . look around . . . by the time you leave, those who knew you will not recognize you," Shari says to me.

I look around for the first time and am amazed by the sheer amount of clothes I see. I touch a simple-looking shirt at random; silk. Even the basic clothes here are anything but. There are racks of clothes everywhere in this shop. I can't even begin to work out the groupings or sections. How am I supposed to find anything in here?

"We are going on our first date and want to look the part. However, he will be choosing my clothes and I will be choosing his," Shari tells the masked woman.

"I like the way you think, mistress," the masked woman says with what sounds like a smile.

"Actually, it was his idea," Shari tells her, pointing to me.

I can't tell if she is looking at me with a newfound respect or like I'm crazy. The mask disguises her features well. I guess that's the point.

"Follow me, mistress. I will be back to help you shortly, sir." The masked woman bows and bids Shari to follow her, which she does, leaving me alone in a vast maze of clothing.

Instead of becoming intimidated, I think about what I want Shari to wear on our date, because I'm sure they have it. Let's see, Shari needs to feel like the beautiful woman she is. After all, she did say Stacey was drop-dead beautiful. Has she seen herself?

So, a dress, but a more feminine one than the black one Latrice bought; something delicate. I walk among the clothes, not knowing where I should be looking, but I know I'm in the wrong spot when I see a clown suit. Would Shari look good in that? Probably. I hear the masked woman's footsteps a couple of seconds before she tries to surprise me.

"Why are you looking at that?" she asks, sounding offended.

"If I'm being honest, I'm lost," I tell her simply.

"Do you know what you have in mind?" she asks me.

"A dress. A delicate one." I think she smiles under the mask. "Please, follow me," she says with approval in her voice.

Yeah, she definitely smiled.

She takes me to what seems like the opposite side of the shop that I was looking at and passes through a revolving mirror. Hesitantly, I follow.

"You do not strike me as a thief. That is why I brought you back here. Now come up here," the masked woman says from atop a shadowing staircase I almost didn't see amidst the stacks of clothing piles on the floor of this back room.

I go up the stairs, taking two at a time, and reach the top with nothing but my chauffeur's hand telling me to stop. Soon, that disappears too. A moment later, a bright light cuts on, revealing the masked woman. Behind her there are ten of the most beautiful dresses I've ever seen. Period. She waves her hand at them.

"Take your time. Feel your woman's personality in the dress before you choose. I shall return after I help your partner," she warns before disappearing down the stairs and out the revolving mirror.

I approach the dresses. How do I know which one to choose? They're all stunning. After some time, I narrow my decision to two dresses. One is golden like my mother's eyes and has a black pattern that dances aggressively yet delicately on both sides. Aggressive and delicate is definitely Shari's personality, but the other one is red, like her hair, and dangerously short. The top of the dress goes over her breast and thins into a loop that starts just over one breast, crosses her body, going up and around her neck, and then back down, crossing back over to cover the other breast. Her shoulders and upper and mid back will be exposed. The bottom of the dress ties in the back just where her back starts to arch above her bottom.

The other dress may be her personality, but Shari is aggressive because of necessity. This dress depicts who she would have been and still wants to be. I hear the revolving mirror turn, and my guide comes up the stairs and stands behind me.

"You love her," the masked woman says.

"Yes, I do," I reply.

"That was not a question. It was a statement," she tells me.

"How did you know?" I ask curiously.

"I've spent some time talking to her. She does not see herself for the beauty she is. I think she believes she is evil or something. This dress will make her uncomfortable and feel vulnerable, but that is exactly what she needs right now," the masked woman tells me, affirming my decision.

I take the dress and hand it to her.

"Permission to do her hair and add underwear that will make her equally uncomfortable?" she asks in thought.

I just nod my consent.

"This may be expensive, but today is a day you will never forget," she says, moving down the stairs. She gets about halfway, then stops. "You are a good man," she adds, not waiting for a response and disappearing out the revolving mirror.

I follow, then head to the front of the shop to wait. About half an hour later, the woman in the mask returns with a bundle of clothes.

"Here. This is for you. Go put them on in there," she says, pointing to a door.

"Is Shari ready?" I ask.

"Not quite. She is having confidence issues right now, but I will take care of that. Then I must do her hair. Never rush a woman. Now, go," she commands me before going back in the direction I saw her take Shari.

Alright, I guess I'll go get dressed.

The room she sent me to is more like a large closet with a body mirror in it and nothing else. Ready to get this over with, I strip naked, then pick up the bundle of clothing. Shari, you devil. No—more like my personal angel. She chose clothing fit for a prince—at least a foreign prince, but a prince nonetheless. I put my legs into an all-white, silk, one piece that has red cuffs on the pant legs and red trimming where my sleeves would start if this one piece had them. She wants me to show off my arms. I'm up for it.

Gold buttons clamp up the middle of the one piece, starting at my pelvis, going up to my neck. I leave the top one undone, showing off the top of my iron-forged chest. I guess she wants to showcase my body. I will not go against her wishes. The only thing left on the floor are some expensive-looking white slip-on shoes that either gender could wear. I just realize she didn't give me underwear. Okay, maybe Shari is part devil, the seductive kind. I smile.

Challenge accepted.

Putting on the slides, then looking into the mirror, I am reminded of a time when Shari and I did not know each other as we do now, back when our lives were a lot easier. We have some good memories, but I do not wish to return to a time where I did not experience her love, even if it was because of my own foolishness.

Leaving my old clothes in the room, I exit and make my way back to the front. I wait, anxious and impatient, for Shari to appear, but instead, the masked female comes from the back and approaches me.

"Oh my," she lets out.

"What?" I ask in concern, looking over the clothing to make sure I have not damaged it.

"Nothing. Shari is a lucky girl. The clothing looks as if it were made for you specifically."

Oh, I thought something was wrong. "Thank you, but where is Shari? Is she ready?" I ask, concerned.

"Oh, she's ready, but she will not come out. She is as we discussed, uncomfortable," the lady in the mask tells me.

"How . . . How does she look?" I ask.

This time I definitely see her smile through the mask.

"Come see for yourself." She leads me in the direction she took Shari in until we approach a red curtain.

She then places her finger on her lips, telling me to be quiet before she disappears to give us privacy. I look at the curtain and my heart races. I am not a sheep I tell myself before I quickly part the curtain and slip through.

"Do not—" Shari starts while staring at me through a body mirror, but the rest falls on deaf ears when I see her.

She slowly lowers her head in the mirror to look at the floor when she sees I am not hearing anything she is saying. She is embarrassed. Why? The red dress hugs her body like a second skin and is indeed dangerously short. She's tugging it down as I look. For the dress to be so tight, I don't see underwear lines. The masked lady did say she got her underwear too, right? Shari's back, shoulders, and belly button are exposed. I didn't notice the small hole there until now. I look at her face through the mirror, and while she still looks down, her hair captivates me.

It is pulled back into a ponytail, but the ponytail is not loose. It is somehow bound into individual balls, and because of her hair's curly nature, the ponytail is beginning to spiral and rest in front of her left shoulder.

She looks beautiful, soft, and delicate. I move to hug her from behind.

"Stop!" she yells at me, freezing me in my tracks.

Her face has not looked up from the floor.

"Are you okay?" I ask, confused and concerned.

"I . . . I cannot do this," she says, voice cracking. Is she about to cry?

"Shari, talk to me. What's wrong? What can't you do?" I ask, trying to console her.

"This!" she shouts, turning to look at me. Tears are building in her eyes. "You want me to be something I'm not. I feel so fragile and so exposed. How can I fight like this? Everyone will see everything. I can't take two steps without this dress rising. The silk against my skin makes it feel like I'm naked . . . Please don't make me do this." Despite everything she said, I smile.

"Why are you smiling? This is not funny!" she yells.

I move too quickly for her to run, but I don't embrace her. I just take her hand. She tries to pull away. I tighten my grip.

"Don't run from me," I say softly. She stops tugging her hand but looks down. "I do not want you to be anything, Shari, except who you already are. You were robbed of the chance to experience being feminine, and so you fear it. But I know you, and there is a part of you who wants this, but you feel like you don't deserve it because of what life has forced you to become. You are wrong. You are every bit a flower as the next woman, more so than them all, to me, even if that flower is a rose," I explain to her. She laughs, barely holding back tears.

"I am not a flower," she says, but the fight in her is gone.

"Wrong again," I say, taking her chin and forcing her to look at me.

I let her see my true eyes. "You are *my* flower."

She just looks at me for a second before a tear finally falls. Then she wraps her arms around my neck and kisses me.

"I don't care how good you are with words, I still don't want to do this," she says, placing her head on my chest and pulling her dress down.

"I will not force you to do anything, but I will be with you through everything you choose to do," I say, trying to hide my disappointment.

Shari sighs, head still on my chest. "You can't hide your feelings from me, my love. Anyway, you should listen better. I said I don't *want* to, not I will not. I will do this, only because you are you and because you might be right," she informs me.

I tilt her head back with one hand and pull her waist against me with the other, then kiss her, tongue flowing in her mouth delicately. She allows this for about ten seconds before pushing me off her.

"You can't arouse me while I wear this underwear. I fear what will happen to them should I become too aroused," she tells me in warning.

I laugh, lightening the mood.

"Underwear. At least you have them," I spout back, still laughing.

Shari cocks her head to the side, then blushes.

"I forgot to pick some when I saw what the lady in the mask brought to me," she says apologetically.

"Don't worry, now we will both be uncomfortable," I say.

She just laughs.

"You are not slick either, Shari . . . Really, having me dress up like a prince?" I say, part in jest, part in reprimand.

She holds her dress down and walks over to me, then leans up to whisper in my ear. "It is your turn to be wrong, my love. I did not dress you up as a prince. I dressed you as my king."

She then pulls her face back and kisses me before slipping through the curtain. I'm conflicted by the thought; king I don't want to be. Her king, however, is a different matter entirely.

I slip through the curtain and find Shari waiting for me. I hold my arm out to her, and she slips hers through it as we walk back to the front where the masked lady waits.

"I trust everything is alright," the masked lady says to us.

"Better than alright. It's perfect," I reply.

"Thank you for all your help," Shari tells her.

"Believe it or not, you two did not need my help. You chose each other's outfits on your own. All I did was your hair, mistress, and find underwear to match the dress in appearance and comfortability, or lack of, in your case," she says, bowing her head.

"How much do we owe you?" I ask, not really caring because Shari's happiness is invaluable.

"It is on the house. I do not get to see such true love in my line of work. Most who come here are rich, in states of lust, or con artists. So I would be happy if beautiful people such as yourselves wore my family's work," she says, sounding grateful.

"So, if you did charge us, what would it cost?" I ask inquisitively.

"Six gold and some," she says knowingly.

I take ten gold out of my bag and place it in her hands. "To beautiful people," I say, pulling Shari out of the shop with me.

We step outside the shop, and I notice the air has taken up a cool breeze that feels great. I will no doubt be thankful for it when the sun heats up the city. Shari tightens her grip on my hand and continues to squeeze. I turn to face her, and her eyes are shut tight in what appears to be discomfort. But why is she blushing?

"We just talked about this, Shari. Relax. I'm here with you, and this is something you can do," I say, completely ignorant of the problem.

"I know I can and will; just give me a second," comes her reply through clenched teeth.

"What's wrong?" I ask.

"Do you have to know?" she asks, embarrassed. I don't, but I want to.

"Are we keeping secrets now?" I ask her in return.

She sighs, then puts my head down to her so she can whisper, "My underwear does not offer much protection from the chill wind coming up this dress, and it feels . . . conflicting between my legs."

I burst out in laughter, causing her to hit me in my stomach.

"That was not meant to be funny, my love," Shari says in reprimand.

"The Crystal Gardens await," I say, bowing before her and sweeping my arm toward the busy dirt roads.

"We are on a date, yes?" Shari asks me after a moment.

I nod the obvious answer.

"Then we will take our time. Walk with me, my love," Shari tells me, pulling down the bottom of her dress while locking arms with me.

"I am in no hurry. Let us make today as memorable as possible," I say to her with a smile.

She kisses me, then starts moving us through the crowd in a random direction.

Shari and I turn heads as we walk together through the city. People have even begun giving us a wide berth as we move through the crowd like we are royalty or something, but I hardly notice. We have been walking and talking for hours now, and I have not grown tired of it, nor do I think I ever could.

At first, Shari was wound tight, completely out of her element. But as we walked, I began to talk of old times in the palace and things I used to do purposefully to try to upset her. Laughter comes easy as she tells me stories of the same kind and we realize how hopelessly in love we've always been. At this moment, Shari is the woman she's always wanted to be, wearing a dress, hair done, out with a man she loves, on a date. I can't help but think, as I stare at her beautiful being, that I'm glad it was me she fell in love with. Shari could have any man she chooses, but sadly, she doesn't even know it.

I come back to my senses when I notice the people in the streets have completely disappeared. I feel them all, even though I can't see them.

"We are surrounded, my love," Shari says in a hurt voice that sounds like something in her just broke.

Shit. Not now. I can feel them and do not fear their number, but why now? Shari was doing so well. I feel her muscles tense just before she drops my arm.

"We know you are there. Your ambush or whatever this is has failed!" I shout down the road, looking in every alley and window and upon every roof. For a second, there is nothing. And then thirty men, all on the ground, move to surround us from all different directions, coming out of the alleyways. Of course, they are King's Hand soldiers, and they can wield the power.

"We don't know who you are, young man, but Ki'ra has issued a bounty for a girl's head matching *her* description, so get lost," one of the men shouts at me.

"Not a chance," I say without even thinking.

"I told you this was not for me," Shari says, in a low, saddened voice, staring at her dress.

Anger in me ignites like a flame as the men surrounding us close in, and thunder rumbles in my head. Just as I am about to unleash the storm's wrath, which I have no memory of summoning, I feel a power that stops me in my tracks, followed by a calm voice.

"If you value your lives, you will leave this alley and forget you ever saw them."

The voice comes from Donte or Storm, whatever you want to call him. He approaches from the opposite end of the alley we are on. I do not fear the thirty, but I fear this one.

"General Storm, sir, Ki'ra has issued a bounty on that girl's head, and we would see it collected, after we have some fun with her, of course. You're welcome to join."

Shari about lunges at the man, but I grab her wrist. We have no weapons, but that is not why I stopped her. Through her own anger, she missed Donte's. The only clue given was a spark of electricity in his eyes.

Yes, electricity in his eyes. So small, I think it went unnoticed by everyone except me. Donte walks right up to the man who spoke to him and whispers in his ear, causing him to go wide-eyed before stepping in the circle and addressing the others.

"Does General Ki'ra outrank me?" he asks the thirty men loudly to make sure he is heard.

"No, sir!" comes the answer in unison from every soldier.

"Then unless you wish to provoke my wrath, be gone."

They don't hesitate. The alley clears faster than a receding tide but does not return. I still don't trust this man. Shari, as if reading my thoughts, speaks for us both.

"If you are looking for a thanks, you will not get one. This seems like too big of a coincidence, Storm."

If he is offended, he doesn't let on.

"May I approach?" he asks, throwing me for a loop.

If he really wanted to, I doubt I could stop him. I tighten my grip on Shari's wrist for a second to let her know not to do anything.

"We couldn't stop you from approaching if you really wanted to, and you know that," I reply.

"That is not what I asked," he says calmly.

"Yes, you may approach," I say, heart thundering in my chest.

Does he know I can feel his power? He walks up to us, stopping about five feet away.

"My apologies for the King's Hand treatment. You will not be harassed anymore, as long as I am here. You have my word," he tells us in a friendly tone.

"What do you want, Storm?" Shari asks aggressively.

"Not as friendly as Latrice. I'm actually here to ask you permission to take her on a date." What? This man makes no sense.

"Latrice is grown, Storm. She can do as she pleases," Shari says when I take too long to reply.

"Yes, but I would rather not have your man, I presume, from how protective you two seem of each other, destroy Altissia because he thought I kidnapped her," he says matter-of-factly.

"Destroy Altissia? I would never do such a thing," I say, offended.

"And I think you believe that. Tell me, have you ever lost control?"

Is he talking about the power?

"That's possible?" I ask.

He cocks his head at me, trying to determine something.

"I see . . . yes, it is, but might I have a word in private?" he asks, eyes cutting to Shari.

I don't even look at her.

"Whatever you need to say, you can say in front of her," I tell him.

Shari grabs my hand and interlocks our fingers.

"I don't know who you are, but the king will find out about your power. For now, you are Latrice's family and therefore my friend, for lack of a better word. But should the king give me the order, and it's only a matter of time at this point, I will do what I must, even if it costs me my life."

He sounds like he regrets what he does, and his threat sounds like it brings him pain.

"You don't seem like a bad man, Donte, so why do you work for the king? I can feel your power. Surely you could make it on your own," I say, interested in the answer.

He shakes his head, giving a light, hollow laugh.

"Sometimes, you must play the hand life deals, but you did not answer my question. May I take Latrice on a date tonight?" he says cryptically before asking about Latrice again.

I want to say no but I remember what Latrice so casually threw in my face: "Was I wrong about you?"

"You have my permission," I say, "even though, as Shari said, Latrice is grown. But do not hurt her or—"

He cuts me off by turning away from me and waving his hand. "I don't wish to hurt her. Quite the opposite, I assure you. I also don't want to face you until I must. Have fun on your own date. You will be harassed no more," he says, walking off.

19 DATE NIGHT

Shari and I stand in the empty alleyway and watch as Donte walks off. He is an odd man, to say the least.

"I know I didn't treat him as such, but I believe Storm is a good man," Shari says, turning to me.

"And I believe you are right. However, you still look more beautiful than any sunrise, and you owe me a date. Can we pick up where we left off, please?" I ask Shari, trying to project need into my voice because I know she still needs this.

The look on her face is unsure, and she's about to call it off, I can feel it, so I don't allow her to talk. Grabbing her waist, I lean down and kiss her. She kisses me back, slowly at first. Eventually she wraps her arms around my neck. I drop my hands down to rest them on her bottom and squeeze. She lets me, but not for long. She moves her hands to mine while maintaining the kiss and tries to move my hands back up. I grip her bottom tighter, causing her dress to come up, and keep her from pulling on my hands.

"Stop!" Shari laughs, pushing me off her and pulling her dress back down. "I would die from embarrassment if anyone saw my underwear," she says, blushing but still laughing.

I've brought the girl back out, I think to myself, smiling at Shari's beautiful face.

"So?" I ask, alluding to my earlier question.

"It would be my pleasure," she says to me seductively before walking up to me and hugging me, placing her head in my chest. "Thank you," she whispers, barely audible.

"I will always be here for you, even when you are not here for yourself. However, we are both wearing silk, so I can feel everything," I say smoothly.

"It is for you to feel, my love," Shari says, not catching my meaning.

"While I appreciate that I do not have on underwear under this silk, we must still walk in public."

Her eyes shoot open, and she looks down toward my crotch, which is indeed tented with my arousal for her. Looking back ahead, she walks in deep thought for a second before coming to a conclusion of some unknown line of thought. She stops before me, pulls the bottom of her dress down, and then turns to place her bottom on my crotch and my hands upon her waist in the front.

"We will walk like this. It solves two problems at once." I can't help but laugh.

"Two problems?" I ask, in question.

"Yes, you will hold my dress down for me, and no other woman will be able to see what is mine alone," she tells me seriously before leaning back for a kiss.

"Now, let's go," she demands, forcing me to find a rhythm so we can walk, stuck together.

What I don't get is how my manhood is supposed to ever grow soft, because as I said before, we are both wearing silk. I can feel everything.

Walking like this, it takes us forever to make any kind of progress, but we are in no rush, so I don't mind. We are silent at first when we join the crowd of people going on about their daily lives, each of us no doubt thinking about what happened, but I do not allow us to slide back away from this date.

Stopping in the middle of the flow of people, I lean down and kiss Shari's neck, lightly biting her. She reaches up, trusting me to hold down her dress, which I do, and places her hands around my neck, warming to the embrace.

"Okay, my love, I get it," she says, wanting me to stop but not moving away.

I stop because we have on silk and are in public. If anyone noticed our brief moment, they didn't comment or linger near us.

"So, how far are we from the Crystal Gardens?" I ask Shari, just to start a conversation.

"Not far at all," she says, pointing to a giant area sectioned off by stone walls that look like they contain a maze inside them.

On the front of either stone wall is a crystal flower embedded in the wall to mark the entrance. We move over slowly and enter the walls to indeed find a maze.

"Ready to get lost?" I ask Shari, looking inside, noting the four pathways we can choose from.

"Neither you nor I can be fooled by a maze like this, and we know it," she says to me, confident in our skills.

"That is, if we were to pay attention. However, today my eyes are only for you," I say, revealing my true eyes to her and pulling her into the third pathway. I drag her backward down the maze quickly, trusting her to turn me when appropriate. Abruptly, I stop, causing Shari to run into me, and I hold her tight.

"Are we lost yet?" I ask her, smiling.

She smiles one of those rare smiles of hers that reveals feminine beauty goddesses would kill for.

"We are, my love, and I wouldn't mind if you were lost in me right now," she says, reaching for my manhood.

I catch her hand.

"In due time, but we will enjoy our date first," I say with hunger in my voice, then add, "Princess."

She leans back as if she is hit with a blow.

"Princess?" she says, unbelievingly.

"Yes. You called me your king, and you are my queen, but despite what you say, I am not a king, at least not yet. So you cannot be a queen and therefore are a princess, my princess," I say, connecting the dots.

"I don't think I can—" Shari starts before I cut her off.

"I don't recall asking a question. I merely made a statement of fact . . . Princess," I say the last, smiling.

Shari looks at me with too many emotions for me to tell what she is thinking.

"I am frightened beyond reason right now, but I will be your princess and everything that comes with that, so that I will be ready to be your queen," Shari says, determination on her face.

I smirk.

"You already have that part down. You just need to enjoy being a princess for a while," I say, trying to lighten the mood.

"You just want me to—oh my God," Shari says, shoving me out the way.

I turn to see what is so important that Shari had to push me away, and I understand her actions completely when my eyes take in what Shari is staring at.

In front of us, resting in a corner of the maze, is a crystal rose, twice my size. Sunlight causes it to glisten with rainbows on the inside. Whoever made it must be a master craftsman. I move behind Shari and embrace her while we stare, speechless, at this work of art.

"I've never seen something so beautiful, not even in the palace," Shari says aloud.

"Why would they just leave it exposed like this? Aren't they afraid someone will steal it?" I ask Shari.

"Well, when something so beautiful belongs to a place, people tend to take pride in it. So even the thieves in Altissia probably respect this place, and from what I've heard, this maze is full of them. It would hardly be a garden with one flower. Shall we?" Shari informs me before moving and hugging me behind her.

We move through the maze as the sun passes through the sky and begins its slow descent, westbound. I think there is more than one creator of this garden because the flowers all have their own personality types. Some are proud, some are aggressive, some are delicate, and some are just simply amazing. As we move through the maze, going deeper, the number of crystal flowers increases until the walls seem practically made of crystal flowers.

"Look! It's a daisy!" Shari shouts, running to a specific flower, holding down her dress.

I move to join her to see what she's excited about. "How can you tell it's a daisy?" I ask, amazed.

"Look at how the flower swirls and at the shape of the petals . . ."

She explains, continuing to go into fuller detail.

She really loves daisies.

"Close your eyes," I tell Shari abruptly.

"Why?" she asks, sounding disrespected.

"Do you trust me?"

She sighs. "With my life," she says, closing her eyes.

I put my hand on one of the crystal flowers and focus on Certus. I summon small blades of force and cut the flower off the wall. The flower I choose is palm-sized. I close my fist around it and continue to cut at it with the sharp blades of force. *Certain, sure, definite, decided, specific, precise*, I chant in my head, willing the blades of force to shape the crystal in the pattern Shari just explained to me.

"Stick your hand out, palm down," I instruct Shari.

She does not hesitate, but I can tell by the look on her face that she is nervous. I slide my creation on her ring finger.

"Open your eyes." She does.

"Oh my God, it's beautiful. How did you make this?" she asks, staring at the crystal daisy ring on her finger.

"I just followed your—"

She cuts me off as realization hits her, and her eyes widen in fear.

"You can't do this. Your mother will kill me," she says, looking terrified. She goes on, "Luca, you are a prince, *the* prince. I am a stray your mother took in because my parents died. I love you and nothing will ever change that, but you are royalty, and I am nothing. People fight wars over marriages like this. I can't let you do this," she says, sounding scared, hurt, yet determined.

I am hurt. I was not proposing. It was just a gift—more like a promise to propose, but hearing her words has shaken me.

"Luca . . . my love . . ." Shari starts, but I cut her off.

"You told me never run from you so that you could run from me? Do you really love me?" I ask in disbelief.

"You know the answer to that," she says, sounding hurt. I do know the answer.

"Then if you love me, why does what anyone else thinks matter? I know my mother would approve," I say, falling down to both knees, sick at the thought of Shari's rejection.

"Luca," she says, moving to comfort me.

"I wasn't even proposing, I just wanted to give you a gift that was personal, a promise," I mutter in defeat to no one in particular.

Shari gasped, realizing her mistake.

"I would go to war with the one true God for you, Shari, and you care about what backgrounds we come from? I didn't know you held me apart from you like that," I say, beginning to accept that she will never fully bridge this gap she's been forced to believe through life's antics.

"I don't hold you apart from me, my love," Shari says, sounding betrayed and upset.

"You may not believe it, but that does not make it true," I say in defeat.

"Stand up, Luca," Shari whispers, sounding hurt.

Well guess what, we're both hurt, Princess. I don't move.

"Stand up, Luca!" Shari shouts in a shaky voice.

This time I do, and because of our height difference, when I do, she is right in my face, tears falling out of her eyes as she openly cries.

"You are not allowed to be mad at me for feeling that I am not good enough for you, because I will never feel like I am good enough for you. But do not mistake that for me holding you at bay, because I'm not. You have all of me that I can give and some that I did not. I will marry you, and we will whether the consequences together, but do not ever question my love for you again," she says, voice escalating from a hurt whisper to an angry shout, crying all the while.

She stands there daring me to contest her again.

I don't.

I raise my arms to hug her and begin to speak. "Shari, I —" She leaps into my arms, squeezing the life out of me, and all the crying she held back bursts forth from her. Not knowing what else to do, I just hold her, rocking slightly, until she calms.

Eventually, she turns her head to lie on my chest after the crying has run its course. I chuckle down at her, still holding and rocking her.

"*What?*" she says, looking up at me, not breaking our embrace.

"I don't think you can marry me if I didn't propose," I say jokingly.

She just rests her head back in my chest. "I do not recall asking a question. I merely made a statement of fact."

I'm starting to realize she's particularly good at that. "Shari, look," I tell her so she can see what I do.

"I don't want to move right now. Just hold me please," she says, sounding tired.

Got it. I do not let her go and turn myself so I cannot see and she can.

"Shari, look behind me," I try again.

She sighs in annoyance but lifts her face from my chest to look. There comes a sharp intake of breath from Shari, and she lets me go and walks behind me, pulling me with her. The sun is beginning to set, and the light is causing the crystal flowers that cover the wall to shoot rainbow light in every direction, constantly shifting as the sun continues to set. Shari and I stand side by side holding hands, watching the rainbow light dance for a second before she speaks.

"Attempting to explain how you make me feel is impossible, but how this looks is a start," Shari says to me, motioning toward the most beautiful view I think I've ever seen, outside of Shari.

I turn to face her and pull her to face me. She looks worn out and tired. I was going to kiss her, but I guess I took too long because she leans up and kisses me. I pull her dress down for her, but then she moves my hands to her butt before placing hers around my neck.

"You look tired. Do you want to go to the Pale Horse so you can rest? It's getting late anyway," I suggest as the sun finally sets.

"Yes, I do want to go to the inn, but not so we can rest. You know I love you, but apparently not how much I love you. After tonight, even if you don't understand my actions, you will never question my love for you again," Shari says in the softest voice possible.

I almost feel like I'm in trouble.

Shari begins to lead us out of the maze that is the Crystal Gardens, and despite my earlier attempt to get us lost, she knows exactly where she is going. We exit the maze, and she stops, turning to me.

"Why do you look troubled, my love?" Shari asks in the same tone of voice.

"Well, because you don't look happy. You look stressed out," I say in all honesty.

She even giggles softly. I don't think I've ever seen her in such a delicate state. "I am beyond happy, my love. You have just made my dreams reality, but the way you did it has me emotionally exhausted. You need to learn to flower your words more at times like this, especially if you want me to be a princess," she says softly, laughing with the last word.

What am I doing wrong? I wonder.

"Don't worry, my love, I listen to this . . ." she puts a hand over my heart ". . . more than this." She leans up to kiss my lips. "Because sometimes that is all your mouth is good for," she jokes, which sets me at ease.

I guess she is just as she says—emotionally exhausted.

"I seem to recall a night with a red moon that adds another skill to the list," I say seductively.

"Oh, I have not forgotten, nor will I ever. You will most definitely do that again tonight, and many more, but I have a few surprises of my own this night," she says, looking me dead in the eye as if I am prey.

I am not a sheep. Then why does the look in her eye make me feel like one?

"What do you mean?" I ask anxiously.

"If I told you, it would hardly be a surprise. But you will not have to wait long to find out. Let's go," she says with a hint of satisfaction in her voice before pulling me through the city.

By the time we arrive outside the Pale Horse, the sexual tension between us has grown so thick I have moved through excitement into fear. We talked on the way here, but her soft tone has not gone anywhere, further adding to my fear.

"Are you ready, my love?" Shari asks with a dangerous gleam in her eye, nodding to the entrance of the Pale Horse.

"Yes, how could I not be?" I ask confidently. She laughs lightly.

"You may believe that, but that does not make it true," she says, letting go of my hand and walking into the inn, expecting me to follow.

I gather my wits and enter moments after she does. She is already halfway up the stairs that lead to our room when I see her. She still hasn't looked back to see if I follow. I rush up the stairs, two at a time, and catch up to her just as she opens the door to our room. Latrice and Stacey sit on the bed looking at us like we just interrupted their conversation.

"Oh my, Shari, you look so beautiful. It feels like I'm doing something wrong just by looking at you," Latrice says in a trance-like state.

"Thank you, Latrice. That means a lot to me, especially right now," Shari says, joining them in sitting on the bed.

Stacey looks caught between running from Shari and admiring her beauty.

"I am sorry we got off to a rough start, Stacey. I would very much like to get to know you and possibly become friends," Shari tells Stacey, taking her hand.

Stacey is stuck for a moment but then comes to. "Only if you show me how you did your hair like that," Stacey jokes, sensing the mood.

I watch all three women laugh from just inside the entrance to the door.

"I didn't do it, but I paid enough attention and will be glad to show you. However, right now, can you two do me a big favor?"

Latrice and Stacey nod in unison, captivated by Shari's feminine beauty.

"I desire the night alone with Luca. He seems to believe my love for him has boundaries. Tonight, I will show him the truth." She says the last as she looks at me longingly, idly fingering her crystal ring.

Latrice's eyes look down at the ring and up at me. "Stacey, darling, let's give these two some privacy," she says, rising from the bed, taking Stacey with her, and moving toward the exit, toward me.

Latrice allows Stacey to leave the room first, lingering a second beyond to speak to me.

"If you hurt Shari—" Latrice begins to whisper to me, to be cut off by both me and Shari.

"I won't."

"He won't," we say in unison.

Latrice looks back at Shari one last time and smiles before exiting the room, closing the door behind her. I make sure I lock the door behind her, and then I turn to face Shari.

Shari stands from the bed, pulling her ponytail to have it lay over her left shoulder. Then, not taking her eyes from mine, she reaches for the dress's loop around her neck and gently pulls it around her head. She then slowly starts to pull the dress down from the top, in a teasing fashion, until her breasts come free. Then the dress finally drops to the floor. Her underwear is scandalous. I can see straight through the red material, but only in bits and pieces, as if someone cut them up, but in a really seductive manner. She smiles at me, and my eyes find hers instead of staring at her underwear. She turns from me and begins to walk to the large hot pool.

As she moves away from me, I see the underwear does not cover her bottom. Only a thin strap goes around her waist and in between her cheeks to attach to the front. Before she steps into the water, she bends over and looks back to me, then slowly begins sliding down her underwear, revealing everything. She then stands back up and walks into the pool until she is entirely underwater. She surfaces a moment later, revealing only her head.

"I didn't ask them to leave so you could stand there," she says in her soft tone. I take a step toward her.

"Drop your disguise, Luca." I strip as fast as possible and then take another step. "Change your eyes and undo your hair. I will see you tonight and nothing else," she demands.

My eyes become golden-black vortexes, and my hair falls from the bun down my back. I look at her for approval before I take another step.

"I am done waiting, my love." I walk into the pool and join her.

Anxiety, fear, and excitement run wild through me as I walk to her in the pool. She moves back from me until her body begins to rise out of the water on the other side. Only then does she stop, lying back on the steps with one leg up. Water drips from her body. I start the rise up the steps to her, and when I get close enough to lie on top of her, she grabs me and switches our positions so she is above me and my back is on the steps. She kisses my lips and then slowly works her way down to my neck, stomach, and thighs.

"Nervous?" she asks, seductively looking at me.

"A little," I say, trying to laugh it off.

"You should be." And before I can respond, she . . . she . . . some things are best left secret. Tonight will undoubtedly be the best secret of my life, our lives.

20 DOWN TIME

I awake to Shari's head on my chest, along with half her body lying atop mine, one of her legs lying over one of my own. She is softly tracing some unknown pattern across my stomach with her finger. We are both still naked, but I am too tired, sore, and sensitive from last night for any more excitement.

"Good morning, my love," comes Shari's voice, sounding less emotionally exhausted and more . . . gratified.

I have not moved, aside from opening my eyes, so how she knows I'm awake is beyond me.

"Good morning, Princess . . ." I say, leaning down and kissing her forehead. "How did you know I was awake?" I ask, a hint of amazement coming off in my voice.

"I've been listening to your heart since I awoke ten minutes ago. It just started beating slightly faster, hardly noticeable really, but it was enough for me to know you were awake," she explains happily.

"You're amazing, you know that?" I tell her, meaning every word.

"And don't forget it," she says, laughing. "But was it enough?" she asks, suddenly sounding self-conscious.

She is asking about last night. She gave herself to me in more ways than I knew possible, and she was not the bold, aggressive Shari I am used to, but the soft, delicate version of herself she keeps hidden, who is already beginning to retreat into the deep that is Shari. I choose my words carefully.

"You are more than enough, more than I deserve, truthfully," I say confidently.

She exhales a breath I didn't realize she was holding.

"Good," she says simply, sounding gratified once more.

"Were you worried?" I ask mockingly with a laugh.

"No, because you're stuck with me, like it or not . . ." she says, holding her ring in my face. "However, I am extremely sore and sensitive right now. I don't know if I could have handled you anymore last night," she finishes.

She doesn't know if she could've handled me anymore! "Shari, I pushed past my own limits for you. I thought that's what you wanted, what you needed," I tell her, somewhat confused.

She laughs in amusement. "Maybe it was," she says thoughtfully, then adds, "but it was a good thing we passed out when we did. Or was I like the only one?" she asks, looking up at me.

"Shari, I don't even remember falling asleep. One moment you were riding me, and the next I was waking up," I inform her truthfully.

"Maybe I can touch the power," she jests, then kisses me on the lips.

"Will you join me in the pool, my love?" Shari asks, sitting up, standing, and then starting to walk to the pool. I watch her move away from me, becoming transfixed in the way her hips sway and bottom jiggles.

"Well?" she asks, turning her head back to me, catching me red-handed. She smiles.

"I would be a fool not to, Princess," I say, standing and following her into the pool.

We move to the far edge, and Shari sits me down and then sits on my lap so only our heads are out of the water. We sit like this for a moment, and I allow my head to lean back against the ground behind me, granting me a view of the sky through the glass sheet. I can't see the sun, and the sky is a lightening blue, so it is still pretty early. I wonder where Latrice and Stacey are.

"You have gotten better at kissing, my love, possibly even better than Latrice. At times I feel as if I could kiss you forever," Shari says to me out of nowhere.

"If I feel the same way about you, why are we not kissing?" I ask playfully.

Her answer is to turn around, straddle me, and grab my face softly with both hands, then begin kissing me. I try to lift my arms, but she pushes them back to the ground outside the pool. So I sit, head back, arms wide, and relaxed as the love of my life sits atop me in a heated pool, holding my face while our tongues explore each other's mouths. If we did this till I died, I would be fulfilled.

Not enough time passes before there comes a knock on the door, followed by Latrice's voice.

"Are you two decent?" she asks through the door.

"No, but you may come in anyway," Shari says playfully after she returns to her original position on my lap.

Latrice comes in looking happy with a cup of tea in her hands, using the key she still has, and closes the door behind her. Stacey is nowhere to be found.

"Do you two not like fresh air? Not that I mind, but—"

I cut Latrice off. "That's not fair; there are no windows in here," I complain.

Latrice walks the edges of the pool to come around to us and hands Shari the cup of tea. What would we do without her?

"Thank you," Shari says gratefully to Latrice.

Latrice pays her no mind, walks back over to the side of the bed closest to us, and places her hand upon a lever, then pushes. The glass sheet in the roof raises at an angle of about five feet, causing the icy morning air to rush through the room, which feels amazing against the contrast of the heated pool.

"No doubt you were too consumed in one another to notice," she says, smiling down to us.

"I will leave you two—"

Shari cuts her off. "You will not," she says simply, nursing a devilish smile.

"Oh no?" Latrice says, smiling a smile of her own.

Whatever understanding has passed between them has completely alluded me.

"You are glowing in a way that I have never seen before. You will join us and tell me all about your date with Storm," Shari says, sounding excited.

That's right, Latrice had a date of her own last night. How could I forget? Then I remember last night with Shari. Easily. Is she really glowing? I can't tell.

"You only say that because you didn't see me with Luca before you came around," Latrice states in jest.

Why would she joke like that? Even for Latrice, that is extreme.

"You will not get out of telling me about your date that easily," Shari says, smiling and enjoying herself.

Personally, my body tensed at Latrice's comment, until Shari stroked my leg under the water to let me know everything was fine. I will never understand women.

"You are growing up before my eyes, Shari," Latrice says, smiling, stripping down to her underwear. She moves to enter the pool with us but is stopped by Shari's voice.

"We are naked, Latrice," Shari says playfully. Latrice surprises me by blushing but at the same time smiling.

"Growing up indeed," Latrice says, unhooking her bra and slipping out of her underwear. I look down.

"It is okay, my love. I don't care if you see her." Her words shock me to the core, but I still don't look up.

"I see one of you still has some growing to do," Latrice laughs before she steps into the pool just as naked as we are, allowing the water to come to her neck.

I feel lost in their world right now.

"I am hardly the only one glowing right now," Latrice says aloud.

"Something changed last night," Shari responds.

"I know, I saw the ring," Latrice says, sounding happy.

"That had something to do with it, but its more. I think Luca broke me last night," Shari explains.

I look up to her, confused and insulted.

"In a good way," she adds.

You can break someone in a good way? I wonder.

"I will gladly tell you how my date went, but only after you tell me how your own went. And I am not only talking to Shari, nor are we the only ones glowing."

I blush as my eyes find Latrice's, and she and Shari share a laugh. "You two confuse me," I say, trying to sound manly.

They laugh even harder.

"So, Luca here suggested we go to a tailor so we could look the part before our date to Crystal Gardens . . ." Shari begins. She tells the entirety of our night, except what happened after Latrice and Stacey left the room.

A secret indeed. I think about Stacey.

"Where is Stacey?" I ask after Shari finishes reciting our tale.

If Shari feels some type of way about me mentioning Stacey, she doesn't let on.

"She went to gather some of her things from her home. She should be here any minute," Latrice says.

As if that was her queue, there is a knock on the door.

"Come in," Latrice shouts.

Stacey comes in. Gone is the traveler's cloak, replaced by a simple yellow dress that covers her shoulders and falls below her knees. She comes in eyeing us in the pool, then sets some bags down by the foot of the bed before going back to the door, closing and locking it.

"You are just in time to join us for my retelling of my date last night. Sadly, you just missed Shari and Luca's, but do join us in the pool, darling," Latrice says to Stacey.

"I would love to," Stacey says, stripping down to her underwear, which matches her dress, and walking up to the pool. I notice Latrice eye Shari on my lap.

"We are all naked, Stacey," Shari says to Stacey just as playfully as she did to Latrice. However, this time I feel her body tense atop mine.

"I don't believe I have been naked in front of people until these last few days, and aside from my experience with the King's Hand, it has been scandalously refreshing," she says, coming out of her underwear, not thinking twice about me.

"Do not look away, my love," Shari whispers for my ears alone, grabbing my hand under the water. Something has indeed changed inside of Shari, and I hope it is for the best. Stacey's beauty and body definitely rival Shari's, but if Stacey were a goddess, I would pray to her and worship her. If Shari was a goddess, I would lust over her and go to war behind her. But maybe that's just because I'm hopelessly in love with Shari. Just before Stacey's naked body enters the water, I stop her with a question.

"Do you think you could show them what you showed me?" I ask Stacey. Her face turns red and she looks away.

"What did she show you?" Latrice asks curiously

Shari stays quiet because she knows I refer to Stacey's power.

Stacey nods at me and walks into the water, keeping her upper body exposed, then moves to the left of the pool since me, Shari, and Latrice are on the right. Latrice eyes me, and I just point to Stacey.

"Watch," I say simply.

Stacey closes her eyes, and just like the first time, large wings made of liquid gold fire spring into existence behind her back.

Shari and Latrice both gasp in awe.

This is my second time seeing it, so I'm not as shocked, but the sight is still just as beautiful. Stacey maintains her wings for about fifteen seconds and then lets them disappear, sinking into the water up to her neck, looking embarrassed. It takes a moment, but finally Shari speaks.

"Why do you look as if you've done something wrong? That was heavenly."

"Aside from Luca, I've never shown anyone, you know, because the king has been taking everybody who can touch Potentia," Stacey replies sheepishly.

"So you use Potentia?" Shari asks her, somewhat protectively.

"I'm not sure. No one has ever taught me, so I don't know the difference," Stacey says seemingly relaxing a little and swimming over to Latrice.

"You should be grateful Stacey just gifted us with that beautiful display of her power, Luca," Latrice says to me just as Stacey sits next to her across from Shari and me.

"Why?" I ask genuinely curious.

"Because I was seconds away from slapping you for what you told

Shari yesterday," she informs me, anger clear on her face.

"What did he tell her?" Stacey asks from her side, eyeing me in what seems like a whole new light.

"He told her that she did not truly love him and kept him at a distance from her heart, even if she did not believe it true," Latrice says venomously.

"You did not," Stacey says to me, refusing to believe.

"I . . . She had just turned down a marriage proposal I didn't even make yet. I was hurt," I say apologetically.

"She was in shock, idiot, she would have said yes as soon as she calmed herself," Latrice yells at me.

Stacey and Latrice both stare at me like I am evil incarnate. Shari takes my hand and gives it a squeeze before moving from my lap and swimming gracefully through the water to sit next to Latrice.

"Oh, Latrice, at least you understand my heart where he cannot," Shari says, smiling at me and then grabbing Latrice's face and pulling her in for a kiss on the lips, which she holds for a couple of seconds.

I now understand why Shari squeezed my hand.

Those words hurt, but I needed to hear them as well as my mistake from Latrice's mouth. I also now understand why Shari was so emotionally exhausted yesterday. I feel like an enormous fool as usual around these two, and now Stacey too.

"As you told me before, Luca is not enlightened to the ways of women, and this creates the innocence in him we love so much," Shari tells Latrice in my defense.

"You're lucky I like Shari, or else . . ." Latrice jokes at me.

"Well, if you like me so much, please gift me with the details of your date with Storm, glowing one," Shari says, taking Latrice's arm.

"Yes, please do tell," Stacey adds, taking Latrice's other arm.

And just like that, I am forgotten as Shari and Stacey listen to Latrice, wrapped up in her every word. Shari is not as wrapped as she appears, though, because she keeps eyeing me every few minutes or so.

Latrice is lost in her own tale, and as she talks, I think I begin to see the glow Shari spoke of. It is an aura of true happiness and love. And sitting in between two goddesses of beauty, Latrice, while not as beautiful as they are, is definitely holding her own, and I am happy for her. Do I make Shari look this way too? I hope so. I can't really tell because Shari has always been unnervingly beautiful to me, but as I stare at her now, she does look happier and more delicate. Two down, one to go, I think, as my eyes find Stacey, who is still wrapped in Latrice's story. I don't know what her life was like before this, but I can still see the fear and worry ingrained in her features from her cruel experiences. I will find a way to return Stacey's happiness to her, and I know Shari and Latrice feel the same. After all, we are the lost.

I only really half listen, absorbed in my own thoughts, but overall, Latrice reveals that Donte, as she calls him, is smart, kind, and passionate. She said he used to have a lover, but he didn't tell her what caused them to break, or she just chose not to tell us. All they did was talk over dinner and a glass of wine, getting to know each other more. She said they kissed after dinner in the moonlight and she actually felt a novice compared to the masterful way he worked his tongue in her mouth, leaving her breathless. To this, Shari and Stacey both make cat calls toward Latrice.

"I know . . . I know . . . I wanted to, but I thought it best to make him wait to see how he handles the time apart, because traveling with you two, well, three now, will surely make this a long-distance relationship. And I had to make sure Shari and Luca were okay with my decision first," Latrice responds to the cat noises.

I wonder what those noises meant.

"Latrice, you're a grown woman. Luca nor I would stop you from pursuing love," Shari says to Latrice, sounding motherly.

I wonder where she learned to do that?

"Yes, I know, but you two are my family, and he is your father's strongest general. I would not pick him over you for any reason. Even if he makes me feel butterflies, like I'm a little girl again," Latrice says, causing all three girls to laugh.

"Love should be denied to no one. Pursue him or allow him to pursue you. That is my approval as well as demand as your family. We will deal with the rest when we must," I say to Latrice, causing all of the girls to look at me, but my eyes are for Latrice alone right now.

"I see you are trying to work your way back into my good graces," Latrice says, causing Shari and Stacey to laugh.

Latrice doesn't laugh. Instead, she mouths to me, "Thank you," from across the pool, eyes full of gratitude, appreciation, happiness, and a hint of sadness.

I wonder why she has cause to be sad.

"You know he speaks for us both, right?" Shari says to Latrice, forcing her attention off on me.

"Me too!" Stacey yells excitedly, and then blushes as all of our eyes turn to her.

Latrice pulls Stacey and Shari close in embrace. "Thank you all," and then looks up to me to let me know I am included in this.

For some reason I think about being caught in an embrace between the three women and blush, looking away. I think Latrice reads my mind because she bursts into laughter loud enough to give Shari and Stacey pause, "What's so funny?" Shari asks Latrice.

"I promise to tell you later. Don't let me forget," Latrice says to Shari, still laughing.

"Can I know too?" Stacey asks excitedly.

"I don't see why not," Latrice says, shrugging her shoulders.

Shit, I don't look forward to being alone with them again after that conversation.

Another half hour passes, which consists of nothing but girl talk as I remain silent, enjoying the water and the sight of Shari getting much-needed girl time.

"I think it is time to get out, as I am starting to become wrinkly," Shari says, standing and then exiting the pool. My eyes drink in her body, and she looks back at me and smiles.

"You are right," Latrice says, getting out of the water and standing next to Shari, followed by Stacey.

Three naked women stand in front of me, two of which are goddesses, and the third not far behind. I can only see their backs and bottoms, but I still turn around to face the wall, out of respect, and to hide my extremely red face.

"Luca, if you love me and are the man we know you to be, you will come out of the pool and get dressed with us," Shari says to me.

I turn back around, and all three women are turned facing me, starring right at me. Their naked bodies glisten and drip with water. This scene provokes my inner man, but luckily, Shari exhausted me last night. So even though I do not understand the game Shari is playing right now, I don't deny her challenge to my love.

I move to exit the water, and just before my manhood comes out of the water, Latrice and Stacey turn away and move to go get dressed. I walk straight up to Shari.

"Did you think I would deny you whatever it is you're playing at?" I ask her.

"Never. I will explain myself in a moment," Shari says to me in a whisper before kissing me quickly and getting dressed in her red dress.

Latrice and Stacey moved to the left side of the bed to get dressed, so Shari and I use the right.

After everyone is dressed, Latrice asks, "Is anyone up for breakfast?"

"Yes, please!" Stacey replies eagerly.

"You two go ahead. We will join you in a minute," Shari says to both Stacey and Latrice.

Latrice just shrugs and takes Stacey by the hand. "Let's go eat, darling," she says to Stacey, leading her out of the room and closing the door.

I turn to Shari.

"I'm sorry if I made you feel uncomfortable," Shari apologizes to me.

"It is fine. I'm with you no matter what you're going through, but can you please help me understand what that might be?" I ask Shari.

She sighs. "You want me to embrace my feminine side, and that is what I'm trying to do," she explains.

"By forcing me to look at other naked women?" I question bluntly.

"It has less to do with you and more to do with me," she says cryptically.

"Go on," I say simply.

"I keep the Princess you are trying to pull out of me hidden because she suffers from an inferiority complex developed by my unfortunate upbringing. I never got the time to develop my inner female, and when I see girls just being themselves around you, it makes me . . . jealous doesn't begin to cover it. As of yesterday, I've begun to let that side of me surface, but I need to be comfortable in my own skin around you in front of other women. Right now is my best chance because Latrice is family and Stacey is soon to be, and they are both beautiful. It will be difficult for me, but if I can do this with them around, I will be fine. I also can't keep getting angry when you are yourself around women, especially when I know your heart. So this is training of a sort for me."

That answers so many questions. Why does she not speak plainly like this all the time?

"You told them this as well?" I ask in shock.

"No, but they sense it. That is why they turned to face you naked with me. We are just created that way. I just happened to be lucky enough to get Latrice and Stacey to help me through this. I believe most women would take advantage of the situation," Shari continues.

"And risk your wrath?" I ask, disbelieving.

"You'd be surprised what women can and will do," she replies simply.

"After last night, I don't think I'll ever be surprised again," I joke, trying to move the conversation to a lighter note.

"No? Well, we will just have to see how true that is when my body is up to the challenge again," Shari says seductively, then kisses me.

I get the chills.

"Any idea when that will be?" I ask playfully, not ready myself.

"Soon, if I'm being honest. Despite what I said earlier, I was about to try to take you in the pool before Latrice came in."

Shari's sexual appetite is monstrous, but then again, so is mine.

"Time for breakfast, unless you desire to be my morning meal, Princess," I say, reaching my hand up Shari's dress slowly. She does not flinch as my hand rubs across her underwear.

"I definitely can't take that right now or I would happily let you, so let's go before your hand changes my mind," she says, staring at me, still not moving my hand. "Don't begin something you can't finish, my love," Shari says in finality.

The hunger in her voice moves my hand for me. I'm scared to disappoint right now.

"I'm glad you were the chicken, because I was bluffing," Shari says, laughing, then pulling down her dress.

God, I love this woman.

***

We join Latrice and Stacey in a booth on the second floor for breakfast. Latrice so kindly already ordered for us, so Shari and I are able to eat as soon as we arrive. Breakfast consists of generous servings of eggs, toast, ham and coffee to drink. We all eat in silence, too busy with our delicious food to talk. I am the first one done, followed by Latrice, who wipes her face before asking Shari a question.

"So, shopping? I most definitely want to buy some things from the shop you got that dress and those underwear from. I'm sure Stacey wouldn't mind either."

"I don't have any money," Stacey cuts in, sounding embarrassed.

"Awww, neither do we. It's his," Latrice says, pointing to me. "And you're more than welcome to it. I'm sure he doesn't mind," she finishes.

Stacey looks up to me in question.

"Honestly, it was given to me, so I really don't even care," I say shrugging my shoulders.

"You girls go have some fun. Just make sure we have enough to survive off of when you're done," I finish in a kindly voice for Stacey.

"So, yes, shopping," Shari says deviously. "Thank you, my love," she adds.

"Yes, you are back in my good graces," Latrice says with a smile.

"You guys are the best thing that's happened to me in like . . . my whole life," Stacey says with childlike glee.

"No, the best thing in your life is the smell of Shari's—" Latrice stops short when she sees Shari blushing furiously.

"See, I told you she blushes," Latrice says to Stacey, laughing.

Stacey stares at Shari with a relaxed smile.

"I see Latrice is a bully," Stacey says to Shari.

"You have no idea," Shari replies, and she and Stacey share a laugh.

As they jest back and forth, I can't help but think, this is what life should be like for everyone. I find myself happily laughing along with them.

We eventually make it back to the room where Shari shows Stacey how to do the hairstyle the woman in the mask gave Shari. And now they both wear matching ponytails made of individual balls. Latrice watched and I pulled out my blue book so I can maybe interpret some more elements when they leave.

"Okay, we're leaving now," Latrice says to everyone in the room, walking to the door and opening it.

Stacey jumps up excitedly and heads out the door with Latrice following.

Shari stops just before the door and says to me, "Come say goodbye, my love."

I set the book aside, then rise from the bed and move to embrace Shari. Shari leans up to kiss me, and I hold her dress down for her.

"So far so good?" Shari asks me, referring to her working on herself.

"There is not a standard you must meet. I just want you to be you and be happy when you're doing it," I correct her.

"I will be happy being myself as long as it's with you," she says after a moment.

"Then you will be happy forever. Now go," I say, kissing her one last time.

She smiles, then turns to walk out the door. I don't know why, but I smack her bottom softly when she steps out the door.

She takes a couple more steps, then turns her face to me while still walking forward. She is blushing and biting her lower lip in somewhat of a seductive snarl. She doesn't say anything; she just turns her head back forward, then disappears down the stairs at the end of the hallway. I close the door when she is gone and ponder the look on her face.

I like it, but I wonder what it means.

Moving back to the bed, I sit propping my back against the massive headboard and pick back up the blue book. With any luck, I can . . . nope, I just flipped back to the page that says, "Mind functions independently of space. You." I concentrate as hard as I can, but the "you" still does not reveal its meaning. I'm about to give up on this one. I flip through some more pages and stop when I notice a page full of a bunch of elements my mind has somehow already interpreted. Wow, this is a lot.

"Difficulties challenge mediocrity and defeat the fearful, but they only stimulate true children of the one true God."

Another one. "The greatest affliction of the cosmos is never to have been afflicted. Mortals only learn wisdom through experiencing tribulation."

Wait, what? But there's more.

"Only a poet can discern poetry in the commonplace prose of routine existence."

That one was really deep.

The last one I can interpret says, "The destiny of eternity is determined moment by moment by the achievements of day-to-day living. The acts of today are the destiny of tomorrow."

I have never been able to interpret so much at once. I feel like I'm having an information overload. Okay, one thing at a time.

Wait, I still never meditated on the last one I read on the journey here: "Seek first higher realities, and the shadows of the material realm will have no choice but to follow."

Okay, just choose one. The one about the poet in the commonplace prose of routine existence. So deflowering that, it takes a poet to find poetry in the words and phrases most commonly used in everyday life. So if I were not a poet, I could hardly understand or appreciate the beauty in everyday language. I am not a poet, and I most certainly do not see poetry in "good mornings" or "good nights."

However, I believe every person feels this way about their craft, respectively. Amy the carpenter would show me the beauty of each stroke of wood. Bron would definitely tell me every hammer blow is a stroke of beauty soon to be reflected in the weapon itself. The masked woman told me to pick a dress to go with Shari's personality because that is what truly makes both person and dress beautiful.

So, in essence, one must devote their lives to something to see the beauty it manifests to the land. The greater the subject of devotion, the more beautiful the personal experience. What if one devoted themselves to the one true God? I wonder what beauty that would yield. I can't help but feel like I'm missing something. What about this one?

"The greatest affliction in the cosmos is never to have been afflicted. Mortals only learn wisdom through experiencing tribulation."

What is "the cosmos?" I do not like this interpretation. Why must we learn through struggle and discomfort? I don't like it because it rings true. When I was a prince, I was ignorant of my father's evil. My body was weak because I had no reason to make it strong. Shari has been around me since I was eight, and only when I lost her did I finally realize I loved her. All of those experiences were uncomfortable and required struggle to varying degrees, but the result is who I've become. If we do not push our limits or experience affliction and tribulation, how will we progress or grow? If I live an easy life forever, I will never discover poetry hidden in routine existence, because I've devoted myself to nothing but pleasure, which disguises itself as happiness until you've been afflicted by truth and learn the wisdom to see through the lie.

I don't know if it is because I was deep in thought or what, but the door sounds like it's kicked open, breaking me from my meditation.

"We're back!" Latrice shouts, sounding all too happy.

I look up to the glass ceiling panel, which is still open. Shit, it's already night and it's cold in here. As I look back down, Shari and Stacey pour in behind Latrice, who closes the door behind them. They've got bags galore.

"Why is it so cold in here?" Shari asks absent-mindedly.

"Because I forgot to close the glass panel," I say, reaching for the lever.

"Don't!" Latrice shouts.

"That is why the pool is heated, and my feet hurt, so I'm about to get in it," Latrice finishes.

"You too?" Shari asks, agreeing with Latrice.

"But before we do that, Luca, look at this dress . . ." Shari says, pulling Stacey into my view from behind them. Stacey is wearing the gold dress with the aggressive black lining down either side I almost chose for Shari.

"It is beautiful, is it not? And Stacey looks like she is of divine origin."

I already thought Stacey looked like a goddess. Now, if I didn't know better, I would believe her to be the one true God or his wife. For Stacey's part, she looks somewhat embarrassed, refusing to make eye contact with me.

"You look marvelous, Stacey, and how you look right now is how you should feel, no matter how you look or what you've been through."

Stacey does not look at me, but smiles and says, "Thank you. But my feet hurt, too, so about that bath . . ." pulling away from Shari and heading toward the pool.

Latrice isn't far behind.

I stand and approach Shari. "I almost bought that dress for you but—" Shari shushes me with a finger, and I hear splashes from the pool as Stacey and Latrice enter.

"Jordanne told me already, and I approve of your decision," Shari tells me.

"Who is Jordanne?" I ask, dumbfounded.

"That is the masked lady's name. Turns out, she's the same age as Latrice and is very exotic looking. Now, can we get in the pool?" Shari asks, kissing me.

"We?" I ask, not sure why I was put in this equation.

"Yes, I desire your company as well, my love. I missed you," she says teasingly.

I know I no longer have an option. Shari and I approach the pool and strip to our underwear before we attempt to step in.

"We are naked," Latrice and Stacey say at the same time, and then look to each other and laugh.

I look at Shari, but she is already coming out of her underwear. I carefully take mine off behind Shari and follow her into the pool, not that Latrice or Stacey are looking. I'm still getting used to this.

Shari and I take our seats directly opposite Stacey and Latrice. Apparently, the girls have done away with modesty because both of their breasts are above water, as are Shari's, who sits on my lap. My manhood reacts, not as exhausted as this morning.

"Oh," Shari whispers in delight so only I can hear. "Do you think Latrice can smell through water?" Shari asks me, clearly debating something.

"I doubt it," I say, not understanding her line of thought.

"We will soon find out," she whispers again.

She adjusts herself and me to begin her sneaky escapade, and I almost moan in pleasure and pain, my body still sensitive. My hands move to the top of her lap so she does not move too much.

"Still sensitive, my love?" she whispers.

"Delightfully, yet excruciatingly so," comes my replied whisper.

"As am I," she whispers simply.

Oh really?

"Enough whispering, you two," Latrice says, turning from her conversation with Stacey.

"Did you girls buy enough clothes?" I ask hurriedly, thinking Latrice has caught us.

"Absolutely. Shari even bought you some more clothes," Latrice replies pleasantly.

"Is that right?" I ask, eyeing Shari.

"It was to be a surprise, my love," Shari says innocently.

"Well, I am surprised, but are we broke?" I ask, looking to the bags piled by the foot of the bed.

"Hardly. Jordanne liked us. She said we were beautiful people and gave us a huge discount. We still have 50 gold and more silver," Latrice says with pride.

Well that's good.

"So what did you learn while we were away?" Latrice asks as she usually does when I read the book.

I think for a minute and decide to answer with a question of my own.

"Would any of you happen to be poets?" I ask, knowing Shari and Latrice's answer.

"No," they all say in unison.

I smile, and move my hand between Shari's legs, continuing my game with her while I start my recollection of my meditations. Latrice and Stacey remain none the wiser because Shari has not moved, not even to stiffen her body.

"Only a poet can discern poetry in the commonplace prose of routine existence," I quote, and then begin to dive into the meaning as I rub Shari in constant circles. I can tell she enjoys it, but she gives off no signs Latrice and Stacey notice, as they are wrapped in my words. After all, my meditation today was rather deep, so they are still clueless as to what goes on beneath the water.

"The greatest affliction in the cosmos is never to have been afflicted. Mortals only learn wisdom through experiencing tribulation," I quote, drawing confused looks from Latrice and Stacey, going into the second half of my meditation.

Refusing to give any visible signs as to what I am doing under the water, I know she must be going crazy inside. I will pay for this.

"So you see, if you live an easy life forever, you will never discover poetry hidden in routine existence because you've devoted your life to nothing but pleasure, which disguises itself as happiness until you've been afflicted by the truth and learn the wisdom to see through the lie," I say with finality as Shari quietly releases on me.

"I . . . I think I've just been inspired," Stacey says, dumbfounded.

"I thought I was the smart one," Latrice says in awe after Stacey.

"It only took all day to think about," I joke.

Shari still has not moved, nor has she commented on my meditation. I wonder if she even heard me.

"Okay, well, my feet don't hurt anymore, and I don't want to turn into a raisin, so I'm getting out," Stacey says, turning to get out of the pool.

Modesty is definitely lost because she carelessly bends over as she gets out, exposing everything to Shari and me.

"Right behind you," Latrice says, following her, but choosing to walk up the stairs out of the pool so she doesn't expose herself.

Shari and I are left alone in the heated pool. Slowly, Shari raises herself off of me, almost causing me to explode, and turns to me and straddles me.

She leans forward and whispers in my ear, "I told you I was sensitive. I was not ready for that. However, I started it, so I did not stop you. I am not mad at you. In fact, I think that was by far the most pleasure I've ever experienced. The rush from doing that in front of two beautiful females was exhilarating, and I felt helpless because I could not move in pleasure or protest lest I give us away. The release was to die for, doubly so because we did not get caught. You will never rid yourself of me, so I hope you're ready. Although I did enjoy this, I still hate feeling helpless, so I will return the favor, my love. I would tell you not to forget, but I honestly don't care. You will be paid back in full," she finishes, then kisses my lips as if she's never kissed them before.

"None of that, you two. Come on, it's bedtime!" Latrice yells as soon as she notices Shari straddling and kissing me.

You're a little late, Latrice, I think and smile. Shari leans back and gracefully swims on her back to the other side, exposing herself to me as she does, and then turns over and exits the pool.

What did I just get myself into?

I wait until I am no longer aroused and then exit the pool. I find the towel Shari used to dry off with and use it for myself.

"I always thought he had a nice butt," Latrice says aloud.

I turn my head only toward the bed and see all three women bunched up under the cover, only their heads exposed.

"It is nice but too firm. It should be softer," Shari complains to Latrice.

Stacey is giggling uncontrollably.

"Excuse me, I'm right here," I say, embarrassed.

"Yeah, and not where you need to be. Hurry up, my love," Shari says, seemingly back to normal.

I sit on the foot of the bed and continue drying off.

"Oh, now he's shy. You guys are mean," Stacey says, sounding genuinely concerned.

Now Latrice and Shari share a laugh.

I move to put on my boxers and ...

"No. No. No. Clothes have been irrelevant for a while now, so stop what you're doing and join us as you are," Shari says, sounding too much like Latrice for my liking.

Latrice definitely told them what I was thinking yesterday. Fine, I will play this game. I stand and turn around completely naked as I move to join Shari on her side of the bed. I notice Latrice and Stacey avert their eyes again and look at each other. They really are doing this for Shari. I need to loosen up and go with the flow, but naked women and the river do not make for a good calm.

I sigh as I get under the cover next to Shari. Latrice turns and cuddles with Stacey, and Shari snuggles up to me, facing me, resting her face on the pillow next to mine.

"Behave, you two, or I will know, and I will teach Stacey how to know as well. Goodnight," Latrice says playfully.

"Teach me to know what?" Stacey asks curiously.

Shari, Latrice, and I all stare, then erupt into laughter. Shortly after, we all fall asleep.

21 DISPERSE

The next few days fly by all too quickly, but they surely will be some of the best treasured memories of my life. All we know is our makeshift family, laughter, good food, and the heated pool, the last two of which are courtesy of Storm. I believe I have seen enough of the naked female body to last me a lifetime, but my eyes and heart only belong to one.

Shari.

For her part, these last few days has indeed opened her up to her inner woman, and her feminine grace has me on my toes. We have not done anything since I pulled that stunt in the pool, and she doesn't even sit by me in the pool anymore. Her kisses are still full of love, though, and she, as of recently, constantly has me squeeze her butt when we kiss, so I don't think she's mad or anything.

I awake to space between Stacey and I; Shari and Latrice are gone. I hear whispers coming from the pool area. I look over to find Shari and Latrice having what appears to be a serious conversation. All good things must come to an end.

I carefully rise from the bed so I do not wake Stacey. Silently, I walk over to the pool, and with their backs turned to me, neither Shari nor Latrice notices my presence until I am already neck-deep in the water, for which I am grateful, because it's just before sunrise, so my manhood is filled with blood for no reason.

"Yeah, but there are only two days left," I hear Latrice whisper before they notice me.

Latrice jumps, but Shari remains calm. She must have heard me.

"Very kind of you to sneak up on us this morning," Latrice says, like I was supposed to be loud while Stacey is still asleep.

"The love of my life is an assassin, and she knew—she just didn't tell you," I whispered back, placing the blame on Shari.

Shari just smiles and walks over to me through the water.

"Good morning, my love," she whispers, walking into me and my hard member to kiss me before returning to her seat next to Latrice.

"Whatever. You're just in time to discuss the important things with us," Latrice says, sounding sad.

"Fill me in," I say.

"So, in two days Ki'ra is supposed to leave through the northern gate via horse at midnight. We do not know if he will be alone or ride with an honor guard, but we will assume the latter due to the information he carries. I would like for you two to set out tonight and head north a little ways so you can scout your environment and choose the battlefield. When you do attack him, try to make it short and quick, no theatrics," Latrice says to me specifically.

"If you cannot make short work of the battle," Latrice continues, "then, Shari, you stick to the King's Hand soldiers, and Luca will keep Ki'ra's attention off you." That is her reminding us about what happened the last time we ran into Ki'ra. "Above all else, neither of you is allowed to die. I would see my home, my family returned to me." Latrice says the last with no small amount of concern in her voice.

Shari leans over and hugs her.

"Wait, you are not coming?" I ask, the thought just now occurring to me.

"Luca, do not be dense," Latrice says, sounding hurt. "I would only be in the way. Besides, someone needs to watch over Stacey and pack our belongings in case something goes wrong and we need to flee," she finishes, staring at the water, looking ashamed.

Shari nods and leans over me as she moves to embrace Latrice. I walk over and embrace them both.

"You've done more than enough, Latrice. Soon you will be able to fight with us, but for now, we've got this part, and we've got you. We will not die, I promise," I say, meaning every word.

"*We* promise," Shari adds.

Latrice looks close to tears and finally embraces us back.

"I love you two," she says quietly.

"And we love you as well," Shari replies for me.

"Finally in control of your thoughts?" Latrice asks, sniffling.

I jump back as if bitten by a snake. I was just hugging Shari and Latrice naked with their breasts pressed against me. I'm so glad this water relaxed my member already. I look away, embarrassed. Latrice and Shari laugh quietly together.

"You just had to point that out, didn't you?" I ask lightly.

"I couldn't help it. You guys were making me feel vulnerable, and I didn't want to be the only one," Latrice says, still in Shari's embrace.

I just smile. This is definitely what family should be like. Mom, where are you?

"When are we going to tell Stacey?" Shari asks both.

"We can tell her when she wakes," I suggest.

"No," Latrice says, shutting me down quickly and stepping away from Shari.

"Why not?" I ask.

"Stacey is very fond of you right now. She feels you are her protection. Let's not bring that problem up until it gets here. I want her to remain happy and comfortable for as long as possible," Latrice says to

Shari and me, referring to me.

"I guess I can see the wisdom in that," Shari says in thought.

Latrice is right again as usual. Randomly, I feel even better about what me and Shari did in her face without her ever knowing.

"So, what should we do with the rest of the day? The sun is about to rise any moment now?" I ask with something already on my mind.

"Let's just . . ." Latrice begins, only to be cut off by Shari.

"We will spend the day as family out in the town, and later in the evening I would like to take Latrice and Stacey to the Crystal Gardens." Shari read my mind exactly.

"I do believe I would enjoy that. I will wake Stacey so we can get ready," Latrice says as the sun's light begins to filter through the glass panel in the ceiling.

She then exits the pool, taking the walk-out stairs.

"So you are a mind reader now?" I ask Shari, meeting her eyes.

She closes the short distance between us in the water, then grabs my hands and places them on her butt.

"Maybe, but I would think it better to say you just know my heart," she tells me, caressing my face with her left hand.

"Of course I know myself," I jest.

"Good answer," she purrs seductively before she kisses me, lingering for a second so I can feel her body pressed against mine, conveying her hunger for me right now.

Then she separates from me and just walks out of the pool and joins Latrice in waking Stacey. I believe I discern the poetry in that.

Not long after our early morning discussion, we find ourselves breakfast in the inn and then go on our adventure through Altissia. The girls decided to wear the same type modest dress, but different colors. Stacey's is black, the color of Latrice's hair; Latrice's is red, the color of

Shari's hair; and Shari's is golden, the color of Stacey's hair. They all have the same hairstyle as well, the same one Jordanna did for Shari for our date. As for me, I am dressed in simple tan sweats and a white, long-sleeved button-up made of silk. I was not given an option. Shari, Latrice, and Stacey came together and chose for me. I know better than to complain. Besides, I look rather good.

The town is just as busy as every day we've been here so far, and true to Storm's word, we have not been harassed any further. Storm, Donte, I wonder what his story is. For now he makes Latrice happy, and that is good enough. I do, however, wonder why he makes it seem like it is he who will not survive me when the time comes. Doesn't he know I fear him? And that I cannot summon half the power I feel radiate from him when he does nothing but walk? I do not look forward to the fight when it comes for three simple reasons. The first and the simplest is I do not think I will win. The second, he is a good man, and that alone kills my desire to fight. Lastly and most importantly, it will tear Latrice apart. How can I stop it from happening?

"Your thoughts are not that important. Attend Shari as I attend Stacey while we traverse this maze," Latrice yells back to me from the entrance to the Crystal Gardens, arm in arm with Stacey.

Have I been in my own head that long? Judging by the color of the sky, the sun will set in forty-five minutes. I proffer my arm to Shari, who gladly accepts with a dazzling smile.

"Shari, I . . ."

She cuts me off, "Was not the only one in your thoughts today, my love. We all were. Latrice and I put on a good show, but I know Stacey can feel what is going on."

She moves so we can keep pace behind Stacey and Latrice.

"Do you think . . . ?" I begin, only to be cut off again.

"Not right now. Enjoy this with me, with them," she says, motioning with her head to the girls in front of us.

She is right: soon we will be on the road again with a full day between us to talk. My concerns can wait.

We walk through the maze, and Latrice and Stacey gasp in wonder at every turn, seeing for the first time the beauty of the Crystal Gardens. Although Stacey has lived in Altissia all her life, she admits to never having come here. While Shari does not gasp due to this being her second visit, I can tell she is just as moved as the first time by the beauty that is the Crystal Garden.

The sun is about to set. "Not trying to rush you, I swear, but hurry up. You must see this," I shout and run. Shari knows what I refer to and keeps my pace easily. Taking two right turns, I make it to the wall that looks as if it's made of crystal flowers, in front of which I gave Shari her ring. We are in time.

"What was all that about?" Latrice asks, huffing and puffing for air, arm still locked together with Stacey's as they come around the corner.

"Oh my God," Stacey shouts, noticing the wall behind me before Latrice.

"It's beautiful!" they both say together, moving past Shari and me to examine the wall and flowers thereon.

"You haven't seen anything yet," Shari says mystically.

Stacey and Latrice immediately turn to us in question. The sun does it's magic, and the pathway in the maze lights up with living rainbows from the refracted sunlight in the crystal flowers. Stacey gasps and covers her mouth as if she's about to cry. Latrice falls down to her knees in awe.

"The Almighty has been brought to her knees," I jest, nudging Shari.

"Do not speak, Peasant. Just enjoy the divine light," Latrice shouts back without taking her eyes off the rainbow lights.

"Did she just . . ." I start, but then Shari grabs my face and starts kissing me.

Shocked, I fight it for half a second, and then begin to lose myself to her. Instinctively, my hands find her butt. We kiss until the sun finally sets, taking with it our rainbow paradise.

"Thank you, Shari," Latrice says, standing.

"It was my pleasure," she replies, looking to me.

I catch up.

"Did you . . . Did you just thank her for shutting me up? And did you actually kiss me just to shut me up?" I question, first Latrice, then Shari.

My answer comes from Stacey. "Do not take this the wrong way, but you were ruining the moment," she says matter-of-factly.

"You see, truth. Thank you, Stacey," Latrice says, looking at me, then motioning to Stacey.

Stacey lets out a nervous laugh, and at that none of us can hold our laughter hostage any further. Good times indeed.

We make it back to our room in the Pale Horse in good time. Upon entering, Shari, Latrice, and I grow serious, knowing what we must tell Stacey, but Stacey surprises us with a statement of her own as she plops down on the bed.

"You guys are leaving me."

She knows.

Me, Shari, and Latrice stare at each other, dumbfounded.

"I enjoyed your kindness, but why all this talk about 'the lost' and being family if you knew you were going to abandon me?" she asks, trying to sound calm but failing.

Latrice recovers fast. "I am not going anywhere. They are, and they are coming back," Latrice says, pointing to us two.

Way to save your own skin.

"Why?" Stacey asks, looking to me with abandonment on her face.

I feel so guilty. Shari moves to sit next to Stacey on the bed.

"Do you remember the man I was looking for when we found you?" Shari asks.

"Ki'ra?" Stacey replies swiftly.

"Yes, he is going to tell the king where Luca and I are in a days' time, and we do not wish him to succeed. So we must stop him," Shari says to her softly. Stacey seems to understand.

"Will you kill him?" Stacey asks next.

I save Shari from looking like a monster. "Yes, if he tells my father where I am, protecting our family will get harder. Ki'ra has already almost taken Shari from us once," I say, kneeling in front of her.

She looks to Shari in horror and worry.

"I do not want you guys to die," Stacey says, looking back down in her lap.

"You and me both, darling. I will be here with you worrying just as much, if not more," Latrice says, sitting on the other side of Stacey.

Stacey looks up to Latrice and pauses for a moment, then hugs her fiercely. Latrice just comforts her. As if realizing that it is Shari leaving and not Latrice, Stacey jumps from embracing Latrice to embracing Shari. Shari laughs lightly and hugs Stacey back just as fiercely. Stacey abruptly stands and is about to hug me, but catches herself and sticks out her hand. That's right, she no longer likes the touch of a man. I smile and take her hand.

"He will not hurt you, Stacey," Shari says.

"I know, but . . ." Stacey begins, but is cut off by Shari.

"You cannot let them define you. Luca is your family as much as Latrice and I are," Shari says hopefully.

Stacey squeezes her eyes shut tight and envelopes me in a bear hug. I hug her back and motion for Shari and Latrice to join us with my head, hoping it will help Stacey more. Shari and Latrice both embrace us, and Stacey begins to cry.

"You are alright, darling," Latrice comforts.

"It's not that," Stacey says through tears.

"Then what is it?" Shari asks, concerned. Stacey shifts so she can hug Shari and me at the same time.

"Come back," she says simply.

"Aww . . . they will, darling, or they will have to deal with me," Latrice jests.

"And me," Stacey says through tears.

We all laugh lightly, still in a group hug.

"So, clothes make it better, Luca?" Latrice says abruptly. We all laugh harder, still not letting go of one another.

"Yes, actually, they do," I say, still laughing.

Latrice is the first one to leave the embrace, after which we all stop hugging, and moves to retrieve something underneath the bed. We all stare at her, wondering what she is searching for. As far as I know, there is nothing under the bed.

"Here it is," Latrice says, pulling something from under the bed we cannot see.

She stands, grunting, and reveals my staff wrapped in a black cloth. From what I can tell, it is pearl white again.

"This is for you," she says, walking over to us and handing me my staff.

"I completely forgot about it," I say, absentmindedly staring at the white of the staff I can see through its black wrap.

"I know. You also forgot about our horses and supplies at the first tavern we visited, remember?" I am speechless.

"I am to blame for that actually," Shari says in my defense.

"Yes, but it is much safer to pick on him," Latrice says causing Shari to blush. Stacey laughs.

"Not to worry, I've retrieved our things and traded our horses in for better ones. Also, it is time to change into these," Latrice says, moving to the other side of the bed and dragging out from under the bed the two King's Hand mail suits she had fitted for me and Shari.

"When did you have time to do all this?" Shari asks accusingly.

"When you two were busy saving Stacey," Latrice replies happily.

"You were supposed to be here safe, awaiting our return," I say sternly.

"But that is how I met Donte. He saw my fight in the first tavern and followed us here to kindly remind me that we had forgotten our things. Donte escorted me the whole time, so I was still safe," she explains to us like a child wanting to be right. The sad part is she was safer with Storm than she is with me.

"So technically, you forgot too," Shari says, quickly piecing that together.

"Ssshhhh. I have a reputation to keep," Latrice says, smiling.

We all laugh together, and then Shari and I set to changing into our chain mail suits.

It only takes a few minutes, after which Latrice and Stacey make a show of handing me my staff again and handing Shari her two black short swords.

"We will be back, so make sure everything is packed, so if need be, we can move with all haste," I say to Latrice.

"Yeah, we've got the hard part over here. Go play with your toys, children," Latrice says back playfully, trying to hide the worry in her voice.

With that, we head out to the tavern's stables to get our horses.

"Room 214, correct?" asks a little boy waiting around back.

I nod, and he disappears into a wood stable.

"Be sure your staff remains fully concealed as we leave through the gates. It will cause us no end of trouble this late in our plan if it is seen," Shari tells me as we wait for our horses.

"I know, Princess. You just stick to the plan and don't engage Ki'ra when the time comes," I say, worried about how little protection I can offer her this time.

"I will not leave you alone, my love," she says, giving me an indirect answer to my question.

"Shari, you . . ."

My thoughts are stolen from me when the boy brings out our horses. Two monstrous black beasts are led out by the young boy. They seem well trained, but just looking at the size of them, I know they were bred for war. A bite in the face from one of these beasts would kill a man, as well as a kick in the sternum from one of their rear legs.

"Shadow and Twilight. Shadow is the male, and he is yours . . ." the boy says, handing me the reins to the bigger of the two horses. "And Twilight is the female. She is yours, pretty lady," he says, handing the other horse's reins to Shari.

"Pretty, am I?" she says, leaning down and giving the boy a kiss.

He nearly faints. I absentmindedly toss him a gold coin.

"Gold!" he exclaims.

I do not respond because I am lost in the beast that is Shadow. He eyes me as I slowly present my hand to him. He continues to stare at me as if I am dumb or something, then suddenly, he whines and kneels. I smile. Shadow is ready to go.

"Do hurry up, my love. Twilight is dancing with anticipation," Shari calls down to me from atop Twilight, who is indeed dancing.

I need no further encouragement. I barely pull myself into the saddle by the time Shadow takes off following his sister, who is galloping through the empty streets in the night, guided by Shari.

It turns out the streets weren't actually empty. People just got out of the street when they saw our massive war horses coming in their direction. We slow our horses to a walk as we approach the northern gateway leading outside the city.

The line is not long at all, 4 or 6 people at most, we make it to the front without even having to stop. 10 King's Hand Soldiers guard the gateway and seem to pay us no mind.

We are almost through when a soldier calls out to me. "Hey, you, stop!" he shouts, stepping in the way of Shadow, who would have walked right through him had I not reined him to a stop.

"Yes?" I say, trying to sound annoyed and in a hurry.

Shari made it through with no problems and now waits just outside the gateway for me.

"What is that across your back?" he asks suspiciously.

I turn my head to look to give myself time to think. Shit, the white staff is showing. This is going to end badly. If it comes to a fight, our plan is as good as ruined. I force myself to calm.

"You know General Storm, yes?" I ask the man instead of answering his question.

"Yes, but what does that . . ." I cut him off.

"I am who he spoke of when he left the instructions not to harass a certain man. And I assure you two things. One, it is for your own safety. Two, I am not just a man," I say, then change my eye color to a blood red like the moon I experienced with Shari.

I see his body tense in fear, and then I change them back to my disguised green eyes.

"Carry on," he says, waving me through, trying to sound like he is still in control.

And like that, I am riding next to Shari at breakneck speed atop war horses into the night, the wind drowning out all other noise.

We ride until we are sure we can no longer be seen and slow our horses to a walk.

"Why did the soldier stop you?" Shari asks as soon as I'm close enough on my horse that she doesn't have to shout.

"He saw a little bit of white from my staff through the black wrap," I tell her honestly.

She looks at me reprovingly. "And what did you tell him?" she questions, raising her eyebrow, wondering how I got past without confrontation.

I smile, then recreate my encounter for her.

"You are so overdramatic," she says through serious bouts of laughter. I can't help but smile.

"It worked," I say simply.

"So what now?" Shari asks after she's done laughing.

"Now we kill time until the sun comes up so we can pick our battlefield," I say, staring back at Altissia.

"Any ideas?" Shari asks, dismounting Twilight. I look back at her as I dismount Shadow.

"I could think of a few that involve less clothes," I say playfully.

Shari smiles. "As much as I would enjoy that, I need my mind to be focused on the task at hand, and it would be weird with the horses watching," she says, sounding more concerned about the latter.

I didn't think about the horses.

"What should we do with the horses?" I ask, still holding on to Shadow's reins.

"They seem well trained, just let them roam free and graze for now," Shari answers knowingly.

"Okay" I say, letting go of Shadow's reins, allowing him to join his sister, who is grazing freely.

"So you had concerns earlier in the Crystal Gardens?" Shari asks, taking my hand and beginning to walk around the horses.

"What will we do when it is time to face Storm?" I ask, seriously worried.

"I do not know. I cannot feel his power as you can, so I am not as worried about it as you are. Besides that, he seems to think it is a fight he will not survive."

So I am not the only one who picked up on that.

"See, and that's another thing that's driving me crazy. Why does he talk like that when his power is so immense, so oppressive, so paramount to mine that . . ."

Shari's eyes silence me. "Oh, you felt that?" Shari says, laughing approvingly.

"I don't know much about the power, but I do know your mother and father are both the best at what they do, respectively, and you are the heir to both bloodlines. So have a little faith in yourself," she says cheerfully.

Easy for her to say.

"I only take after my mother's side, and Certus will not win me a fight against Storm," I say plainly.

"Will you let me die?" Shari asks me abruptly.

"No, never," I say, a little off put.

"Then we will win because when that time comes, I refuse to let you die, so victory is the only other option," Shari says lightly, as if it's just that simple.

I sigh. This will get us nowhere, so I will just hope she is right.

"Relax, my love, one thing at a time. Right now, we have a different fight ahead of us. Let us focus on that," Shari says, wheeling me to face her and then kissing me.

She is trying to calm my mind, but it's not possible. There is just too much going on, with too much at stake.

"I appreciate what you're trying to do, Princess, but it's not working," I say softly.

"No? Well then tell me what your rapid, all-encompassing mind says we should do about all these things," Shari says, then waits patiently for my answers.

"I don't know," I say, feeling useless and unworthy.

"Neither do I, and that is my point. Do not let stress consume you, my love. All we can do is all we can do. And we will find a way," she says encouragingly.

Her confidence in me—no, in us—is calming, contagious, and emboldening. I feel my chest swell with pride.

"There he is," Shari jests, looking me in the eye. "You know I love you, right?" I say passionately. She flashes her crystal ring in my face.

"You know you no longer have a choice, right?" she says jokingly, but dead serious.

I lean down and kiss her. We kiss underneath the stars for what feels like a lifetime while Shadow and Twilight graze in the grasslands. Shari ends our kiss by pushing me back softly enough that only my head moves.

"Seeing as how we can't scout our terrain until daytime, lie with me and watch the stars," Shari suggests, and I can tell by her tone, this is one of those things she's always wanted to do but was never afforded the opportunity.

"That sounds like a wonderful idea," I say, falling back and pulling her down with me.

She laughs as we go down. I lie flat on my back, and Shari lies with her head on my chest and a leg over one of mine. We do not speak, but right now words would be empty and vacant. Shari slips her hand under my chain mail suit onto my bare chest right over my heart and keeps it there. I just smile and continue my vigil under the stars.

22 THE WIND BLOWS

Lips caress mine, awakening me from a sleep I never knew I was in.

"It is time to go work, my love, Shari whispers from my side, hand still resting over my heart.

"I'm sorry. Were you awake that whole time?" I ask her, feeling inconsiderate.

"No, I just awoke myself when the sun started peeking in from the east."

Good. And she hasn't been up for long because the morning sky is still pinkish purple, but it is fading fast.

"Are you ready?" I ask her, more to give myself time to mentally prepare.

"Am I by your side?" she asks me.

"Yes," I state, the answer obvious.

"Well then, there you have it," she says, kissing me once more and then rising and helping me to my feet.

Shadow and Twilight seem to be doing just fine not far from where we left them to stargaze.

From our current location, movement can be seen in all directions, especially on horses. "I suggest we travel farther north and look for more favorable terrain," Shari says, looking around.

She is right. We can still see the city from here, but that is just because of its sheer size, grassland spread out in every direction for as far as the eye can see. No one will surprise anyone in terrain like this.

"I agree, let's go. Shadow!" I shout the beast's name.

His head rises, and he begins to trot my way, his sister following not far behind.

"Ready to run?" I ask him enthusiastically. He just snickers in response.

I grab his harness and jump on, then await Shari to do the same. Soon, we are farther North, the city just barely visible from our vantage, but the terrain is all the same. I'm starting to feel like we might have a better shot just ambushing him in the city like the King's Hand tried to do to Shari and me.

"Look ahead, my love. We might be in luck," Shari yells from atop her horse so she is heard through the wind pointing directly ahead of us.

I look to where she points, and there is indeed something on the horizon. From here it looks like nothing but a bush. However, for me to see a bush from this distance means when we get closer it will probably reveal itself to be a forest. I smile to myself. This will be perfect.

About an hour more of riding delivers us to the front of a forest just as massive as the one in which my grandfather trained me. The only difference is there is a dirt road down the center of this one for fast travel, which is only big enough for one horse to run through at a time. The one true God must be favoring us today because with this forest, our plan couldn't get any easier.

"Are you alright, my love?" Shari asks from beside me, already off of her horse.

"Yes, why do you ask?" I ask, confused.

"Well, because you have been staring at this forest for five minutes now," she points out.

I smile, then dismount Shadow, leaving him be for now, to join Shari.

"I'm just excited is all," I say, picking her up and spinning her through the air.

She doesn't fight it, but instead leans back and embraces the experience. When I finally get her down, she blushes, then kisses me before asking, "Why so excited all of a sudden? What happened to anxiety boy?"

Anxiety boy, what's that supposed to mean? Doesn't matter. "How can I not be excited? Look at this forest. With this, the battle is won before it has even started," I say happily.

"I am missing something. Explain."

I look to the sun. It isn't even high rise yet. We have time. "I'd rather show you. Catch me if you can," I say, darting into the forest.

I look behind me, and Shari is chasing me with a smile on her face. I can hear her every step in the forest. She may be an assassin, but in here she might as well be a trumpeter. I take her in a loop to see if she notices. She doesn't. I feel bad for what I am about to do. My grandfather made me run in the forest every day until I could move like a wraith. It is time to disappear.

"Luca, what is this about? You cannot . . ."

I sidestep behind a tree from a dead run, and when Shari bends the tree, I am gone.

". . . Luca? . . . Luca?" Shari calls my name, searching for me, not understanding how I've just disappeared.

"Do you believe in ghosts?" I ask her, then silently move in a different direction.

"No!" Shari shouts, turning to where my voice came from and hurrying in that direction.

"That is because you've never met one."

Shari stops dead in her tracks, my voice coming from the opposite direction.

"You are not funny," Shari says timidly.

"Is that fear I hear in your voice?" I ask her, then climb up a tree.

"No, you are not a ghost. Ghosts are just fairy tales made to scare children," she says, fear rising in her voice as she moves to the tree I just climbed up.

I now sit on a branch and watch her wander like a lost child. All she has to do is look up, and she would see me. I wonder why people don't look up in the forest. I know I didn't when my training first began.

"Okay, Luca, you've proved your point. You can come out now," Shari says, sounding terrified.

I wait until she passes beneath me and fall from the branch, silently landing on my feet behind her. She will try to cut me open when I scare her, so I place my hands right above the hilt of her swords.

"Boo," I whisper in her ear.

And as I thought, both of her hands move to her blades. I catch her wrist and lightly tap the back of her knee with my foot, dropping her to her back, and kiss her before she can scream at me.

She fights the kiss for half a second and then closes her eyes and surrenders to it once she realizes it's just me. I let go of her wrist, and she reaches up and grabs me behind my neck, pulling me down to kiss on her neck.

"Please do not . . . do that again . . . at least not while . . . we have important . . . things to do," she says, clearly sexually aroused, letting groans escape between words.

"Why?" I ask, barely lifting my mouth from her neck.

My pause in kissing is enough to break the spell. She pushes me from behind her.

"Because that got my heart going, and something about feeling the rush turns me on. We have things to do and people to kill. I need to remain focused," she says lightheartedly.

"Can't you see, Shari?" I ask, gesturing to the forest around us. "The fight is already won. My grandfather trained me for this. They won't even know what hit them. I don't even need your help anymore," I say excitedly, admiring the forest view.

"Oh," comes Shari's one-word reply in a tone devoid of emotion.

I turn around quickly and see her staring at the floor, looking hurt.

"Shari, you have to know I didn't mean that in a bad way," I say hurriedly, rushing over to her.

"Not in a bad way, you say. Well explain to me what other way you could possibly mean it," she says to me, sounding betrayed.

Shit. I need to pick my words more carefully.

"I just meant that you'd be safe and I wouldn't have to worry about losing you. I will always need you," I say, ashamed and looking at the floor.

A moment of silence stretches for a while. Finally, I hear Shari giggle, and I look up. She is all smiles and laughter. What happened to her hurt and feelings of betrayal?

"I already knew what you meant, but it didn't hurt to hear you say it aloud. That should teach you better than to scare me," she says as if she's proved a point.

Now I'm even more confused.

"But I thought you just said you liked the rush," I say, at a loss for understanding.

"I love the rush, but that doesn't mean I wasn't scared," she says playfully.

"You're cruel," I say simply.

"Oh, come now. You don't believe that," she says, leaning up to kiss me.

"No, I don't, but it felt good to say at the moment," I shoot back, then kiss her.

We kiss for a moment longer before she pulls back.

"Do you really believe it will be so easy now?" she asks me hopefully.

"I do," I say, smiling, knowing she will hear those words from me again someday. She picks up on it.

"You do, huh?" she asks, playfully tracing a finger across my lips.

Before I can answer, she silences me with the same finger. "Do you smell that?" Shari asks suspiciously. I sniff the air. "Rain," I say, catching the scent of water in the air.

"Do you recall seeing any storm clouds in the sky on the ride here?" Shari asks, even though she knows the answer.

"Let's go check on the horses," I say, beginning a light jog through the forest, back the way we came, holding Shari's hand so she does not get lost.

When she realizes what I'm doing, she snatches her hand back from mine and moves to run past me as if saying, "How dare you believe I would get lost or left behind." I've got a good one.

We make it back to the entrance of the forest and spot Shadow and Twilight grazing where we left them. However, the sky is graying at an unnatural pace, and storm clouds are rolling over each other in the direction of Altissia.

"I've never seen anything like it. What do you think it means?" Shari asks, taking my hand.

I have never seen anything like it either. One moment the sky was blue with hardly any clouds, and the next, it looks as if tornadoes could touch down any second. Even the wind has turned cold and picked up speed drastically. My anxiety shoots through the roof as fear begins to try to override my body. There is no need to guess what is causing this. I can feel him.

"Storm is coming," I say to Shari, fear evident in my voice.

"What do you mean he is coming? He doesn't even know where we are," Shari says, not feeling what I can.

"Just as I can feel him, he can also feel me, so he knows exactly where we are, and he is closing in fast," I say, not understanding what my senses are telling me because I see no one, only the gray clouds that have finally made it overhead.

"Ridiculous, I see no one," Shari says, looking the way we came. Heavy rain suddenly starts to fall from the sky as we watch for any signs of Storm's approach. Lightning begins to streak across the clouds. This man's power is staggering. Wait, that is not how lightning behaves. There is only one bolt and it is shooting through the clouds directly to us.

"He comes," I say, pointing to the lightning bolt in the sky.

"He can fly?" Shari asks, thunderstruck.

I do not have time to answer because the bolt of lightning crashes into the ground directly in front of us, causing a deafening boom and a flash of bright white light, which we have to shield our faces from. I pull Shari behind me as I do so. When the light fades, I see Storm walking toward us, hands behind his back. For all the insanity involved with his entry, the ground still remains undisturbed.

"You said we were good for now, Storm. Why are you here?" I ask, pulling my staff from my back.

At the movement, Shari draws her blades too. Nothing good is about to happen right now. I just hope I can keep Shari alive. Storm stops when we pull our weapons.

"Whoa, calm, friends," he says, raising his hands.

"You want us to be calm when you just summoned a storm and flew through the sky as lightning itself to get to us. What exactly are we supposed to be calm about?" Shari asks angrily.

"Well if you put it like that, I suppose you're right. But we don't have time for this. Plans have changed. Ki'ra will not be leaving via the north gate anymore. Instead, he will go through the southern gate. You need to leave now."

Shit, that's the opposite direction. But why, what happened? "Why did he change his plans? And why are you helping us?" Shari asks for me.

Storm sighs impatiently.

"Something about a red-eyed demon wearing a man skin leaving the northern gate last night. As silly as it sounds, he is taking no chances. Apparently, the information he is to deliver is vital," Storm tells us.

Shari and I eye each other. Shit, my plan to get me out the gates worked too well. Storm sees the look we share and raises an eyebrow in question.

"I was pulled over leaving the northern gate and could not afford to be searched for obvious reasons, so I may have used a little theatrics," I say grudgingly.

"Red-eyed demon?" Storm questions. I make my eyes flash red in answer. Storm doubles over laughing.

His laughter sets me at ease, and I lower my staff. Following my lead, Shari sheaths her blades.

"Forgive me. That was quite funny. I am here because you are Latrice's family, so I thought I should help you. Also, I believe you to be a good person, and this may be the last time we are on the same side," he says, still trying to calm his laughter.

The last thing he says makes me tense in fear.

"What . . . what do you mean by that?" I ask, confounded.

"There is a contingent of fifty King's Hand soldiers currently en route to deliver me some information concerning a man with a white staff."

His eyes flick to my staff and back. "Whatever it is will not be good for—" He doesn't finish what he's about to say.

"You . . . you came to warn us, so why can you not just help us?" Shari asks almost pleadingly.

"I wish I could, but I cannot be seen rebelling against the king. I have my own reasons," he says sorrowfully, stepping backward.

Latrice was right. This man in not bad. In fact, I believe he is lost.

"Donte," I call, before he . . . I'm not sure what he was about to do.

"Yes?" he says, turning to me.

"Before you switch sides, or whatever, do me a favor and check on Latrice, please," I ask sincerely.

"Done," he says smiling. He turns back around.

"Good luck," he shouts before turning into a lightning bolt and shooting back into the stormy sky from which he came.

Shari and I just watch his bolt recede from which it came, in awe.

Soon the rain stops, then the air warms, and finally, the sky clears.

"I take it back. He is someone we need to worry about," Shari says, grabbing my hand.

I never believed otherwise.

"We need to get South and fast," I say, still staring at the sky. "Too bad you can't fly, my love," Shari says jokingly, then whistles for Twilight.

I know she is just trying to lighten the mood, but I can't help but wonder what that feels like.

Twilight comes quickly, and Shadow is right behind her.

"Well, I can't fly, but our horses can do something akin to it," I say, jumping on Shadow.

"We will have to go wide around the city to avoid being seen, and that will take time," Shari informs me.

"Time we do not have. Let's go," I say, launching Shadow into a run.

Storm frightens me, but he is not my enemy right now. Ki'ra is, and I will see him dead before he tells my father anything. But then what? Assuming I do not die, where am I supposed to go from there? And I am no longer alone. Shari, Latrice, and Stacey are all with me now, and they are all family. So where do we go from there?

Shadow and Twilight eat distance like children devouring sweets, and at the pace at which we push them, they will crash just like those same children in a couple of hours.

We cannot afford that, I think to myself. I wonder if I can heal the horse's exhaustion. It won't hurt to try. Placing my hand on the back of Shadow's neck, I reach for Certus, and just like I would heal anyone, I allow power to flow from my body into the horses, willing it to right whatever is wrong. Shadow neighs in pleasure and picks up speed. Slowly we begin to outpace Shari and his sister. I slow him down so they can catch back up. I can tell he is none too happy about that from the way he snorts.

I ride him close enough to Twilight that I could pull one of Shari's blades if I wanted to. Shari just looks at me, trust and worry warring on her face. One wrong step from either horse, and this will end badly.

Slowly I reach over and place my hand on Twilight's neck and send a wave of healing through her body. She reacts much the same as Shadow, neighing in pleasure and picking up speed. I carefully guide Shadow apart from Twilight, then allow him to pick up speed. It's about two hours past high rise, and we still have a long way to go.

The sun moves westward in the sky and slowly begins to sink toward the horizon as time becomes nothing more than the wind rushing against my face and the sound of Shadow's and Twilight's hooves beating the earth. We started eastward around the city first, and by what I can tell, we were about halfway from our desired location, directly opposite the position we just held North of Altissia. I believe we will make it in time to cut off Ki'ra and his possible guard, but scouting the terrain so we can choose the battlefield is out of the question. We simply don't have that kind of time anymore. The only saving grace is the fact that since he's headed south first, now we will be familiar with the landscape, having already traveled that way coming to Altissia from Last Stop.

Remembering what Ki'ra did in Last Stop, almost killing Shari, makes me believe that familiarity with the land alone will not be a big enough advantage. It also wakes a slumbering friend inside me. Anger fills my veins, recalling my failures of that time. Bron was beheaded trying to get information for me. Countless people in Last Stop were beheaded because they chose to harbor me instead of give me up. Shari was captured and almost killed. All I can do is hope for forgiveness from the dead, but Shari is alive, and that will not change today.

The faintest sound of thunder rumbles in my head as I call to the storm slowly, allowing it to take its time to gather its destructive might, the object of my wrath, Ki'ra. Shari told me not to summon the storm again. She will just have to be upset with me because I'd prefer her alive and upset rather than dead and gone.

My hands grip tightly on Shadow's reins, and he neighs excitedly. Can he feel my zeal for wiping Ki'ra from existence? As if to answer my thoughts, Shadow jumps mid-stride for no reason. This horse might be my spirit animal, if such a thing exists. With one more healing for each horse, we continue our mad dash through the grasslands as the sun finally sets, practically making Shadow and Twilight invisible in the starlight.

I start to believe we are making better time than I originally anticipated when Shari pulls Twilight in close to me and points to something on the horizon. I look toward the direction she points and spot six white horses carrying men south into the night.

Shit, they left early. Now how are we supposed to stop them, especially without Shari attracting Ki'ra's attention? I should have come alone. Then I would not have to . . . Shari turns Twilight in another direction. What is she doing? Trusting in her as she does me, I wheel Shadow to follow.

I watch as our target disappears from view, blind trust the only thing keeping me following Shari. After a few minutes, I am about to cut her off and ask what this is all about, but then I recognize our surroundings and smile. She is headed toward the massive hole in the land that used to be Alterain, and judging by the group's slight angle westbound, so are they. Now we will arrive on the opposite side of the crater with minutes to spare before they appear. How could I have ever entertained the thought of coming without her?

Shari, I love you.

Shari's horse slows as we crest a hill and comes to a stop just before land gives way to nothingness. I must slow Shadow by pulling on his reins hard. He would have jumped right over the ledge had I not. I pull him right next to Shari so our horses face opposite directions, and we look each other right in the eye.

"We don't have much time, love. What is your plan?"

I kiss her in the mouth hard, then pull her head to mine so our foreheads touch. "You are a genius, Princess. As for a plan, we don't have time for one. Besides, they always go bad. We will just do what we do best. I will attract their attention, and you kill from the shadows," I say softly with lightning beginning to crackle, loyalty in my head but voice full of love.

"Latrice is the genius; I merely have common sense. So we will go opposite directions around this?" Shari motions to the crater.

"Yes, be sure not to attract Ki'ra's attention. I will see you soon, Princess," I say, moving Shadow into a light canter around the edges of what used to be Alterain.

"Control your anger, my love," Shari calls back to me. I look back to her so she knows I heard her, but I do not respond.

It is far too late for that, and by the look on her face, she knows it too.

As I circle around to the other side, I can't help but wonder what would bring them here of all places. I know Storm told us their plans had changed because of my theatrics, but why here? As I complete my half circle around the cavity in the ground, I see that I will not have to wait long to find out. Six white horses materialize in the distance, headed my way but not directly toward me. I realize I would rather not fight with this massive hole at my back, so counting on Shadow's black coat to keep us concealed in the night, I set him on a path that will bring us up behind them and put the hole at their backs. Of course, they will see me, but that is going to happen regardless. As long as Shari can remain unseen, I will be fine.

I successfully swoop in behind the six riders and watch them come to a stop as the assembly reaches what was Alterain. I keep going straight toward them.

Soon I am able to discern men on top of the horses wearing typical King's Hand gear, and at their head in his same black-and-red-trimmed robes sits Ki'ra on top of a white stallion bigger than the rest. Storm was right: Ki'ra thinks too highly of himself. I hate the ugly smirk on his face I see when I stop Shadow after coming as close as I dare to my enemies.

Wind is blowing hard in my head, muting out much of the background noise, which is reality. The storm is ready to make landfall, but I hold it back for now. I can feel its pressure building.

"You are so predictable," Ki'ra shouts, smiling from atop his horse.

I have no desire to talk to this man, but my grandfather's lessons have not been forgotten: flow like the river and strike like a dragon. Right now, it is time to go with the flow.

"And you are running. Don't tell me a red-eyed demon wearing a man's skin scared you off your chosen path," I mock, trying to provoke him into rash actions, making my eyes flash red so he knows who he ran from.

To my surprise, he laughs. "I had a feeling it was you, and that is why we are here." He gestures to the hole behind him.

"So you and your men can jump to your deaths like cowards instead of fight me? Well, that's expected," I taunt.

"On the contrary, the hole is for you to go in. The king seems to want you alive, but you have pestered me long enough, no matter who you might be. So when you die, I will throw you in there, leaving no evidence, and tell the king you left me no choice."

No matter who I might be . . . Does he know who I am? No, because if he did, he wouldn't dare try to kill me.

"Where is the assassin?" Ki'ra asks suddenly when I take too long to reply.

"I left her behind, no distractions this time, just me and you," I say, letting anger slide into my voice.

"Well that was dumb. I brought you here to kill you. Do you really believe I will give you a fair fight?" he asks, disbelieving me.

"Six of you and one of me, I'd say you're still at a disadvantage," I bluff, trying to keep his attention on me.

"No, you are not dumb. She is out there somewhere. I can feel it in my bones," he says, dismounting his horse as his men do the same, then motioning for two of them to search for Shari in the dark.

Shit.

"Now your chances are even slimmer, but that is your loss, not mine," I say, looking to the sky as if in thought, then adding, "It doesn't even matter if she's really out there or not."

Then, I, too, jump off my horse.

"And why is that?" Ki'ra asks, indulging me.

"Because you will not live long enough to find out."

23 REVELATIONS

Including Ki'ra, four men surround me, Ki'ra himself directly in front of me with that ugly smirk still on his face. I am not calm. I feel like I am about to have a heart attack, not from fear but from holding the storm at bay for so long. I need to release, and I have an idea.

"I will find the assassin and make her my personal pleasure toy, and when I tire of her, I will give her to my men," Ki'ra says, trying to break my focus as he and his men close in on me.

The thought punctures a hole in whatever I was using to hold the storm back. I ball my fist and feel the ground beneath me, but instead of turning it into sand, I compact even tighter into rock then shoot a platform upward under the man to Ki'ra's immediate right, launching him backward into the air. The release of energy slows my rapidly beating heart but only slightly, I still might have a heart attack. I do not hear the man hit the ground in the distance. He must have fallen in the hole.

"There's one man down the hole, your odds suddenly decrease," I taunt. But Ki'ra is done talking.

A ring of fire materializes around me in midair and then grows upward toward the sky and downward toward the ground until I am surrounded by flames ten feet high. Slowly the fire begins to close in on me, inviting me to a blazing death. Not today. I am already shielded, so I step outside the makeshift pyre. As soon as I clear the flames, three fists connect with my shielded jaw, almost breaking it. I try to look up into the night and realize my eyes are having trouble adjusting to the darkness of night again after seeing the brightness of flames so close. I'm effectively blinded, but I hear no movement around me, so they were fists of force.

Get it together, Luca. All these men can touch the power. Forget that again, and I will probably die. After I remind myself, I pull my white staff out and assume position one.

"You cannot expect to win a contest of power with a simple white staff. Maybe you are dumb," Ki'ra says, chuckling.

Arrogant to a fault, he effectively stole my vision, but now thanks to his need to brag, I know where he is. I charge the direction his voice came from.

Suddenly, the ground under my feet softens. I jump as high as I can, and my vision returns while I'm in the air. I spot Ki'ra fifteen feet in front of me, his two remaining men to either side of him.

My intuition tells me I didn't jump far enough to make it out of the area one of his men turned into sand, so I throw my staff at the ground like my grandfather did when he landed on his own staff like a god. I've tried this before and failed; however, this time I do not have to land atop it. I just need to use it as a stepping stone to jump again and land on solid ground. I also do not have the luxury of failing. Ki'ra shoots a ball of fire at me as my foot touches the staff, which is standing upright halfway buried in sand. I push off of it, back into the air, flowing into position 17 to dodge the blast.

34, 21, 5 . . . and three more he threw while I was still in the air.

My feet hit solid ground, and I roll, predicting the fists of air that whistles past my face, avoiding them. Springing up from the roll, I launch myself into a dead run at Ki'ra. He will shoot a wall of fire or some such to keep me from reaching him. I bank right as he does exactly as I thought he would. Now who's predictable?

My new path takes me right into the man who made the ground soft. This I assume because he hasn't shot fists of force at me yet or even moved his hands to do so. I am about to see how he likes being sunk into the earth, when my eyes find Shari, killing one of the men Ki'ra sent to find her with a short sword from behind through the heart because he thought it would be more exciting to watch.

Excellent job, Princess.

I must continue to do my job and keep their attention on me, not her. That alone saves the life of the man in front of me. Stopping, I backflip over what could have possibly been fists of force. I will never know for sure because they never touched me. I land and run toward the man who is shooting fists of air because he is in the opposite direction of Shari and he is rather annoying at the moment.

"Now who is running, boy? It will not save you, only prolong your death," Ki'ra shouts, sounding frustrated.

My heart feels like it's about to burst again, so I solidify the ground under my feet and the man's who hit me with the fist of air, making platforms that push up out of the ground to shoot us toward each other.

I can tell he was not ready for that by the way his arms flail as he sails through the air. Nor is he ready for my fist as it connects with his jaw, shattering it from the joint force of our momentum. We hit the ground, and he lands on his back, screaming in pain and grabbing at his face.

"That's how you throw a punch," I say, feeling the beating of my heart slow from the release of energy.

I can't hold the storm at bay much longer.

It is said pride can kill a man, and it nearly does now as I stand over the man whose jaw I just shattered with my back to Ki'ra, feeling high off what I just did.

It is too late by the time I hear Ki'ra's voice. "Now you die," he shouts in anger.

I turn and see a ball of fire bigger than the one he shot at Shari, and it's heading right toward me. However, this fire is not red, but blue. Fire that hot will cook me alive through my shield, but through his anger, he couldn't center the blast on me. I take off running, knowing I will not make it. If I could just . . . I will not make it out of the range of the explosion, but I do not slow. The ground shudders from the impact of the blue ball of fire.

"Move, move, move," I scream at myself.

I can feel the heat at my back as the flames swiftly catch me. Time seems to slow as death draws near. I stare at a patch of land that I assume is safe and wonder as I am about to die what Shari will do without me. Suddenly, the world shifts around me, and I begin to blink rapidly from being disoriented as I hear the roar from the explosion of blue flame in the distance.

"What just happened?" I say aloud even though no one can hear me.

I look around and notice that I am somehow in the same place I thought would be safe from the explosion.

"Did I just travel through space?" I ask myself aloud.

Suddenly the elements from the blue book come to my mind, and the interpretation is as clear as day.

"Mind functions independently from space. You have mind; therefore, you can transcend space."

Shit. Holy shit. I just jumped through space itself.

"He is dead," Ki'ra says, sounding much too gratified.

His voice breaks me from my spell.

I look to myself and recall the feeling of wanting to be somewhere else and then making it so. I jump three feet to my left, not literally jump but move without moving, transcend space. It is very disorienting, but I will get used to that. I need to act before Shari loses her cool and exposes herself.

"You couldn't kill me if your life depended on it. Oh wait . . . it does," I shout at Ki'ra.

Both him and his soldier turn to face me.

As the fire clears, I see his man's ashes right where he layed grabbing his broken jaw in pain. Ki'ra killed his own man with no hesitation.

"How?" Ki'ra asks confusedly.

I see Shari creeping up behind his man in the night. Shit, she thinks I'm dead. Why else would she do something so risky?

"I am faster than I look!" I shout extra loud so Shari can hear me as I walk over toward Ki'ra.

Shari stops dead in her tracks and looks as if she has seen a ghost when she hears my voice. Theatrics. I need to buy more time.

"Your man told you I am a demon wearing a man's skin. Did you not believe him?" I ask, turning my eyes red and letting them stay that way.

"There is a reason the king wants me alive. Take me to him, and I will allow you to keep your life," I say, lying through my teeth.

Shari has gotten a hold of herself but continues to creep behind Ki'ra's man. I pick up my pace.

"You are no more demon than I am king. I do not fear you," Ki'ra says hesitantly.

Keep the act going and attention on you, I chide myself mentally.

"It is beneath you to lie. I can smell the fear in your blood," I say, smiling as the sun begins to rise on the horizon.

I stop moving ten feet away from him.

"You are stalling, but what for?" Ki'ra questions, squinting his eyes at me.

Shit.

"The assassin," he shouts in realization, but it's too late. Shari's blade comes out the front of the soldier's mouth as Ki'ra turns his head to her, and I . . .

Everything shifts, and I find myself tackling Ki'ra.

"Shari, go!" I shout, punching Ki'ra in the mouth as I pin him to the ground.

I wasn't really thinking when I tackled him and pinned him to the ground, but as I stare into his eyes, I realize I have made a mistake. Fire begins to dance in his eyes just as lightning did Storm's that day. He then inhales a deep breath of air and exhales a blast of fire through his mouth with enough force to send me flying through the air. Because I am shielded, I am not burnt, but the impact from landing on my back when I hit the ground drives the air from my lungs.

"I knew you were here; it is time for you to die," I hear Ki'ra say to Shari, causing me to sit up.

I am much too far to help her. Shari has managed to put about a twenty-foot gap between herself and Ki'ra, but it is still not enough. Jets of flame leave Ki'ra's hands and barrel their way toward Shari. She will die.

Or so I think, until she does something neither Ki'ra nor myself expects. She crosses her black blades in front of her to shield her from the flames, but will that work?

The blades begin to absorb Ki'ra's flame and effectively protect Shari from his raging inferno, causing them to glow and turn a deep red color.

"Luca!" Shari screams my name for help pleadingly. The blades will not protect her forever.

Whatever was holding the storm at bay gives. I stand and punch a fist upward in the air, causing the ground under Ki'ra to shoot upward ten feet from the earth, launching him straight up into the air farther than the eye can see. I jump to Shari and stand her up.

"Luca . . . how did you . . ."

I cut her off. "Shari, leave now. That will not have killed him," I say, trying to keep the storm out of my voice but failing.

"Luca, I will not . . ." she begins, only to be cut off again

"Shari. Leave. Now!" I shout at her as I never have before, causing her to flinch away from me.

I feel bad, but I will not see her die today. She turns from me looking hurt and whistles before beginning a slow jog. I see Shadow and Twilight come to her in the distance she has put between us. That is enough for me.

I turn and look up and see Ki'ra's body begin to descend through the air, but he is falling as if he is standing on land. About a hundred feet from the ground, flames erupt from his hands, which are facing downward at the ground. His descent begins to slow rapidly until he touches the ground, lightly. The land to either side of him is burned to a crisp. Flame still dances in his eyes.

If I can transcend space, I wonder if . . . "Certain, sure, definite, decided, specific, precise," I chant aloud, unable to do so in my head due to the storm's energy flooding through me and the object of its wrath in my face.

"Cheap trick . . . what are you . . . ?" Ki'ra begins distastefully before stopping as three replicas of me surround him.

I can see what they see and hear what they hear, but I know I can't use the power through them. Truth be told, I'm glad, because just this alone is almost a sensory overload in my mind right now.

"I have figured out who you are," Ki'ra says, looking more aggravated than I've ever seen him.

"Oh, you have now? I seriously doubt it," I say nonchalantly because I really do not care; I'm just stalling to figure out what else I can do with these replicas of myself.

"The power you possess and the name the assassin called you by—you are the king's son, of that there is no doubt."

Okay, so I can control their movements, and from what I feel, they can't make physical impact on reality.

"I do not have a father," I say, feeling the storm's energy surge within me, begging me to act now.

"Wrong, but he will cease to have a son after today," Ki'ra says, hurling blue flames at one of my replicas.

It disappears from my mind as the fire consumes it.

I begin to run a circle around Ki'ra and use my mind to make my two remaining replicas do the same. He begins to hurl blue flames at us—well, me—at random. All he can do is hurl fire? How was I ever afraid of this man? Compared to what I saw Storm do just to relay a message to me, Ki'ra is a joke. I run by the fallen soldier Shari most recently killed and scoop up the bow on his back. Suddenly, my replicas manifest the same type of bows in their hands. Interesting.

I do not have arrows, and if I fire an arrow made of the power, he will know which one I am, my replicas being unable to fire arrows of their own. Me and the replicas weave in and out of his wild flames with ease. Having three pairs of eyes in one mind watching him from different angles lets me know his every move as soon as he makes it.

Time for a test.

I charge him and keep my two replicas circling him. He turns to me and predictably throws a massive ball of flame at me. I wait until the absolute last second before impact, and jump. My world disorients. I am around a hundred yards away from him and my replicas, who still circle him, and about thirty yards in front of the absence of Alterain. The senses my replicas relay to me have not diminished in the slightest. Great.

Closing my own eyes but still seeing through those of my replicas and guiding their movements, I nock an arrow of power and then funnel all the energy of the storm into it. It takes a while to channel the wrath of the storm into something so small, but I lose myself to thoughts of everything that has driven me to this point as I do it.

My family was a lie; my father is the greatest evil this land knows. Bron is dead. People in Last Stop are dead. The King's Hand treats people like dirt. My father is the reason Latrice's parents left her.

Latrice.

When I remember her, I begin to think of the positive experiences I've had up until this point. Meeting Latrice, finding Shari, rescuing Stacey.

Stacey.

They tried to—no, they did rape Stacey. Anger returns.

The storm has almost poured its wrath in its entirety into this single shot. Lightning crackles next to my ear, but I do not notice with my eyes closed and mind focused on guiding the replicas. The time approaches.

Suddenly I charge Ki'ra with both the replicas, one from in front of him and one from behind. When they get about five feet from him, blue flame erupts from within a semi-sphere above the ground bigger than anything I've ever seen him conjure. The ground quakes lightly under me as I lose the extra senses of my last two replicas.

My knees shake as the last of the destructive power of the storm flows into the arrow.

This man would have killed Shari.

With that thought I open my eyes and release the arrow that is no longer an arrow but a bolt of lightning the width of which is the size of a person. The last thing I see is Ki'ra begin to turn my direction, but I know it is too late for him.

The reason that is the last thing I see is not because I pass out, but because the recoil from that shot sent me flying backward with breakneck force.

Fortunately, my neck does not break, but I feel like I have just jumped with the way the world disorients around me. My body is drained entirely as I fly through the air. The storm took everything with it when I let that arrow fly.

My vision begins to adjust itself, but that does nothing to slow my momentum. I am traveling toward what is left of Alterain, and fast. I feel my body begin to slow, but I don't think I will slow fast enough not to go into the nothingness my father left behind.

I am right and I am wrong. Gravity reasserts itself on my body, causing me to hit the ground just before the hole and skid across the dirt, rolling into what surely leads to oblivion. I reach my hand up at the last second as my body begins its descent and grab the edge of the drop above me with an iron grip, causing my body to swing into the wall of the solid rock now in front of me so hard that my vision goes black.

I now hang on the edge of life and death, powerless to pull myself up.

My vision eventually returns, but my strength does not, and I can't reach up and grab the ledge with my other arm because it is dislocated from the recoil of my shot.

Did I shoot lightning, or did I imagine that? I had to have imagined that because that would mean using Potentia, and I clearly took after my mother, who uses Certus.

Would have been cool though.

I try to use the power to jump back to land, but for whatever reason, I am unable. Next, I try to make the rock wall in front of me shoot out a platform for me to stand or sit on, but still, nothing happens. I'm too spent. Lastly, I try to make the ground in which my fingers are currently gripped more solid because I am losing strength in my hand. Even that doesn't work. When my grip gives out, I will fall to my death. If only I hadn't sent Shari away. Why did I do that? Oh well, at least she is alive and safe. I can go to my death happily knowing that is the case.

My fingers slip, and I stare at the blue of the sky one last time, knowing death awaits me at the bottom of this hole. I wish I could have seen the sun, too, but I will take what I can get. It's not like I have a choice. I drop all of three inches before a hand clamps around my wrist, causing me to look up.

"And where do you think you're going?" an out-of-breath Shari asks me with tears in her eyes and mixed emotions in her voice.

Do my eyes deceive me, or did I already die?

"Shari?" I say her name questioningly.

"Yes, I do believe that is my name" she says jokingly even though tears still fall down her face freely. "Hang on, my love," she says before pulling me up and back over the edge onto solid ground, positioning me so that my head lies in her lap.

I am exhausted. I could not move if I tried, but right now, I could not think of any place in the world I would rather be.

"Is this real?" I ask, still in disbelief.

"Is this real?" she questions me back before kissing me slowly and delicately.

"You know I've never been able to quite figure out what reality is when you kiss me," I joke when our lips separate.

"Shut up," she says playfully, rocking back and forth, tears dripping onto my face.

I see the sun behind her. I thought I would never see it again, but there it is. Something moves to block the sun; my eyes focus in on it, and it is a face I have not seen in a while.

"Grandfather? I must be dead," I say uncomprehendingly.

"You are hardly dead if you can ask dumb questions. I will give you two a moment, but hurry up; time is short," he says before disappearing and allowing the sun to shine on my face once more.

"Stop saying you are dead already. I'm having a hard enough time believing it as it is, after everything I just saw," Shari complains.

"Why did you not leave?" I ask out of curiosity.

"The same reason you asked me to, because I love you," she says longingly.

"I'm sorry for what I said, but I'm glad you understood. Never have I been happier that you didn't listen to me," I say apologetically.

"I told you I listen to this not that," she says, placing her finger first on my heart and then on my lips. "Besides, you could tell me to leave you for the rest of your life and I wouldn't," she says playfully, showing me her crystal ring.

I just smile until another question assaults my mind.

"Ki'ra, is he . . . ?"

"Dead," Shari answers, cutting me off.

"That lightning arrow was quite a spectacle. His body is missing its top half but still stands rooted to the ground from all that electricity. Look." She raises my head so Ki'ra's body, or what is left of it, is in my line of sight.

"Why does his blood mist upward to the sky like that instead of spill on the ground in normal liquid form?" I question, the sight being very odd.

"I do not know for sure, but if I had to wager a guess, that heat from the bolt of lightning boiled his blood on impact. Mist is all that remains," Shari explains her thoughts.

"Wait, so I really shot lightning?" I ask, disbelieving that too.

Shari looks at me questioningly. "Did you not intend to?" she asks in return.

"I don't know what I intended to do. I just poured the wrath of the storm into the one shot," I say, then catch my mistake. "Shari, I had to," I begin before she silences me with a finger to my lips.

"I knew what you had done when you did not respond to my warning about controlling your anger. You are forgiven," she says, smiling down at me. "But we will talk more about it later," she finishes.

Fair enough. Last question. "Do you know my grandfather?" I ask her.

"No, only what you told me of him. Why?" she replies.

"You did not seem shocked when he appeared over your shoulder," I point out to her.

"He appeared out of thin air behind me as I watched your fight from a distance. At first, I tried to fight him, but when he began to move, it reminded me of you. Then I saw golden eyes, and they gave me pause. When I thought about it, he was not even trying to fight back. Then recalling your stories, I knew who he was," she explains to me.

"Did you hit him?" I ask, not able to help myself.

She shakes her head no, reliving the experience.

"I thought you were fast. My eyes couldn't even keep up with him," she says, sounding defeated.

I chuckle.

"Did he tell you his name?" I ask hopefully.

"When I asked, he was about to answer, and then he eyed my ring. He instead asked me if you gave it to me, to which I answered yes, and then he just said 'old man' would suffice," she explains.

So much for that.

"He did not help you pull me out of the hole. Why?" I ask suddenly, feeling irritated at him again like I did when he trained me.

"He said it was very unlikely you would die; he said that the powers that lie within you would react in a way that would keep you alive. He said it was more likely we would experience something akin to a natural disaster. That was when I stopped listening and ran over to save you. I do not care what he knew; I could not let you fall," Shari says, the last full of love.

"He was not going to die, I assure you. Can you walk, Luca?" My grandfather addresses Shari first and then me from somewhere behind Shari.

"Shari, help me stand, please," I tell her. She kisses me first, then obliges, helping me find my feet carefully.

"Is this good enough old man?" I ask with my arm around Shari's shoulder.

"For a sheep," he says, amused. Something about this man irritates my soul. I am about to explode in anger when Shari pinches my side, distracting me.

"I see you have tempered your anger, young man," my grandfather says proudly with a smile. "If I'm being honest, after seeing everything you just did, I'm impressed that you're even conscious, let alone able to stand even with help," he finishes.

I do not know how Shari knew that was a test, but she is my princess.

"Thank you," I mutter out, knowing I should have failed that test and unused to praise from the old man. Then another thought crosses my mind. "How much of the fight did you see?" I ask, knowing I am going to dislike his answer.

"All of it," he smiles knowingly. Even Shari squints her eyes at him.

"You watched the whole fight and did nothing—?"

He cuts me off. "Not only did I watch the whole fight, but I've watched your every move since you assumed I left you just outside of Last Stop until you entered Altissia. With no way to hide my golden eyes, I would not make it past the gate without causing problems," the old man tells us boldly. He then adds, "Speaking of eyes, fix yours."

I forgot they were red. I quickly change them to match Shari's.

I want nothing more than to hit this man for what he just told us, but instead I turn to Shari and simply say, "I told you ghosts exist."

For the first time ever, I hear my grandfather laugh—and not a light chuckle, a real laugh, the type that makes you hold your stomach, which he is currently doing. His laugh is infectious, and soon Shari and I laugh along with him. After a few minutes or so, my grandfather's bout of laughter is over and his face grows serious again.

"It is time to go," the old man says, whistling for the horses.

"Go? Go where?" I ask, not really understanding.

For a while now I have been used to being part of the plan-making, or at least present for it. Suddenly he is back in control, and I know nothing.

"To see your mother," he says excitedly. If my body could have tensed up, it would have. Shari's does.

"Yuna?"

"Mom?" Shari and I say at the same time.

"Yes, Yuna is my daughter's name, and, yes, she is your mother. Are we done with the foolish questions? Time is of the essence."

"Latrice and . . ."

My grandfather waves off my concerns. ". . . has already been contacted and will meet us outside Altissia by the western gate with a carriage containing all your things. Now can we go?" The horses choose this moment to trot up to us, neighing eagerly to get moving, but there is only Shadow and Twilight.

"There are only two horses. How will you get back?" I ask him.

Shari answers, "You are in no condition to ride a horse, so we will share one. You hold on to me, and he will take the other."

My grandfather smiles at Shari. "I like her." Shari blushes and looks down, smiling.

"How did you get here, old man?" I ask, annunciating every word.

"Does he still worry this much about everything?" the old man asks Shari.

"Unfortunately," she replies, laughing lightly. I close my eyes to soothe my mind.

"Your mother," he answers. But that makes no sense. "More questions will lead to more answers that will only provoke more questions that will eventually get answered when you get to your mom. Now, let us go," he explains in finality, jumping on Shadow and riding off.

"Calm yourself, my love. For now, let's just go. We have accomplished what we came to do. We are both still among the living, and that is more than enough for now," she says before kissing me and then jumping onto Twilight and holding her hand down to me.

I take it, and between the two of us, I manage to mount Twilight behind her and hang on as she gallops after her brother.

My eyes stay closed for the entirety of the ride. The smell of Shari's hair, the wind on my face, and the sound of hooves beating are all I know. My body needs this rest. As the hours pass and the air warms, my energy begins to slowly return. I am nowhere near recovered, but I can walk on my own if necessary. I feel the horse slow but still refuse to open my eyes. The sound of carriage wheels hits my ears next.

"Is he asleep?"

"Hello, Latrice. I see you did all the hard work," I jest.

"Don't be mean. She was worried about you," Shari says back to me.

"Correction, I was worried about the pair of you. And it is quite alright: if he can joke, I know he is well," Latrice says to Shari, smiling at both of us.

"Where is Stacey?" I ask.

Latrice is currently driving a two-horse carriage, and Stacey is nowhere to be found.

"She is inside the carriage. She didn't want to be seen by the King's Hand when we left Altissia, and I do not blame her.

"Besides, I believe she is scared. Altissia is all she has ever known, and today she left it. So give her some time to herself."

Stacey did leave her home as Latrice left hers. Shari and I . . . I left my staff.

"My staff!" I shout rather loudly in concern.

Latrice just points in front of her. I follow the direction she points with my eyes and see my grandfather riding Shadow a little way ahead of us with my staff strapped across his back. At least he's good for something.

"So that is the legend, huh?" Latrice asks Shari and me.

"He is not a legend," I say distastefully.

"He may not be a legend, but he is the fastest human I've ever seen," Shari says in awe.

"He looks like an old god of war or something," Latrice says, still staring at his back.

That he does. "You haven't even seen him with his shirt off," I concede grudgingly.

"I'm not sure I want to. He's already terrifying enough," Latrice chooses to whisper.

"Agreed," Shari whispers back.

"So obviously we are somewhere to the west of Altissia, but do you know where we are headed?" I ask, hoping Latrice has an answer.

"No, I was just told by some random person at the inn that I was to meet you guys out by the west gate with a carriage holding all of our things," she says, just as clueless as Shari and me.

"And you just believed this random person?" I ask not understanding why Latrice would do such a thing.

"They knew your real name," she says to me, explaining her reasoning.

Well, that is a good enough reason, I suppose.

"We are here," my grandfather's voice shouts back as he brings

Shadow to a halt.

Shari and Latrice do the same with their horses.

"We're here? But I do not see my mother," I say skeptically, eliciting no response from anyone.

Shari's hand finds my thigh as she inhales a deep breath.

"Look," Shari whispers to me, not taking her eyes off whatever is in front of her.

I get off the horse and move toward her line of sight, then stop dead in my tracks. We are in the grasslands where you can see nothing else in any direction besides Altissia behind us and this apparent doorway with no door frame to speak of, which is large enough to fit the carriage through, that leads to a foggy beach. It looks like somewhere the sun has not yet risen.

"Before you ask, it is called a portal, and your mother created it with her power, so I do not know anything about it," my grandfather says, then moves through the doorway, through reality.

My mind is not functioning properly now. How is such a thing even possible?

"Are you going to go in, my love?" Shari asks from behind me with fear present in her voice.

If I don't, my grandfather will surely come back through and call me a sheep.

"We don't have much of a choice. Besides, I know you want to see my mother as much as I do," I say without looking back, then wave my hand for them to follow as I walk through.

As I pass through the portal for a brief instant, I feel like I can feel everything that went into making it, and the application of Certus is staggering. I would not even know where to begin weaving the delicate threads of power that pass through reality itself. I knew my mother was the best, but not until just now did I have any inkling of what that meant.

I exit the other side to indeed find a beach on which visibility is extremely low due to the fog. It is also very cold here, but I keep walking until I find my grandfather standing next to Shadow in the sand just outside the reach of the water. In front of him is a boat big enough to admit us and our belongings but small enough to go undetected by bigger vessels in this fog. Nothing is special about the boat. In fact, it is too plain—no sails, no paddles, and no wheel required for steering.

"How exactly are we supposed to get anywhere in that?" I ask my grandfather.

"Your mother has done something with the power that will make the boat take us where we are headed when we are ready to depart. I do not know more than that," he replies, sounding as if he does not entirely trust it himself.

"Why didn't she just make the portal take us to her?" I ask, thinking it is the simpler choice.

"Portals leave residue of power behind that can be traced and possibly reopened, or so she says. No one can know where we are going. It is a secret older than you," he says in his cryptic voice.

"It's cold out here," Stacey's voice comes from behind us as she exits the carriage.

My grandfather's eyes lock onto her with an intensity I have never seen.

"Well, we are on a foggy beach and the sun has not yet risen," Latrice says, climbing down from the driver's seat of the carriage.

"Why do you look like that, old man?" Shari asks, moving past both me and the old man to inspect the boat.

"Who is she?" my grandfather asks loudly, referring to Stacey.

"Her name is Stacey, and she is family. I thought you said you watched my every move." I say the latter jokingly.

"He said he watched your every move until we entered Altissia,"

Shari corrects, moving to stand by my grandfather.

Latrice and Stacey move to stand on either side of me. My grandfather's eyes have not left Stacey's face.

"Is there a problem, old man?" I ask hesitantly.

He takes a moment to reply. "I do not know her. She cannot come," he says finally and in finality.

Me and the three women all exchange looks.

"Why? You left me alone, and I found a family of which she is a part. I vouch for her," I say in Stacey's defense.

"As do I," Shari adds.

"And me," Latrice seconds.

"I just told you this secret is older than you. More lives are at stake than your own here. She cannot go," the old man says assertively.

I take Stacey's hand into my own. For her part, she has been quiet during the whole conversation.

"If she cannot go, then neither will I. I will not leave her," I say with finality.

He will not leave without me.

Shari and Latrice wear masks of worry on their faces, and Stacey just looks at the sand in fear, gripping my hand tighter. Suddenly, my grandfather smiles.

"You have become a good man, and I am proud of you, but we do not have time for this," he says respectfully.

I see it on his face. What does he regret?

Quicker than any of us can react, he pulls Shari's black short sword from its resting place in the sheath on her back and rams it right into my forehead, flipping it at the last moment so the hilt connects with my head instead of the blade. My last thought before the world goes black is, how much stronger will I have to become before I can protect my family?

SHATTER

ABOUT THE AUTHOR

Nicholas Wolfe's path to authorship is as gripping as the story he tells. Wrongly accused and imprisoned, Wolfe was cut off from the world-but not from his imagination. With no access to computers or traditional writing tools, he saved what little he had to buy notebooks and pencils, crafting Shatter entirely by hand, page by page. Fantasy became both his escape and his way of reclaiming his identity. What started as a lifeline in confinement evolved into a raw, personal exploration of fate, power, and self-worth. Shatter isn't just a novel-it's a bold testament to the power of storytelling, born from injustice and transformed into art. Now free, Wolfe is dedicated to sharing his voice and world, proving that even in the darkest places, creativity not only survive – it thrives.